A Land Without Hope:

The Return of Lord Nebula

Sebastian Perez-Martinez

Imperial Star Publishing

FLORIDA

IMPERIAL STAR PUBLISHING

An imprint of Imperial Star Publishing, LLC.

First Edition, December 2024

2 4 6 8 10 9 7 5 4 3 1

A Land Without Hope: The Return of Lord Nebula Copyright © 2024 by Sebastian Perez-Martinez

Cover Design by miblart

The text of this book was set in Adobe Garamond and Baskerville Old Face

Manufactured in the United States of America

ISBN 979-8-9923820-2-0

This book is dedicated to my mother Susana Perez and to my wonderful Grammar School teacher, Anita Bland. Without your support and love, I would never have been able to achieve my dreams.

TABLE OF CONTENTS

A Land Without Hope:

The Return of Lord Nebula

PART I - THE HOLY WAR

PROLOGUE

A thick cloud of toxic ash encased the Earth, forcing the sun's rays to retreat. The ferocious waves of the ocean clashed against the island paradise of Hy-Brasil, as fire rained down from the sky, decimating the lush jungle. Time stood still, as if the fabric of existence were torn in two by the fierce battle underway. Mankind was extinguished, and the life forms that remained would soon meet the same fate. The bloodstained battlefield remained silent. The war between the rapturous angels and tyrannical demons was long, revolting, and proceeded with many casualties. Their bodies lined the battlefield, and the insects that inhabited the ground feasted on their corpses. The war between God and Satan was nearly at an end.

Trumpets resonated as God descended from the sky. His massive black wings crackled like thunder. Without hesitation, he grabbed two battleaxes from his harness and ripped through the higher demons that protected his adversary. Hundreds of creatures with multiple arms, disfigured faces, and mutated bodies. In the scuffle, one of the demons managed to rip off his mask, revealing his scarred face. God's doting angels, rushed to his side to secure his mask and conceal his imperfection. Beautiful beings in golden armor surrounded him. Their white wings spanning six feet. Each feather capable of piercing metal. As he rose from the floor, his golden pauldrons were drenched in blood as he stood over Satan's body. Corrupted by darkness, his skin was now purple, only infuriating his father even more. The four black wings on his back were damaged and burned to the bone. He took great satisfaction in this victory. God placed his golden, armored boot on the demon's neck as he applied pressure. Looking into Satan' eyes, he was filled with regret. He could not bring himself to deliver the final blow. In pain, Satan whispered out his name.

"Hyperion!"

It was a name too few remembered. Hearing it murmured only infuriated him more. He was God! This foul creature did not deserve to speak his name, the black eyes staring back enthralled him. He removed his boot, and with a whip of his hand, Satan slowly rose from the floor. Disgraced and afraid, he slowly raised his head and locked eyes with Hyperion. Even in his defeat, his face still glimmered with pride. Mankind's eradication was retribution for Hyperion's betrayal, but in the end, Satan could not prevail.

The wounded demon would not go down so easily. His hatred gave him strength, and with every breath he took, he regained power. He gazed into his creator's eyes and a smile escaped his lips. Hyperion's intentions were clear. He could not bring himself to destroy his first creation. No matter how destructive, or how revolting he was. The immense darkness within him could not be extinguished so easily. Where light thrives, so does darkness. Hyperion could not disrupt that everlasting balance without consequence. Satan's death would only allow that darkness to inhabit a new host.

Fear and confusion clouded the mind of the Almighty God. Mutual destruction was ensured; however, Hyperion saw an opportunity form before his very eyes. A funnel of wind wrapped around him as he called out to the heavens. The toxic skies thundered with rage, and a vast surge of lightning poured down onto the battlefield, claiming the lives of those still clinging to existence. The angels and demons found themselves prey to the devastation as well. The smoke retreated toward Hyperion's hand, and once it cleared, a golden book etched in runes rested on his palm. Satan's blackened eyes bulged as he realized his fate.

The pages of the book whistled, as they turned and landed on an illustration. Hyperion hesitated at first, but he finally gave in and placed his hand on the image. He cried out in pain as it drew blood from him. The book fell out of his hands and landed on the ground, emitting a massive shockwave. Behind Satan, the ground quaked as a monumental archway assembled from the earth. With his remaining strength, he motioned his left hand toward his son. The demon's body began to twitch and sizzled as it moved closer to its prison. A spark ignited in the center of the archway, and a portal materialized.

With a deep exhale, he sent Satan's body hurdling toward it. His heart pounded against his chest as the portal sealed shut. He collapsed to the ground as his blood-soaked hand drenched the soil. His victory turned sour as he watched the stone archway change in appearance. Its stones corrupted and turned black, resonating with a darker aura, giving off a violet glow. With all his enemies gone, Hyperion was left alone to rebuild from the ashes of chaos.

His hand was no longer bleeding, his eyes shifted toward his battleaxes. Every inch was covered in blood except for a ruby stone embedded in the shoulder. It housed Hyperion's infinite power – the Flame of Aterma. With it, he would cleanse the universe and rebuild. He waved his hand over the book, causing it to disappear. He flapped his wings and ripped through the atmosphere, soaring into the vacuum of space. As he glided through the darkness, the horrors of his past flooded his mind. Glimpses of his grandfather flashed before his eyes. His dishonor filled him with grief. He grabbed the hilts of his axes and forged them together. The ruby stones ignited, and the merged axes, changing their shape into a spear. Grabbing ahold of the spear, the stones ignited once more, releasing an intense flame that encased his body until it exploded. A massive white light decimated everything it touched. The multiverse died for a new paradise to be born.

CHAPTER

1

REBIRTH

From the cosmic ashes, he created a singular system in the vacuum of darkness. Hyperion's attitude toward his accomplishment showed a new, dark, and malevolent side. The emptiness he felt inside was nearly erased. His new prized jewel was called: Helvaya.

Destroying the multiverse came with complications. A cosmic storm formed from the residual energy left behind. It ravaged the primitive planets. Hyperion could only contain a fraction of the cosmic storm and created a landmass from it, stationing it above a baron planet. Heaven was now reborn, but tranquility would not come easily. Every millennium the storm would return and trigger chaos. For centuries, Hyperion fought against the storm, trying to contain it, but even he could not win against it. It forced him to delay recreating new life. Hyperion brought forth temples, large meadows, and enormous mountains to fill his new kingdom. The beauty of heaven was darkened by silence. There was no laughter. No cheers for battle. No prayers. Knowing that his beloved angels were impure and prideful he still contemplated their revival. He re-envisioned their might and their beauty.

Knowing that the cosmic storm could destroy everything he loved, he still went forward with his plans. The Angelic Race would fill his lands with much-needed joy. As their numbers increased, they were divided into factions. Their strength was tested, and they were placed into three groups.

The first nine warrior factions became the Celestial Order. The next three became Generals – the Order of Aterma. The Generals reported to Hyperion's elite protectors – the High Council. Perched above his great citadel, he watched them flourish.

Happiness quickly turned to paranoia. He believed enemies could flourish from the shadows. Lacking the abilities to make his new children immune to corruption made him feel weak. From his essence, he created four God-like warriors. The Horsemen of the Apocalypse as they were named took orders from no one. Their sole purpose consisted of bringing an end to life. They slumbered as statues in his citadel, and only through his blood could they be awakened.

Hyperion's vision was coming together, but it still was not complete. There was emptiness still in his heart. The laughter and praise of the angels were not enough to fuel him. A god needed more to survive; without it, he would slowly lose his powers and decay. Satan turned his people against him long ago and weakened him. He dwelled on the idea of creating a new race of humans. His confusion led to centuries of sorrow. He watched his angels thrive but yearned for humans as they could repopulate and give him back his eternal strength. Hyperion did not want the ghost of his past to haunt him, but deep inside his decision was already made.

His emotions grew unstable, and the heavens thundered. His sorrow forced him to flee his palace. The barren planet below was flooded with his tears. Its magnificent glory called to him. Hyperion shimmered into light and floated down to the world, and as his feet touched down onto the cold water, it caused him to reveal himself. He waved his hand, and the water tossed and turned until sections of the bedrock rose from the depths and settled onto the surface. He landed on one of the landmasses and closed his eyes to meditate. By placing his hands on the floor, he could feel the vibrations in the ground.

The Creator took a deep breath and, as he opened his eyes, released a surge of energy. He jolted his hand into the ground and ripped through the bedrock, creating an island in the middle of the landmass. He flung his arm to the east and the ground separated once more, creating an opening for water to pour in around the island. A monstrous mountain stood before him. He sculpted the beauty into a huge fortress. The enchanting masterpiece would serve as a home for his new creation.

The shimmering sun cascaded its light across the Creator's face. The whispering wind overtook the island paradise and swirled around the mountain fortress before dancing off into the sun. Hyperion gazed at its beauty as he felt the moist dirt beneath his feet. As his toes dug into the dirt, faded memories resurfaced. The birth of mankind was his greatest accomplishment. He wanted to please his father so much, but in the end, he became a plague upon his family. Disappointment crossed his face as his memories faded from happiness to gloom. The fall of mankind was his doing. Secrets that he believed were buried; rose to the surface. His own children revolted against him. The visions of chaos caused him to grimace.

Even through the darkness, he still managed to smile. Praise and power drove his madness. This vast new world was larger than Earth in size and would be suitable for a much larger population. Grabbing the dirt from the floor, he sprinkled it in front of himself. The dirt spun into a funnel cloud and rapidly took the shape of a man. Standing at six feet tall, he had a very muscular physique. His majestic blue eyes were soulless until Hyperion breathed into his mouth. The sun's light gleamed off his sandy brown hair as the god took notice of his cream-colored skin. His body remained in its perfectly nude state. The Creator found him very handsome and admired his sublime creature.

Without delay, Hyperion gave him the task of overseeing the growth of mankind and its protection should anything happen to jeopardize it.

"My child, I bestow upon you the name, Sir Erin Whitespear."

Hyperion knew he could not entrust one person with supremacy. For reproduction to continue, a woman was needed. The name Lady Eileen Snowstar was bestowed upon her. She stood as tall as Sir Erin. Her eyes were an elegant green; her hair was as thick as vines and gave off a solemn green glow. The beautiful woman appeared like a goddess before him. They would rule as equals from the great fortress.

Humans were not the only dominant species on Earth. As a child, Hyperion witnessed countless creatures birthed by his grandfather. Many became extinct prior to the rise of mankind. He collected their DNA so one day he could repopulate the world once mankind withered away. Hyperion raised his hand into the air, the clouds began to darken, and the winds roared around them. Lightning struck down onto his palm, bringing forth his book once more. On the cover of the book was a single word:

Tarsem. It contained old, magical spells and charms that were used during the early reign of his family, known as the Time of the Elementals. One of the spells within the book brought forth a vault that contained samples of each creature.

He entrusted them to Sir Erin and Lady Eileen. They alone could not control these magnificent creatures. During the Time of the Elementals, the gods kept the balance between the World of Man and the World of Beast. Mankind and beast were kept in line by the wrath of the gods. Each of them was an elemental manipulator of the natural world and used their abilities to protect their subjects and enforce their reign. His new children would carry this trait. He gave life to four humans that would continue this legacy and give rise to the *Ilihi*.

Hyperion waved his hand toward the river and brought forth its water. From it, he created a woman that towered over him. She was rather slender and pale. Unlike Sir Erin she was not naked, she wore a dress that exposed much of her physique. A silver pendant, resembling two crescent moons, held her white satin dress together. It was positioned on her lower back, and from the crescent moons came a single strand of cloth that split in two as it got closer to her neck. The strands cascaded over her breasts and reached her belly button before continuing down as one strand. It continued between her legs and attached to the pendant. She wore a shredded skirt that exposed much of her pelvis and legs. The longest of the strands began at her lower back and trailed the floor behind her.

She was even more beautiful than Lady Eileen. Hyperion drew closer to her and breathed life into her, causing her eyes to light up. Her celeste-colored eyes captivated her creator as he gently touched her lips. A beauty such as she deserved a strong name, Lady Udana Moonspark. She held dominion over water. Her powers were seemingly limitless; with the passing of each full moon, she would grow stronger. Hyperion placed two silver cuffs on her wrist to keep her abilities from becoming a threat.

Hyperion then called to the ground and brought forth the dirt beneath him once more. With the wave of his hand the stones piled up creating a man. The stone man's physique was more muscular than Sir Erin. Hyperion grabbed hold of his face, and the ridges faded as his emerald eyes dilated. Releasing his face, the man took his first breath. His olive skin was hairier than Sir Erin's. He had long brown hair that cascaded down his back. His beard and mustache were full and trimmed neatly. His naked body drew attention from both Lady Udana and Lady Eileen. Hyperion covered him in deep purple and emerald robes.

To Hyperion's amazement, his creation assembled a staff of rocks from the ground and at the top of the staff stood a huge emerald. He would be able to manipulate anything that contained minerals from the bedrock of the planet. The Creator gave him the name Lord Celeio Teradom.

Hyperion's power was plummeting, but he was far from done. He drew fire from the sun and formed a man. Hyperion favored this one over the others since they shared similar abilities over fire manipulation. Hyperion's manipulation of light evolved from his control of fire. His creation stood as tall as the rest with jet black hair down his back and bright red eyes. He wanted to spoil his child, so he brought forth a meteorite from his kingdom and created a suit of black armor as tough as dragon scales. The remaining fragments of the meteorite were used to create a helmet, sword and shield. As the Creator handed him his weapons, he kissed his child on the forehead and deemed him - Lord Marlusha Infernoheart.

Hyperion nearly collapsed. He was overexerting himself. The longer he was away from his citadel, the weaker he became. He could not falter. There was one more to be created. Taking in a deep breath, he exhaled a mighty whistle that caused a massive whirlwind to form. He twirled his fingers into it, and something odd appeared before him. This man was slender and very old. Hyperion grew worried as he noticed the man was covered in a tattooed language he could not decipher. This omen caused a panic. The man was not perfection, as the others. His hair was long and as white as snow, and he was also blind. He blamed the imperfection on his depleting stamina. He drew from solar energy and created golden robes for him to hide the markings. Gifted with control of the winds, the tender, old man was given the name Lord Grevis Stormlight.

Hyperion grew weaker and collapsed onto Sir Erin. His children rushed to his side as they noticed blood dripping from his nose. His protective aura flickered as he nearly lost consciousness. Lord Celeio created a throne from the dirt and placed his father on it. His children lowered themselves to the ground and tended to him as he tried to regain his focus. Lady Eileen rubbed her father's head as he closed his eyes. He tasked each of them with a duty to carry out. The Divine Lords, as he called them, would work under the direction of Sir Erin and Lady Eileen.

It was done. The seeds of creation were planted. Hyperion erupted into a bright light and took off into the setting sun. The Creator returned to his empire and allowed Sir Erin and Lady Eileen to rule without interference. Mankind began to flourish; Sir Erin and Lady Eileen gave birth to their first son, King Habagin Whitespear, while the other Divine Lords mated and populated their own regions. As King Habagin got older, he married Calista Stormlight, a daughter of Lady Udana and Lord Grevis. In his adulthood, King Habagin was a massive man towering over his father at eight feet with a muscular physique. The only feature he inherited from his mother was her green eyes. His wife was also a sight of beauty. Her white, flowing hair and blue eyes were lusted over by many. She catered to her husband, with the ambition she would rule one day after his parents were dead, but they had other plans for their son.

Tartarus, a mountain fortress surrounded by Nightfeather Forest, became their home. King Habagin and his descendants became Wardens of the Dead, tasked with ferrying souls to Heaven. His four oldest children became fearsome Ilihi, but those that came afterward were born mortal. With each passing day, countless souls were ferried into the afterlight. Hyperion had to take additional precautions. Taking on this cosmic form, he descended from the heavens to visit Sir Erin and Lady Eileen. In order to survive and live longer lives, many of the creatures had to be removed. Lady Eileen did not see eye to eye with her creator and was displeased with his actions.

Her insolence reminded him of Eve. She too was strong-willed and rebellious against her creator when he created the first humans on Earth, but unlike Eve, if Lady Eileen did not submit, he surely would make her.

As he did before, he called the Tarsem forth from the heavens. He enacted spells that would place them under an eternal slumber and hid them away where no human would wander. Time would run its course, and all that would remain of them would be ash and bone. After the last of the beasts were taken away, he met with Lady Eileen and Sir Erin to discuss what was to come. When their meeting was complete, he took flight into the sky and engulfed the world in his glorious light. The memories of the colossal creatures were wiped from their collective minds.

Hyperion's light was fading rapidly. The Flame of Aterma was pushing its limits to sustain him in this form. The Creator needed to regain his strength and magnify his power. Without delay, he ordered the High

Council to forge a crystal out of his throne. His cosmic form was placed within it as well as the Flame of Aterma. His armor was melted down and he ordered his Solaris Angels - a sect within the High Council – to forge an hourglass from it. Referred to as the Dordim, it would house the Flame once he drew enough energy from it. If used by God, it would start the countdown to eradicating life once more.

The Solaris Angels were left with a gift, naming the world. Collectively, they chose LunaSol. With Hyperion out of commission, deception and treason followed. Satan planned his downfall. He waited for the right moment to make his move against his creator. His decaying body was held in place by four chains appearing from the dark abyss around him. Two chains held his arms levitated above, while the other two kept his feet chained to a stone tablet.

Satan could hear the joy of the outside world, as the chains burned at his flesh. His prison was placed on the moon, so no human would be drawn to his darkness. His priority was to break free from his chains. He concentrated his energy onto the chains and created a glowing fire. The chains were shattered, and he was set at ease knowing he was able to walk freely in the abyss.

Overconfident in his success, he then focused all his dark energy into his hands. If he could create a rift in the abyss, he would be able to weaken his prison. With that he would have access to the outside world. Satan tried to meditate and take full control of his darkness, but it was harder than he thought. The prison was meant to keep his energy scattered. His mind was assaulted with pain. Hyperion did not want him to regain full control of his powers. With all his might, he tried, and he tried, until a ray of hope emerged. He managed to create a small rift in the abyss, but it was not enough.

This new alternative source of energy gave Satan a brilliant idea. If he could harness enough of its energy and project it onto the gateway, it would ricochet back to him and recharge his own power. The idea was ludicrous, but he had to try something. The prison was eating away at his crumbling mind. Satan took in a deep breath, placed his fingertips in a circle, and focused his energy into a ball. It was a huge, eerie sphere of darkness. Sparks erupted from the ball and started condensing the energy. Once all his energy was in the palm of his hands, he shot it at the door, and the door redirected it back at him. He erupted into a black cloud, and the energy ball shot right through him, stunning him. The sparks forced him into his demonic form. With this new energy pulsating through his veins, he turned and attacked the gate once more. He directed the energy into his mouth and let out a mighty roar.

The roar sparked the entire abyss, and he was able to finally inflict damage onto the surface of the gate. A small crack appeared in the center. It was not big enough to inflict any real damage against his father, but it was a start. The attack weakened him greatly and left him nearly dead. The demonic angel needed time to recuperate, so he could draw energy from the darkness around him. He fell asleep at the base of the stone tablet.

A loud ringing overtook the heavens and overshadowed the fracture of the gate. The angels abandoned their day-to-day activities and gazed upon the great citadel. They watched as their Generals flew toward the call. In the citadel, Hyperion's essence glowed with radiance. It was time for him to usher in his final stage-the Era of Eternal Life. Earth was never able to reach this level of existence due to the fall of mankind. Early humans lived to about one thousand years before death, but on LunaSol they would be gifted with longer life spans. Hyperion emerged from his crystal in his new form. His servants were worried, because his appearance was not normal. He aged rapidly. His hair was pure white, and his skin was burned. The Flame took life from him rather than restoring it.

Returning to LunaSol, he met the Divine Lords and Royals at the royal fortress. Drawing on their power he engulfed the world in his light. The immeasurable blast shook the ground, rendering various slumber spells to be undone. A wave of energy slipped into the crack of Satan's prison, burning it even further.

While Satan began to hatch his demonic plan, Sir Erin and Lady Eileen were doing some planning of their own. Hyperion's actions to rid the world of beasts weighed heavily on them. Secrets that he thought were hidden came to light. Sir Erin and Lady Eileen were fearful of challenging him directly. They knew the day would come when they had no choice but to stop him.

CHAPTER
2

THE FALL

For thousands of years, LunaSol prospered while Hyperion watched from the heavens. Sir Erin and Lady Eileen had countless children, but they were expecting another one any day now. Satan had already amassed enough energy to infect the child with evil. On the day of the child's birth, a lunar eclipse loomed overhead. Satan could feel Lady Eileen trying to push out the baby.

He released a shock wave that cracked the gate even more. By using his darkness, he took control of the baby's mind while still partially in the womb. Satan would use her as a pawn to finally rid himself of Hyperion. The child would help him do so when she came of age and mastered her abilities. Lady Eileen gave one final push, and into the world came her new baby girl. She held the child in her arms and named her Princess Eris Snowstar.

Fearing that he would get caught, Satan used this moment to infect one of Hyperion's Solaris Angels. Amongst the humans, angels typically remained in their fiery state, but in Heaven they were creatures of beauty. Lucus, the angel infected, bore twelve white wings. His armor had a lion face etched onto its center. He instructed his servant to shield the child until the time was right. He also had another mission: steal the Tarsem. Within its pages was the clue to finally killing his creator. Satan could not move too quickly without being caught in the act. Time had to take its course if his plan was going to work.

While Satan was stuck in his prison, he learned new tricks that allowed him to gain more control. He knew Hyperion was filled with malice and tried his best to steer clear of him, but the infection was growing. His greed for power drove him insane. His conquest and unparalleled control led him to destroy his family, but Satan would return the favor. He knew how to tap into Hyperion's greed to his advantage. With Hyperion's darkness growing, Satan could not allow that energy to be wasted. He slowly fed on that greed from a distance without ever raising an alarm.

While Satan waited, Lady Eileen gave birth to another child - Princess Ionica Snowstar. A thousand years passed before she would give birth again to a baby boy - Prince Adam Whitespear. A few thousand years passed before Lady Eileen gave birth to her final child. The labor of her last child left her incredibly weak. This allowed for Satan to move forward with his plans. Princess Eris was the first of his pawns to be moved into place. Her training was finally over, and now the real battle was ahead of her.

She had surpassed both her parents in strength. Her power even rivaled the Divine Lords. War was declared, and Satan's plan went off like clockwork. Princess Eris waited until the dead of night and used her mastery over the shadows to slip into her parents' bedroom as they slept peacefully. Her piercing purple eyes watched them as they slumbered. She slowly approached their bedside. Her black nails caressed their lips, and without hesitation or remorse she stood over them and placed her hands a short distance from their mouths. Shadows sprung from her hands and into their bodies, consuming their souls. Lady Eileen and Sir Erin jolted in their sleep, as their bodies turned to dust.

An alarm went off in the heavens that vibrated through the ground. Satan's plan was breached. The angels gathered from their resting grounds to the citadel in fear. Their father's light flickered in terror. That alarm only meant one thing – someone was murdered. Lucus panicked and was eager to fulfill his task. His eyes turned purple; he grabbed his sword and ferociously killed the two angels that were guarding the relics he needed. Killing them corrupted his heart even further. His body mutated into a darker form and his white-feathered wings turned black.

Hyperion took on his angelic form once more, as he heard the commotion outside of his throne room. Even in his decaying state he still had vigor. He grabbed a sword and blew open the doors. To his surprise, Lucus was orchestrating a civil war. His light turned purple as he infected hordes of angels with his demonic powers. He ordered them to stop, but Lucus laughed at the Supreme Being. His infected servants addressed him as Lord Dark Lucus, which infuriated Hyperion. He slammed his foot into the ground sending out a shock wave of energy that knocked many of them back, but Lord Dark Lucus dodged it and fled the heavens.

The war spilled over onto LunaSol. Eris and Lord Dark Lucus attacked the Divine Lords, who were protecting the Royal Family. The Divine Lords were able to hold Eris off, but they did not anticipate the brute strength of the corrupted angels. They held them at bay for as long as they could, but their fate was sealed. They were betrayed by one of their own. Lord Marlusha weakened the collective and delivered them to the enemy. Lady Udana, Lord Grevis, and Lord Celeio were no more. Those that remained loyal to Hyperion were too late. They descended from the heavens and attacked the traitors. Lord Marlusha took his leave in search of the children.

Hyperion sent down two of his Solaris Angels, Antillias, and Soldiel to return the Royal Family to his side. The two Generals were concealed in fire. They would not reveal their true forms to lesser beings. They found what remained of the Royal Family and brought them to Heaven. Antillias stared at the children as they awaited the Creator. The children were still in their sleepwear. Princess Ionica's blue robe concealed the baby prince. He was nuzzled against her chest. She did not trust them. Prince Adam with his messy brown hair held onto his sister's hand as he tried to focus on the shimmering flames in front of him. After the death of her parents, she knew the angels could not protect them. This evil went unnoticed even by Hyperion.

Princess Ionica watched their every movement. Evil still loomed in the heavens, and the princess worried it would come for them. She knew more about Hyperion than even his own servants. The princess voiced her concerns and wanted to escape before he returned. Antillias grew infuriated with the princess for speaking ill of the Creator. She refused to listen, but Soldiel could feel something was not right. Antillias was called away to destroy the infected creatures that were ravaging the planet.

While Antillias was away, Soldiel grabbed Princess Ionica and the children and returned them back to LunaSol. He could sense something was not right with his father. Hyperion's only concern was the baby prince. He left their side to check on Satan's prison, only to find it opened. The prison stood intact for centuries, and for what? Soldiel always questioned why Hyperion kept him as a trophy. He sought the wisdom of The Keepers (three angelic sisters with immense abilities) to get answers. It took Soldiel a while to return to the Royal Family, but when he returned, he came bearing bad news. Hyperion was no longer himself. The baby prince was in danger, and if he found him, he would have slaughtered him. Princess Ionica was confused. Why would their god want to kill her baby brother? Soldiel knew more than he was letting on, but he had a plan to save the prince. He took them to the Temple of Notus - one of the four spiritual temples protected by The Keepers. Within the temple, there was a huge archway that lay in ruin. He removed a scroll fragment from his armor and levitated it in front of him.

The children stood nearby and watched as he began to chant.

Păzitorii timpului, deschide-ți porțile.

Întunericul a apărut pentru a ne corupe soarta.

Permiteți-mi puterea de a începe o nouă ardezie.

(Guardians of time, open your gates.

Darkness has arisen to corrupt our fate.

Allow me the strength to start a new slate.)

The pieces of rock that lay on the floor began to repair themselves. The ruined rocks reanimated and recreated the archway. Once completed, a portal appeared in the center of it. The portal was shimmering and presented a calming presence. Soldiel gestured for the princess to hand him the child. He took the baby and told the princess that he was sending the prince to live in a realm where Hyperion could never reach him. He entered the portal and appeared in a primitive world of volcanic destruction. Soldiel had no time to waste and could not afford to let the rift of time stay open too long. If the portal remained open, it would cause chaos to the time flux.

He hid the child and returned through the portal, he found himself surrounded by Hyperion and a squad of angels. The Creator stared at the archway in utter disbelief. Rebellion. His angels once again betrayed him.

Enemies on all sides. Hyperion's dark history was unfolding before his very eyes.

"Where is the child?"

"Somewhere you will never find him."

His disbelief turned into rage. The mighty Solaris Angel stood his ground and did not show any shame in his actions. He could sense the Royal Family escaped unharmed. Soldiel breathed a sigh of relief knowing Hyperion did not have them.

His sigh triggered anger amongst the others. They attacked him to appease Hyperion. Soldiel's brute strength overwhelmed them, but he could not stand alone against their creator. With a snap of his fingers, all the angels were forced back into the heavens. He tortured Soldiel in front of his peers. The High Council and Order of Aterma pleaded with Hyperion, but he only turned his rage onto them. He allowed the darkness to consume him and infect his physical form. Hyperion revealed that in order to stop Eris and Lord Dark Lucus, he had to absorb Satan's power. He was too weak to fight it, and it infected his mind. He ordered his servants to address him as Lord Nebula. The angels quickly took action to keep him at bay.

While they fought in the heavens, Princess Ionica and Prince Adam were whisked away to safety. Loyalists prepared by Lady Eileen separated the children and escorted the princess to Luna Mountain and the prince to Sol Mountain. Hidden within were shrines built to house the mightiest of beasts - *dragons*. Only their amulets could awaken them from their slumber.

Following instructions, they each presented their amulets and spoke the ancient tongue, releasing them from their slumber. The Sapphire Dragon was covered in white scales with a soft blue tone on the tips. Multiple sapphire gems were embedded into her body; the main one was on her chest. Her horns resembled antlers. They were sharp and white as well. The Ruby Dragon was covered in red scales and had multiple ruby gems embedded into his body. His claws were black and sharper than any metal. His horns were black and protruded from a ruby crown on his forehead.

The royals were fearful; dragons were said to have become extinct during Eris' birth. There was an instant bond between them. Prince Adam and Princess Ionica mounted their dragons and took off into the sky. The mighty dragons soared above the skies, witnessing the world below ravaged by chaos. The continents were ripped apart, and new landmasses were created. Lord Dark Lucus was to blame. He separated the four continents of Anahata, Adva, Terra Firma, and Lavos and formed three new ones.

Eris and Lord Dark Lucus could sense a powerful foe approaching. They waged war on the newly formed continent of Weguard. They were able to take control of the land and set their eyes on the continent of Valhalla. Driven by greed, they thought they were unbeatable. Countless cities burned to the ground as they celebrated their victories. However, their victories ended when Eris was pierced by a shard of ice from the sky. The ice climbed up her body, and all that remained visible was her head. Lord Dark Lucus tried to flee, but he was surrounded and caged in fire.

Princess Ionica and Prince Adam descended from the sky. In a fight against dragons, they knew they would surely die. The two marvelous creatures descended from the sky and witnessed an army of Fae creatures. As mighty as they were, they could not take on the horde by themselves. With their ferocious roar, they awakened an army of their own. The opposition rose against the darkness, and the war escalated.

While the Holy War consumed the planet, the heavens plunged into darkness. Lord Nebula crucified countless servants and set others ablaze. His angels used the Flame of Aterma to bind him. They created chains from the flame. The Solaris Angels brought forth the Tarsem and used a spell that would bind the demonic being and drain his power into relics of their choosing. Lord Nebula's power was finally sealed away in the heavens. Now, the World of Man needed them most. They descended from the heavens and slaughtered those that remained loyal to Lord Nebula. Chaos and hatred nearly brought the world to its knees.

With the Creator gone, the angels had no leader. The law of the Tarsem was clear; they could no longer interfere in mankind's affairs. After the Holy War they abandoned them and returned to the heavens, so they could restore it to its former glory. Evil still thrived in the shadows as Eris and Lord Dark Lucus were still at large. Mankind would have to stand alone against this enemy.

PART II - NEW BEGINNINGS

CHAPTER
3

ALEXANDER

"All right, it's time to close the book; it's time for bed. You have to wake up tomorrow for your first day of school."

"But dad, I want to finish reading about what happened to the baby. Did he ever return to LunaSol? Was he reunited with his family?" The fragile boy with golden, spiky hair pleaded with him.

"Alexander! Go to bed; you can finish reading the book tomorrow night," demanded Drail.

Drail Chamberling was a tall and strapping man. His blond hair was combed back and away from his face. His full beard shifted in colors, from blond to white. Nothing was left to the imagination since his cerulean robe fit him like a glove. The robes had beautiful, cool gray trimming. He was a man of importance, being the Duke of Hellenic and a humble servant of Queen Rania Khair. She was one of the ruling monarchs; Hellenic was her seat of power and one of the ten countries that comprised the continent of Laurasia. It was a southern country near the Tethys Sea. Across the sea was a massive continent that remained mostly untouched by mankind: Gondwana. It was mostly jungle. The small portions that were colonized by people were the subjects of Queen Rania. Drail's job was to oversee the colonies. Over the years he was gifted pieces of land including the castle where he and his son lived. They called the Villa d'Padamo home.

For a long time, Alexander was homeschooled, but in the morning, he was finally going to attend an Ivy League high school. It was also his sixteenth birthday. The green-eyed boy pulled his black covers over his body, so only his head could be seen. His messy blond hair nearly covered his eyes. He was very persistent to read more of the story. Since childhood, Drail would write stories of this fantasy world - LunaSol. They were never published, but only for Alexander's entertainment. Drail could not help but look at his son and stroke the top of his head with sympathy.

"Okay, okay!" Alexander knew he was not going to win this argument. His futile attempts would only make his father more upset. The window next to him remained open, and the gentle breeze patted his face. His father turned off the table lamp and exited the room. The restless child kept tossing and turning, pondering the story. Sleep was a luxury he was fighting for, but once obtained, he was out like a light.

His mind was filled with dreams of LunaSol, but they soon turned to nightmares. This dream was more vivid than any other. He was in a dark room and could barely see anything around him. The smell of burnt flesh filled his nose. The hair on the back of his neck stood up as he heard someone breathing. He frantically turned his head and could see purple-piercing eyes staring at him from across the room.

He woke up in fear and soaked the bed in his sweat. The shimmering moonlight beamed through the open window and called to him. The midnight breeze filled the room and calmed his spirits. It filled his soul with strength as he walked over to the window and held onto the banister, as he looked across the castle grounds. The full moon reflected off the pond and cascaded its light throughout the garden.

The beautiful blue diamond orchards danced in the twilight hours whispering to him. Alexander was fixating on a fantasy and needed to get some rest. He went back to his bed and fell asleep once more. He could not afford to have his father walk in and scream at him.

The next morning, the sun beamed in and covered the room in a satisfying glow. Alexander awoke to the sound of his door being opened. It was his handsome butler. Towering six feet, wearing his black and white suit. His stunning blue eyes met Alexander's. He entered with his breakfast and sat it on the bed. While the boy ate like an animal feasting on its last meal, his butler entered the closet to fetch him an outfit. He came out with a green polo and white shorts.

Alarmed by the sounds, the butler looked toward the boy. With judgment, his eyes burned through him, and Alexander raised his head in embarrassment. They shared a satisfying laugh, and he made Alexander hurry up before he was late for school. After he finished with the crumbs on his plate he washed up and got dressed. The sound of his butler's voice rushing him; he ran downstairs to meet the driver.

As Alexander reached the bottom of the stairs, he noticed that the house seemed rather different. His eyes were drawn to his father's study. The glass windows overlooking the living room were closed rapidly. A loud ringing pulsated in his ear and made his heart race. He could barely stand and grabbed onto the rail for a few minutes until the sound went away. Thinking nothing of it, he grabbed his backpack from the sofa and put on his sneakers as he ran to the front door.

He ran down the marble staircase and down the cobblestone road to the limousine. The limousine driver was also exquisite to look at. Everyone who worked for his father looked like they were selected from a magazine. He was also wearing a black and white suit, his eyes were green, his hair spikey and golden like Alexander's. He opened the door and stepped back as Alexander got into the car. He closed the door and went around to the driver's seat. The young boy's mind replayed each story he heard before bed. He was fixated on this world and the rich and vibrant imagination his father put into each story.

He wanted so badly to believe LunaSol could exist. Having been homeschooled, he had the best teacher's money could buy. Learning astronomy from Dr. Livite, he knew his world was a smaller fragment of a bigger universe. The man was a genius. He was five foot-four and was bald on top with curls on the side of his head. He talked about the formation of the universe and all the stars and planets. He prayed that one day his government would find life on another planet. The idea frightened him. What would happen if an Ilihi lived on Earth? What would his government do? On one side the government would use them as soldiers, while the others would kill them because they were different.

Hellenic was the most powerful country in the world. The laws under the queen were not accepting of all people. She was also the governing figure of religion. The majority of those within her boarders belonged to the Congregation of the Divine. Their main teachings revolved around spirituality and divine rule. Religious leaders working for the crown passed on these teachings, which came from a single book that was passed down from God. Their supreme being is never mentioned by name in any of their religious texts. Hundreds of temples were erected for the masses to worship. Hellenic was bordered by Celtica and Cisalpina which shared the same religion. Drail always taught Alexander to keep an open mind.

His daydreams continued to fill his mind as the limousine made its way further away from the castle to his school. The Academy for Privileged Individuals was a private high school in Hellenic. The school only opened its doors to families of wealth. It provided the best education in the country and allowed the students to have a healthy learning environment. It was an old castle that was revamped with modern technology and turned into a high-tech school. It was located on a hill, overlooking the town of Atpolis. The car ride seemed forever with all the twists and turns. The streets were filled with old monuments and buildings that were erected thousands of years ago.

Alexander gazed over all the buildings and statues that they passed, but all he could think about was the dream that haunted him. Inside of him there was a longing for a connection to Drail's story. He felt like an outcast here; he was living alone with his father and barely had interactions with anyone outside of his house. Drail told him that his mother died giving birth to him due to complications. Their house contained no memories of her, not even a picture. His father barely spoke about her. He could not even bring himself to describe how she looked. He became emotional and began to cry quietly in the backseat. As tears escaped his eyes, they landed on the floor. A quake overtook the road, causing the car to jolt sideways. After a few minutes, the driver was able to regain control of the car. He glared through the mirror and saw the boy's face. This was not a natural tremor.

The school became visible as they reached the top of the hill. The students were still outside waiting for the bell to ring. The driver opened the door and allowed Alexander out. Everyone was staring at him. His golden spikes glistened in the sun. His green eyes locked onto a group of kids whispering. He bypassed them and walked toward an administrator who was holding up a sign with his name. It was the Orientation Administrator, Mr. Quintin. A small, red-haired man with glasses. He was escorted into the school and taken into the office. He was provided with his school schedule and shown to his first class.

First period consisted of World History with Mr. Kakos. He was a slender man with choppy black hair and a full beard. He welcomed Alexander and assigned him a seat. Timidly, he walked past two boys who were whispering about him. The boy behind them kicked their chairs and ordered them to shut up. Out of fear, they did what he said. Alexander locked eyes with the boy. His green eyes were mesmerizing, and his perfect white smile made him blush. The boy was sixteen as well and introduced himself as Gabriel Buros. His brown hair was combed back and he wore a blue polo shirt and white-washed jeans. His father was the owner of Jade Circle Developments, a real estate developer. He shook Alexander's hand as he took his seat.

The classroom consisted of smaller groups of twenty-five students to ensure adequate learning. Alexander took out his books as the class passed around the assignment. They were instructed to pair up in teams of two to complete a project by week's end. Gabriel jumped at the chance to work with him. The assignment required them to complete a research paper on Religion. After reviewing the list, Gabriel was upset when he noticed something was missing.

"Professor, why did you omit the Creed of Lykos?"

The students looked around at one another in confusion. The professor stared at Gabriel and swallowed abruptly.

"The Creed of Lykos was omitted because it is not considered a religion of Laurasia."

"So, excuse my confusion. Is this assignment supposed to be about religions that are practiced by the majority or to research and shed light on religions so that we can learn more about them?"

Gabriel's comment stirred the class to laughter. He was known to have a bit of a temper. The professor shook his head and silenced the class.

"If it means that much to you to write about the Creed of Lykos then you have my permission."

Alexander noticed Gabriel wanted the final word, but he placed his hand on his forearm to try and get him to submit. He did not realize it was going to work. Gabriel did not say another word. He turned to his partner and smiled. For the remaining hour of the class, they logged into the computer stations and began working on their assignment. Gabriel took the lead and began searching for sites with references about the religion. Alexander watched him from the corner of his eye. He was so infatuated with him that he could not concentrate. The boy noticed and punched him in his arm as he laughed.

"We need to focus!"

"Sorry about that."

"Don't worry. I would stare at you all day if I could."

The comment made Alexander blush. He changed subjects, scared that the other students would make fun of them. He asked Gabriel why he was interested in researching this religion. He closed his eyes and shook his head before answering.

"My mother was a practicing Lykos before she died. I began practicing it because of her."

The conversation stopped. Alexander felt guilty for making him relive a painful moment. He too was motherless and confessed that his mother died during childbirth. Gabriel turned to him and pushed his shoulder against Alexander, trying to lighten the mood. Before he could learn anything about the Creed of Lykos, the bell rang for second period. Gabriel wrote down his phone number and placed it in Alexander's hand. He wanted to meet up after school so they could continue working on the project.

As he headed to second period, he noticed the girls smiling and winking at him. He never reacted to girls the same way he reacted to guys. For the rest of the day, he shifted from class to class, but his mind was on Gabriel. He now had something else to focus on rather than the stories of LunaSol. He hoped their friendship would flourish into something more, but that reality disappeared as he entered his last class. The professor was nowhere in sight, and the students were fooling around throwing paper airplanes at one another. In the back of the class, he noticed Gabriel was holding onto a girl's waist. He could not see her face, but she was curvy with long wavey hair. She wore a white shirt with a yellow and black plaid skirt. He did not realize Alexander was in the same class as him again. Alexander watched as he kissed the girl on the lips. He turned his face and took a seat in the front. The girl next to him noticed he was upset by what he saw.

"Don't let those two lovebirds get to you. Gabriel and Natasha have been together since primary school."

"Why would they get to me?"

40

The girl chose not to respond. She knew he was not ready to admit he was jealous. She rather introduced herself as Amira St. Clair. She had a darker skin complexion than him. Her head and neck were covered by a pink hijab, and she wore a white shirt and pink jeans. She extended her hand to him and shook his hand. Gabriel finally noticed he was in the room and pushed off Natasha and took his seat. He tried to get Alexander's attention, but he ignored him and continued talking to Amira. Before Gabriel could interrupt their conversation, the professor entered the room and had everyone take their seats. He gave his opening remarks for Anatomy 101 and provided them with their syllabus for the remainder of the year.

Amira handed Alexander his book, and when he opened the front cover, he noticed someone had drawn a symbol of a sun and a moon intertwined. He rubbed his finger over it and noticed it was drawn in blood. It sparkled upon touch and then he was hit with a massive migraine. The purple menacing eyes flashed in his mind again. Amira noticed something was wrong with him and asked the professor if she could take him to the nurse. Gabriel tried to follow, but Natasha grabbed him by his arm and made him sit down.

Alexander walked to the nurse's station, but the floor seemed to disappear beneath his feet. He collapsed onto the floor and faded into darkness. He slowly regained his senses and noticed his clothes were wet. The first thought to cross his mind was that he peed himself. He opened his eyes and noticed he was not in his school anymore. A vast lake stood between him and what appeared to be a palace. He rubbed his eyes and noticed a woman standing in the middle of the lake calling out to him. The words coming out of her mouth were foreign to him. He tried to step forward, but his feet were trapped in the mud. It pulled him down into the water, and as he drowned, he finally awoke from the dream.

He was lying on a bed in the nurse's station. Amira was explaining to the nurse what happened in the hallway. She noticed he was finally waking up and she ran to him.

"You scared me! What happened back there?"

"What do you mean? We were in Anatomy. Why am I here?"

"You don't remember you had a headache, and we started walking to the nurse?"

He did not remember the headache or even walking with her. He shook his head no and asked if had called his father. The nurse stated she was able to get in touch with his father and he was on his way. The nurse asked for Amira to return to class, but she refused to leave his side. The nurse walked away and allowed them some time to talk. Once the nurse was out of sight, Amira questioned Alexander some more.

"Tell me the truth. What do you remember?"

"I had the craziest dream."

Amira's eyes lit up. "Tell me!"

"I woke up in a lake. There was a woman calling to me, but she was speaking in a different language. It was hard for me to understand. My feet were stuck in mud, and I began to drown, and I woke up here."

Amira gave him a devilish grin. She rubbed his shoulder and told him to get some more rest until his father got there. Alexander refused to close his eyes; he worried he would have another nightmare. Minutes turned to hours, and finally Drail appeared. He rushed into the school and saw his son lying on the bed. The nurse tried to calm him down and explained the situation to him. Drail just stared at his son with sorrow. The school was aware that the boy had a long history of medical issues. As a child, he had horrible seizures. He had unbearable night terrors and would fall asleep for days at a time. With the best physicians, Drail thought his son had pushed past these issues. Alexander rose from the bed, walked toward his father and gave him a hug. Drail ordered his driver, Marcelo, to help his son to the car. Drail remained behind to collect his things.

He noticed a girl staring at him from the end of the hall. He stopped dead in his tracks and watched as a white python slithered out of her pant leg. A loud ringing noise caused him to close his eyes, and when he opened them, the girl vanished. He rushed out of the school and took his son back home.

CHAPTER

4

SECRETS

Upon their arrival the butler, Hans, and the Security Manager, Unic, greeted them. Unic towered over the staff. He was very muscular. He had a neck tattoo and a bunch on his arms. He kept them covered with his suit. He communicated with his officers through his earpiece. They noticed the worried look on Drail's face. Without question, they helped Alexander into the house and into bed. Drail ordered everyone to follow him into his office, while the boy rested.

"Something is not right with my son. We need to keep an eye on him," ordered Drail.

Unic responded, "I sense there is something you are not telling us."

Drail reluctantly spoke, "I saw something odd at his school. There was a girl staring at me after I got Alexander. A white python appeared from her pant leg."

The maids broke out into whispers, "The Demon Mother! It can't be."

Hans grew nervous, "The boy is in danger. We cannot let him go back to that school."

Drail screamed, "Enough. The boy is protected. Whatever she is, we will deal with it."

Drail ordered everyone back to their post. He wanted to be left alone. Hans took his leave, but Unic remained behind.

"Master, this is not good. Are you sure it was a white python?" Unic muttered.

"Yes."

Hans was listening from the door. He worried about Alexander and went to check on him, but he was not in his room. Panicked, he ran throughout the house looking for him. The maids revealed that he had a guest, and they were in the garden. The boy apparently got his address from peeking at his file in the nurse's room. Hans informed Drail, and they watched from the office balcony as Alexander and the boy sat in the garden talking. Gabriel was worried about him. He wanted to make sure he was okay.

Gabriel noticed Alexander was acting distant with him. "What's on your mind?"

"You!"

Gabriel paused before he answered, "What about me?"

"Nothing. I'm just glad you're here."

Gabriel hugged Alexander and kissed him on the cheek. Drail was disturbed by the boy's actions and ordered Hans to have the boy removed from the premises. Before Hans could leave the room, he was called back to the balcony. The maids had allowed someone else into the house.

"Hans, she is here."

"Master, who?"

"The girl!"

Hans stared into the garden and noticed the young girl with a pink hijab. She sat next to Alexander and played with his hair. She noticed they were being watched and looked up toward the balcony and waved. Drail grimaced and tried to keep his composure. He left the balcony and searched his office for a book. He found what he was looking for and took a seat. Hans continued to watch them as they pulled out their schoolbooks to study. Drail needed answers to what he saw. The book in his hands was bound in leather and contained old paintings. The paintings had hidden text in the images. As he turned the pages, he stopped on one that depicted two children beneath an apple tree and a white python slithering down from it. As he read the text, his body tensed up. He closed the book and rushed toward the balcony.

"We need to separate them, NOW!"

"Sir, what is going on?"

Hans picked up the book that his master left on the desk. As he turned the pages, his stomach began to turn. The book entitled; 'Genesis' was forbidden in Hellenic; if the Queen was to find out, she would have him killed. The book was written by a Shaman in the jungles of Gondwana. The first few pages depicted the death of God. The following pages depicted the ancient tribes that sprung to life before the Great Flood wiped out everything and humans were the only ones to survive. The white python was the sigil for the Tribe of Demons.

"Why would you think she is a demon?"

"The night terrors, him collapsing at school, my vision of the white python. Someone is playing a deadly game with my boy."

Drail stared at the girl intensely. As they were studying, Alexander noticed a drop of blood next to him. He looked up at Amira and noticed blood was falling from her ear. He pointed it out and called for help. She refused assistance and asked him to show her to the bathroom to clean up. Drail noticed the blood too and urged Hans to follow them. He would not tell Hans why. Hans feared causing a scene but did as commanded. He found Alexander waiting for her outside of first floor bathroom.

"Is everything okay, little one?"

"My friend Amira, she was bleeding," replied Alexander.

The mere mention of her name summoned her from the bathroom.

"Everything is fine. I just need to get home."

Hans responded, "Let us take you home."

His offer was denied. Her driver was still waiting for her outside. She had her bag and books in hand as she rushed out the front door and into her car. Hans found the girl's actions rather odd. He asked Alexander if his friend was staying for dinner. He was going to make lasagna. With a nod of his head yes, he returned to the garden to study. Gabriel had laid out all the papers he printed for their project and let Alexander into his world.

He was one of eight hundred people who identified with the Creed of Lykos. Those who practiced the religion were very tight lipped about it. The religion was founded by the people of Gondwana. Even though the continent was vastly unsettled, there were small settlements that were untainted by colonization. Their teachings ended up in Laurasia but were not accepted by the vast majority. They were characterized as a cult because they believed in magic. They believed mankind was descended from three tribes: elves, demons, and shapeshifters. This differed from the teaching of the Congregation of the Divine. The Divine Text spoke about a garden and a man and a woman populating the world. This story was upheld by many of the religious teachings in Laurasia.

Alexander was mesmerized by the images. He thought his father's stories of LunaSol were amazing, but now learning about the Creed of Lykos was even better. He stared at Gabriel as he flipped each page and continued down memory lane. Alexander placed his hand over Gabriel's as they came to an image of an apple tree. Beneath it was a pack of wolves. A smile escaped his lips as he looked up at Alexander, enclosing his fingers with his own.

"This was my mother's favorite story."

The shapeshifting tribe was unlike the others. They had no origin story. After centuries of fighting between the Elves and Demons, they stumbled upon a mountain. Within that mountain was a glorious tree with shimmering petals. The hypnotic lights faded as the intruders desecrated the ground with their war. They sought to eat the apples from the tree, only to find a new enemy awaited them. The massive wolves awoke from their slumber and tore through the elves and the demons. Once they had their fill of blood, they emerged into the world scared and confused. The light of the sun forced them to change shape and revert to their humanoid form. After centuries of crossbreeding, humans came into being.

Alexander was ecstatic that Gabriel chose to share this side of himself. He geeked out at the idea of having a friend that believed in this kind of stuff. Before he could turn the page, Alexander stopped him.

"So, what does the Creed of Lykos have to do with these stories?"

Gabriel replied, "They are the descendants of Elves!"

His words made Alexander laugh uncontrollably. Gabriel grew uneasy watching him laugh. He took his religion seriously and found it offensive. Alexander composed himself and finally was able to explain himself. He was in awe of the story. He wanted more. Gabriel's annoyance changed to joy. He was glad to be able to share a side of himself that he kept hidden from others.

Alexander's attentive ears were ready. He was surprised to learn that the Creed of Lykos believed they were descended from the Lykos Tribe of Elves. They were the oldest clan of pureblood elves that nearly died out during the Great Flood. The sole survivors were scattered and had no choice but to mate with the human survivors. When he turned the page, it was the same tree with two kids and a snake.

"What story does this picture tell?"

"The story of Demons."

"What is all of this talk about DEMONS?"

Gabriel quickly closed his book as Drail approached them. "Nothing sir. We are just working on our project."

Drail stared at the book in his hands and noticed it resembled the one he had in his office. Gabriel quickly packed the book into his bag. He asked the boys to get ready for dinner. Alexander and Gabriel gathered their papers and took everything inside. They washed up and took their seats at the dinner table. The massive twelve-seat table was filled with food and desserts. Drail watched as the children ate up a storm. He pondered over the book he saw Gabriel with and cautiously questioned the boy.

"What project are you working on?"

Before Gabriel could come up with a lie, Alexander opened his mouth.

"A history project on religion."

Drail laughed at the idea. "For someone who doesn't practice religion, you are very excited about the topic."

"Gabriel is teaching me about his religion."

Drail could see the topic was making the boy uneasy. "As a citizen of Hellenic, you do not practice the customary religion. So, Gabriel, tell me. What is your religion?"

"I belong to the Creed of Lykos."

The maids nearly dropped the silverware. Drail's eyes darted back and forward between the two boys. Alexander could see the look of fear on his face. This was the first time he saw fear in his father's eyes. Drail excused himself from the table and went in search of Unic. Gabriel grabbed Alexander by the hand and whispered to him to show him out. Alexander was baffled. What was going on? Why did Gabriel want to leave so soon? Before Drail could return, Gabriel was already gone. Baffled by his actions, Alexander looked to his father for answers. His father had concerns about the boy being inside their house. He believed the Creed of Lykos were fanatics and were involved in hundreds of disappearances. The news shocked Alexander to his core. He was sheltered in his own reality that he was too blind to see the cruelty in others. He knew his father wanted what was best for him, but he was drawn to Gabriel. He could not end a friendship that was just flourishing.

Alexander agreed to keep Gabriel away from the house but would not agree to keep his distance from the boy. He yearned for friends so badly and would not subject them to his father's paranoia. Alexander exited the conversation to get ready for bed. He showered and prepared his clothes for school. Sleep was a luxury he needed after the long day he had. The balcony doors were left open to allow the moonlight in. Within seconds he belonged to his dreams. Once again, he found himself in a dark, damp room. The sounds of screams echoed around him. When he turned around, he screamed, as he was face-to-face with the eerie purple eyes. This time the shadow spoke.

"I finally found you."

Alexander awoke from his dream petrified. He could barely catch his breath. Hans heard his screams and rushed to his side. Drail was summoned from his chambers as well. Alexander was coughing up blood. He bit his tongue too hard. Hans cleaned out his mouth and made sure there were no other wounds. Hans took his leave, allowing Alexander to recount the night terror to his father. Drail wanted to take him to his psychiatrist to prescribe him pills again, but Alexander declined. The pills were extreme and kept him paralyzed in his own body. He just wanted to get back to bed.

Drail kissed his son goodnight but did not return to his bed. He made his way to the office and retrieved the book he was reading earlier. He stared at the image of the apple tree and the two children. Unic entered the room quietly.

"What are you reading?"

Drail replied, "Alexander's friend had a book similar to my own."

Drail turned the book to show Unic. The color in his face faded.

"The boy belongs to the Creed of Lykos!"

Unic gasped, "What does the Creed of Lykos know about the boy?"

Drail whispered, "Everything!"

Drail closed the book and ordered Unic to increase security around the premises. He feared they would come for his son. There was nothing more they could do at this point. Drail needed to get to bed so he could work in the morning.

CHAPTER
5

FRIEND OR FOE

Dawn broke and the rays of the sun danced throughout the corridors. Alexander once again found himself waking up to a much-needed breakfast. He showered and got dressed while Marcelo brought the car around. Drail was waiting at the door with Alexander's book bag and kissed his forehead. The drive to school seemed longer the second time around. The winding streets nearly made him sick. He was fatigued and wanted to go back to bed. The only excitement he felt was to see Gabriel and Amira again.

The car arrived at the school, and it was a madhouse. All the students were outside. The building was on fire. The local authorities were trying to put out the fire. Marcelo wanted to turn the car around, but Alexander wanted to see what happened. He pushed open his door and walked toward Mr. Kakos.

"How did it happen?"

"Arson, someone tried to burn down the school," responded Mr. Kakos.

Alexander watched as the flames intensified. His attention was drawn to Gabriel, who was arguing with Amira. He could not hear what was going on, but from the look on their faces it was heated. He approached them in order to quell the fighting, but by the time he got to them Amira had walked away.

"What were you two arguing about?"

"You!"

Puzzled by his reaction, he turned to walk away from Gabriel, but he grabbed his hand. He apologized for screaming at him and led him away from the school. There was a desolate path on the other side of the school. It led down the cliff to a secluded landing. The view of Atpolis was spectacular. The Tethys Sea sparkled in the distance. There were rocks pushed together to form seats. It was a hangout for the students when they skipped school. Gabriel wanted to be alone with Alexander. They each sat down and absorbed the surroundings. Gabriel leaned his head against Alexander's shoulder and closed his eyes.

"I wish things were different," Gabriel sighed.

"Why do you say that?"

"My heart is torn between wanting to pursue getting to know you and what's comfortable for me," Gabriel responded.

Alexander took a deep breath. "You mean your girlfriend?"

Gabriel shook his head yes.

Ever since he was little, he knew he was different. Whenever he went out with his father, the other kids made fun of him because he was slimmer than most. He was always well put together and had soft features. He was a target of cruelty and torture. This new school was a blank canvas for him to begin anew. His emotions were always on overdrive and at this point he was infatuated with Gabriel. He knew if he said the wrong thing, he would regret it.

"Comfort is not what I am looking for. I just want a friend. I want something real."

Gabriel replied, "Please don't be like that!"

Without even looking at Gabriel, he got up from the stones and made his way back up to school. The fire was finally under control and all the students were already sent home. Amira and a few others remained behind and were hanging out by the entrance. She saw him coming out of the bushes and rushed toward him to hug him. His sadness called to her. No words were exchanged. Alexander softly cried into her shoulder. She walked him back to his car and kissed him on his head. His eyelids became heavy, and he fell asleep in the back of the car.

His dream was finally different. The room around him was no longer dark. He was standing in a prison. The screams of torture resonated around him. He closed his eyes, trying to wake himself up, but it was useless. Alexander was driving himself insane. Laughter broke through the screams. The scraping of chains drew his attention behind him. It was as if the air was sucked out of the room. There was a massive woman suspended from the ground. Her hands and feet were bound in chains. Twelve wings protruded from her back and were chained to the wall. Her body was covered in scars.

"You can see me!"

He tried to approach her, but his feet would not move. Laughter from the dark corner of the room caught his attention. Purple piercing eyes were staring at him again.

"Now, I can see you!"

The uncanny voice shocked him back to reality. Marcelo stopped the car to check on him. He was sweating and bleeding from his ears. He rushed him back home and called Drail with the news. It was time to see the psychiatrist again. The villa was swarming with security upon their arrival. Alexander was taken to his room to rest. Hans immediately called Drail to advise him. He was still working in the royal palace. The queen had acquired new land and wanted him to come up with a plan to build on it. He had to put a pause on it. As he was cleaning up his office to leave, he heard a commotion outside of the door. One man pushed through his security in order to gain an audience with the duke.

"Leave my office at once!" Drail commanded.

"This involves your son!"

Drail began to tremble. He placed his briefcase on the table and took a seat. He ordered his security to wait outside while he spoke with the man. He wore a black suit beneath his long trench coat. He proceeded to remove his leather gloves as he took a seat. His green eyes were fixated on Drail. He introduced himself as Nathaniel Buros, the father of Gabriel. The Creed of Lykos learned of their friendship and wanted an audience. He abruptly rose from his chair to escort Nathaniel out, but his guest had more to say.

"Have the night terrors started?"

Drail removed his hand from the doorknob. His chest tightened and his thoughts evaporated. He could not escape this conversation.

"How do you know about those?"

Nathaniel slowly moved his eyes from Drail to his chair, as if telling him to sit down. Drail took a seat as they continued their conversation. Gabriel was having night terrors as well. They were unable to decipher what the dreams meant until he mentioned that Alexander appeared within his nightmare. He could see the terror in his face as he watched from the shadows. He witnessed an angel hanging by her arms in a dungeon. When he caught a glimpse of Alexander, he tried to run toward him but was restrained as a woman appeared from the darkness. As he described her, Drail dug his nails into the chair.

"She has seen his face now. For some reason, my son is connected to yours. He has been having the same dreams," growled Nathaniel.

"I do not want the Creed involved in this."

"We are involved because of you."

"I will take it from here."

"You should have thought about that before you involved us in this fight. When you first appeared in this world you used us, or have you forgotten?"

Drail refused to engage in arguing. He slowly rose from his seat, and so did Nathaniel.

"She now knows where he is. She will come for him," replied Nathaniel.

"I will protect him at all costs!" roared Drail.

Compromise was out of the question, but Nathaniel had more information. He pulled out an envelope with the arson report from the school that showed a filing cabinet of information was taken. Alexander's personal records were in there as well. Whoever started the fire used it as a smoke screen to gain access to his documents. Drail looked over the records and his eyes lit up as he noticed the chemical traits.

"She has help."

"Someone is going through great lengths to find the boy. We need to work together otherwise he will be lost to you. Head home. The Creed will collect you in the morning."

Nathaniel showed himself out as Drail collected his things and ordered security to take him home. On the ride home, he stared out the window and yearned for simpler days. Why now? Why would she risk it all? A faded memory of holding Alexander in his arms as a baby filled his eyes with tears. Sixteen years the boy went unnoticed. What changed? He pulled out the envelope and stared at the arson report again. Sulfur was found all over the area, a component in demonic blood. His concentration was broken as a massive tremor took over the road. His car began to swerve on the road. A huge fissure began at the side of the road and managed to go as far as the mountain range. An unnerving chill was in the air.

Drail's security managed to get him home safely before nightfall. The roads were damaged and many of the power lines were down. Fortunately for him, the solar panels on the property had their own generators and still powered the house. The villa's gray iron gates opened, allowing him entry. Unic was patiently waiting at the door for him with news. Fingerprints were taken from the school after the fire and the authorities had a suspect. The prints traced back to Amira St. Clair. Drail had a disturbed look on his face and made his way to his office so they could continue the conversation in private.

"Why would she want his records?"

"His doctor. You provided his psychiatrist's name on his medical reports."

Drail punched the table so hard it cracked. She was playing a dangerous game. He ordered his security to locate the psychiatrist and bring him to the villa. Unic led the command and took ten men with him. Hans was listening in; he had dinner prepared. The table was set, but Drail would be eating alone. Alexander was still sleeping. Hans watched as Drail ate and finally gained the courage to voice his concerns.

"Alexander needs to know the truth."

"What truth would that be? The one that he is being hunted like an animal?"

"He is a sitting duck."

"ENOUGH. No one will tell me how to protect my son!"

Drail continued to eat and ended the conversation, or so he thought. He looked to his side and saw Hans was inches away from him. He stabbed a fork into the table.

"HE IS OUR SON. I was the first one to take your side."

Hans released his grip on the fork and left the dining room. The dimly lit lights flickered as he approached Alexander's room. He could hear sounds coming from the room. Pressing his ear against the door he tried to make out what he was saying. The language escaped him. Hans pushed the doors open, but the boy was alone. Everything seemed untouched. The balcony doors were open and allowed a cool breeze to fill the room. Tiptoeing into the room, he noticed muddy footprints on the floor. They began on the balcony and stopped inches from the bed. Alerting security would only cause a panic. He cleaned up the floor and closed the balcony doors. Near his bed was a cabinet filled with healing stones that had been given to him as gifts since he was little. Hans grabbed two fluorite crystals and placed them in the corners of the balcony door for protection.

He grabbed a chair and a book and sat by Alexander's side all night until he heard banging coming from the front door. He raced through the corridors until he reached the balcony overlooking the living room. Drail was sitting in his wingback chair, drinking red wine. The maids opened the door allowing Unic and his men to pile in. Many of them were wounded. The shattering of glass silenced the moans.

"What happened?" questioned Drail.

"We were too late. The psychiatrist is dead."

"Do we know what she was after?"

"Alexander's blood."

Drail's eyes darted back and forth trying to understand how the psychiatrist still had vials of his blood. Unic stumbled onto his files before they were attacked. The psychiatrist knew Alexander's blood was unnatural. He was studying it in a lab. Amira left him badly injured. Unic and his team followed her to the lab where his blood was stored. She was covert and agile. She managed to tear through them without haste.

Hans' acute hearing picked up on movement upstairs. Staring at them from the balcony was Alexander. The look of terror was written all over his face. Drail ordered the maids to tend to their wounds. They were escorted to the medical wing of the villa. Hans rushed up the stairs to console Alexander and explain what was going on. He was gasping for air.

"I had another night terror."

"What did you see this time?"

"A lake. A woman calling my name."

Hans held the boy as he began to cry. Each doctor he went to labeled him with night terrors and could not put an end to his hallucinations. Alexander felt crazy. His world was upside down. He was helpless in his own mind. Hans released the boy, allowing Drail to take him into his arms. Lifting him from the ground he carried him back to his bed.

"Dad, what happened downstairs?"

"We had intruders. Everything is fine now."

Lying came naturally to Drail, but this time Alexander could sense he was not telling the truth. He felt it in his bones. His father tucked him back into bed and kissed him goodnight. He stationed guards outside of his door and bolted to his office. His world was unraveling around him. Nothing made sense anymore. He turned on his computer to research the girl and her family. There was scarce information on the internet. An article dated two years prior illustrated a car crash and the death of her parents.

Her parents, Akeem St. Clair and Sada Joshwa owned Serpentine; an oil drilling company near the southern point of Gondwana. Her father's history was spotless. He came from humble beginnings, but her mother's history was very limited. There were no records of her before the start of her company fourteen years ago. He dove deep into her records, looking into her taxes, property records, and others. There was one that stood out – a photo from an expedition into the jungles of Gondwana. The photo was over a hundred years old. The research team uncovered a shrine with thirteen statues. After its discovery, the statues were stolen. In the center of the photo was a woman who looked identical to Sada.

He was like a dog with a bone. What was their connection? Why was this family interested in Alexander? Drail would not sleep until he got to the bottom of it. He followed the new clues until it led him to a passage from a five-hundred-year-old book, written by a prophet of the Creed of Lykos:

> *Light destroyed the multiverse and from it a*
> *distortion of reality was born. The Savior of*
> *Mankind, the curse, the boy, born of the*
> *Emerald Queen. Stolen and raised on Earth*
> *until maturity by traitor and servant. Upon*
> *the breaking of the three seals will he return*
> *to the world of the sun and moon. Blood of*

the Servant, Blood of the Spawn, and Blood
of his Blood. Alexander, the Eclipse, of the
land of Hell and Enic will dawn this world in
his shadow.

Drail closed his computer and called for Hans' assistance. He professed everything he learned. Alexander was no longer safe under his roof. They needed the Creed of Lykos.

"How will you communicate with them?"

"Tomorrow, Gabriel's father is coming. We will share our findings with him. He can help us!"

Hans poured Drail some tea before leaving the room. His eyes grew heavy, and his vision clouded. Hans drugged him. He locked the office door behind him. He pulled a chair from outside of the office and stood guard.

CHAPTER
6

TRUTH REVEALED

The following morning, Hans awoke to an upset Master. Drail was standing over him ready to pounce. Hans just stared up at him and told him to shower. His intentions were pure. All he wanted was for Drail to get some rest. He was burning himself out by falling down a rabbit hole. The shower water did him some justice. It relaxed his muscles and eased his worries for the moment. Hans was standing ready with his clothes. After he made sure the duke was ready, he made his way to Alexander's wing.

Loud snoring pulsated from his room. Hans was glad he was getting the much-needed sleep he deserved. To the outside world he was sleeping, but Alexander was a prisoner in his own body. His vivid dreams had taken control of him. The young child found himself surrounded by mountains. The smell of wet grass pierced his senses. He was once again at the foot of a lake. As he took a step forward, his foot did not sink into the mud. He could barely make out the images in the distance. From the water rose a woman who cried out to him as she held her arms out.

The elegant woman stood as tall as a tree. Her presence was familiar. Her vague image haunted him. She began to call out his name and then she spoke one last time, "My son, return to me!"

He could finally understand what she was saying. His body began to convulse, and he dropped into the lake. He awoke to Hans' shaking him awake. He was being rushed to get dressed. Drail was taking him on a trip. Alexander was excited. It was ages since his father and him went on a trip together. He showered and got ready. Everyone was already downstairs waiting for him. Alexander entered the living room and was surprised to see so many people. One of the men stood out the most to him. His features reminded him of Gabriel.

His suspicions were confirmed when Drail introduced him as Gabriel's father. Nathaniel extended his hand to the boy and shook it firmly. He had a boat ready to take them to Alkebu, where his company was headquartered. He had a private mansion on the beach that he rented to Drail for a few weeks. Alexander thought he would get to spend some time with Gabriel, but his hopes were shot down. It would only be him and his father going. No one could know they were there. He found the request odd. Why were they being so secretive? He grabbed his bags and followed Marcelo to the car. Alexander entered the car alone. Drail and the others piled into four black trucks. Two of the trucks drove in front of Alexander's car and the other two stood inches behind them as they left the villa.

Alexander's mind wandered into oblivion. For days his nightmares haunted him. The only thing that set him at ease was his father's stories. He visualized LunaSol, the Royal Family, and the Divine Lords. As he stared at the floor, engaged in the thought of Lady Eileen, the floor began to peel away like magic. He jumped in shock and gazed over his surroundings. Once again, he was standing near a lake. The smell of damp grass filled the air. A glowing ball of blue light fell gracefully down from the sky and tapped the water. A ripple consumed the lake, and a woman in a blue and silver dress appeared from the light. She stared at him with sorrow in her eyes.

She expanded her arms out to him and called to him, "My son, you are in danger. Return to us!"

The woman finally stopped speaking, and he extended his hands to her. He did not realize he was walking on top of the water. When he touched her hands, he was surrounded by a white light and suddenly snapped out of his daydream. Alexander was dripping in sweat. He could not believe he had the same dream again. This was beginning to freak him out.

Alexander snapped out of it and was now sitting in the limousine once more. The floor seemed the same, as did everything else. The road quaked with envy and caused the cars to crash into one another. His attention was on his hand. It burned with fury and as he looked down, he was holding a golden amulet; a sun and crescent moon forged together. In the center there was an emerald jewel. His breathing quickened and his heart began to palpitate. He had a disconcerted look on his face. Marcelo came around to his door to make sure he was not injured. He noticed the boy frozen in terror and was staring at his hand quivering. Alexander held up the amulet and shifted toward the driver. The driver's face reassured him that he was not imagining it at all.

The driver froze in panic and asked him where he found that. Alexander did not answer him; all he could do was stare at the amulet. Marcelo left his side to inform Drail. Silence followed, and the driver returned to the car and detoured from their route, heading back to the villa. The entire ride, Marcelo could not wrap his mind around what he saw. Alexander paid little attention to the words coming out of his mouth. All he kept looking at was the amulet in his hand. The woman's voice whispered to him from the amulet. He found it odd that he was able to bring something out of his daydream.

The limousine picked up speed, and they raced down the road. Alexander did not even care to notice it. He could not help but stare at the amulet that glistened in the sunlight. The light entering through the sunroof set the amulet ablaze in lights. Marcelo noticed the lights being emitted from the amulet and had no choice but to close the sunroof. Alexander clenched the amulet in his hand and could feel an odd tingle overtake his body.

The limousine came to a complete stop, and Marcelo flung his door open and rushed to get Alexander inside as Nathaniel and Drial followed. Hans forced him into a chair outside of Drail's office, while they whispered to one another. The brows on Drail's face stood at attention. His eyes shimmered with the sun and began to shake. He nearly collapsed onto the table as his body trembled.

Drail picked up his ring from the table. On the ring was an image of two swords with a flame behind them. For the first time he actually paid close attention to his father's ring and thought about the images he would draw as a child for the Solaris Angels. They were very similar. They both walked over to the boy, and Hans told him to hold out his hand. He did as he was instructed, revealing the amulet. His father was terrified and bit his bottom lip. Alexander explained what happened and how the amulet appeared in his hand. The boy was scared and wanted to know what he was holding.

Drail could not divert his eyes from the floor. Nathaniel continued to whisper into his ear, only making matters worse. This omen could only mean one thing: the secrets and the lies were coming to an end. He battled with the idea of telling him the truth. Lost in thought, his son became annoyed as he watched him ponder in silence. He felt his father was going to explode.

Drail finally snapped back to reality.

"Alexander! Listen to me: I do not know how you came to possess this thing, but you must give it to me. This is for your own safety!"

He felt his heart tied in two and could not come to grips with handing over the amulet to his father. Whatever secret he was keeping, it was going to end here.

"I keep having this same dream of a woman calling out to me from a lake. She kept calling me her son. Why is this happening to me? I have a right to know!"

The blood in Drail's veins boiled. The veins on his neck bulged. He shifted his eyes to the butler. Drail then shifted his eyes back onto Alexander. His voice became very demanding as he lashed out on his son, **"I SAID HAND IT OVER NOW!!!"**

His eyes grew; his father never screamed at him like this before. The fearful child got the courage to battle back and yelled out, "NO!!" As he yelled out against his father, Drail went to grab his hand. Alexander moved his hand quickly and the amulet began to glow. He pushed his father's hand away, and Drail was sent flying back into his chair. The impact caused the entire castle to tremble. Alexander's heart raced as he stared at his hand. He could not believe what had just happened. He cried out to his father.

Nathaniel whimpered, "Oh, no!"

Hans ran to the aid of his master. Alexander's hands began to glow red, blue, yellow, and lastly green. Fear, anger, hate, disappointment, and even joy overcame the small boy. He dropped to his knees and could not resist his tears. His life was normal, and now it seemed like it was falling apart right in front of him. Drail got up from the destroyed throne with the help of the butler and limped toward his son. His father picked him up and embraced him. As he picked up his son, Alexander's hands stopped glowing.

The frightened boy took a seat across from his father as the lies were stripped away. Drail was not his true father, and Earth was not his home. He was in fact the last son of Sir Erin Whitespear and Lady Eileen Snowstar. Drail's heart broke with every truth he revealed to the young boy. He could no longer deny the newly recognized prince the truth. Drail finally confessed that he was Soldiel.

The truth killed him. Each word ripped apart the stitches, keeping his heart afloat. The stories were no longer stories, but his distorted life. Filled with mixed emotions, all he could do was cry. His entire life was based on a lie, and now the truth seemed unreal. He finally stopped sobbing, pushed Soldiel away from him, and ran off into the corridors. The whimpering child continued running until he reached the massive doors leading into his room. Soldiel looked at Hans and gestured for him to bring him a book off the shelf. Walking over to the wicker bookshelf, he levitated up and grabbed a book from the twentieth shelf.

The book was aged with golden stitching down the side. The words on the cover and along the side were written in another language. The butler allowed the words, '**_Libro Incantamenta_**' to escape his lips. He placed the book on a nearby stand as Soldiel and Nathaniel left in search of the boy. Soldiel walked through the corridors and approached the prince's room. With the wave of his hand, he unlocked the door, and the doors opened for him as he walked through. The prince was sitting there motionless on the side of his bed. He was staring out his window at the majestic and tranquil garden that lay at the bottom.

Soldiel placed his hand on the prince's shoulder and gently caressed him. He betrayed his trust. All he could do now was comfort the boy.

"Nothing can undo this sense of betrayal you are feeling. I am still your father. I have loved you since the moment you were placed in my arms. Even though we are not of the same blood, I have cared for you ever since. It was my job to protect you. I prayed you would never have to return to LunaSol and see the horrors that remain."

Alexander moved his teary eyes from the garden onto Soldiel's face. Learning that he was a prince was one thing but learning that a god wanted him dead was another. His mind could not fathom the idea, and it disturbed him to his core. He could not hold his anger back anymore and allowed his emotions to get the best of him.

"How could you lie to me for all these years? You filled my head with stories that stirred emotions in me. So, tell me, why have you watched over me all these years and why was the lady from the lake calling out to me?"

Soldiel bit his lip trying to maul over his words. The lies were finally crumbling. Hans could see his pain and intervened.

"I believe it is your mother."

Alexander stared into Hans' eyes. "How is this possible?"

He turned to Soldiel and interrogated him.

"Ever since I was little, I have been having night terrors. They have gotten clearer and more vivid. What is the connection with my mother and the woman with the purple eyes?"

Soldiel could not bring himself to lie again. Knowing the danger involved he needed to repair their trust. He confessed that he believed Eris was trying to lure him out of hiding. The amulet was supposed to be passed down to her, but Lady Eileen enchanted it before her death to go to Alexander. The mental barriers that were placed on him as a child were ripped away. His heart ached to hear that he was deceived. His night terrors were nothing compared to the emotions he felt when he was near Lady Eileen.

Hearing that the woman in the lake was his mother only made him feel worst. Growing up in the villa there was not even a whisper of her name. No image of her face for him to hold on to. It was lot for him to take in. He wished all his life to have a normal upbringing with two parents. The emotional toll of not having his mother weighed heavily on him. His tears burned his cheeks as Soldiel continued to speak.

"I could not tell you the truth because I was trying to protect your mind from corruption. LunaSol is filled with darkness. I needed to keep you alive."

Alexander moved from the bed and stood beside the open window. He gazed at the pond and the fish swimming within it. He could feel the heat of the sun warm the blood in his veins. He turned around and looked at Gabriel's father. What was his role in all of this? Before he could interrogate him, he locked eyes with Drail and unleashed his rage.

"All these years I thought you were my father and now you tell me this. I have always felt like an outcast here and alone. Now you tell me I have brothers and sisters. There is a place out there where I matter. I have no purpose here; at least there they will be by my side. You have no idea the feeling of emptiness I have felt all these years, not knowing the real me, and now all of that can change."

The winds began to pick up speed outside with the rising echoes of his voice.

"Take me back!!!"

Soldiel noticed that his dormant powers were revealing themselves. With all the magical protections he placed on the prince, he was amazed to see how quickly he was decimating them and how his powers grew just from being in contact with the amulet.

Soldiel paused and took a deep breath in before he spoke, "Son, that is an impossible task you ask of me. The gate was shut, so no one could follow us through it. I needed to keep you safe."

As the words escaped his lips, he mauled over the thought of how the prince could encounter the spirit of his mother and the amulet if the gate was shut. The time flux was undisrupted until now.

"If your mother was indeed able to communicate with you something must be wrong with the gate."

Alexander inhaled heavily and the winds outside were doing the same. Storm clouds appeared outside, and lightning struck the ground. Soldiel could sense it was the prince's doing, and he needed to stop him before he got out of control. He raced to his side and held him tight and helped the prince break his concentration.

Soldiel continued to hug the prince and the clouds slowly subsided, but his attention broke once more as he felt an earthquake strike. The floor shook with passion and flung objects across the room shattering them. A strange feeling overtook the prince's body as he gazed out the window. He could feel a dark and ominous presence. The earthquake was only the beginning; the sun darkened as the moon got into position in front of it. The eclipse brought heavy rain and devastating winds. The rain pummeled the ground like a drum. Lightning ravaged the lands causing destruction in its path. Soldiel was worried and left the room quickly. His cape blew in the wind, as he raced through the corridor and enlisted the assistance of Hans. Nathaniel rushed after him and they locked themselves in the office. Hans handed him the book he required and Soldiel used a green piece of chalk to draw runes on the floor. He placed a dozen candles around him in a circle.

"Soldiel, what could it be?"

He whipped off his cape revealing his armored tunic and pants. Attached to his hip were two swords with the same symbol that was on his ring. The symbol was also on his chest plate.

"I can sense it too. When I first brought the prince through the portal a Solar Eclipse also appeared. If it's happening again, that means something came through. I am going to Mt. Alymus to check on the gate and the tomb of the Imperial Knights."

Nathaniel and his agents from the Creed of Lykos agreed to assist Soldiel in his mission. They got in the middle of the circle and the symbols ignited with savagery and engulfed them in its mesmerizing light. Soldiel's ring glistened as Hans chanted.

"Quod datum redde nune. Et Lucernae
ardentes in aeternum veniunt in.
Crepidinis et potestatibus, de quibus in.
Penitusque laxant serenitas magna."
(That which has been given, return it now.
Lights of the Everlasting come burning down.
Powers given up settle back in.
Unlock your great serenity deep within.)

CHAPTER
7

ERIS

Hans stood behind to ensure Soldiel's plan did not backfire, but he did not account for Alexander eavesdropping from outside the door. He pushed the doors open and demanded to know where Soldiel went. Hans' eyes betrayed him and jolted from side to side as lies slipped from his lips. Knowing better than to believe him, Alexander paced around the room further causing Hans to panic. The symbols on the floor were starting to ignite again and drew his attention. Hans tried to escort him out, but he kept moving away from him. He refused to leave until he learned the truth.

"This is madness. Stop snooping and just listen. Soldiel left to check on the villa and the staff. There is nothing to worry about my child. Just return to your room."

"Enough with the lies."

Anger got the best of him, and his amulet began to glow. It blasted Hans and contorted his body into the air. He was lowered back onto the ground and his movements were no longer his own. The amulet forced him to reveal how Soldiel teleported out of the villa. The amulet reignited the ritual circle and opened a portal. He was staring through it and could see snow on the other side. He stepped through the split and Hans jumped in as well. The ground was covered in a thick blanket of snow.

Standing before them was a huge stone archway carved into the mountain. Massive runes were etched into the rim. A tear in the fabric of reality rippled in the center of it. Green, red, and blue lights sparkled from the split. The amulet ignited once more and ripped the tear open until the mountaintop was blinded in lights. It began to rearrange the colors until they faded, and an image appeared on the other side. He could see a thick and savage forest hidden in the dead of night.

Alexander walked closer to the archway, but a huge crash redirected his attention. His eyes were drawn to the side as he saw Soldiel fighting a colossal, armored centaur. He was beneath the creature's hooves and was inches from being crushed. Words could not escape his mouth. Even after Soldiel revealed he was from another world, a part of him still had his doubts, but now seeing a creature that appeared in fairy tales made it that much more real. Soldiel gripped the hooves of the beast, and a shockwave of energy exuded from his hands and electrified the beast. He was able to toss the creature off him and stumble to his feet. Out of the distance, another creature appeared that paralyzed the prince in fear. The creature appeared to be a bipedal dragon. He had the severed head of one of Nathaniel's agents in his hand. Soldiel was unaware that the creature was approaching. Alexander cried for him to look out.

He shifted in the snow and leaped into the sky. As he flipped, twelve massive wings broke through his armored tunic and expanded outward. Soldiel took off into the sky for protection. The creature turned his attention to the boy and charged him. Hans jumped in front of the prince and raised his hands parallel to his waist and roared, "*Einfrieren.*" Green sparks jolted from his fingertips and knocked the creature back into a pile of frozen snow.

Hans roared out for the prince to run and hide. His magic could not hold the creature back too long. Alexander watched his butler in utter disbelief. Nothing was as it seemed. He tried to fend off the beast, but he broke free and grabbed the butler by the neck. His magic was weakened since he did not use it often. The creature tossed him aside and turned his attention back towards the prince. Nathaniel leaped from a nearby stone and sliced the creature in the face. The massive beast grabbed him by the leg and flung him across the snow-covered ground. He would not stop until he had the boy. The creature grabbed an axe from his back and attacked the prince. Alexander tried to run, but he tripped and fell face first into the snow.

The beast grabbed him by the jacket and raised him into the air. The young prince was now his. He clenched his grip around the boy's body tighter than before, crushing the life out of him. Alexander could feel his ribs being crushed. Hans was lying on the ground unable to do anything and the members of the Creed of Lykos were all beheaded. Their blood stained the mountaintop. Alexander struggled to stay conscious. He was holding the amulet in his hand but could not get it to work.

The beast smelled him and chuckled. "So, you are the child everyone is searching for."

He applied more pressure onto his hips causing the prince to scream out in pain. Alexander could barely breathe. He peered into the eyes of the monster and asked, "Who is searching for me? Who are you?" The prince was very frightful as he tried to release himself from the monster's grip with no luck.

From a distance he realized he had been betrayed. Amira slowly approached the colossal beast and patted him on his leg. The creature's metallic wings expanded as she spoke, "I see you have met Dynas, he was once an Imperial Knight and protector of this world. Now he is one of our servants."

"Amira, why?"

"My mother was killed, because she stumbled onto your secret."

Amira's mother was one of the few demons that survived the Great Flood. She watched Soldiel build this world as its false god. She stalked him from the shadows and learned that he had a child. The news was unimaginable. The child could not have been his own. As a pureblood demon, she retained her magical abilities, broke into his villa, and took a blanket that the prince was wrapped in. She learned about the gateway after slaughtering those that survived the Great Flood. She learned of Alexander's identity and enlisted help from the gateway. With her blood she broke the first seal. When the Creed of Lykos learned that she was tampering with the magical seals placed on the gateway, she was murdered.

Why am I still alive? It was a question that repeated in Alexander's head. If Soldiel brought him through the portal when this world was nothing more than volcanic chaos, how did he survive this long and with no memory of it?

"Amira, I am sorry about your mother, but you cannot blame me for her death. I had nothing..."

He was cut off by a dark and spine-chilling laugh from the distance. Shadows turned, bent, and expanded. The laugh came from the rock formation near the prince.

"Yes, yes, yes. You were lied to and deceived by your kidnapper. Held all these years without knowledge of who you are. Prince Alexander Whitespear. I have been waiting for this very moment!"

A woman appeared from the shadows near the boulder. Alexander's heart began to race faster than it was. Sweat rolled down his forehead as he tried to get the words out. "Eris!" He tried to gather his thoughts as the fiend laughed at his pain.

Eris glided toward them. Her dark black and purple hair flowed in the wind as she stared at her brother. She was disgusted at how much they looked alike. The gentle boy was face-to-face with his parents' murderer. He imagined her differently. She was tall and very fit and wore little clothing. Her dress covered her breast, her core, and pelvis. The sides of her body were exposed to the elements. Eris was a sexual being and was not afraid to flaunt her body. The prince was enraged that she still wore her crown. She ran her long scaly nail on the side of his face.

"Good boy. I am glad to see Soldiel has taught you about us. You and I are connected. I have been searching for you. I knew one day my efforts would lead me to you."

"How are you here?"

Amira interjected, "With my help."

Eris laughed and kissed Amira on the cheek.

She was interrupted as Nathaniel crept behind her and stabbed her in the chest. The sword dematerialized upon contact. He tried to distract her so Hans could get away, but another Imperial Knight grabbed him. This soldier had the face of a leopard and two massive-feathered wings. Rather than killing him, he dropped him at Eris' feet. Nathaniel was subdued as well and chained to Hans.

"I see you have made friends."

"Do not hurt them."

"You are in no position to command me."

Eris ran her long nail across Nathaniel's face, drawing blood from him. She placed her finger on Amira's lips and her eyes turned red. Amira was half demon and half elf. Her skin ripped and her true form was revealed. Gray like a corpse, cracked skin under the eyes, hoofed feet, pointed ears, and hair as white as snow. Behind her was a long rattlesnake tail. Through her blood the second seal was broken. The angelic essence of Soldiel drew her attention. With Amira's help and a vial of blood from the prince, she was able to open the gateway and allow Eris through. She infected the knights to keep the Solaris Angel occupied, until she had what she came for.

Amira was able to drop the prince's mental barriers. The eclipse symbol she drew was embedded with magic. When he ran his finger across it, the enchantment from the ink soaked into his blood stream. The infection allowed his mother's enchantment to finally reach out to him.

"You do not have to do this!"

"I want what is rightfully mine. Give me the amulet. I know you have it."

The prince was terrified of Eris. He was not going to give up the amulet without a fight. The prince gathered all his courage and roared out, "No! I will never hand it over to you!"

Eris' body was consumed by shadows as she stepped away from Amira. "Brother, you leave me no alternative." She gestured for the beast to end his life.

Dynas threw him against the floor and the impact broke the ground. His ribs cracked on impact and now he was in even more tormenting pain. Blood gushed from his mouth as he tried to breathe. He clenched his axe ready to strike. The terrified prince stared at the dried blood on the steel of the axe. His eyes trembled as he waited for his death.

Dynas placed his axe on the prince's neck. The apple in his neck slowly went up and down as he swallowed. From the corner of his eye, he noticed an object speeding toward him. As he turned to see it, a huge bolt of light blasted the two Imperial Knights and slammed them into a nearby pillar. Hans used the opportunity to blind Eris and Amira with a spell and helped Nathaniel escape behind a boulder. Soldiel raced over to the prince and picked him up from the floor. The prince's mind was clouded in confusion and pain. He continued to cough up blood and one of his eyes had blood in it. He was out of breath and was near the point of passing out. Hans moved toward the prince and tended to his wounds.

Eris could not stand by and see them regain their strength. The hatred that ran through her veins kept her clinging to life; to see the day her brother would meet his death by her hand. She needed to attack now, but before she could do anything, Hans took the prince behind some rubble. Soldiel could not battle Eris in his human state. After years of hiding, he embraced his calling and transformed into his angelic form. The bright light encased the peak of the mountain and caused Eris to lower her head in disgrace of the glory that stood before her. Alexander peaked over the boulder with anticipation of finally seeing the true form of a Solaris Angel.

Soldiel stood a towering six feet, five inches. White robes and golden armor guarded his body. Two swords were attached to his waist and Alexander noticed a machine around his wrist that held little arrows. Tattoos appeared on both of his forearms. Soldiel's wings were enormous, and his feathers were very sharp. The transformation was finally complete. Eris and Soldiel circled one another as they waited to see who would attack first. Eris knew the angel would not attack first. He focused on her breathing pattern to see where her next attack would come from. She created a ball of shadow in her hand and launched it at him. With accuracy he drew one of the swords from his waist and shredded the energy ball before it even got close.

Eris could not stand the sight of her foe. She grimaced at the very sight of him. He was a complication that had to be dealt with. She wanted her brother dead and needed his amulet. Soldiel removed his hand from the sword. He knew that Eris would not dare attack him yet. She was a manipulator and loved to toy with the mind of her prey. Once she was fully charged, she would strike back against him. He circled Eris and began to question her actions.

"You went into hiding like the coward you are and now you have the nerve to show your face. Do you really think you can win in a battle against me?"

Eris busted out laughing at the top of her lungs. She glanced over and saw the little prince hiding. As she glanced over at him, she gave him a wink and a smirk.

"As memory serves, I did not go into hiding after the Holy War. I merely went to recover from the fight. Why should I explain myself to you? You are one to talk. As I recall, you gave up protecting the heavens. You left to protect a child that was doomed to die. You are a pathetic fool!"

With every fiber of his being Soldiel tried not to fall into her trap. Nathaniel watched as they prepared for battle. He pressed a button on his watch and called for assistance. Alexander had to be protected at all costs. The mighty angel looked over at the young prince who remained hidden behind the boulder staring over. A child filled with such innocence was stained with devastating tragedy. His heart filled with compassion and love. He could not allow Eris to succeed. He pulled out his second sword and aimed it at her throat. "Prince Alexander will destroy that abomination you call God."

Eris swallowed abruptly and laughed again. She still needed more time. She was going to finish this now and finally rid herself of the angel. Her hands were charged with enough energy now. He pressed his sword forward, but Eris took on her shadow form before he could slice at her flesh. She pressed against Soldiel's chest and grabbed his inner arm as she flipped over him. He was consumed by white lights and attacked her while trying to wiggle his way out of her grip. Alexander and Hans saw the shadow and light intermingling. Eris managed to get her way and got him to drop his swords.

She managed to get face-to-face with Soldiel once more. She released him from her grip long enough to direct a huge arrow of dark energy straight into his chest. The impact of the attack threw him back and he landed in the snowy meadow. Soldiel's body sparked with purple lightning and caused him to shiver. The prince screamed out an earth-shattering cry. He raced over to his fallen protector with tear filled eyes. Eris floated above them in glee. Pain and agony erupted in his soul. Everything seemed to slip into chaos. Nothing seemed to go right for him. He blamed himself as he watched Soldiel died. He held him tight as tears flooded his eyes and fell over the lifeless body of his protector and onto the amulet.

The amulet began to glow and consume the prince. The pain and torture he felt turned into something else. Rage and frustration filled his heart. The world went still, and it was as if time had frozen. The very fabric of existence greeted the prince and welcomed his vengeance against that which stood in his way. He walked forward and the ground around him shook at his glory. The snow-covered ground split and ascended into the sky.

Eris was a sitting duck. The boy lived an average life and left LunaSol before he could manifest his abilities as an Ilihi. She could not understand how a mere boy could retain such power. There was only one person in existence that exuded this power, and he was imprisoned. She launched a shadow ball at him, but the attack was in vain. Alexander moved his head to the side, and it evaporated as it got closer. Eris could not believe what she was witnessing. His aura was emitting huge amounts of energy that caused his surroundings to dematerialize. The vast pressure surrounding him forced her to her knees.

The words, "What are you?" escaped her lips.

Alexander's power skyrocketed as his mind unraveled. His mind was wrapped in a blanket of rage. He kept replaying Soldiel's last moments. They were embedded into his mind and the last teardrop escaped his eyes. He could no longer hold back his frustration and released his true power. A huge force escaped from his body as he screamed out in pain and blew everything around him away.

The floor was no longer covered in snow, but it was now whirling around in the air. His energy levitated boulders, trees, and even shards from the ground. Eris was consumed by fear as she stared at him in amazement. In his fragile state he was more dangerous than anything she faced. She could only imagine what would happen if he was allowed to survive and find someone to properly train him. He had to die. Without warning she jolted her hand toward his heart, but his aura stopped her. Her hand was paralyzed and then her fingers broke from the immense surge of power around the prince. His eyes changed from golden brown to white. No matter how much she tried to vanish into the shadows, his immense power kept her in her human form. She stared into his soulless eyes.

"YOU SHALL PAY FOR WHAT YOU HAVE DONE!!!" As the prince spoke, his voice echoed through the mountaintop. This mere child possessed something Eris could not. His rage was fueled by compassion. Her train of thought was cut short when her brother raised his hand and waved it in the motion of a tidal wave. The snow that circled in the air dropped down and knocked her to the ground. She was covered in snow.

Eris blasted the snow off her as she tried to get to her feet. She was not leaving without the amulet. She waved her hands and the light around her turned into darkness. The corruption of the light created sparks. The prince knew what she was preparing for. It was called Shade Lightning. Soldiel mentioned it countless times in his stories of how she used it to kill Lady Udana. She shot a bolt of lightning straight at the prince, but once it got closer, he redirected it back toward her. It was as if he was a puppet, and someone was pulling his strings. Eris tried to dodge it, but he clenched his hand and kept her from running. The lightning overtook her body; sparks caused her to convulse in agony. The atoms in her body were destroyed. Her hair floated in the air one last time as she dropped to her knees. Piece by piece she vanished into thin air. The prince gestured his hand forward quickly and clenched his hand keeping the shadows from floating away. He drew the shadows closer and flung them into the archway. He stared at the portal as it invited Eris' soul in.

Alexander's energy depleted rapidly. His eyes changed back to their golden-brown color. The weight of his energy made his knees buckle. He let out one final scream that shook the mountain with unbelievable force. The man who raised him, the father he knew all his life was gone.

Hans looked over the boulder to check if the coast was clear. He walked over to the prince and comforted him. Nothing could be done in this world to bring back the prince's happiness. Everything he wished for came true, but at a cost, a very expensive cost. The prince was still in tears. He could not believe that the father he had known all his life was no longer there. His heart yearned for the love of his father and to hear his voice once more. Hans could sense the confusion and conflicting emotions in the young prince's heart. He held him tight as he cried.

Nathaniel stood watch as they spoke. He noticed Amira regained consciousness and set her sights on the prince. Her earth-shattering scream shifted the debris from Dynas and the other Imperial Knight. In the nick of time, Nathaniel's call to the Creed of Lykos was answered. The mountaintop was overflowing with protectors who battled with the knights to keep them at bay. Without Soldiel the prince would surely die. Nathaniel ordered the prince to return to LunaSol and seek shelter.

"Soldiel's death cannot go unanswered. You may have stopped Eris today, but this is far from over."

"Nathaniel, this is not the time for heroics. The boy is in pain," argued Hans.

"The Creed can only do so much to hold them back. If the remaining knights were freed, he would be slaughtered. We cannot protect the prince without Soldiel. He must return to LunaSol for his own safety."

The mountain entrance grabbed his attention as he gazed at the beautiful sight. The runes around the archway shimmered with magic. Hans noticed they were written in the language of the gods. Having studied under

Soldiel's guidance he was able to make out the message. It was a warning to all those that entered. It stated only death, and destruction awaited the poor soul seeking hope in LunaSol. It was a message that would surely upset the prince, so he decided it was best not to mention it.

The prince began to question himself. *Could he really do this?* If he returned, he would truly be in danger. His lips began to quiver as he spoke. He wanted Hans to enter the portal with him. It was not a task he could do on his own. He knew he must overcome his fears and travel into a foreign world where everyone wanted him dead.

PART III - LANDS OF SHADOW

CHAPTER

8

LUNASOL

The prince and Hans moved toward the portal with uncertainty. Amira's voice drew their attention as she rushed toward them. The Creed of Lykos tried to subdue her as the prince and Hans moved through the threshold. Before the portal could disappear, she managed to enter as well. The runes on the archway ignited. Time was undone and the destroyed ruins on the mountaintop reanimated. Temples rose from the floor and citadels skyrocketed into the sky. Thousands of statues were reassembled and illustrated creatures of immense strength. The final pieces of rubble reanimated into thrones. The souls that once rested beneath the ruins were awakened. The ancient Imperial Knights emerged from the dirt as the Creed of Lykos protected the entrance to LunaSol.

Hans and the prince had no idea what destruction they left behind. Blinded by darkness, they found themselves in a dense forest. They peered up into the sky expecting to see stars, but to their surprise they could only see a stone ceiling. The wild forest had grown within a building. They kept close to one another as they made their way through the bushes. Filled with heartache, Hans began to silently cry. He abandoned his fellow kin to be slaughtered. Eris' power was mighty if she was able to manipulate the Imperial Knights. Only three of them were topside upon their departure.

The longer they were away, the harder it would be for them to undo the knight's influence.

Alexander could see the look of dread on Hans' face. The prince held his hand, forcing Hans to face him. The knot in his stomach was growing. He needed to know what danger he left behind by coming to LunaSol.

"What are the Imperial Knights?"

Alexander's question burned in his mind. Hans, unlike Soldiel, could not face lying to him anymore. Lord Nebula's ascension not only created an alternate reality, but it birthed new gods. Hyperion and his family still thrived in their reality, but this version of Earth was still young. It did not face the tribulations of its predecessor. Soldiel recruited the Imperial Knights and destroyed the gods to avoid Hyperion's rise to power. The knights were the last gods to live amongst the natives. Soldiel entombed the knights for trying to rebel and open the portal into LunaSol. Whispers from the archway entranced them and corrupted their minds. With Eris' arrival, Hans believed it had to be her meddling with the time flux. His words became faint, as he feared the forest had ears.

As Hans continued to talk, they came upon a dirt road, but soon he found himself caught in a trap. He stepped onto a rope and a cage of vines entangled him. The prince tried to break him out of it, but glaring yellow eyes stopped him dead in his tracks. Before long a prehistoric lion, a mutated white tiger, and a Corsac fox surrounded them. They were massive in size compared to the animals he had seen. The prince fell alongside the cage in dread. They appeared crazed with saliva dripping from their fangs.

The creatures began to circle the boy as they inhaled his scent. The terrified prince could hear them speaking to one another. This terrified Hans, as he could only hear them growling.

Hans noticing the lion was ready to pounce, screamed out, "Stop. This is Prince Alexander Whitespear."

The lion retracted his claws and sniffed around the child, "No one has seen the prince for over sixteen thousand years. Is this a joke?"

The prince stood up slowly, trying not to make any sudden movements. He looked over to the lion, "Fourteen thousand years?"

LunaSol was unlike Earth. Time was slower. Age was a thing of the past. One Earth year was equivalent to one thousand years on LunaSol. The life span of the average LunaSolarian could last fifty to seventy thousand years before being considered old.

The fox leaped around the tiger and growled, "They speak lies. This boy is not our prince. He was killed by the Solaris Angel."

Alexander's heart exploded at the vulgar lies. He argued with the fox and explained that Soldiel raised him on Earth after they escaped through a time rift. The prince ran toward the snow-colored fox to kick him but was stopped in his tracks as the lion jumped in the way.

"ROARRRRRRRRRRRRRRRR." The fearsome sound caused the leaves of the forest to stand still. The lion found truth in his words. He would not allow harm to befall the child. He wanted to hear more. The prince did not know whom to trust. Could these creatures be working for Eris? He took a chance and told them how Soldiel used a scroll given to him by the Keepers to open the time rift. With utter sorrow, he had to relive every lie and story he was told growing up. Alexander explained that Eris found a way to reopen the portal and came looking for him. The lion learned that the prince's protector was no more.

The white tiger roared at the very notion that Eris could out best a Solaris Angel. The lion moved toward the prince and inhaled his scent once more. There was an eerie aura surrounding him. No one outside of the Royal Family had seen him after he was born. The creatures continued to inhale his scent. Any movement the prince made could easily offend them and cause them to attack.

Hans thought by blurting out that he was an Elf would help their cause. The lion took interest even more. Each of the creatures looked at one another with disbelief. They approached the cage and inhaled his scent. Rather than an elf, they smelled a combination of demonic and human scents. The tiger laughed at Hans and then growled. Even though Hans could not understand them he could sense his pleas were falling on deaf ears. Only in his true form would he be able to connect with the creatures and understand their tongue. Hans attacked the cage with spells, but none seemed to work. Only the prince would be able to free him. Hans gestured with his eyes to the amulet.

It was about time, he thought. He aimed it at his butler and the amulet drew on the prince's aura. A bolt of light blasted the cage, turning it to dust.

The dazzling light encased him, and his physical appearance changed. The man that stood before him was a slim white elf in a green and gold squire outfit with long blond hair. His skin was flawless, and his hair was tied in place by two thin braids that wrapped from the sides of his head and traveled around toward the back revealing his pointy ears.

The Corsac fox growled at the prince. "WAIT! This cannot be! He holds the Eclipse Amulet."

Hans could finally understand their native tongue. The three creatures were astounded and each of them kneeled at the prince's feet. He felt more at ease knowing that he would live to see another day. They were in the presence of Narnarie, Leogard, and Nacilias. Each of whom protected the Temple of Notus from intruders. Nacilias' kind roamed the colder areas, they were native to Earth. Narnarie was a Panthera Leo Spaleaea; they were once fierce cave lions. Leogard was a Massiritis white tiger; their kin were much older and were used by the Imperial Gods as hunters. Parts of their body were replaced with machinery. They were genetically advanced Smilodon's with an accuracy that was unmatched. Each of them leaped on the prince, licking him in submission. A shimmer of hope had returned to them. Narnarie wanted to get the prince to safety. It was only a matter of time before Lord Nebula's forces learned of his arrival.

He gestured for the prince and elf to mount his saddle. Once they were seated, Narnarie took off like a bullet. Leogard and Nacilias were right behind him. They braced themselves as they approached the temple entrance. A slight breeze caressed the prince's face as the light from the outside world guided them into another realm of mystery. Furious waves crashed against the island. From the mountaintop, the prince could see magnificent meadows lining the bottom of the mountains. To the north, the silhouette of a massive landmass could be seen through a fog blanket. Without warning Narnarie inhaled the majestic breeze and raced down the jagged cliff.

The prehistoric lion was the first one down, but he was not alone. As the others approached, his fur became still and hard. His teeth grew in length and the beast turned his attention to the empty meadow. He roared at the emptiness and the sound of his voice cut through the air like a razor. The very trees became as stiff as a nail and the leaves lost their dance appeal in the shifting winds. The three beasts could sense danger was coming.

Hans and the prince took cover, as a dark cloud shot down from the sky and jolted toward him from across the field. He was able to leap out of the way before it made impact. The dark cloud faded revealing a soldier. He was built like a mountain and was covered in black armor etched with purple runes. Two lion heads protruded outward from his pauldrons and the tunic and robes he wore underneath his armor were purple. Attached to his waist was a sword that caught the prince's attention. His nightmare became a reality when Narnarie roared for them to stay clear of Lord Dark Lucus. His presence shocked even the lion. It was rare for Lord Nebula's generals to reveal themselves.

Lord Dark Lucus smirked at the proud beasts and flexed his wings. His twelve wings were not like Soldiel's; they were filled with black feathers. Without warning he charged toward the prince and struck the mighty lion to the floor. Narnarie jolted up from the ground and growled at the fiend. The Solaris Angel motioned his hands into a circle creating a ball of dark energy. He flung the ball toward the lion, but Narnarie was able to dodge it and raced through the meadow.

He spotted an overgrown tree next to the hovering brute and used it to leap onto Lord Nebula's General. In their struggle the mighty lion managed to claw and maul at his flesh. He ripped his wings, tearing away at them. Lord Dark Lucus grabbed the lion by his paws and flung him into the mountainside. The impact crushed his bones, but he did not go down without a fight. Prince Alexander could not stand idly by and watch him die. He jumped down from the tree and tried to save him, but Leogard intervened. Narnarie was too weak to continue the battle. The heroic lion laid motionless on the floor, as Lord Dark Lucus bathed in the glory of his victory.

The aura around the angel's foot darkened as he placed it on the lion's neck. The weakened beast bit into his foot and caused him to stumble. Narnarie was able to push him back with his weakened body and made a run for it. Lord Dark Lucus tried to fly off into the sky, but his wings were badly damaged. He concentrated his energy and launched multiple attacks at the lion as he raced toward him, but Hans redirected them. The lion's agility had decreased, but he was still able to leap onto him. Lord Dark Lucus was consumed by a purple veil and tried to disappear, but Narnarie bit through his armor and into his shoulder. He managed to pin him down to the floor.

It was an amazing sight for the prince to see the lion holding his own against an angel. Something was different about Narnarie. The prince wondered how they were evenly matched. His attention was drawn elsewhere as two strands of dark mist shot down from the sky to assist Lord Dark Lucus. Still concealed in darkness, the two figures tackled Narnarie to the ground. He was able to bite into one of their arms and subdue the target, but the other one was able to free the General. Leogard and Nacilias aided their friends in battle and pushed their enemies back. Lord Dark Lucus was shrouded by shadows and retreated.

Alexander and Hans came out of hiding to aid the wounded lion. They saw extensive damage inflicted on his body. His wounds were deep, and blood poured out like a stream. They were infected and burned at his flesh. Narnarie needed immediate attention.

"You cannot leave me now!" muttered the prince. His heart ached to see such a proud and majestic creature on the verge of death. Narnarie could not travel with the prince under these conditions. The dead weight would only slow them down. He instructed Nacilias to guide the prince to his sister. She was their only hope of protecting him. Leogard would tend to the lion and spread the word of the prince's return.

Alexander knew it was the right thing to do. He helped Narnarie from the floor and parted ways. Hans, Nacilias, and the prince cleared the meadow into an opening to the west of the mountain. The cunning fox would lead them to the place where it all began - the Kingdom of Haven, the fortress and home of the Royal Family.

Alexander could not help but think about the voyage. He could not deal with losing any more friends along the way.

Narnarie's battle with Lord Dark Lucus weighed heavily on his mind. The angel could have easily taken out the lion, but they were evenly matched. Narnarie was more than meets the eye. There was something special about the lion and the prince wanted to know what it was. He had a blank stare on his face as he mauled over his thoughts. Hans glanced over at the worried prince and could see the devastation in his eyes.

A strange vibration echoed into Hans' mind. The feeling of carnage overtook his body. The narrow path reeked of it. He gently glided his fingertips across the sides of the mountain and was overcome by a vision. A bloody war orchestrated by a man with a dragon helmet. Hans walked amongst the dead bodies that lined the floor until he reached the diabolical figure responsible for so much carnage.

"What happened here?"

Hans was in a trance-like state as they turned to look at him.

"What are you seeing?" questioned the prince.

Hans replied, "DEATH!"

Nacilias shared that Lord Marlusha was enraged with the inhabitants of Templaro for aiding in the escape of the Royal Family that he destroyed all those who called the Temple of Notus home, leaving it abandoned. The angels needed to secure the temple, so they forced the ground to shift and created mountains to protect it from another invasion.

Soldiel's bedtime stories rushed into his mind. They were nothing compared to the dark and twisted reality that was unfolding before his eyes. Alexander was frustrated and wanted to know more. His stubbornness and impatience were getting the best of him. The three continued on their voyage through the caverns. Nacilias kept a keen eye out and made sure no one was following them, but his nose caught a nasty whiff, and his white fur slowly spiked to attention. Something was heading toward them.

Hans grabbed the prince by the hand and told Nacilias to follow his lead. He waved his hands and chanted, "*Migalis Totalis!*" Their bodies became invisible just in time. They backed up against the wall of the mountainside, as three shadowy figures got closer. With each step they took the floor trembled. The prince tried to focus on their faces and noticed they were deformed, their teeth sharp and stained with blood. They were monumental in size and overweight. The stench of death followed on their torn clothing. The dark, slate gray creatures did not notice them and continued through the mountain pass.

While their adrenaline was still pumping, they raced through the caverns and came upon a new valley. They left behind the stench of death and breathed in the fragrant flowers that grew below. Exotic plants such as the Agapetes ludgvan cross and Blue Angel's Trumpets thrived in the valley. Parrot Lilies and the fabled blue amaryllis were among these exotic plants. The plants gave the valley its elegant grace. Overcome by such beauty, the tired prince took a second to rest. A place that once thrived with life was now overrun with nature's glory.

The majestic wildlife now called it home. Clydesdales ran wild and catered to their young, while water buffaloes roamed the valley consuming the grass. The prince reveled at the amazing sight. His heart was set at ease even with all the chaos awaiting him. He was glad to see something good come out of it and that the animals used the valley as a haven. He felt at home at this very moment. In the distance stood the remains of what appeared to be a broken mountain and buildings. In the other direction a shrine. Hans and Nacilias walked down the little slope into the valley to make their way to the ruins. Still consumed by his senses, Alexander noticed it was hard to breathe.

"What were those things?" questioned the prince.

"They are called *ogres*. These beasts rarely leave their caves unless they are hunting."

Alexander and Hans looked at one another in distress. They needed to create more distance between themselves and the ogres. Hans looked over to the prince and gave him a nod to continue walking. The mist in the air electrified his senses. He was filled with sorrow over the thought of seeing his parents' home. His breathing was impaired, and his body was overwhelmed. A loud thump caused Hans and Nacilias to turn around. The prince was unconscious on the floor. His breathing was shallow, and his heartbeat was slowing down. Being raised on Earth made his soul weaker and he could not handle the transition back to LunaSol.

CHAPTER
9

HAVEN

Hans knew very well that the prince's life force was fading. Panicked with the thought of losing the only family he had left, he recalled Soldiel's teachings. There was a dangerous spell that could energize his aura, but it would come at a cost. He held onto the prince's hands as he chanted.

"Sidera vires supra vires da lunae solisque coitum.
Itum est donum spiritus vitae ut vivificet hoc totis
viribus meis."

*(Powers of the stars above, grant me the powers
of the moon and the sun. Allow me the gift of the
Breath of Life, so that I may revive this being with
all my might.)*

The sky darkened and the winds whistled and roared around them. A fog of green light escaped from Hans' mouth and wrapped around the prince. His body levitated into the air and the fog electrified him. His eyes bolted open, and he floated gracefully back down onto his two feet, but his senses were magnified. Still trying to catch his breath, he turned to Hans for answers. In his mind he was prepared for even more secrets and lies, but Hans caved in and confessed. The prince was dying. His soul was fractured and oozing out energy. Soldiel's interference nearly killed him. Earth's atmosphere was not suitable for humans. Upon his arrival, he had to use an Oricale Shard to preserve the prince's essence and keep him in a cryogenic sleep until civilization had formed; its magic was waning now that he returned home.

Hans could no longer keep the truth from him. The Oricale Shard that saved the prince from dying once belonged to a larger relic, the Tri-Oricale Crystal, before being broken apart. It was a power source used by '*The All Mother*,' a title given to the first female humanoid. It was a celestine blue obelisk with three crystal shards that formed a crown at the top.

Soldiel had no clue the power it held, but whenever he held it, it spoke to him. The prince was already familiar with how he received it, but he wasn't sure how the Keepers came into possession of it. Hans revealed that Lady Eileen discovered this relic on one of her visits to Heaven. Hyperion had a room filled with mystical trinkets. In its presence, she heard a voice call to her. Drawn to the obelisk she touched it and witnessed visions of the Multiverse and its true creation before Hyperion restarted the clock. She absorbed energy from the obelisk that cut off her connection to Hyperion's influence.

The voice that called to her was 'The All Mother.' Her most notable name was Oricale. She was created by a techno-organic race called the First Ones. She encountered a dying star and absorbed its power without dying. With the assistance of her children, she created an anchor for its limitless energy. The Tri-Oricale Crystal are the key to that anchor. Hyperion amassed an inventory of stolen power. The relics were his trophies from his victories.

Hearing that even his mother was rebellious brought a smile to his face. They shared at least one thing in common. His thoughts broke as he learned that his mother was captured by 'The Keepers'. Lady Eileen could not allow them to report back to Hyperion, so she attacked them. To their surprise she was gifted with abilities that rivaled even their powers. By placing her forehead on theirs she was able to break their bond to their creator and show them the truth. The Keepers helped Lady Eileen steal the relic and created a replica. She could not afford for it to be tracked, so she broke it into four pieces. The obelisk remained with her, but she gave the three shards that made up the crown away for safe keeping.

Nacilias was astounded to hear how much Hans knew about her. As one of her four familiars, he witnessed many challenges she faced holding onto secret knowledge. Storytime had to wait. They needed to find cover. The valley was massive, and they were only halfway there. They came to a lone rock formation and a loud screeching could be heard overhead. Hans looked up, but the glare of the sun blinded him. A falcon-like warrior landed on the rock causing the elf to draw his bow and arrow. He aimed it at the creature's head. His cool gray and white feathers were groomed neatly. Around his waist was a kilt made of brown leather with a pouch on one side. His weapon of choice was a sharp fencing sword. Nacilias was glad to see him, while the others were filled with dread.

He came with urgent news for Nacilias. The three ogres were sent by Lord Marlusha to search for Eris. He was aware that she had found the prince and was going after him, but she was uncounted for. The ogres were seen leaving the temple heading back their way.

"Thank you, Barbal. We will reach the palace before nightfall."

Barbal intrigued the prince. He extended his hand to greet him. His hands were soft and fuzzy, but he was hiding something in his palm so the others could not see. He whispered to the prince to open it when he was alone. Out in the distance a huge red-tailed hawk glided down and landed near him. The majestic bird came bearing more news. Narnarie was safely aboard a ship heading to a secluded location for them to tend to his wounds.

"Novai is right, I must go! Take care my dear friend; Tramedo is waiting for our report." With that said, Barbal and Novai took off into the sky.

All the animal voices were too much for Alexander to handle at once. He was losing his grip and noticed blood dripping from his inner eye. Before anyone else could notice, he wiped it off. Nacilias realized the prince was still fatigued and wanted him to rest for a bit. The prince just wanted to get to the palace. Hans on the other hand was excited to see a Frayjain. Soldiel always spoke highly of them. They were once prophets and sears. Frayjains were immune to magical spells and were even used by the gods of Earth as protectors.

With Barbal gone, the white fox raced through the meadow for shelter. Hans held onto the prince as they raced to catch up. The sun was setting on the great planet and the animals that grazed nearby began taking refuge for the night. The whispering wind flowed through the plants, setting the creatures at ease. As they ran through the flowers, they startled a herd of bull elks. The creatures stomped around until they cleared out and reached the ruined fortress.

The beautiful mountain palace once stood twelve stories high with cast iron gates etched with the symbols of the sun and moon. All that remained were his bedtime stories. The immaculate fortress was reduced to rubble. It was once the most exhilarating sight in all the lands. The palace itself was a bronze color. It was also covered in emerald, ruby, and sapphire stones. Circular towers, courtyards, and libraries were once filled with life. Nothing in LunaSol could surpass its beauty.

The emotional prince could not find it in his heart to bypass the hatred he had for Eris. How could she do this to her own parents? Things were not making sense to him. Why bring him here? Why would they want him to relive this pain? He could no longer stand to hear any more stories about the palace, so he stormed off into the ruins to look around. Hans gawked at the bricks covered with scorch marks; tons of them lined the floor. Soldiel made no mention of an attack on Haven. Nacilias went after the prince to make sure he did not wander too far by himself. Hans picked up one of the bricks and whispered, "*Demimatas*," his body jerked quickly and was taken back to the day of the attack.

Hans opened his eyes and witnessed a full-fledged assault. Lord Marlusha was leading an army of creatures in his black chariot. Pulling his chariot were two serpent-faced, winged beasts. The Divine Lord called for Prince Adam and Princess Ionica to surrender. The prince and princess emerged from the balcony and ordered him to stop or suffer the consequences. Instead, he ordered his hoard to kill them all. Prince Adam leaped off the balcony and was shrouded in fire. He landed in front of the army of ogres and their commanders - *the trolls.* Creatures, as big as elephants with skin made of stone. They only had four fingers which held massive clubs with spikes. He blasted them with a wheel of fire that burned at their flesh. Even on fire and in excruciating pain they still charged at the prince. Princess Ionica raised her amulet into the sky and yelled for Narsacil. A whirlwind was released from her amulet and engulfed the sky above. Gigantic wings descended from the clouds and a massive sapphire dragon appeared.

Lord Marlusha released the serpent beasts, and they engaged Narsacil. Prince Adam was preoccupied and could not summon his ruby dragon. Fire erupted from his hands and decimated those that approached.

The sapphire dragon bested the creatures, she ripped off their heads with her bare claws. She turned her attention onto Lord Marlusha's army. While Narsacil took care of the creatures, Princess Ionica ran inside the palace as she saw catapults with iron boulders being brought forth.

Narsacil swooped down to stop the machines, but it was too late. Hundreds of boulders were ejected and destroyed the fortress walls. Princess Ionica was not able to get everyone out. Lord Marlusha's army stormed the palace claiming the lives of many. They were too strong for just two of them to handle. Princess Ionica reappeared to help her brother, and it was a close call. Lord Marlusha had Prince Adam in his clutches while her dragon drove his armies away. The princess could not lose another brother. Narsacil could sense her pain and soared back to her aid. Princess Ionica held her ground against the Divine Lord.

She summoned the water from the broken fountain and blasted Lord Marlusha off his feet and into his chariot. Prince Adam dropped to his feet and ran toward his sister. At that moment, her dragon appeared behind him and tried to devour the Divine Lord. He laughed at the great dragon, and as she used her ice breath to attack him, he was consumed by fire. He blasted the area around him before taking off into the sky. Narsacil's face was scarred. At that moment, Hans felt someone touching him and he awoke from his vision. Nacilias was crawling at him to get his attention. He found the prince and needed Hans to comfort him.

Hans dropped the brick and moved with Nacilias through the open corridors. They got close enough to see the torment on the prince's face. They stood at a distance and let him absorb his surroundings. Nacilias did not want to push the subject and reopen his wounds. He was flooded with overpowering emotions. Everything was hitting him at once and was taking its toll. They walked from room to room and the ghosts of the past haunted the ruins. Scorch marks and boulders paved the way to the great travesty that took place. Alexander stared at the collapsed walls with a blank look on his face. He was trying to visualize how something like this could happen.

Hans would not dare cause the prince any more pain, so he buried the vision. The prince walked into one room and saw the remains of two thrones. They were untouched by war. A shooting pain paralyzed his body. It was as if the palace was speaking to him. Seated on the thrones were a man and a woman. Their faces were blurry. At their feet stood four children playing with one another. The pain subsided and the room went back to normal.

At the back of the throne room was a desolate hallway that led into the fractured mountain. They ascended the staircase and were led to the bedrooms. Each of the doors looked like they contained names at one point. The names were all scratched out. The door at the end of the hallway had an eight-pointed star on it.

Alexander tried to open the door but was met with resistance. With one finally push he fell into the room. They found themselves on the peak of the mountain in a room exposed to the world. He hesitated at the threshold as he looked around.

"This was their bedroom!"

Once a place filled with warmth and laughter. Now, it was a silent testament to their absence. The room remained untouched since it was ravaged. The ceiling was destroyed, and the walls were broken by what appeared to be the remains of huge boulders. The only difference was the room was not riddled with scorch marks. Hans was relieved to know that Lord Marlusha's army didn't make it this far. All that remained intact was the limestone bed and its pillars. The prince stood at the foot of the bed and sighed.

He caressed the pillars and touched the coldness of the bed. A strange presence watched over them. Hans and Nacilias stood in the doorway and watched as the prince ran his hands up and down the sides of the bed and the pillars. A lump formed in his throat, he imagined all of the memories stolen from him; bedtime stories, lullabies, and running around with his siblings. He sank to his knees, his fingers clutching to the grooves of the pillar. The enormity of his grief, held at bay for so long, but seeing the empty room up close, it broke free. It was a feeling unlike anything he had ever felt. Anger settled into his heart and tears flowed from his eyes. At every turn he felt the remains of a broken heart. Nothing could mend the wounds that were leaking within. Knowing that he was ripped away from his family and that he would never be able to physically be in his parents' arms caused the most pain of all.

The room bore silent witness to his emotions, the walls absorbing his cries. It was as if the very essence of his mother reached out to comfort him, urging him to find solace in her love for him. As the storm of his emotions slowly subsided, Alexander rose from the floor. Hans moved closer and held him. He stopped crying as he heard whispers surrounding him. They were the very whispers that haunted his dreams. "She is here...I can feel her...Tell me what I am supposed to do?"

Hans slapped the paranoid prince back to reality. He was straining himself and rambling on. His magic could help clear the prince's mind to figure out what was going on with him. He whispered into the prince's ear and relaxed his mind. He took a deep breath and closed his eyes. The world around him faded and Hans could hear a female voice. Her face materialized within his mind. It was Lady Eileen. The rest of her body materialized as the prince focused on her. She was statuesque and elegant. Her long curly hair gracefully fell to her breast. The queen stood before him in an emerald dress that revealed her upper body and midsection. It wrapped around and expanded into a long cathedral style trail. Lady Eileen wore a belt with an eight-pointed star. Her face was foreign to him. Growing up with Soldiel there were no images of her. His emotions were skyrocketing as she ran to him and embraced him. She cried as she smothered him with kisses.

"It has been ages since I have held you in my arms. I have missed you so much. I finally have you here," cried Lady Eileen.

"I cannot believe this."

He wished to bring her back to life, but it was too late for her. The fragments of her soul only survived to guide him. She could not stay long otherwise Eris would find him. She needed the prince to follow her instructions. Beneath the room stood the Hall of Records, where the Tablet of Anagar was located. It was a relic that would help him. She turned to Hans and placed her hands on his face, "Protect him!"

They embraced each other one last time. His body quivered as his soul reconnected with his mind. Without hesitation, he rushed to do as his mother told him. He tried to move the bed on his own, but it was too heavy for him. The limestone pillars weighed a ton. Hans lifted his hands and uttered, "*Surgere.*" The bed lifted from the floor and became unbalanced. He was not able to control where the bed landed, and his spell smashed it into the wall. The wall was destroyed on impact. Alexander's eyes were glued to the floor. There was an eight-pointed star covered in dust etched into it.

He tried to locate a handle to open it, but there was no opening. Hans inspected the symbol and realized it was imbued with magic. He ran his index finger along the lines of the symbol as he chanted.

"Magna stellain Oricale, aperi vives tuas, mihi!"

(Great Star of the Oricale, open your powers to me!)

The ground quivered with vengeance. The stone around the symbol began to crack and the metal beneath it was revealed. The metallic symbol was engulfed in an emerald flame. The skies darkened with rage and the air became very moist with precipitation. Hans' eyes began to glow. A huge bolt of light shot up from the floor and lit the sky ablaze with emerald sparks. The emerald light spread like wildfire throughout the clouds.

As emerald lightning filled the sky, thousands flocked to gaze in its glory. In a desert land, a young man rushed from his golden sculptured bed to watch the glorious sight from his palace balcony. In another part of the world, a distinguished princess stood in her garden and cried with ecstasy. In the death infected parts of the world a hooded figure gawked in loathing from his black tower. He roared over his lands and summoned creatures that were dormant in the fiery wasteland below. The world knew that this spectacle could only mean one thing, the promised savior had returned

CHAPTER
10

VISION QUEST

Nacilias and the prince watched as Hans' eyes shot open, causing the emerald lights to spin into pandemonium. They rushed for cover as lightning ravaged the ruined fortress. The fox was nearly clipped by a thunderbolt and was thrown into a rock. The sparks receded into the eye of the storm and assailed the elf. His essence was encircled in a protective cloud. Lightning flowed through his body and electrified the iron symbol on the floor creating a funnel of dust around him. As the dust spun around the symbol, it glowed with the same fury as the sky. The emerald glow spiraled back down from the sky and vanished as it dazzled the iron symbol. Smoke sizzled from his body as he fell to his knees. The prince panicked and ran toward Hans.

Still in a trance-like state, Hans' fist was surrounded by a greenish glow. He jumped into the air and punched the symbol on the ground shattering it. From the rubble a spiral staircase was revealed, it descended into the depths of the crumbling palace. Hans gestured for them to follow him. They took great care to descend into the darkness until they reached the final step.

The room was cold and damp. Hans slid his hands across the walls and could sense there was an unlit torch nearby. In the Elven tongue he spoke the word, '*Imluminite!*' The darkness began to fade as the torches that lined the wall lit up with flames. A hallway stood before them, and they could see a vast iron gate at the end. They carefully made their way through the corridor keeping an eye out for booby traps.

In the center of the gate was an opening that mirrored the Eclipse Amulet. Alexander removed the amulet from around his neck and placed it in the opening. Cranking noises exploded from within the massive gate and it slowly opened. The room was enormous in size. Bookshelves lined the circular room and touched the ceiling. It was dimly lit with artificial lights, lighting the corners of the room. In the center stood a monumental stone tablet with orbs of light circling it. The Tablet of Anagar was a sight of beauty and mystery.

They made their way across silk rugs and noticed a marble staircase that led to the stone tablet. The tablet was lined with carvings that caused a force of euphoria to flow through the prince. He felt drawn to the ancient writing and seemed to understand it, unlike Hans and Nacilias. He walked over to it and touched the markings. The prince could feel boundless energy from the stone. A thick white cloud of fog seeped out from the bottom of the tablet and nullified their senses as the crystal at the top of it ignited.

Hans could barely scream out the words, "Watch out!"

The prince looked up in fear and was blinded by light. His blurry vision finally faded and now he was standing on a gigantic landmass surrounded by clouds. Overhead the sun was beaming on his skin. At the opposite end of the landmass stood a man four times his size. Massive like a mountain, built for war. His clothes were torn and burnt. His olive skin was bruised and cut. The sentinel of a man called to the prince.

"I am Anagar, the spirit of the tablet."

"Where am I?" questioned the prince.

"Not where, when?"

Reality shifted before his eyes. They were standing on a volcanic surface with hundreds of mountains. The ground beneath them shifted and exploded and now they were standing in a garden.

"What are you doing?"

"This is not my doing, this is you."

Anagar's cryptic riddles were causing the prince to get annoyed, "Enough!" As he screamed, reality stopped shifting. They were floating through the sky on a giant landmass. Anagar stood up, lifted the prince, and sat him on his shoulder.

"Time to leave."

Anagar grabbed a knife he had tucked away and with it he cut through time and space. Stepping through the tear they found themselves floating through the vacuum of space.

"Where are we?" questioned the prince.

This time they were on solid ground surrounded by hundreds of statues. Each unique resembling a creature or humanoid of some kind. Anagar called it the Valley of Possibilities. Every statue was a potential person or creature he would soon meet. Some statues had a buzzing sound that called to the prince. Strings of destiny pulling him toward them. Like a maze he walked through the statues until the buzzing noise stopped.

He stood before a hooded figure with four floating spheres circling him.

Anagar looked down at the prince, "Chaos calls to you."

The prince reached out and touched the statue. He was teleported into the emptiness of space. In the distance there appeared to be a man and then an explosion. Cosmic dust and dark matter were scattered throughout. As these particles spun together, they formed a dust cloud. After eons of condensing, a spark ignited. Later that spark became a cry. A baby's cry. His skin was as black as night, eyes white, and his veins were violet and illuminated as he breathed.

Alexander moved toward the being. He was witnessing the birth of Earth's first God - Chaos. Anagar confessed the man he saw before the explosion was an Alulim and descendant of 'The All Mother.' Chaos was his creation and ancestor of Hyperion.

Anagar returned them to the Valley of Possibilities. Before walking away, he bowed to the statue and kissed his feet. Alexander found it odd. Seeing the confusion on his face, Anagar revealed he was connected to Chaos through his father Hyperion. The news startled Alexander. He learned Hyperion bore seven children, Anagar being his third. An abomination in his eyes and a threat. Through art, he could depict events from the past and the future. Having a child like that could jeopardize his reign, but he also saw it as an opportunity to experiment on his son. Hyperion was fixated on stealing this ability. To walk through time and space would allow him to rule multiple realities. He failed and resorted to the destruction of the multiverse.

"Seeing the future is a tricky thing. Many outcomes, depending on the road you take, but all stained with blood."

Alexander continued through the valley until he came upon a sculpture of a tortoise, a phoenix, a dragon, and a wolf fighting an angel stood before him.

Upon touch, he was dragged into another vision. A war. A beautiful angelic warrior fought against five massive creatures. A hydra-like tortoise, a four eyed wolf, a crystal dragon, and a six-winged phoenix. Leading them into battle was a stone serpent. The angelic warrior's face was scarred, and he was left for dead. The closer the prince got to him, the angel looked up at him and reached for him. Anagar pulled him out of the vision.

"He saw you."

"What?"

"You got too close."

The prince was getting tired of his short responses. Shifting between the statues he heard the calling again. As they walked, Anagar grabbed his hand. The prince could feel his protectiveness. He was worried.

"What was that back there?"

"A final gambit," answered Anagar.

The Gods of Earth were hanging on by a thread. Hyperion massacred the majority of them. Those that still lingered brought forth the Cardinal Deities of Earth and declared war against the traitor. He managed to infect one and turn it against the others so he could cling to life. Prior to their mission, they flourished on their respective primordial planets. Ewonbi of Nephtisis, Baru of Yoin, Zuagio of Magna Dragonis, Invertu of Astranein and Alzamther of Earth. These were five of the eight planets comprising the Solis System where Chaos and his descendants called home.

Nephtisis was the closest to Earth in the habitable zone; humans could breathe its air, but it was completely overrun by trees and enormous deserts. Unlike Earth with its many oceans, Nephtisis had hundreds of lakes and rivers connecting to one another. Magna Dragonis was closer to the Sun. A barren red desert of volcanoes and mountains. Astranein was a gas realm with mountainous terrain. Yoin was further from the Sun, a frozen wasteland. Chaos before his death, called Abyss home. It was the farthest planet in the Solis System. Heaven being the closest to the Sun and Vordaris was another gas realm with mountainous terrain. Their names changed as mankind learned astronomy.

Walking through the endless statues they finally came upon the buzzing; it was neither human nor beast, but a symbol. A hieroglyph of an eye surrounded by flames.

"No, not that one..." Anagar tried to pull his hand back, but he was too late. He was standing at the base of a mountain. By his side was a man in purple and emerald robes. He was amazed to see it was Lord Celeio. The prince watched him and his Magnus' excavating the mountain. Runes were etched into the entrance to protect them from Hyperion's gaze. Days turned into years and the heart of the mountain became a temple. Within the temple, the Magnus' forged a massive eye of iron and embedded it into the floor. Encircled around it, stood fourteen stone griffins erected on their hind legs. The Divine Lord commanded each of his servants to stand in front of them and enact the ritual.

"Jeg kaller frem All Seeing Eye.
Slipp din store makt på himmelen.
Jeg kaller deg frem i navnet til vår mor.
Gaea gi oss styrke hverandre."

(I call forth the All-Seeing Eye.
Release your great power onto the sky.
I call you forth in the name of our mother.
Gaea, grant us the strength of one another.)

"Blasphemy. We should not be here," roared Anagar.

"Why?" questioned Alexander.

Anagar responded, "Mother was a traitor."

His words alarmed the prince. '*Mother.*' Above the ritual site within the temple was an oculus. It was directly in line with the opening at the peak of the mountain. The sky above darkened as a solar eclipse engulfed the world. Everyone rejoiced for the celestial event. The ground shook incredibly fast and a golden light burst from beneath the rock and set ablaze the eyes of the griffins. The stone items that they each held materialized into gold. The symbol on the floor was no longer stone, but gold as well. The symbol cracked open, and two items floated out of it. One was a golden book, and the other was a necklace that resembled the eye on the ground. He ordered his servants to remove the items from each of the griffins.

Prince Alexander noticed Lord Celeio's aura changed as he spoke.

"Today is a victory for us! We have successfully performed the Revival Ritual for our rightful goddess - Gaea. As her Gaeatonic Guardians, it is our duty to protect the heir."

Anagar ripped the prince from the vision and returned him to the valley. "This is not the way. He is not the heir. Lord Nebula is no longer your only threat."

"What are you talking about, Anagar? Take a breath, you're scaring me."

"You should be."

"Gaea is no one to trifle with. If she is tethered to your future, you must be careful."

Sweat pooled at his brow. Anagar seemed genuinely worried about him. Hearing Lord Celeio speak about their rightful goddess only intrigued him more. While listening to his inner voice, he lost Anagar amongst the statues. Chasing after him, he noticed him standing before the image of a baby being held up to the sun. Tears flowed down his face. "My brother..."

This time it was not the prince who placed his hand upon the statue, but Anagar. His eyes glazed over and now his feet were covered in sand. Golden brown sand blew in the wind. The sun was extremely hot and sweat appeared at the tip of his brows. A monumental shrine stood in the center of the barren wastelands. Seven figures appeared wearing purple hooded robes. They stepped into the shrine as Lord Celeio appeared with a package in his hands. He walked up the stairs and onto the platform.

The seven figures surrounded him and the baby. Alexander tried to get a closer look at their faces. Each of them held in their possession a relic that radiated magical properties. One held a sword, another a star, one held a staff, and another held out in their hand a spear with a golden eye in the center. The others followed suit. One removed their hood and revealed a golden helmet. The last two revealed their items; one held in their hand a pendant and the other lifted her hood to reveal a tiara. Each of the items glowed in the presence of the child. His attention was drawn to a statuesque woman with olive skin. As she spoke, the sound disappeared. The prince could not make out what she was saying. He watched as Lord Celeio handed her the child and she placed him in a basinet in the middle of the shrine. The sound returned and the prince could hear her humming. The basinet was lifted by a golden hand that materialized from the ground. The others began chanting his name - Saturos.

A bright light exploded and flung them back into the valley.

"I should not have done that," stuttered Anagar.

"You wanted to see your brother. It's okay."

"No, it is not. I am interfering. My gift. My curse. I am only supposed to guide you."

Prince Alexander took his hand. Smiled and led the way. The buzzing noise had returned. For miles they walked until they reached the end. One solitary statue on a metallic platform. A woman on her knees, holding a star in her hand. Twelve wings folded downward. As the prince approached, Anagar bowed to the statue.

"It's The All Mother."

A sense of joy filled the prince's heart. It was as if he knew her. He longed for her. Touching her face, he was plunged into darkness. He was witnessing Creation. It started millennia ago when dark matter and cosmic dust gave birth to the first star - the Nebula. It was the first highly intelligent being to foster life in the darkness of space. It exploded, creating a rift and gave life to the multiverse. From its ashes it recreated itself again, but this time a second intelligent being came out of its destruction. It became known as the Sentient Source. The first planet to circle its sun. Life evolved on the planet becoming known as the Sentients or the First Ones.

The Nebula grew envious and malice. Only it could be the sole creator of life. Life on the planet soon felt its wrath. The sun grew intense, making it inhospitable on the surface of the planet. The life forms sought refuge inside the planet. Seeing them adapt, only enraged it more. It infected the Sentients, and a war erupted between two factions. The Nebula became a source of darkness and torment, infecting anything it touched. Those that survived gave birth to The All Mother and the first generation of Alulims.

Her birth caused the vision to change once more. This time they were standing before a tribunal of female angels. He could see them clearly as day. Their skin milk chocolate, radiating with the glow of the sun. Each wearing a golden disk tiara atop their white hair, which flowed down their back and styled in dreadlocks and curls. Each of them wore a golden-armored corset and a white silk skirt that kissed the floor. They circled an angel that was on his knees.

"Soldiel," the prince called out.

The Keepers were interrogating him. He came seeking their guidance, but they did not believe him. His mission to collect the remaining

101

Royal Family was questionable. Words spoken were deemed heresy. Soldiel was bound before he had the opportunity to flee and tell Hyperion. He was forced to see the truth. Hyperion wanted the baby prince murdered. Their creator was not the beacon of light that he portrayed himself to be. He was already infected by the Nebula before merging with Satan. During the prince's birth he had a vision of the boy usurping him. The child was the only hope against Lord Nebula's reign.

The Keepers ordered Soldiel to keep the prince safe. Even with his mind open to the truth, how could he protect this baby. Hyperion was omnipotent. The Keepers laughed at Soldiel's lack of faith. They bestowed upon him the Oricale Shard that was used to preserve the prince's life force.

The vision released him and tossed him back into the valley. Anagar began to fade. His fingertips dissolved.

"Anagar, what is happening?"

With a mighty scream, the statues shook with vigor. The sand turned black. "There is a corruption in your mind."

Anagar's words only caused the sand to explode and shatter some of the statues. Oricale's statue was no longer alone. The sand constructed its own statue; A hooded figure holding a book.

"Father!" whispered Anagar.

Alexander was bewitched. A cold whisper in his ear called to him. He slowly approached the statue with his arm out.

"Stop."

Anagar's words fell on deaf ears. Just a single finger was all it needed to suck him in. He was now standing on white marble. Runes were carved into the floor and dusted in gold. A massive throne stood in the center of the room with a broken crystal behind it. Golden pillars as high as the eye could see lined the walkway toward the entrance of the room. He realized he was standing in Lord Nebula's throne room and Soldiel was lying motionless on the floor.

Another angel pleaded with him to stop. It was Antillias. A beauty as radiant as the sun. Her blond hair flowed down her back as she banged on the floor for Soldiel to answer the creator. Tears flowed from her blue eyes. Her armor was a combination of blue and silver. Her stag-encrested helmet laid by her feet.

Soldiel looked at her with blood dripping from his ears. Lord Nebula clenched his claws, and his body contorted, and his bones snapped. He was his puppet. The dark fiend laughed at the Angel's pain as he continued twisting and turning his hands. His voice crackled like ice. "The Keepers have betrayed me. Lady Eileen's children will die today for her treason. You will tell me where they are!"

He roared out vulgar words against the Angel. He clenched his hand once more and the Angel's wings began to burn. Soldiel let out a mighty roar in sorrow. Lord Nebula approached him and took away his ability to scream out in pain. He kicked his Solaris Angel in the face and pressed his face into the ground. Darkness and electricity merged into the palm of his hand.

Antillias roared out, "No!" As she flung her spear into her creator's chest.

He mustered a laugh and pulled the spear out before tossing it aside. Antillias rushed out of the room. Lord Nebula continued to inflict pain until Soldiel was at the point of passing out. He lifted him from the ground and held him up, so they were face-to-face. Before he could press his hand forward into the angel's heart, two angels descended into the room and pinned Lord Nebula against the wall. Their faces were not visible, but blurs. Lord Nebula was placed on his knees in the center of the room. Antillias entered the room with other angels and helped Soldiel to safety. She was given the pleasure of binding Lord Nebula's ankles.

"Death would be too great a reward for you, I will torture each of you for eternity," laughed Lord Nebula.

"You will never get the chance again."

Alexander stared at the angel who spoke. He was massive. Standing at ten feet. Unlike the others he could see his face. Muscular frame with long black hair and gray eyes. Half of his body was covered in tattoos. His green and golden armor complimented his body. Hidden in his armor were short daggers that he could pull out to slaughter his enemies and on his hip was a double-headed Warhammer.

"Apocartha...I gave life to you, and this is how you repay me. Without me this world will crumble, and death will come to you all."

"We are not going to kill you. You will suffer great torment. Lucifer, bring me the Tarsem."

The angel he called to was still in his fiery form. Lucifer handed Apocartha the ancient book and prepared for Lord Nebula's imprisonment. The angels loosened the chains and Apocartha lifted the Creator as he spoke the words, '*Se ridice in picioare.*' The angels carved symbols onto the floor around him. Lord Nebula laughed as the chains burned through his skin. Apocartha roared out, "*Leviteze*" and the chains levitated. They wrapped around the pillars, keeping his arms elongated.

The angels chanted, and as they did, the symbols glowed one by one.

"Great Gate că, odată închis sufletele, ridica de
la sol și sigilați dușman nostru. Aduceți -vă
puterea, lumina voastra maiestuos, astfel încât
să putem scăpa aceastâ lume de aceastâ
noapte fârâ sfârșit.'
(Great Gate that once imprisoned souls, rise
from the ground and seal our foe. Bring
forth your power, your majestic light, so that
we may rid this world of this endless night.)

Lord Nebula gave out a frightful laugh, and frigid air swept through the room. Gusts of wind swept around them, and the floor began to rumble. A stone gateway appeared within the circle of symbols. It was twice the size of Satan's prison. Lord Nebula lowered his head and muttered his own curse against the angels in a language puzzling even to them. Six of them raised their hands into the sky and bound six stars into a crystalized form, while Apocartha recited the chant again. A portal appeared in the center of the archway and sucked in everything it could. The angels held their ground as Apocartha released the chains from the pillars. Lord Nebula's body was sucked into the portal, but he clenched onto the outer rim as he tried to escape.

Apocartha raised his right hand toward Lord Nebula and a shock wave caused him to lose his grip on the rim. The angels tossed the stars into the portal as a door began to appear. The stars drew Lord Nebula's power into them and turned to stone. Lucifer collected the stars and disappeared with them.

The gateway changed in appearance. A cloaked angel appeared above the archway with its hands folded downward. A symbol appeared on the door and connected the indents where the stars were removed. Apocartha, Antillias, and Soldiel torched the gate. The stone melted slowly, and it gave Eris and Lord Dark Lucus time to infiltrate the throne room. They attacked the angels, tossing them into the wall. Eris snapped her fingers, and a dark mist consumed the gate.

Anagar was able to pull the prince from the vision. He was no longer whole. Half of his arm was gone. One of his legs was now being eaten away. The prince tried to hold the broken man up.

"Something is wrong. My spirit is being attacked. I cannot hold this world together much longer.

"Anagar, I need to learn how to defeat Lord Nebula. These visions have shown me nothing."

"They have shown you everything you need to know."

Anagar refused to say any more. He pushed off the prince and finally faded into the dark sand. Alexander was left alone. The sand around him formed an archway, as he crossed it, he was transported to Earth, a much more primitive version. The water was boiling and there was only one island that was suitable for life. The island was under construction by mysterious beings. The buildings were built with advanced technology and there were hundreds of flying ships moving equipment onto the island. His body was flung into the water and taken into a cavern. Within the cavern there were hundreds of marble statues. In the center of the room stood an altar. Soldiel studied the statues in the altar and stood in the center of them. Thirteen statues surrounded him.

He removed the Oricale Shard from around his neck and held it in his hands. The crystal radiated against his skin and burned through his palms. He aimed it at the statues and their marble skin cracked away. The thirteen statues were imprisoned creatures. Soldiel was not alone; he noticed he was being watched. The goddess introduced herself as Gaea. She stood a towering ten feet tall. Lush green vines descended her back as hair. Her skin resembled bark from a tree. Her forehead had four tree branches protruding from it and intertwined into a crown. Green moss covered her body like a dress. The goddess levitated over the shrine as he pleaded with her. He informed her that Hyperion must die for mankind to survive. Gaea could not see her masterpiece fall into chaos.

Gaea would not allow Hyperion to amass enormous power. She ordered him to remain in the shadows and use the Imperial Knights that he had awakened to rid the world of gods before Hyperion could betray them. If he was caught and Hyperion learned of the time rift, it could potentially lead down to a darker future. Prince Alexander noticed Dynas among the thirteen creatures and the centaur that attacked them.

"Imperial Knights, I call you forth to protect this world from the gods. This world will see death and destruction at their hands. Show them no mercy. Leave none of them alive."

Soldiel wanted to give this version of Earth its best chance. He could not afford the tyrannical god to gain the powers of his brethren. The Imperial Gods would face the consequences of their actions and would be wiped from existence.

Prince Alexander's astral body finally evaporated. The tablet shook and time began to flow in the Hall of Records. Hans and Nacilias were running in slow motion as his astral body returned to the physical world and slammed into his body. His vision quest left him.

CHAPTER
11

GLORY OR DEATH

"My prince, what happened?" questioned Hans.

"The tablet. It's alive. Hyperion's son, Anagar, is trapped in there. He showed me the past."

"Anything of value?"

"No, nothing of importance."

Nacilias glared around the room. "We are in your mother's study. Why don't we have a look around and see if we can find something that could help."

Hans showed more excitement than the prince. He peeled back the cover of as many books as he could find, but many of them were in languages, not even he understood. As he walked past each of the bookshelves, he ran his finger across their spines. His heart was tugging in one direction. Hidden deep in the shelves was a set of journals written by his mother. They were all bound together with a string. He ripped the string off and opened the first journal. It was about a woman called the Mystic Otrant. He continued through the others, and they were each titled after a person - Ro, Asphera, and Servilia. The last one had his name on it.

The first few pages recounted the day she found out she was pregnant. She was leaving her palace to inspect the Elemental Towers after a solar flare disrupted the magnetic fields of the planet. Hyperion's power was also affected, and his angels had to place him into a stasis sleep. Lady Eileen was escorted through Anahata, the once great continent ruled by Lord Grevis. The journey to Mercure Tower was trying on her body. They had to set up camp many times before they could even reach the tower. Lord Grevis' son, King Silverpeak Stormlight was sent to collect the queen. Upon his arrival, he noticed she had fallen ill. She could not be moved in her current state. He summoned his mother, Lady Udana, for guidance. She arrived within a day and found the queen in her fragile state. Lady Udana placed her hand on the queen's chest and could sense the water flowing through her body. She noticed one heartbeat and then a second. The news devastated the queen. She feared the news would reach Hyperion. She urged them to get her to safety.

As the prince continued to read, Nacilias and Hans continued to look for answers. The library was vast. None of the books they came across could assist them. Hans found himself in a corner of the room with a mural on the wall. It was a family tree. It even had names. Images of Sir Erin and Lady Eileen were at the top. Their lines connected to King Habagin, Sir Amos, Princess Ezmeralda, Sir Gabriel, Lady Nymaya, Sir Gesen, Prince Marteo, Servilia, Asphera, Admiral Nelson, Lady Nima, Lady Amil, Princess Eris, Princess Ionica, Prince Adam, and Prince Alexander.

Additional lines descended from their older children depicting their descendants. Hundreds of lines intersected. Hans called out for the prince to come see, but he ignored the call. Hans caught up with Nacilias and they found him plopped on the floor with his face glued to the book. The color in his face had faded like he had seen a ghost. Nacilias sat next to him and placed his head on his shoulder. He noticed the queen's handwriting. They stood in silence as the boy continued to read.

In one of the passages, she recounted her conversation with Lord Grevis. She had finally arrived at Mercure Tower, but rather than inspect the building for damage she was concerned about the weapons that were being built to combat Hyperion. During their conversation, she confessed she was pregnant to him. He cried for her and the baby. She placed her hand on her stomach worried what he would become. The prince closed the journal and stared down at the floor.

"She feared me. She feared what I would become. Why?"

Nacilias looked at Hans and shook his head. They were both in agreement, he could not know. Alexander rose from the floor and kept the journals in his hand as he returned to the Tablet of Anagar. He screamed at it for answers; waiting to see if it would communicate with him again, but it did not. His body was still feeling the effects of having his soul ripped from his body. His hands were trembling. Instead, the floor beneath the stone tablet separated and drew the tablet in. The lights that hovered above disappeared. Hans could see the disappointment in his eyes.

Nacilias' ears caught the faintest sounds from above. Someone had infiltrated the ruins.

"We need to move now."

Alexander's eyes bulged. He held onto the journals tightly as he followed Nacilias out of the room.

Hans did not want to leave the Hall of Records behind. "I have an idea. Let's take it with us!"

He placed his hands on the iron doors.

"*Rumpfensch!*"

The room began to shrink before their very eyes. Hans picked up the iron chamber and held it in his hand as he followed the others down the hallway. As they ascended into the room once more the sun was rising overhead. They were no longer the only ones there. At the entrance of the door stood a man wearing a red pirate hat with red robes and a red cloth over his mouth. His wavey black hair was shoulder length. Next to him was a white Pegasus.

Nacilias recognized them as Paku and Artamisa. Paku was a Magnus sworn to protect the Royal Family. He served as guardian of the Shrine of Glory, a vault that housed Sir Erin's treasures. As a Magnus he was able to practice magic. Their kind were divided into colors, so the LunaSolarian's would be able to identify what type of magic they utilized. As a Red Magnus he practiced fire magic. They also had the added ability to replicate the magical abilities of others. Paku came with urgent news, the ogres had returned with other foul creatures. They caught wind of the prince's scent and would arrive shortly. Paku mounted Artamisa and took off into the valley. There was only a small window of opportunity to get to safety. Hans' fingertips electrified with energy as he whipped his hands around and materialized a backpack. He placed the journals and the Hall of Records into the bag and gave it to the prince. Nacilias led them into the

109

main courtyard toward an exposed corridor. It led further away from the fortress until they arrived at the shrine.

It was a sight of beauty comprised of marble and covered in purple passion flowers. The graceful flower was in full bloom, and the fruits lining the pillars. The shrine was home to many protectors, a unicorn, a panther, and another Magnus. She wore emerald robes with an eight-pointed star to honor Oricale. Alexander moved toward the center of the shrine but was grabbed by her before he could fall into a pit.

Latoria introduced herself as a handmaiden of Lady Eileen. She was one of the first High Magnus'. As a spellcaster they are similar to Ilihi. They rely on nature and the elemental properties around them, but they are different. Magnus' are practitioners of magic and use spells, rituals, and incantations to achieve a wide range of effects. Ilihi tap into the natural world, they can feel the primal source within the element and manipulate it to their advantage. Magnus' are born mortal and rely on learned magical knowledge.

As they spoke, a panther approached from her right side. Latoria explained that Shistia was one of four familiars belonging to Lady Eileen and was sent away before her death with the Eclipse Amulet. They were surprised to see the amulet around the prince's neck when it was supposed to be at the bottom of the pit. The palace extended all the way to the shrine before Sir Erin had the catacombs destroyed. Eris wanted its treasures for herself. She sought to use them to gain favor with Lord Nebula. Alexander was disgusted. If it were not for her, he would have grown up with parents. If it were not for her, Soldiel would still be alive.

The thought of his amulet being corrupted by darkness infuriated him. The amulet was not the only relic she wanted. Latoria explained how Oricale's children betrayed their mother and tried to use her power to take control of the multiverse. It backfired against them, and they were cut off from the anchor. When his mother stole the Tri-Oricale Crystal it granted her abilities and shielded her mind from Hyperion's influence. Once Lord Marlusha learned of its existence, he made it his mission to find it.

Latoria summoned the unicorn, Shoxz, that once served Soldiel. He left her behind in the event he returned with the prince to reclaim his world. She rubbed her head against the prince's shoulder as he caressed her white mane. She would join the prince in his quest. Before he could leave, there was a ritual that had to be completed in order for him to use the full

110

force of the amulet. Latoria and Paku stood on opposite sides of the pit. Following her lead, Paku drew on her energy and echoed her chants. Their chanting darkened the sky, and the clouds blocked out the sun. The valley was overrun with harsh winds. The animals in the valley cried out in fear and sought shelter. The roars of the ogres reached the shrine. They were no longer alone; trolls and goblins were now rushing through the valley as well.

Latoria encased the shrine in protective charms, as the roars grew closer. Alexander moved toward the tip of the pit and was ordered to throw the amulet in, but as he was about to do so, a shadowy figure jolted down from the sky. It broke through the charms and flung the prince into the valley. Two other figures encased in shadows held him down. Latoria rushed toward the prince and disabled their spells protecting their identity. The first to come into sight was Eris. As the shadows faded from the other two, their golden robes and black trimming caught the prince's eye. On their armored chest plate was the sigil of a golden eye. Lord Celeio's Gaeatonic Guardians were allied with his enemies.

Latoria set up new wards to protect the shrine, "MAGNUS' OF SALAHEA, HOW DARE YOU BETRAY THE CROWN. LEAVE OUR LANDS AT ONCE!"

"We have the boy, we are leaving now," laughed the hooded figure.

Latoria summoned two emerald whips and attacked the two men. Eris grabbed her brother by the hair and dragged him further back.

"You look surprised brother!" Eris let out a dark and ominous laugh.

"Beast, be gone!" Paku ignited his hands with a spell and launched fireballs at Eris causing her to lose her grip. The prince rushed toward the shrine. Dozens of small, grotesque creatures chased after him. Their skin ranging from green to rust and sharp teeth like sharks. Hans summoned his bow and started shooting arrows at the goblins that chased after the prince.

Paku challenged the two Gaeatonic Guardians, but they deflected each of his spells. He uttered the words, '*Vatra Mija*,' and with a flick of his hand he created a flaming chain that he transformed into a serpent of fire. The flaming serpent overpowered them.

"Hand over the prince, or all of you will die."

"Only in death!" With that said, Hans shot an arrow that landed in front of the two enemy Magnus' and exploded. This gave the group time to

111

run for cover in the shrine. Latoria cut her hand and allowed the blood to soak the grass and summoned a thick barrier of thorn bushes. Eris was the only one who managed to get through the barrier. The Gaeatonic Guardians were entangled.

Eris' gaze was no longer locked onto her brother. She set her eyes on the elf. As they were running back, a cloud of shadow appeared before them and grabbed Hans by the neck. It twisted and turned, and the shadow reappeared outside of the barrier. Eris reemerged and called for Paku and Latoria to release her army, otherwise, Hans would die. Alexander's heart and mind raced uncontrollably. He told them to do as she asked. He could not risk the life of his friend.

She laughed at them as they watched Hans' body quiver in her hands. The prince walked down the steps of the shrine and tried to surrender. Paku and Latoria pleaded with him to reconsider what he was doing. The thorn bushes dissolved, and Eris waited until her brother was in the hands of her Magnus'. They took off into the sky covered in dark mist first with the prince while Eris stood behind. While they were in midair, Latoria jolted energy spears at them causing them to drop the prince.

Eris had enough of Latoria's meddling. She saw an opportunity to cause her brother pain. Dark sparks appeared on her fingertips, as she placed her hands near the side of Hans' head. The frightened elf stared at the prince and signaled for him to close his eyes. With tears cascading down his cheeks, he ran toward them. Paku tackled him to the ground. Kicking and screaming, he was dragged back to the shrine. Heart racing and sound nullified; he closed his eyes. Eris electrified Hans' brain and his body let out one final quiver before the life in his eyes faded. The world slowed around him as he took his breaths. The prince finally opened his bloodshot eyes. Death was something he knew too well and could not deal with again.

Hans' body began to fade with the wind as she tossed him into the air. Screams of anger and sorrow echoed across the valley. The creatures that once took shelter became crazed and violent. They attacked and overwhelmed Eris' army, as the prince pushed Paku and Latoria away from him. Their eyes locked onto one another as Eris smiled. Paku and Latoria implored the prince to see reason. His aura intensified and they noticed the animals were becoming more ferocious. They could not have done anything to save Hans. He dropped to his knees as he cried uncontrollably. Tears rolled down his cheeks as the unsettling feeling of emptiness took over his heart. He looked down to the floor and noticed the grass was not absorbing the water. The water levitated around his hands and glowed with every breath he took.

The prince would not listen. He jumped up from the floor and focused on his hands. The water crystallized into shards. He launched them toward his sister, but she absorbed the attack. The prince raced toward her as she launched shadow balls at him. He was not skilled in combat and was in over his head. Paku chased after him and finally caught up to him before tackling him down to the ground. The look of devastation filled his eyes. No words could change what he was feeling. The Red Magnus ordered the prince to stand down and let him take care of Eris. The ice shards that remained in his hands liquefied and soaked the ground. Paku removed a white feather from his hat and engulfed it in flames. He blew the ashes toward the ground and created a barrier around him and the prince.

"Eris, you shall pay for what you have done!"

Paku glanced at his side and saw the prince was no longer with him. His eyes were pitch black and with every breath he took the wind around him increased. Eris stepped back in fear. This time his energy was even more powerful than their first encounter. The Gaeatonic Guardians abandoned Eris and cloaked themselves in darkness before taking off into the sky. Eris inhaled and electrified her body in dark energy. Purple sparks formed at her fingertips. She kept her index and middle fingers elongated while she closed her hands. She waved them from left to right and the sparks became ropes of purple lightning. She whipped the lightning directly at her brother.

The prince smirked at his sister and simply stood at an angle and with both hands he split the lightning. The impact shattered the ropes and tossed Eris back, burning her hands. The ground around him became putrid and the flowers decomposed. He grabbed her face, and his hands burned through her flesh. Smoke radiated from her body and the shadows slowly claimed her.

"I will make sure you die this time!"

Eris laughed as she looked into her brother's eyes.

"You will join the elf in death before long!"

The prince's black eyes changed to emerald. Like a puppet, he was being controlled. He placed his hand over her forehead and concentrated. Eris screamed out in pain as her body began to harden in darkness. His revenge was short lived. A shadow raced from the distance and attacked him. It broke their connection and Eris' body returned to normal. The shadow twisted and turned, and Amira appeared in her demonic form.

"Glad to see you made it home. I will be back for you!"

Amira took off into the sky and disappeared. Everyone raced to the prince's side and returned him to the shrine. The color in his eyes returned to normal. Eris' troops retreated to safety. Paku held the prince up as he tried to comfort him. No words could ever fill the hole in his heart. He kept replaying Hans' final moments in his mind. Latoria broke his concentration.

"We cannot wait another second. This ritual must be completed!"

The amulet was already at the bottom of the pit. Latoria, Paku, and the prince stood across from one another.

Latoria chanted, "From dusk to dawn, hear our call. Sleeping giant of the Emerald Light rise once more and take flight."

Paku chanted after her and it was as if a bullet shot into the sky. Thunder roared overhead and a huge twister shot down from the darkened sky and entered the pit. The prince stood back in wonder as he saw the Eclipse Amulet levitate inside the twister. The amulet reached the top and shattered. Once shattered, it sent a ripple down into the pit. The jewel fragments sparkled with energy and enveloped the twister. The ground shook and a huge flash of light blasted into the sky. The sky cleared up and the dust began to settle. Emerald scales glistened like lightning. Six horns stuck out of its head like a crown. An infant dragon about the size of the prince's arm glided down toward him.

"The Emerald Dragon, Fang is now yours to command. This ritual has released him from his slumber."

With a snap of her fingers, the amulet reconstructed itself. She placed it around his neck as she whipped the tears from his eyes. Holding him in her arms only made him feel more alone. The father he once knew was dead. The man who helped raised him was now dead. He was alone in a world with people who wanted him dead. Finding his sister was imperative. Princess Ionica ruled over the country of Seraqus. It was one of the bigger realms on the continent of Weguard. The spell they were going to use would teleport him close enough to her palace. She whispered in his ear that she was truly sorry for the loss of his friend. He fought back the tears as he walked back to Nacilias and Shoxz. Latoria and Paku held hands as they chanted.

"Divisum per tempus et terrarum spatio pontis
extruamus nobis deleri non potest.
Concede nobis facultatem solute moveatur
ac libere, ut hac arte destinatum pervenire."

*(Lands that are divided through time and space,
build us a bridge that cannot be erased.
Allow us the ability to move at will, so that we
may reach our destination with this skill.)*

A huge spark of light devoured the travelers. Latoria and Paku were set at ease knowing the prince would soon be with his sister. Latoria feared the prince's abilities. Seeing how unstable he was without proper training. Paku confessed he too feared what the prince would become. He noticed the boy could speak with animals and influenced wildlife. It was a rarity. Paku stared into the sky and watched the strand of light that held the prince, and his companions moved further away from the island. Artamisa was sent to find Narnarie and warn him of the attack.

The strand of light finally touched down on Seraqus and the impact burned the flowers around them. Alexander opened his eyes and noticed they were transported into a garden. The breath-taking scenery overtook his heart. It brought him back to happier times in his own garden with Hans and Soldiel. The garden thrived with blue mystique orchids and Alstroemeria isabellana. Massive fields of purple torch of the clouds, Begonia fusca and yellow birds of paradise expanded over the hills. Dozens of blue angel impatiens, blue dreams, and bed Bolivian fuchsias covered the meadow as far as the eye could see. Accenting the gardens were fields of orange sunset bomareas and candelabra lilies.

The plants created a lavish painting to the traveler's eyes. The field also contained bushes arranged in the formation of animals. The garden had a peaceful ambiance that the group fell in love with. Shoxz separated from the others and walked toward the field of flowers. She inhaled the aroma that the plants were excreting. The flowers placed her in a trance; it sent a tingle down her spine and overtook her mind. She turned to the group with happy news.

"My dear friends, we are in the Meadow of Seraqus; the garden that surrounds your sister's empire."

PART IV - EMPIRE OF SERAQUS

CHAPTER
12

PRINCESS IONICA

The morning breeze blew a heavy cold mist through the air. Pollen from the flowers covered the prince's face. He tried to move but his body was solid like stone. Fang licked his eye lids, removing the pollen. Flapping his wings, he removed the rest that remained on the prince's body. His thoughts were scattered, and his memories were fuzzy and distorted. The prince was finally able to raise his head when he realized he was lying on the ground. He tried to pick himself up, but his legs were paralyzed. As he turned his head, he realized the others had fallen asleep, but how? He tried to focus on what happened before he passed out. The last thing the prince could remember was Shoxz telling them that they had arrived in the Meadow of Seraqus. The prince slowly regained feeling in his hands and he crawled over to the others and cleaned the pollen off their faces. Each of them opened their eyes and slowly began to regain feeling in their bodies. Shoxz realized that the flowers she sniffed contained enchanted pollen to keep out unwanted visitors.

For as far as the eye could see there was nothing more than a gigantic garden. Nearby, there were three bull elks that grazed on a bush of roses. Nacilias approached them for assistance, but they would not comply. They ordered the prince and his companions to leave. Prince Alexander thought by introducing himself they would budge, but it ended in failure. Shoxz was overcome by rage at this point and flared her wings at the creatures. Her piercing white horn glowed as she charged at the beasts, but the prince interfered. He would not allow her to ruin his chances of seeing his sister.

Her threat was not taken lightly. The secret veil that protected the empire cracked open behind the bull elks and a woman walked through. Her sandy blond hair was cropped just above her shoulders. Her face was exquisite and enchanting. She had very high cheekbones and elegant eyes. She wore a cropped red shirt that revealed parts of her breast down to her midsection and red sheer pants. She was wearing a belt with darts that were engraved with an eight-pointed star in the center. She examined the child and the creatures he called friends. The baby dragon clung to the prince like he was its mother.

"You bring a creature of destruction into this meadow. Leave at once!"

"We mean no harm. We were just asking for directions to the Empire of Seraqus."

Laughter overtook the woman, "You think you can communicate with these animals?"

The prince's ignorance nearly exposed him. His abilities were not common amongst the others. He had to tread lightly, otherwise he could put himself in harm's way. There was no way to know who friend or foe was.

Fang snarled at the woman as his emerald scales sparkled to life.

"Easy, little one. I got this. I am Prince Alexander Whitespear. I wish to speak with my sister."

"Child, go home. Turn away and leave this place."

Nacilias growled and Shoxz flared her wings. The woman spun around quickly, grabbing her darts, but the prince removed the amulet from around his neck and its light blinded them. The princess' forces were on high alert. The whispers of his return caused panic and false sightings. The prince lowered his amulet and apologized for his forcefulness. The warrior dropped to her knees.

"Apologies, my prince."

Prince Alexander lowered himself to her and helped her up from the floor. "It is foolish of me to presume you would welcome me with open arms. None of you truly know me. Please help us."

"Your Majesty, my name is May. Please gather your friends and follow me."

May whirled her hand and opened the veil once more. She allowed the prince to enter first and the others followed behind her. They came across a coastline that was hidden in the meadow. The majestic blue water cascaded against the shoreline and in the distance stood a massive fortress. The architecture was superb. The massive Doric, Ionic, and Corinthian columns were visible from the shoreline. The tufa limestone buildings were covered in frost and glistened with the shining sun still rising overhead. The fortress was surrounded by a black metallic wall, but the wall also appeared to have a thick glacier sheet encased around it to withstand an onslaught. Rock formations held the base of the fortress in place, as waterfalls formed and fell into the water around it.

At the edge of the shore there was boat made from hickory wood. May led them aboard as she grabbed an oar to help move the boat from the sand into the water. The prince grabbed another oar, and they made their way toward the fortress. His nerves were getting the best of him. He stared into the water and could see a shadow in the distance. The boat began to rock as waves crashed against the side. The shadow hit the side of the boat, but that was not their only problem. From a distance something massive was heading their way. She roared for everyone to brace for impact. The shadow beneath the water got closer and with a huge splash a serpent comprised of water penetrated through the surface. The creature attacked the boat with full force, causing the prince's amulet to ignite and shield the boat from the creature's vengeance. Shoxz noticed something else swimming under the water, and she flared her wings, warning them of the impending ambush.

The creature launched itself onto the rear of the boat at incredible speeds. May quickly turned and flung a ninja star at the beast. It merely ricocheted off it. It was as black as night with scales mixed into its fur. Wings spanned from its wrist to its shoulders. Its tail was at least six feet long and spiked with razors. Its face resembled that of a panther. Fythos were a rare beauty. Most of their kin were slaughtered during the Holy War. Fang snarled at the creature, and smoke blew out his nose. May was relieved to see it was an envoy sent to collect them.

121

"It's only Shonux. Samistha must have sent him to investigate the boat. He will not harm us."

With a sigh of relief, their anxiety diminished. Shonux jumped into the air and whirl-pooled into the water. The water serpent positioned itself in front of the boat and created two strands of water that attached itself around May's hands to ferry them to the empire. The serpent rumbled and sank into the lake as they neared the docks. The prince's impression of the empire faded. The docks were tattered and old. The statues that once stood to harbor the boats, stood in ruins.

As they docked, Samistha appeared from behind one of the statues. She was covered in ornate embroidered robes with a high collar and large billowing sleeves. Alexander noticed that she had a graceful circlet, and an ornate headdress engraved with runes. She wielded an elegantly crafted staff encrusted with a gem on top. Her robes were a heavenly blue color and had silver trimmings. Samistha was ecstatic to see him. Shonux jumped out of the water and stood beside her. She rubbed the Fythos' head as she addressed the prince.

"Your arrival is a blessing from the stars. These are dark times, and we are in a constant state of war."

"We must notify the princess of his arrival," explained May.

"I will take you to her," replied Samistha.

Samistha was a Blue Magnus and was able to manipulate water with spells but could also heal. They followed Samistha through Cobblestone streets. The buildings were riddled with images of the empire's rise. The impressive architecture seemed supernatural. It was filled with clock towers, bell towers, countless courtyards, buildings of great magnitude, and great cathedrals. The courtyards were filled with laughter and cheers as the children played. The essence of joy radiated from the buildings. Hope was everlasting, and the citizens of this empire knew that very well. The beam of the sun glistened as it rebounded off the sapphire buildings and sculptures that lined the streets. Sculptures of dragons and humans reflected the ancient culture of Seraqus, but this advanced culture was also depicted by its formation of buildings and machines used within its walls.

Samistha escorted them into a courtyard that stood in front of a monumental palace. It was newly crafted, and expansion renovations were underway. Fang's head tilted sideways as a rumbling caught his attention. The call of another dragon. Fang opened his mouth, and the whines of a baby escaped. The courtyard was flooded with hooded figures. One of which, approached them. This woman was taller than the rest. On the center of her silver hood was an eight-pointed star, surrounded by three circles, and in the center was a blue flame. Her robes were silver and trimmed in royal blue. The woman had a silver waist plate and, in the center, had the same symbol that she wore on her hood. She clenched in her hand a carefully crafted staff made of mahogany wood. The tip of the staff resembled a tree during its winter season with its leafless branches, and in the center stood a glowing green crystal. She raised her head and took off the hood.

"You abandoned your post to usher strangers before her majesty's palace?"

Samistha stepped forward and addressed her with a bow, "You stand in the presence of Prince Alexander Whitespear, brother to her majesty."

Whispers erupted in the courtyard as the woman approached the prince and touched his face. His emerald dragon gripping him for dear life lashed his tongue out against her. Her eyes darted down to his neck as she noticed the Eclipse Amulet.

"Welcome home. I am Anri, High Magnus to Princess Ionica."

The High Magnus led them into the palace. Its gates were made of dense ice, and as she waved her hand, she chanted the words, '*Odmrznuti.*' The ice became transparent, and it allowed them entry. The transparent parts of the gate became solid once they were all through. Cobblestone floors, lined with sculptures of dragons standing in armored uniforms, were covered in the powder of winter. As they passed each statue, they noticed they were holding their swords downward, so the tip was facing the floor. Down the shaft of the sword were runes. At the end of the walkway stood a marble staircase leading into the room beyond.

Upon entry, the snow-covered ground was no more. This room was filled with golden walls with images carved into them. The floor was covered in demantoid garnet, but once it reached the center of the room it was replaced by green and blue marble. The marble was formed in a circular image with triangle figures and in the center of the circle stood a geyser that shot out a stream of water. Another staircase stood at the far end of the room. Soldiers halted them as the princess was descending the stairs.

123

Alexander's heart dropped as he stared at her grace. She wore a blue and silver topped corset that was connected to a long white skirt and white sleeves. The bottom of the sleeves and skirt had a splash of blue. She wore a diamond diadem on her head that shimmered in the light. The soldiers stopped moving and circled the prince and his companions. Anri bowed to the princess and the princess moved her hand forward allowing the High Magnus to kiss it. She rose from the floor and stepped to the princess' side.

The stories that filled his mind every night before bed were finally coming true. His heart was consumed by mixed emotions. Princess Ionica lowered herself to him and placed her hand on his chin. The princess' actions caused a commotion amongst the Royal Guard, but Anri silenced them. She raised him from the floor and embraced him. The princess sobbed on his shoulder and held him for what seemed like hours. She finally released him and lowered herself to his feet.

Her actions caused everyone else to bow as well. The feeling of having those around you acknowledge your presence and glorify you was something the prince could not fathom. He thought of himself as a child who had made countless mistakes since arriving in LunaSol, but in this instant he was praised for who he was. It was a feeling the prince could not describe.

Anri rose to her feet and could not allow any more time to pass. "Princess, we must hurry to the throne room and speak with your brother. Let us take our leave!"

The princess rose from the floor, and everyone followed suit. She gestured to her guards to leave them at once as she proceeded to walk up the stairs. Prince Alexander and his companions followed her into the throne room. The oculus in the ceiling allowed for natural light. In the center of the room stood a pond of water that was home to a crystal obelisk. It had hieroglyphic writing that consumed one side and on the other side the words, *Nos Animadverto Totus*. From his encounter with Anagar, he realized the obelisk was the base of the Tri-Oricale Crystal. The prince wanted to get a closer look at it, but Nacilias nudged him to focus. Princess Ionica took her place on the throne while Anri took her place on a smaller throne near her. Shonux stood at the side of the High Magnus while the doors were sealed behind them. She rubbed the head of Fythos as she addressed the room. Within the throne room she would be able to speak freely without being overhead.

"Why the secrecy?" questioned the prince.

Anri responded, "The empire has been infiltrated by spies. Many of our tactical plans have been stolen. We could not risk anyone listening to our conversation."

"How can this be?" questioned the prince.

"This person is shielded by greater magic, and I cannot sense their identity."

The princess studied the prince's face, his gestures, his tone. Her eyes darted from the fox to the unicorn, then to the baby dragon.

"How is this possible? How are you alive?"

Anri stopped speaking as she fixated on the prince's face. His innocence stirred fear in her. Since their separation, the story passed down was Soldiel murdered him before fleeing through a portal. The angels even presented them with a body to bury in the catacombs. His words cut through her core. All these years, Soldiel raised him in secret, but Eris still hunted him like an animal. Breaking through the barrier of reality, she found him with the help of a demon. A demon who followed him into LunaSol. Her darkness seemed to touch every corner of reality. He smiled as he recalled his childhood with Hans and Soldiel on Earth. His life was amazing and filled with joy, even though there were moments of depression and self-injury due to his night terrors. Anri showed interest in his night terrors and the winged figure he saw. From the corner of her eye, she locked eyes with the princess. Even more danger awaited them.

He also confessed that in his battle with Eris, his abilities manifested. Princess Ionica grew worried that she was moving freely when they were supposed to be trapped behind enchantments. Since the prince was taken at such a young age, no one knew if he was an Ilihi or mortal. A sharp pain crushed Anri's focus. Her face shriveled up and she was no longer involved in the conversation. The obelisk radiated as she slowly approached it. Fires erupted throughout the meadow. The inhabitants fled for their lives. She rubbed her hand over the obelisk, and she could see the meadow clearly. Her three bull elks were slaughtered, and two unknown figures attacked the barrier.

Anri noticed two red foxes hiding in the grass. She used her magic to see through their eyes. The red fox lifted his head and witnessed two Fire

Ilihi set the barrier aflame. The High Magnus held out her hand to the princess and uttered, "*Telepatija.*" The spell allowed her to connect with the princess for her to witness the destruction. The perpetrator's faces became recognizable; it was Lord Marlusha's children Cort and Jenna. Her world grew smaller. The angelic enchantments that were placed over Lord Marlusha's lands were meant to keep them locked away forever, but here they were. Flaunting their freedom. '*How did they get out?*' was all she could think about.

Cort's distinctive physical features made him a memorable figure. At five feet ten inches he was of average height amongst his peers. His hair, short and choppy, and jet black. On the right side of his head, three carefully crafted braids hung. Underneath his cloak was a set of formidable black armor with red robes like his father's.

Jenna was the same height. Her flowing red hair was pushed back into a ponytail and tied together with two metal chopsticks. Her nails were long and accented with small daggers at the tip. She also wore similar armor and robes like her brother.

"This is a nightmare. His lands have been secured for centuries, and now this. We must find out how they can leave Martilo freely?" Princess Ionica explained.

"Princess, our focus should be securing the barrier. If they break through it, we could be attacked from all sides. We need reinforcements," pleaded Anri.

Anri waved her hands at the obelisk and chanted, "*Objaviti svoju dušu.*" She retrieved two crystals from the obelisk and smashed them onto the floor. Purple gases emerged from the shattered pieces, and they took on the form of two men. She introduced them as Dementorol and Jecxas. Her spell summoned them from a previous mission.

Dementorol was a Wind Ilihi. His beautiful amber eyes met the prince's. He smiled and his white teeth lit up the room. He had his brown shoulder length hair in a man bun with pieces of his hair falling down the sides of his face. He wore gray robes with golden accents.

Jecxas was a Water Ilihi. He had six earrings in his left ear. Both sides of his head were shaven, and the top of his hair was long, but tightly braided into box-braids. His navy-blue robes were accented with white symbols.

She instructed them to destroy Cort and Jenna before they could bring down the barrier. One evaporated into the air while the other dematerialized into water and took off through the oculus. Dementorol turned himself into a whirlwind and blasted through the barrier. He flung Jenna into a tree and knocked her out. Jecxas jolted through the barrier on the back of a wave and froze Prince Cort's hands in ice.

All that remained of the meadow was burnt land and the remnants of plant life. Anri whispered, "*Priključak*" and flung her hand at the obelisk. Alexander and the others were able to see the battle as well. Lord Marlusha's children retreated to one another. Their objective was completed and within seconds they were consumed by flames and vanished.

The damage was too extensive. The flames ate away at the protective charms. The magic keeping the barrier up was fading quickly and causing cracks to appear on it. The cracks worked their way up to the top of the barrier and piece-by-piece it dissolved right before their eyes. The citizens of the Empire of Seraqus feared what this dark omen could bring upon them. Princess Ionica called for Dementorol and Jecxas to return to the palace at once. They needed to regroup and protect the citizens from potential harm. The empire was vulnerable to a full-scale invasion. They feared the princess' wrath, but she was not disappointed at all. This called for a plan of action.

Anri gave the order to the High Magnus' to secure the perimeter. Princess Ionica instructed the Royal Guard to enforce a curfew amongst her citizens until the traitor could be found. She turned toward her brother and saw he was deep in thought.

"What is weighing on your mind?"

"I fear that this is not going to end well. They want me, and they will stop at nothing to see me dead."

"That is why you have us. We will never let anything happen to you. Lord Nebula may be powerful, but his servants are far from locating the keys to revive him. They seek you out to destroy you and buy time to locate the keys for his release, but you have time to learn all the things necessary to defeat this great evil. Trust in us!"

Her words sparked his memory. The tablet showed him the star fragments that kept Lord Nebula's prison closed. The angels scattered them, and they needed to remain hidden. Alexander needed to get her away from the others so he could find out where the stones were.

"I do trust in all of you. I just have little faith in myself."

Anri could not take any more of the prince's whining. He was young and could easily be trained, given the proper guidance. He had been babied far too long and did not know what it meant to fend for himself. Anri gave him a taste of harsh reality; his perfect life was over. The kingdoms of LunaSol were tortured by Lord Dark Lucus and Eris. They needed a beacon of hope. The room was shocked and appalled with Anri's actions; disrespect of a royal could cost her head. The room remained silent to see what the princess would do, but the prince appreciated her honesty. He broke through the silence and welcomed her remarks. She reminded him of Hans. He appreciated her perspective and understood her intent. Throughout his life, he was shielded from discord and kept locked away from the truth. He could no longer hide behind others. Anri apologized for her harsh words; she grabbed his hands and looked into his eyes. She could see the loss, the sadness, and the fear. He needed a guiding hand. Without proper structure, he would never learn how to defeat his enemy. She offered to teach him how to fight and educate him in their customs.

No matter how happy she was to see her brother, there was still a spark of resentment. For years she was the reigning force keeping the continent together and now his arrival could destabilize her control. Not once did Lord Nebula's generals try to attack her empire head on, but since his return they were emboldened. Princess Ionica believed her and Prince Adam controlled the last remaining dragons, but seeing Prince Alexander with an Emerald Dragon in arm stirred concerns.
She pointed at the creature.

"How did you come across such a beast?"

"His name is Fang! He was hidden by servants of our mother at the Shrine of Glory."

She clenched the side of her dress as she called for Anri to join her at the obelisk. With the appearance of an Emerald Dragon, it was time to consult with a higher power.

"Dragons are fearsome beasts. Fang, as you call him, was meant for Eris, but here he is clinging to you. We thought she corrupted his egg during the war and housed him in secret."

"We must take him below," smiled Anri.

The sunlight from the oculus was directly overhead and revealed a glowing object in its center. Anri chanted, "***Obeliscus ex Oricale, revelet***

Deus absconsa tua." (*Obelisk of the Oricale, reveal your secrets.*) At the end, she uttered the words, '***Nos Animadverto Totus.***' The words and symbols on the obelisk began to glow, and the light encased the entire obelisk.

The white light changed to emerald and soared through the oculus. The entire throne room was illuminated in its glow. Ripples in the fabric of time appeared all around them like strings. Time seemed to slow down, and all movement was stiffened. Anri seemed to be the only one who was not stiffened by the spell. She approached the obelisk and tapped it with her staff. It melted downward into the lake, revealing a smaller crystal glowing in its core. She used the crystal at the tip of her staff to touch the floating object. The connection caused the floating crystal to spiral out of control. The emerald light retreated toward the heart of the crystal, and the Oricale Star appeared on it.

A vortex opened beneath the pond, and they were dragged into a hidden chamber. Alexander saw the vortex close above them and the obelisk reappeared. They found themselves in a frozen chamber with huge icicles hanging from the ceiling and icicles lining the floor. The emblem of a crescent moon was etched onto the walls. Statues of sapphire dragons lined every corner of the room. The prince noticed an archway that remained hidden behind a frozen stream of water. Anri touched the ice and dissolved it. She parted the steam, revealing a long corridor.

The princess led them down the corridor and into a huge stone bunker beneath the lake. It appeared to be a haven for the empire, but it was home to something greater. The rumbling that they heard before was from the mighty beast resting beneath the surface. It was Narsacil, the sapphire dragon lifted her long neck and peered down at the prince. The little dragon flared its wings, causing the prince to release it. Fang growled at the other dragon, forcing it to lower its head. Narsacil's head was the size of elephant. Its teeth were as sharp as swords. Soldiel's stories did not do her justice. Her white antler-style horns were majestic and the sapphire on her chest dazzled him. The smaller ones on her forearms were like blades. Down her spine was a white mane that reached her spear-like tail. She had patches of hair on her shoulder blades and down her forearm to her wrist. She blew snow from her nose causing the little dragon to fall back. For the first time, Fang opened his mouth and breathed fire.

"A beauty, she is. I keep her down here, so my people do not fear being eaten."

"She is a prisoner down here," hissed the prince. His words only angered the princess. Who was he to question her?

"How dare you?"

Her words only enraged the prince more. He could not hear the creatures' thoughts. Same with Fang. Princess Ionica was known for her temper. He kept his mouth quiet after that. Anri noticed the tension shift. She brought his attention to the gigantic chasm in the ground. Four huge columns surrounded it, supporting the ceiling. There was a staircase nearby that led to a platform overlooking the abyss below.

"We must present the creature."

Prince Alexander's eyebrows flared. What was she about to do? Anri made her way to the staircase and ascended to the platform. She walked to the edge and on the floor stood a panel with a small opening in the center. She placed the tip of her staff into it and turned the panel. It clicked like she had unlocked a door. She descended from the platform and joined the others. "This room is sacred space. Oricale's tomb lies in that chasm. During her reign, not only did the Alulim thrive, but so did the precursors of the dragons. A group known as the Basileus were among some of the rarest and favored The All Mother.

Comprised of Purple, Crystal, Emerald, Sapphire, Ruby, and Pink Dragons. As an Emerald Dragon, we must present him to his Mistress."

Anri placed her staff into another indent in the ground, parallel to the platform above and chanted,

"Prope es tu a principio ad finem; Hic habitare
vos clamo. Afferte, et ascensura est de abysso,
ignem accenderent ; ut possimus et accipe
gradum potestatis."
(From beginning to end you have been near;
I call you forth to settle here. Bring forth
your great flame and rise from the depths,
so that we may gain power and take the next step.)

A massive explosion of emerald fire soared from the depths. Its color changed to blue as it engulfed the platform. An intense wave of energy consumed the room, followed by a calming sensation. Narsacil's and Fang's

130

scales lit up. Two strains of fire entangled the emerald dragon and the prince. It jolted into their mouths like a parasite.

"They are now one!"

They each collapsed as the flame exited their mouths. May and Samistha rushed to tend to the dragon. Shoxz held the prince up, preventing him from falling face first. The air in the room was stale and humid. Alexander rubbed the side of Shoxz in comfort. The great unicorn stood at attention as she watched the look of disgust on the princess' face.

Whispering to the prince she warned him, "Your sister is not happy about this. She has hatred in her eyes. Look at her!"

Noticing her face, he could see she was fighting back her emotions. Trying not to let on that she was annoyed, but why? Moments ago, she was happy about his return. What changed? Anri cleared her throat to gain the princess' attention. Her menacing stare was witnessed by all. The blood in her body boiled. She was power, regent, and protector of the realm, he was nothing more than a child playing at a man. Her thoughts corrupted and vile caused her body to react. Water manifested in the form of a dagger and turned to ice in her palm.

Her actions triggered the flame. It shook the foundation and soared into the sky causing her to drop it. A voice manifested in a song crippling their minds with visions. The prince was the only one untouched. He could not hear her song, but rather her voice, warning him. The first stone was found. Lord Nebula's foothold grew stronger.

Oricale released them all. Anri saw it as an act of anger. She ordered them all to leave the Chamber of Dragons. Princess Ionica was the last to leave. She stared at the cavern in disbelief. She protected her tomb for years and now she turned on her the minute her brother arrived. Her jealousy opened her up to darker thoughts. She left the room, and they all returned to the throne room.

She had her High Magnus gather the others and take them to their rooms for the night. Once she was alone, she gripped the sides of her throne and screamed out in pain. The room shook with vigor and the ice walls cracked. With each breath she took she only grew even more upset. *Why him?* She kept repeating the same question in her head. She came to learn about Oricale once she took over the Empire of Seraqus. She fought to protect Oricale's secrets and now she was repaid with nothing more than a headache. The Empire of Seraqus was not always her home. She came to rule it after the previous inhabitants vanished.

Her thoughts spiraled downward, and her anger grew intense. The ice walls shook and shattered, but a knock at the door snapped her back to reality. She looked around the room and saw the destruction. She manipulated the ice and reassembled the room before allowing Anri back in. Anri noticed something was wrong, but knew it was better not to ask questions.

"We should talk about what happened in the pit."

"There is nothing to talk about. She made her choice. HIM!"

"That is not what I mean. We each had a vision. What did you see?" questioned the High Magnus.

Princess Ionica toyed with her hair. She closed her eyes and held her breath. She could not bring herself to repeat it.

Anri on the other hand confessed her vision. She saw the first key to Lord Nebula's prison being used.

"We need to notify the other royals!"

"We will do no such thing. It will only cause panic. The prince is back. This is his burden to bear."

Anri could not believe her ears. All her life, the princess prayed to have her brother back and for this war to end. What changed? Why was she acting like this? She took a step forward to speak, but the princess lifted her hand commanding her to silence herself. She was too exhausted to continue the conversation. Anri left the room and walked past the prince's chambers. His door was still open. Shoxz took her place by the prince's bedside. The prince jumped into the bed and Nacilias found a spot at the foot of his bed. She wished them a good night's rest as she closed the door. May and Samistha were already in their beds sleeping. Shonux took his leave from the palace and returned to his post.

Anri returned to her room and settled in for the night. Before bed she would always brush her hair and stare out across the kingdom from her window. She could see lit torches from a nearby courtyard and the sounds of a night sermon echoing below. Even in her moment of relaxation, she was still tense. She asked Oricale for answers, but what she got in return was silence. Oricale would not speak of the events that took place in the hidden chambers. She feared the princess' actions would hurt the empire if she did not take these events more seriously. One of the star fragments had already been found, but she would not call on the other royals to rally with her. Why? What did she hope to gain from keeping this news from the others? She had no choice but to disobey the princess. Everyone had a right to know. She would send word to the others in the morning. She turned out the flames from the candles and turned in for the night.

Alexander could be heard snoring from the next room, but his mind would not allow him peace. Hans and Soldiel were all he could think about. Just a few days ago he was a normal kid and now he was fighting in a war against a god. As he slumbered, he faded into his dreams and found himself running in a dark forest. Red piercing eyes followed him, and razor-sharp claws ripped at his flesh. The child prince woke up drenched in sweat. The room was silent and in the cloak of darkness, thousands gathered to lay waste to the Empire of Seraqus. Lord Marlusha's secret army was on the move. He returned to his slumber and was finally able to set his mind at ease.

CHAPTER

13

LESSONS

The morning sun woke the prince as it radiated throughout the room. Shoxz and Nacilias were already groomed and waiting for the prince to bathe and get ready. Fang remained at the head of the prince's pillow. As he entered the bath, one of the princess' servants came into the room with breakfast and clothes for the prince. He finished bathing and dried off his hair as he got dressed. His royal blue pants fit him like a glove. He sat at the edge of the bed and pulled his socks up and then his brown boots. He had trouble getting his tunic on since an armored chest plate was embedded into it. He finally got his head through the opening and wrapped a long yellow scarf around his neck.

Anri stood at the door and called for them to assemble in the throne room. Once they were ready, they joined the princess and her servants. She was noticeably irritated upon their arrival and was colder than yesterday.

"With all of the excitement we faced yesterday, we did not have a chance to actually talk."

Unlike yesterday, the princess chose to keep the Royal Guard and a few of her Magnus' at her side. She was unconcerned with upholding secrecy regarding their discussions today. She asked for her brother to elaborate on his return. Her line of questioning made the prince feel uncomfortable. Even though he wanted to trust her, knowing that her court was compromised made him more skeptical. Before he could get a word out, Nacilias clawed at his boot for his attention.

"She is laying a trap for the traitor."

Nacilias was right, he almost forgot about it. The traitor was someone in the room, whatever he said would get back to Lord Marlusha. Without revealing the most important details, he explained the events of his arrival and his encounter with Lord Dark Lucus. His travels to the ruins of Haven. Being found by Paku in the ruins and being taken to the Shrine of Glory. The room was in awe as they listened to the prince recount his battle against Eris and how his guardian died at her hands. He explained how Fang was summoned from the pit. The princess was more intrigued to learn that servants of Lord Celeio were working with Eris. The prince continued to look down at Nacilias as he spoke, causing the princess to stir.

"Brother! You look to the fox as if you are seeking permission to speak. Why is that?"

Nacilias and Shoxz were appalled. How dare she? Nacilias growled at the comment and Shoxz' horn lit up. The prince could not risk letting his sister know he could speak with animals. That would surely unravel. The prince composed himself before speaking.

"This was mother's familiar. I look to my companions for comfort. They are not pets, and I would not allow anyone to treat them less than."

The tension in the room grew thicker. The prince's words were an attack against his sister. She would not be challenged in front of her subjects.

"The creatures of LunaSol are ours to command. They are tools to be wielded for our benefit, it would be wise to remember that."

"If our mother were here to hear you say that she would be disappointed!"

His words cut her like a knife. Everyone gasped in all. They were one in the same. Each of them wanted to have the last word. The princess was shaking with anger, that Anri had to step in and clear the room. The show was over.

"Our mother...How dare you? You weren't even raised by the woman!"

Prince Alexander was not going to entertain her nonsense. The crown was blinding her sense of reality. Her heart was cold. The prince stared at her as she paced back and forth yelling at the top of her lungs that what he said was uncalled for. In her fit of rage, she stormed up to him, but Shoxz's feathered wings separated them. She realized if she had gotten close to him that she would have slapped him. Her eyes darted to the unicorn.

"Control your beast!"

"Learn to control yourself!"

The princess walked back to her throne and held her head in her hands. Not having her family around had made her cynical. She did not know how to properly express her feelings. For years she had the love of her people, but ever since his return all anyone could talk about was him. Her fingertips began to freeze. With each breath she took the room grew colder.

Anri sensed the chaos stirring in the princess. She slammed the end of her staff into the ground and the room began to warm up.

"Now that we worked ourselves up. Can we discuss the next course of action?"

Princess Ionica looked toward her brother, "He must leave the palace at once. Before he can learn how to master nature, he must learn how to fight."

Anri stepped forward to disagree, but the princess shot her a look that caused her to step back. Alexander was confused. They had just reunited, and she wanted to send him away. Was she acting on impulse? The prince, unlike the High Magnus, had to say his piece.

"Why are you doing this?"

"What do you mean little brother?"

"Anri, has agreed to train me to fight. What about what I want?"

Princess Ionica laughed. He thought his opinion mattered in her court. She was in charge and would not allow him to forget it.

"Anri is a servant of Seraqus. She is mine to command and has an obligation to our people. We cannot deter from our duties. Your trainer will be able to focus on you rather than splitting it."

Anri's blood began to boil. She was not a slave. In all her years of servitude, she was never treated like this. She refused to cause a scene in front of the court, but she would have words with the princess later. Prince Alexander grew up as an only child and now that he was with his sister, he was ruining it. Like Anri said, their customs were a lot different than what he was used to. He insulted her in front of her guards. If it were anyone else, they would have been dealt with differently.

The prince looked over at Anri with disappointment. They stood by and watched as the princess introduced him to another Magnus, who would guide him to one of the Kings of Seraqus. She introduced her as Damitai, the White Witch. The White Witch was a beautiful creature by design. Her skin was pale white and her eyes an alluring Prussian blue. Her high trimmed brows and soft pink lips captivated the young prince. Her high cheekbones and hourglass figure made for a sight of wonder. Damitai's white flowing hair blended into her ceremonial dress. Alexander had to remove his eyes from her gaze as her beauty spellbound him.

As a White Magnus she had the ability to manipulate fire in its purest form - light. She could blind enemies, generate protective shields, illuminate her aura in dark areas, heal and enter the dreams of others. The White Witch was entrusted to bring the prince to King Silverskull Darkarrow to begin training. Hearing the surname sparked more interest.

As his inner thoughts spoke to him, he caught his sister staring at him. He had just reunited with her and now it was time for him to go. They barely had time to connect and be a family. Was his excitement to reunite with his family more than what they wanted? Did time run its course and made their love for him fade? Alexander stared into her eyes and could see her emotions. She was conflicted.

The words 'I'm sorry' escaped his lips. Princess Ionica could not hold onto her anger; she walked over to her brother and gave him a kiss on his forehead and an unbreakable hug. The hardening of his heart subsided, but once again he was being pulled away. Damitai gestured to them to hurry because it was time for them to go. She escorted the prince and his friends out of the palace, and they made their way through the courtyards and streets until they reached the docks. Samistha got their boat ready for their journey and ushered them away from the empire. She resurrected her serpent to pull the boat to shore. The White Witch descended first, followed by the prince and Nacilias. Shoxz and May followed soon after and witnessed the great glaciers that once stood as a barrier falling apart. The barrier would be gone by the next sunrise. The prince blamed himself as the flames still roared and claimed more of the fields. Princess Ionica's servants were fighting hard to subdue the flames, but it was too much for them to handle.

Damitai unrolled a map of Seraqus to explain their route. To reach Castle Silverskull, they would first need to reach Shaman Mountains. From there they would travel through the countryside, past Mt. Olympia, and the village of Yallam before reaching Forgon Forest. In the heart of the forest stood their destination. They walked through the meadow as the sun took its place high in the sky. The meadow was large in diameter. May's feet were aching. Shoxz allowed her to rest on her back as the others continued to walk through the fields. They made their way toward a small town on the outskirts of the meadow. After countless hours, Damitai was relieved to see the town of Crux. It was filled with merchants and sea traders. It was a town of money and trinkets of all sorts; relics lost to the sea. It was one of the few towns that bordered the meadow. Alexander watched in amazement as they passed the outer rim of the town. Dozens of travelers gathered to buy and sell jewels.

They traveled onward until they came to the separation of grass and bedrock. Damitai showed them that they were closing in on the mountain range. The mountains were a beautiful sight to behold. As they drew closer, they came upon the opening into the mountainside. Fang growled into the darkness.

She nodded to the prince as he took the lead. He took his amulet out, and it began to glow as they entered the darkness. May dismounted Shoxz and followed behind. Nacilias and Shoxz were worried they were going to run into a trap once they got far enough into the cave. They traveled deeper, for what seemed like hours with no end, but to their surprise there was an opening. The prince exited the cavern and found an abandoned village. Nacilias stopped Prince Alexander from moving any further. Shoxz and Nacilias could sense old magic sprinkled onto the floor around them. The name of the strange village even escaped the White Witch's memory. Fang tossed and turned in the prince's arms until he released him. He flapped his little wings, and the golden dust sprinkled on the flowers danced around them.

Nacilias sniffed the floor and shot the prince a quick glance. The magical properties were not evil. Shoxz' wings flared as the valley was overtaken by a buzzing noise. Flashes of light surrounded them in legions. The Eclipse Amulet burned the prince's palm, causing him to drop it. A blast of emerald light shot through the valley and revealed they were not alone. The valley was filled with little, flying creatures. They had pale skin and wore clothing made from flowers and leaves. Alexander was excited to see them, but the others were worried.

They had stumbled upon a village of pixies. Soldiel used to read him stories about them. They were Hyperion's failed attempt at creating humans. He made them immortal beings, and they stood a whopping twelve inches tall. Not all pixies were good; some of them were tricksters; each pixie had access to magic.

A pixie flew over to the prince, and he opened his hand, "You can see us?"

"Yes, I can!"

"Why have you entered Shaman Village? I am Holone. Who are you?"

May and Damitai could not understand them. All they could hear was buzzing sounds. They stared at the prince, puzzled that he was communicating with them. He would speak the common tongue, and the pixie would buzz back at him. He divulged their names and Holone welcomed him. She was vibrant, her most striking feature was her dress, crafted from delicate pink rose petals. Each one was perfectly shaped, overlapping gently to form a fluttering skirt. Leaves and vines were stitched together to form a top. Her hair a cascade of black waves. Her eyes are a deep emerald green, sparkling with mischief. She was excited to introduce him to their queen.

Before the prince could continue speaking with the pixie, Damitai roared out, "Pixies cannot be trusted. They betrayed us in the war and went into hiding!"

Nothing she said mattered to the prince. She was a servant of his sister. She was not trusted counsel. He looked to Nacilias and Shoxz for confirmation. Nacilias was not on board with his plan to follow her, but Shoxz was. Holone landed on the prince's shoulder, and he followed the others toward the village. May and Damitai stood by his side, as Nacilias and Shoxz scoped out the valley. Seeing the prince interact with the pixies astounded them. They knew none of the Ilihi could speak with the creatures of LunaSol. Centuries ago, the beasts of the world stopped communicating with humans. They became isolated and distrustful of them. The prince was a rarity. Walking through the streets of the village, they noticed it was once inhabited by humans. In the village square was a statue of Lord Celeio. At the foot of the statue stood a bigger pixie. Fang laid at her feet as she stroked the horns on his head.

Holone stood by her side as she introduced her, "This is Queen Asparaes, she is our mother."

Alexander bowed, "It is an honor to meet you."

Queen Asparaes bowed and kissed the prince's hand. She was two feet tall, and her clothes were elegant and made of fabrics instead of leaves. She wanted the prince to dine with her so they could speak. Contrary to the outburst about her race, she explained she worshipped Lady Eileen. When the war broke out, they were released from their prisons and sought out the queen, but she was already dead. Eris and Lord Dark Lucus sought out magical creatures to fuel Lord Nebula, so they went into hiding. She welcomed the prince to stay for as long as he could. The prince kindly declined, but Queen Asparaes insisted. There was more to her invitation than she was leading on.

"Please stay. I see you are traveling with a Magnus. She wears the symbol of the Blue Flame. Have you seen it?"

Her intrusive questioning angered the prince. He turned to the others and told them about her question. Damitai grabbed the prince by the arm as May summoned her throwing stars. Why was he so trusting of others?

Fang roared out and flared his wings, defending the Pixie Queen.

"How...how...how did you know that? Were you spying on us?" Alexander moved himself away from the White Witch and adjusted himself in front of Queen Asparaes.

"You have it all wrong."

"How do you know about the flame?" questioned the prince.

"I was there when it fell from the sky!"

Alexander stopped his line of questioning and sat back down. May and the White Witch followed his lead. They were out of their element. Not being able to have a normal conversation and listen to what the queen was saying was only making their frustration worsen. He continued to listen as she explained; the pixies, fairies, elves, and gnomes were called upon to examine the flame. Their combined magic drew out Oricale and she entrusted them with a fraction of her power. The Nine Kings feared her power falling into the wrong hands, so they hid the flame from those who would steal its power. The Nine Kings of LunaSol instructed them to build a chamber around the flame. Once the chamber was built, a fortress was erected on top of it. It became vacant after their deaths, and soon after, Princess Ionica became the new occupant. She explained that the flame visited her in her dreams. It was in danger.

Alexander looked toward May and Damitai and advised them that she had news of the traitor.

Damitai grew paranoid and could not keep herself together. She questioned the queen to the point that Alexander screamed at her. Queen Asparaes laughed at her as if she could understand what the White Witch wanted.

"Damitai...let me handle this."

The prince returned to his conversation with the queen. He knew he could trust the pixies and needed their support in the coming war. Shoxz and Nacilias were still on the fence with the horde of pixies. As a peace offering, she summoned a relic that would be of interest to him. The prince extended his hand, and the Queen of the Pixies handed him the Star of Orion; a stone fragment and a piece needed to resurrect Lord Nebula. The prince's heart sprinted as he stared at the relic. In his visions, he was already shown that one piece was placed on the gate; now he held one.

"Why would you give this to me?"

"Lord Dark Lucus and Eris are doing everything they can to track down these keys. We cannot protect it. It may be safer with you."

Fang soared toward the prince and stood on his shoulder and let his tail drag off the other. The White Witch stared at the prince with excitement. The pixies urged the prince to hide it somewhere safe. Alexander hugged the queen and promised he would.

The travelers had no time to waste and needed to find King Silverskull. They raced through the valley to another cavern that led them out of the mountains. Queen Asparaes chanted the word, '*Verschwinden*' and faded into the wind with her clan. A single breeze overtook the prince's face. He felt the staleness of emotion in the air. The world of LunaSol was falling apart. The prince mounted Shoxz and rode her through the cavern while Damitai and Nacilias followed suit. Nothing stood in their way now. The White Witch could no longer make the trip on foot and spun in a circle and chanted the word, '*Flucht*.' A radiating white light flicked around her and allowed her to fly.

She led them through the mountain and toward the bog that surrounded Mt. Olympia. It was one of the few mountains that no one dared to voyage to. The dirt around it was tainted and poisoned. Hundreds of dead trees were uprooted and sealed off the original path toward its base. Nacilias divulged that it was sealed off, but rumors claimed it was a vault of some sort. It was abandoned centuries ago, but no one has traveled to the peak to investigate. The sun was making its way west, while the prince and his friends finally passed the city of Yallam. Thousands of farmers and their cattle were tending to their crops.

As they made their way further and further away from the city, she pointed to the dense forest that stood behind the borders of Yallam. Forgon Forest was one of the oldest in LunaSol. It was the forest where the Divine Lords battled Eris and Lord Dark Lucus. Alexander stood on the hilltop, looking down at the lavish green forest.

The trees stood an amazing twenty feet tall. The roots were visible and protruded from the ground and lay on the bedrock. The prince wanted to rest for the night before heading into the forest. The sun finally made its way west toward the tip of the world, and the darkness of night began to overtake the land. Troubled in his own mind, he turned to his mother's journal.

The cache of weapons that Lady Eileen came to inspect would be transported back with her to Haven. The sky was still ablaze with the remnants of the solar flare. The angels of Heaven restricted access to Hyperion until it was over. His gaze upon his creation was blinded. Lady Udana used this opportunity to summon her High Magnus' to evaluate the queen's pregnancy. She removed her gown atop the tower and submerged herself in a pool of water. The High Magnus chanted as they circled the floating queen. The altar where the water flowed from began to discolor as the relic within it ignited.

The High Magnus' noticed the power radiating from the relic and stopped chanting. It was reacting to the baby. It called to him. Lady Udana attempted to manipulate the water, but it was not hers to control. The water would not dance at her command, not even with the spells of her servants. Nothing in the world could nullify her abilities, but this child was interfering. The baby prince used Lady Eileen's body to absorb the water. Her eyes glazed over as she collapsed onto the floor. The veins in her body pulsated as the water cycled through her, cleaning out an infection. She was poisoned.

Someone within her court knew she was pregnant and wanted the baby dead. Even in utero, the child's defenses astounded them. No Ilihi alive had such power. The thought scared him. What made him more powerful than even a Divine Lord? Without Hans to help guide him, he felt lost and isolated, but his mother's handwriting brought him comfort. He rubbed the parchment pages as he closed the journal and finally closed his eyes to sleep.

CHAPTER
14

POTULIARI

The night breeze chilled the air as Damitai walked around the campsite. She stared at the massive forest as the trees whispered in the wind. Snoring from the prince's tent caught her attention. His breathing intensified. She opened his tent, and a sleeping Fang opened his eyes and stared at her. She watched the prince sleeping. His pale skin turned bright red as the blood in his body began to simmer. The White Witch could feel his energy rising and straddled him to hold him down. Fang growled as he watched her. She placed her index fingers on the prince's forehead and entered his mind. She was standing on a platform and glimpsed the prince in front of a stone archway. She took a step forward and was surrounded by fire. She jumped through the flames and managed to pull the prince out of his dreams. The prince awoke and was puzzled to see Damitai on top of him as the others rested. Fang jumped on his face and started licking him. She picked herself up from the floor and told him to follow her.

"Damitai, what happened back there?"

The White Witch sat the prince down on a broken tree as her fear dwindled. Fang stood beside him like a guard dog, growling at her the entire time.

"You were going into shock, and your blood was boiling. Your organs would have shut down if I did not pull you out."

"Thank you for waking me up."

His calmness caused Fang to settle down and rest at his feet. The prince looked into her eyes and could see that she was holding something back. "There is something you are not telling me!"

Damitai paused before she responded.

"You were trying to astral project, and I interfered."

The prince began to tremble in confusion. His mother's journal depicted a glimpse of his power, but nothing like this. His body was working against him ever since he arrived in LunaSol, and it was driving him insane. What was he becoming? The White Witch grabbed both of his hands and tried to get him to focus. She was amazed to see such abilities manifesting within him. No one within the Royal Family could speak with animals, let alone astral project.

LunaSol was rich in its population of creatures, but the four human classes that inhabited the world: mortals, Magnus, Ilihi, and Potuliari had a hierarchy. Mortals were the lowest of humanity since they had no abilities. Magnus' were once mortal but learned how to use magic and relied on verbal spells, hand gestures, or wands. The elite and ruling class were the Ilihi; they were the personified forces of nature - earth, wind, water, fire, and lightning. Among them were rare Purity Ilihi that could manipulate light and shade, Eris being one of them. The rarest of humans, Potuliari, were special compared to the others. They were gifted with unnatural abilities at birth.

Damitai confessed rumors of Alulim living amongst them. Prince Alexander was surprised to hear she knew about them. He was tight-lipped and made sure not to spill what he knew about the Alulim. She heard rumors that they fell from the sky during a meteor shower. She thought the Potuliari may have been their offspring since they had special abilities. There were even rumors that the angels had offsprings with humans and gave birth to - *Engchlich*.

In her travels, Damitai encountered a Potuliari when she was a child living in the Realm of Dolphins, a fortress city on the Island of Nazila. As a baby, his powers were extremely dangerous. His high-pitched screams could blind and deafen anyone in a one-mile radius. The baby was killed at the direction of the queen. For a time, many countries viewed Potuliari as a threat since they had abilities that were deemed extreme. They were

146

rounded up and killed or used as weapons for the Elite. Hearing how inhumanly they were treated only upset the prince even more. He was disgusted to hear how divisive the humans were on LunaSol. He was beginning to understand why his mother feared what he would become.

It only made him more curious, and he jumped at the idea of mastering a new ability. He wanted Damitai to help him astral project. If he were able to complete it, his body would manifest in a spirit form outside of his body. The White Witch was more than happy to assist; she laid the prince down on the floor and grabbed a few branches to create a circle around him. She began to hum as she told the prince to close his eyes and focus on her voice. Her enchantments resonated through the branches and would ignite in flames once he entered the astral plane. She instructed him to focus on breathing and imagine himself standing up and exiting his body. She stood over his body as it began to convulse. She extended his arms towards the branches and watched as the energy left his body and ignited the branches around him. The flames turned from red to white and petrified Damitai. She waited to see if his astral form would appear, but it did not. Franticly touching his face, she noticed he no longer had a pulse. His body was an empty vessel.

Filled with greed, she used this opportunity to try and steal the Star of Orion. She searched his pockets for it, but the prince did not have it. Fang opened his mouth, and a thin cloud of smoke erupted. He was taunting her. The white flames subsided and caused her to panic. She had to find his soul before everyone woke up. She traveled the dream world, but every turn ended in failure.

Alexander opened his eyes, and his worry began to subside. He was sitting on the ground, the moon still overhead. Damitai and Forgon Forest were nowhere in sight. His newfound ability had betrayed him, and it landed him in the body of another. Breasts hung beneath his chin, and his body was covered in a black tunic and red skintight pants. Through the woman's eyes, he saw a phoenix pendant hanging around her neck. Her feet became visible as she ran through the sand dunes and came across a small pond and splashed her face. She extended her arms towards a stack of broken branches on the ground, and they floated into her hands. Her breath kindled the branches with flames to give her warmth. With ease, he tapped into her memories. First her name, Lady Phoebe Nightfeather, the same surname as his brother King Habagin.

Her past came into focus as he concentrated on her. He observed a basket floating in a lake. The cries of a child echoed into the neighboring town, and a single boat came to rescue it. When she was removed from the basket, her powers ripped through the lake and created a whirlpool. The couple that found her took her in. She was unaware of her powers, until one day, while she was playing with a group of children, they began to make fun of her. Her anger was unleashed, and she blasted them away with just a thought. The children ran screaming for help as the poor girl cried. Lady Phoebe was kept in the house after that. She started coming into even more power, as she grew older. Her abilities consisted of fire manipulation, flight, telekinesis, telepathy, and generating force fields. Her thoughts went still and for a second. A whisper called to the prince. A small flicker of fire burned in the depths of her mind. Calm and relaxing.

His connection was broken, and he was once again peering through her eyes. Lady Phoebe ran for cover and extinguished the fire. Her feet pushed through the sandy floor and made her way up a hill of dunes. As she reached the top, she gazed over a sleeping city. Her attention was pulled as a huge blast sent her rolling down the sand; she was able to catch her footing and ran as fast as she could. Servants of Lord Marlusha followed her into the city. She ran into an abandoned house, seeking shelter. Lord Marlusha's servants filled the square in search of her. Lady Phoebe made her way up a flight of stairs to the second floor. She peered out of an opening in the boards that shielded the window. The creatures smelled the floor to track her. Her mind caught the whispers of another in the room.

"The rumors are true then. You have returned to Gazi!!"

Lady Phoebe jumped back as she turned to see a man standing in the shadows. "Show yourself!!" She twirled her hand and fire manifested. He walked forward and revealed himself to her. "Oh my god, can it be...John Vader, it has been ages since we last saw one another."

The man she recognized kept half of his face hidden behind a golden mask. His eyes were bright red, an unnatural color for a human. His hair was pitch black and cut right above his shoulders. It was hidden beneath the hood he was wearing. The prince turned his eyes to his chest-plate, which was gold and black. There was no sigil, only runes. The runes were not Angelic or Elven. Beneath his armor, he wore a black shirt and black pants that were tucked into his boots. He walked over to Lady Phoebe and gave her a slight kiss on the cheek.

148

"It is so good to see you. I have news from Martilo; Lord Marlusha is hunting Potuliari. If the prince does not come to our aid, only you can stand a chance against him. We must move quickly."

"The prince was last seen headed to the Empire of Seraqus. I must get to him, but first, how are we going to get out of this mess?"

"We still have some fight in us!"

Lady Phoebe's memories of John flowed into his mind. His childhood was clouded in mystery like Lady Phoebe. A family that lived in Magma City took him and his brother in. They fled to Sharaa to escape from Lord Marlusha. Their parents were killed, and John and his brother separated and went into hiding. John was first able to create fire in his hands and then in his eyes. The day came when Lord Marlusha's troops attacked Gazi once more and sought to kill him. He was attacked, and his body was consumed by the very sunlight. His body was set ablaze and consumed the flesh of anyone standing close enough to him. Those that sought to kill him did not understand the full extent of his powers. The prince was shaken out of her memory.

Lady Phoebe and John saw an opportunity when their enemies were not looking. He jumped through the boarded window, and Lady Phoebe followed. There was nowhere to run. They were surrounded and outnumbered. The creatures wasted no time and attacked. Lady Phoebe created an energy field to guard them against attacks. She could not concentrate fully on the battle; she sensed her mind was fractured. With each attempt, the force field would fade.

More and more enemies appeared as the others fell. John was limited; the sun was not overhead to assist him. Lady Phoebe's force field finally gave out, and Lord Marlusha's servants were able to grab John. They gagged his mouth and tied him in chains that suppressed his abilities. They came for her next, but she immobilized them with a telepathic shockwave. Lady Phoebe tried hard to refocus her mind but could not do so. As she gained focus, she saw a face. She forced the image outside of her body and stood face-to-face with the prince.

"WHO ARE YOU? HOW DID YOU GET INSIDE MY MIND?"

The prince tried to explain that he was trying to astral project and somehow ended up within her mind. He apologized for the disruption he was causing her. Lady Phoebe examined the prince and noticed the amulet around his neck. No words could express her excitement to finally see the child everyone was talking about. She could not hold her enemies back much longer. Materializing the prince in his astral form and keeping her enemies stunned was too much for her mind. Lady Phoebe gestured for the prince to step aside. She sat on the floor and meditated. He watched as flames overtook her aura and caused a massive backlash. The flames reseeded back to her aura and intensified. She finally had control of her powers once again.

The creatures were unfrozen and began to lead their charge against her. She breathed in, and with a wave of her left hand she sent them crashing into a nearby building. She waved her right hand toward John and freed him from those that bound him. Lady Phoebe placed her hands together and kept them at a distance from her chest. She channeled all her energy into her core. Her aura burned brighter, and her eyes burned a fiery red. Flares sparked from her eyes as her body lit up in flames. Her hair floated in the air as she moved forward toward the creatures.

As she walked toward them, the floor began to crack. Her psychic energy was so strong it radiated from her aura. Reality warped around her. She roared out, and then "BOOM," a huge shock wave of fire and telekinetic energy rippled through their bodies. Lady Phoebe's flame was unlike any other fire. Her fire cut through the very fabric of reality and caused the atoms within all matter to rumble and implode on itself. Their bodies exploded, and the fire consumed their very molecules. John was able to absorb the backlash of her energy as fuel. He blasted the creatures around him with heat energy and caused them to turn to ash. Lady Phoebe's mind was on a rampage; the prince's astral form intensified her abilities. She vowed to find him before releasing him from her body.

Damitai noticed the white flames appear once again and then subsided as the prince's eyes shot open. His heart was racing, and his head was on fire, but he was amazed he returned in one piece. Witnessing the power of Lady Phoebe only made the prince want to continue and learn more. He was not done yet; he wanted to try again and get back to her. He had so many questions. Damitai was astounded at the news that he was not only able to astral project, but to invade the body of another. An ability Lord Nebula would surely enjoy. She would not dare try the ritual again since it did work as intended. The prince only wanted her to stand by his side as he tried to do it on his own. She finally agreed.

He laid his head back down and stared at the full moon overhead. He once again closed his eyes and faded into darkness. His thoughts were clear, and his objective appeared in sight. His astral form took life once more, but not as he intended. Jagged rocks surrounded him, and his body appeared to levitate over a small body of water within a marble shrine. The prince's feet gently touched the water as he walked over it and stepped onto the stairs of the shrine. He was stopped by a scream coming from behind him.

"INTRUDER. STOP! HOW DID YOU GET IN HERE?"

Alexander turned to notice that the person was speaking to him. This time he was not gazing through the eyes of another but rather standing there. He looked down into the reflection of the water and saw his body glistening blue. He gave the man a puzzled look and replied. "I am Prince Alexander. What is this place?"

The man did not know what to do. He had the astral form of a boy standing in front of him, claiming to be the child prince. Alexander studied his clothing. He wore clothing like those in Seraqus. His blue boots and vest bore the Star of the Oricale. His vest was kept open, but the midsection was tied with a golden cloth. The top of his boots was covered in fur, and he had gloves to match. He gripped his sword and shield, as he drew closer to the prince. Alexander noticed the shield had Oricale runes. When the man got closer, he saw the amulet around his neck and breathed a sigh of relief.

"I am so sorry. My name is Piers; I am the High Magnus of the Shrine of Visions. You are beneath the Palace of Otrant. Why have you come here?"

It was like destiny was tugging at him – another name from his mother's journals. In his mind, Piers would lead him to this Otrant person, so he decided he could be trusted with the truth.

"I astral projected into the mind of Lady Phoebe Nightfeather, and I was trying to go back to make sure she was safe."

"Safe?"

"Lord Marlusha is hunting Potuliari."

The words caused great concern to fester. Piers gestured for the prince to stand aside and follow him as he walked toward a massive set of stairs that stood in between the cracks of what appeared to be a mountain. He guided the prince up the stairs and into a huge meeting hall. Dozens of cloaked figures walked through the corridors as they entered and exited.

Piers escorted him into a corridor of massive height with stained glass ceilings. At the end of the corridor stood a golden gate that was engraved with Oricale runes.

Piers opened the door, and within the room stood five marble thrones, and four of them were occupied. Alexander recognized one of the women in the room; she appeared in his visions. Her features were very foreign to him. They were unlike the others. She was darker in complexion and spoke in a different tongue. The prince admired the elegant being. An aura of radiance flowed over her as she rose and called for Piers to take a seat on his throne.

Piers left the prince's side and did as instructed. The room was cylindrical in nature. The floors were formed from mosaic tiles. There were five windows positioned at a great distance from each throne. The windows were stained glass with images of angels, but only four of them were narrow. The main window and the biggest in the room depicted three angels surrounding a huge stone ball. He noticed the Corinthian-style columns that held the ceiling in place. The exotic woman that the prince was transfixed on waved her hand, and the ground beneath his feet rumbled, and a throne was created from the tiles.

The air was thick with the tension of first meetings. Piers was the first to break the air, "Great Council of Otrant, I have brought Prince Alexander forth. I found his astral form floating around the shrine. He comes with a warning. The Potuliari are being hunted."

The council whispered to one another.

"My dear child, who is hunting Potuliari?"

Prince Alexnader stared into the eyes of the most majestic woman he has seen. Her skin, a deep and rich hue, carrying the warmth of the sun. Her high cheekbones and full lips added to her commanding presence and natural allure. Her eyes, golden and expressive; reflecting her spirited nature. Her hair, a crown of tight lush curls, cascading down her shoulders. Adorning her smooth skin was a golden dress, draped elegantly over her curved form. The fabric was decorated with beads, adding texture and depth.

"Lord Marlusha. I was in the mind of Lady Phoebe Nightfeather and witnessed the attack."

"Did she escape?" questioned the woman.

"I believe so. I tried to get back to her, but I ended up here."

"It is great that you have arrived. I am Amaris, Head Guardian of the Palace of Otrant."

Amaris was perfection. Prince Alexander could see the color of her aura. He was brought here because of her. She stood before the prince and revealed her abilities. Her veins sparkled and from her fingertips electricity flowed. With a single wave of her hand, a gust of wind ravaged the room. She could also fly and manipulate the weather. She was called a 'Weather Witch.'

The hooded figure that sat to the right of her rose and lowered his hood. His skin was darker in tone than Amaris. He was bald and wore kohl on the inner eyelid and lash line. He had a gold marking that covered his left eye. His robes resembled those worn by the Magnus' that attacked the prince in the Shrine of Glory. "I am Odin."

As Odin took his seat, another figure rose. She removed her hood, and her pale white skin and white hair stood out from the others. The prince noticed blue scars on the right side of her face. She was the only one in her circle that did not have almond skin. His unweaving eyes made her uncomfortable. She extended her arm forward and waved it to the side as she bowed to the prince.

"Child, I am a foreigner in these lands, just like you are. I am Kera."

Prince Alexander smiled as she took her seat. He then turned his attention to the woman who sat to the left of Amaris. She was the one he was fascinated with. She wore a very low collared white silk dress. The trimmings were gold, and a gold rope was wrapped around her waist. His eyes shifted up to her eyes, and he noticed they were sea foam. Her hair was covered in a tightly woven scarf. What stood out the most was her golden tiara. At the center of the tiara was the Gaeatonic Eye.

The woman rose and slightly tilted her head. "Prince Alexander, I have anticipated this day for centuries. I am Cleopatra."

"You are one of the Gaeatonic Guardians!"

Cleopatra gasped. The Gaeatonic Guardians were kept secret for centuries. The title confused everyone in the room. She questioned the prince as to how he came across this information, but he would not answer. He allowed his tongue to get in front of his mind. The prince was aware of her secret and refused to explain anything to her. He swore to keep the visions to himself, but he was not very good at secrets. Piers and Amaris

153

stared at Cleopatra then turned their gaze to the prince awaiting his response. He would not speak.

Amaris returned to the conversation of the Potuliari being hunted. She reassured the prince her lands were protected by an enchanted barrier and vast deserts. No one was coming for her, or so she thought.

Odin's eyes widened, as screams echoed in the outside halls. His words held true. They were coming for her. Amaris was no longer safe within their walls. Alexander rose to his feet as he saw the morning sun glistening through the stained-glass windows. The sun rose with the grace of a thousand gods, and he could feel his astral form being pulled back to his earthly body. His spiritual connection to them was fading rapidly.

"They are here. Go to my sister's palace! I will meet you there."

Amaris and the others prepared for an onslaught. The council watched the gates that stood closed behind the prince rumble, and in seconds they were destroyed. His astral body could no longer maintain its form. He could hear his name being called, and his astral body was pulled back to its host.

CHAPTER

15

CASTLE SILVERSKULL

The sun was blazing overhead as the prince franticly jumped out of his sleep. Damitai was holding him down as May and the others rushed from their tents as they heard the screams. The prince was drenched in sweat. The cool morning breeze grazed against his face, giving him some comfort. Damitai allowed May to pick him up from the floor and studied his eyes; they were bloodshot. He chose to omit her involvement in the events that unfolded during the night. The prince's abilities didn't line up with any of the LunaSolarian races. Only the Elder Races, such as elves, gnomes, and fairies, shared a fraction of the prince's ability.

May cautioned the prince, "Using your abilities like you did last night, was unwise."

Her words did not faze him. He was focused on returning to his sister and hoping that Lady Phoebe and Amaris would find their way to him. Damitai stared at the richly populated forest in displeasure. A deep seeded hatred was imprinted on her face. The prince grabbed his bag, which he hid during the night. Fang stood by his side, growling at the spellcaster. She led them down the hill toward the dense forest. Thousands of overgrown trees lined their view. It was filled with the beautiful songs of the birds. The dancing winds blew through the treetops, giving life to the trees and allowing them to dance in the sun's presence. The majestic and impenetrable forest took on a life of its own as they made their way deeper. The massive trees prevented the sunlight from penetrating the further reaches of the forest. The prince's eyes were drawn to the exquisite plant life. The enchanting pink color of the Aechmea distichantha made the forest greenery pop. Nacilias inhaled the aroma of the magic dogwoods as Shoxz pushed past hundreds of Winged-Stem Passion Flowers.

Dozens of uprooted trees cascaded down the steep hill. Alexander tried to help May descend the entangled roots, but her foot was met with resistance from the Bleeding Hearts at the bottom of the landing. Nacilias bit away at them. Damitai had created a great distance between them. She did not even bother to look back and make sure the others were okay. The others continued to trail her, while the prince was fixated on something else. With each step he took, the wind whispered to him. They twirled around the leaves, creating faint voices. He stared at them for a few seconds to see if he could hear them again, but nothing. Fang's scales lit up as the wind breezed past him. He felt like they were being watched. He followed behind May and Nacilias. His paranoia got the best of him, and he kept a keen eye on his surroundings. The forest was a gigantic maze with no end in sight. Their destination seemed further and further away.

The tree roots shook as the winds zoomed through them. Once again, the prince heard the trees whispering. The words, 'BETRAYAL' and 'MAGNUS' echoed in his ears. Overcome with fear, he ran to catch up with May, thinking she was playing a trick on him, but she was just as surprised. He thought he was hallucinating. Nacilias asked the prince what the trees were saying. The fox's eyes dilated as the prince confessed. An unspoken secret remained between them. The fox warned the prince to silence the voices; otherwise, they would drive him mad. He knew what they were - *Dryads*. With every fiber of his being, the prince tried to silence the noise, but in the distant corner of his eye something caught his attention.

Women in white-laced tunics ran through the trees as the wind echoed around them. Their faces shimmered in the small fragments of sunlight. Alexander turned his head quickly, but in that split second the women were gone. The nervous prince nearly trampled Nacilias to tell him what he saw. The fox could no longer hide his fear; they were being hunted. The prince roared out to May and Damitai to stop and brief them.

"The dryads will not attack us here. They are waiting. Let's keep moving! Do not let them enchant you in their spell. These creatures were cursed to live within the very forest they protect. They are venomous and lead travelers to their doom." Damitai seemed reluctant to investigate it further.

Nacilias howled to the forest as a plea. Unbeknownst to him, the forest deemed him worthy and whispered back to him, 'TRAITOR' and 'TRAP.' Their warning was real. Alexander turned to him and realized they heard the same thing. The trees warned them that Damitai was the traitor.

They were so caught up in the whispers that they did not realize they had arrived at Castle Silverskull. Not much of a castle by appearance, but the remains of a destroyed volcano. The structure was over seventy feet tall. There was a moat around it filled with lava. The entire area was treeless except for the two green Ash trees that stood near the hickory drawbridge leading into the castle. Damitai approached the bridge, but her advances were short lived. One of the tree branches came out of nowhere and tossed her backwards. The trees began to sway and change in appearance. Pieces of bark fell off, revealing eyes and a mouth. The roots bound together creating, legs for them to walk.

They were in big trouble. Aiars were formidable adversaries. They were unpredictable and easily angered. They could easily crush a lion under its foot. They were shepherds of the forest and protected the trees from those who sought to tear them down. The ancient race towered over the prince. One of the trees had two branches downward on what appeared to be its hips.

The prince quivered as the annoyed tree spoke out. "WHAT BUSSINESS DO YOU HAVE HERE?"

Damitai picked herself up from the floor and charged energy into her hands. Alexander intervened before she could attack them.

"Great tree...we mean you no harm. I am Prince Alexander. I have come to train with King Silverskull."

The trees backed away from the prince and howled at each other. Damitai and the others were baffled that the prince understood them. Whistles, growls, flicks of the tongue, and banging sounds were all they heard. The trees were known as Iuvart and Aragiel. They would not allow traitors into the castle. The prince pleaded for answers to find out who the traitor amongst them was. Confessing the whispers from the dryads.

Turning to the others, the prince spoke, "A traitor walks amongst us, and they will not allow us access until they are revealed."

Words could not express the look on Damitai's face. She could not allow them to reveal her secret. If she did not act now, her cover would be blown. Her fingertips were enveloped with energy as she launched an attack on the prince. Fang wrestled out of his arms taking the full force of the blast. The baby dragon dropped to the floor in pain. Prince Alexander's face turned pale. Shallow breaths became fainter and fainter until none were left. Fang laid motionless on the floor. Tears poured from the prince's eyes as he released a hollow scream.

May pinned her to a tree with her flying darts. Damitai tried to escape, but the prince's rage manifested once more. She was unable to dematerialize. The ground around them trembled with fury. The Aiars retreated as his power intensified. He had no control over it. His emotions were in control. His eyes once again were clouded over and soulless. His energy erupted like a force of nature and decimated the ground around him. Shards of rocks levitated, and with a wave of his hand, he launched them at Damitai. Blood poured from her wounds. Uttering the words, '*Pretvoriti u prah*,' she burned the shards away and cauterized the wound. She flung her hair back and smiled at the prince. There was no remorse in her eyes, only anger.

"Why would you turn on us?" questioned May.

"Lord Nebula has given me a glimpse of his power, and it feels incredible. The Empire of Seraqus will fall, and so will the Great Flame."

Damitai's words only enthralled the prince in his rage. A gust of wind surrounded him, and the floor cracked even more. With a wave of his hand, he began to drain the traitor of oxygen. She clawed at her neck as she tried to breathe. May stood by and watched in terror. The prince was an abnormality; not only did he possess unusual abilities, but he could also manipulate multiple elements. Damitai's eyes began to bulge, but she managed to utter the word, '*Zasita*,' and created a protective light barrier around her. She collapsed to the floor as she tried to regain enough breath to speak. May tried to intervene, but the Aiars stopped her. If she interfered, the prince could kill her in his possessed state. The trees tossed and turned in the ground as the wind around him intensified. The White Magnus embraced the Nebula and drew on its dark energy; her fingertips became putrid, her veins blackened and the soil around her darkened. Damitai tapped into dark magic. She launched spears of purple energy at the prince. He split them with his hand and redirected them to her.

May intervened, causing the Aiars to step in. Her feet were entangled by roots. They dragged her back to the foot of the drawbridge. Iuvart dug his foot into the ground, and hundreds of roots sprung up in front of them, creating a wall between them and the fighting. May cut at the roots imprisoning her and tried to break through the wall, but with each hole she made, another root covered it up.

"We cannot stand by and let the prince fight her alone." May roared at them as if they understood.

The Aiars, once again, whistled, growled, and banged on their barks, this time calling to the spirits of the forest. The wind ripped the leaves from the trees, causing them to dance around the prince and take shape, revealing nearly a dozen dryads and nymphs.

Nymphs were very pale-skinned creatures with long golden curls. A crown of turquoise puya plants sat atop their heads. Blue flowing dresses with a golden rope around their waist sparkled as they danced, their beauty enslaving. The dryads were different, on the other hand. Their skin ranged in color, and they wore white dresses. Vines grew from their dresses as the wind pressed against their bodies. Working together, they used the tree roots to bind the traitor. With Damitai subdued for the moment, they circled the prince and teased him with their beauty. The prince was unaffected by the creatures. They bathed in the fragments of sunlight they were denied for centuries.

The graceful women surrounded the prince from behind as he walked toward the traitor. The opening in the trees revealed that the sky above Forgon Forest darkened. The wind accelerated, and the Aiars had to hold everyone down with their roots. The nymphs and the dryads held onto one another as the prince's rage upset the balance of nature. He stood over her body and placed his right hand on her head.

"You have tainted this world. Never again shall you use magic for evil."

Damitai screamed out in agonizing pain as the prince's hand was encased in an emerald glow. Her skin began to turn gray as her soul was slowly eradicated. Even facing death, she laughed at the prince.

"You have no idea what is coming."

Those were the last words she would ever say. Her eyes turned black, and her body collapsed to the side as the tree roots released her. In the distance, Amira watched them, studying him. She would not dare attack in his current state. She was patient. Before she could turn to leave, she was knocked out cold and dragged away. The prince swayed, and May ran to aid him before he hit the ground. The dryads and the nymphs tended to the corpse as the prince stumbled to get up. May and Nacilias worried about him. In this altered state, he could not remember his actions. He feared he was losing himself to the amulet and its power. It was corrupting his mind. The prince pleaded with Nacilias to help him understand what was going on, but the fox was just as confused. He promised they would get to the bottom of it.

In his weakened state, the prince turned his frustration onto the Aiars. "You knew she was a traitor and did nothing. You could have warned King Silverskull."

The Aiars were not sworn to the king. Since the Holy War, they were forbidden from communicating with humans. They allowed her to travel through their forest to Martilo without provocation. This only angered the prince more.

"How did she get into Martilo, it's supposed to be closed off?" questioned the prince.

"They have help. Angelic help."

Their words stunned the prince. The Black Gates of Martilo were raised by the angels to keep the armies of darkness behind its wall, but many of their troops had slipped out. Now, they knew the truth. An angel was helping them lower the wards and slowly releasing his armies upon the world.

As Elder Beings they could sense its power. For too long they were used as pawns by the Ilihi to gain power and influence, ultimately betraying them and stripping them of their statuses. The royals could not be trusted. The only reason they revealed the truth was because of the prince. Seeing the amulet ignited faith in them again. Divisiveness would plunge the world into chaos. Unity was their strongest weapon facing the enemy. Prince Alexander asked them to join in the coming war. Without hesitation, the call was answered. They would come when summoned.

Lost in conversation, the prince realized Fang was not clinging to him. He turned to May and the others, searching for his companion. He

160

trembled as he stared at the dragon on the floor. Rushing to his side, he held onto him, crying. There was no pulse. The dryads could feel his pain manifesting again, but this time controlled. With each breath, electricity sparked in his palms. He let out a gut-wrenching cry and electrified the dragon's body. His scales illuminated, and Fang blew fire as he tussled to get off his back. Leaping onto the prince, the dragon licked his face.

Fang was no ordinary creature. Nacilias thought it odd. The spirits of all living beings, when they die on LunaSol, travel to Goul for reaping. Immortal beings returned to the dirt when killed, but Fang's soul clung to his body. Prince Alexander was happy to have his friend back. Bound by their promise, the Aiars and the forest spirits returned to the trees until the coming war. May held the prince by his waist as they crossed the bridge into the castle. Its halls were illuminated with vast torches. Its walls etched with depictions of the Holy War. His eyes were fixated on an image that was embedded in his mind: three angels circling a sphere. First, it was at the Palace of Otrant and now here. What relevance did the image have? He studied it, but his attention was called elsewhere as the others continued deeper. The floors were designed with perfectly cut cobblestones and dusted in gold.

Carved from the remains of a volcano, the fortress was circular and wide. The corridor led them to a staircase that descended deeper into the heart of the volcano. Overhead, rivers of lava flowed down and eradicated portions of the steps. Trying to avoid the lava, they proceeded with caution and found themselves in a massive underground cavern, shrouded in darkness. Without torches to guide them, they proceeded into the unknown. Further down was a shrine formed from the bodies of three dragon statues. In the center of it stood an angelic warrior piercing its sword through a stone sphere. The four torches that lit the shrine exploded in a fiery rage and spiraled out of control. The fire darted around the stone sculpture of the angel. The statue was enchanted to guide them the rest of the way. It pointed toward the dark void behind itself and re-lit hundreds of torches that continued down another staircase toward the bottom of the volcano.

The statue seemed to smirk as the prince passed it and made his way around it and down the stairs. The hardened magma stones were perfectly aligned. They traveled for miles down the staircase with no end. A rumbling noise overtook the cavern. The staircase was collapsing. They all

161

fell into the shadowy abyss below. Before their bodies slammed into the floor, chanting on the cavern floor saved them. Their faces were inches from the ground.

The smell of burning rock filled their lungs. A dark and ominous feeling sent a chill up the prince's spine. The bottom of the cavern was well lit with huge stone sentinels holding massive torches. A nicely carved archway stood before the travelers. The prince and Nacilias noticed the sentinels were riddled with carvings. These massive golden polished sentinels appeared human in nature, but each looked different from the other.

Nacilias pulled at the prince's pant leg to grab his attention. Two elves were approaching. The elves had starlike eyes; their faces were brighter than the sun and their hair shimmed a radiant gold. They were tall, slim, and regal in frame. They had very pale skin with pointed ears. May's eyes were drawn to their tunics. Compared to the clothes worn in Seraqus, Elven clothing was phenomenal. Their tunics were embroidered with Elven runes for protection. Golden gauntlets protected their arms. Atop their heads were a metallic tiara that extended down the sides of their face and could turn into a helmet in battle. Skin as pale as milk, flawless and ageless. Each of the female elves had their hair pulled back into a high ponytail. Nothing surprised the prince more than their armored plated sandals. They were forged from blue steel and wrapped around their ankles up until their knees.

The two elves bowed and kissed the prince's hands. "We have waited so long for you. I am Thalanidl and this is Ulelessa. Follow us."

From their outfits, Nacilias deduced they were High Elves, an elite branch of elves. The elven clans were broken down into factions; M'var, N'dora, Il'vi, Pandemonium, Dark, High, and Elves of the Twilight. The M'var honored the moon. N'dora honored the sun. Il'vi were forest dwellers and protected the creatures of the natural world. Pandemonium Elves were female elves tainted by dark magic. Dark Elves were male elves tainted by dark magic. High Elves practiced light magic while Elves of the Twilight could practice both dark and light magic.

Upon entering the throne room there were vast natrolite crystals. As the prince passed them, they lit up vigorously. They lined the staircase to the king's throne. He sat there petting an enormous griffin. Once their eyes met, the king rose from his throne causing the griffin to flare its wings and screech. King Silverskull was an enormous man; a towering seven feet tall with broad shoulders and a body craved from marble. His hair, golden blond, draped down his back. His beard was overgrown and tied into three braids. His chest was oily and made the prince feel uncomfortable as his muscles flexed. Around his waist, an armored kilt held together by a silver belt. On the center of the belt was the sigil of Princess Ionica - a crescent moon. Hanging from his belt like jewels were ten tiny silver skulls. The prince's mind marveled over the gorgeous man and all his glory, while feeling insecure over his tiny body.

How could a man this huge be responsible for his training the prince thought. He would crush him. Formalities had to wait. Prince Alexander informed King Silverskull of Damitai's betrayal and urged him to send word to Princess Ionica. The news startled him, she managed to bypass all the Elven charms placed over the forest with ease right under his nose. He only wanted the prince; he instructed the elves to escort the others out of the room.

The prince's attention was drawn to the spectacular creature that King Silverskull called his guardian. He kissed the griffin on the head and introduced him as Rocc. Unlike his sister, it appeared King Silverskull appreciated the creatures of LunaSol. He grabbed a quill and ink and a piece of parchment paper. The events that unfolded outside of his castle were documented. Rocc was sent to deliver it to the Princess. At the back of the room were golden doors that led to the king's training room.

King Silverskull explained that each country had a fighting style; Seraqus was known for - Capoy. It was influenced by aerial-acrobatic martial arts. Having exerted himself, the prince was not up for training. The elves returned and escorted him to his room. It was comprised of bronze and volcanic rock. He washed up in a hot spring. He took this time to learn more about his birth. Aside from his other abilities, now he could take souls. He opened his bag and grabbed his mother's journal again. He turned to the page where he left off.

His mother finally regained her strength to travel. Knowing that she was poisoned gave her the unforeseen advantage. She would not return to court until all the Elemental Towers were weaponized. She sent word to Lord Celeio to meet her at Venus Tower, but upon her arrival she was alone. The enchantments placed on the facility would not allow her entry. She found it rather peculiar and demanded an audience with the Divine

Lord. Her visit was met with resistance. The Lord of Terra Firma was not hospitable. She was forced to leave without explanation. Lady Udana was dealing with her own situation and summoned her to Adva. A meteorite had fallen from the sky. Within it were beings that predated their existence. The Elders, as they were known, were servants of the First Ones. They remained hidden in a crack within space. Their objective was to collect the fallen Alulim that came during another meteor shower.

Lady Eileen promised to protect them. They noticed she was pregnant. Using their ship, they dug into the ground until they reached a hidden spring. With their advanced technology and science, they infused the water with healing properties. Test after test were ran. They were astounded to learn that the fetus was siphoning her life force to survive. The fetus could potentially possess more power than the Alulims they sought out.

Prince Alexander was neither. An abnormality. Any source of energy he was exposed to could be used to fuel his abilities. Untrained, he could become a destructive force of nature. With their help after the baby was born, they could study his abilities and train him to fight against Hyperion. Lady Eileen refused to use her children in battle.

The words on the page began to blur in his eyes. It was a long and emotional day for him. In the morning, he would begin his training with King Silverskull. He closed the book and placed it nearby to avoid getting it wet. The hot spring relaxed his body as he soaked in it. After a relaxing bath, it was finally time for bed. He was expecting to sleep on a hard-stone bed, but instead he was amazed with the silk sheets and a goose feather bed. It was like floating on air. Nacilias slept by his side as Shoxz slept at the foot of the bed.

CHAPTER
16

LOCKED AWAY

The obnoxious snoring from the prince's chambers was a sign he finally got a good night's rest. Slumber was not an expense he could relish in. As the day began, the elves knocked on the chamber doors. They brought clothing for the prince and left to tend to the king. Nacilias and Shoxz tugged on the prince to wake up since his training with the king was limited. The tired prince recounted the journal entry of his mother and rushed to grab the book to show the others. He read the entry as he placed a brown sleeveless vest and brown baggy pants on. He needed to read more about his mother's encounter.

The Elders had a hard time convincing Lady Eileen to allow them to train the child. She was too weak to argue her point. Lady Udana could feel her heart rate spiking. One of the Elders placed her on the floor and reached into its body and withdrew a sphere. The sphere was placed on her stomach and drew energy from the fetus. The Elder analyzed the sphere, and it contained remnants of earth, water, shade, light, wind, fire, thunder, and spiritual properties. For Lady Eileen to be saved, the prince's power would need to be anchored. He would continue to syphon from her until he killed her. To Lady Udana's surprise, the meteorite they arrived on was a cosmic craft. Among many of the items on the ship, there were eight incubation tubes. They were guarding the next generation of gods to challenge Lord Nebula.

The Elders changed their plans and offered to use the children as anchors for the prince. It was decided that a fraction of his soul would be given to each fetus; they would be separated and given to families who could not conceive children. They would be raised as Ilihi, and when the time came, they would be reunited with the prince to overthrow the enemy. Removing a fraction of the prince's soul would keep him from becoming unstable and destructive. The prince abruptly closed the journal in resentment. How could his mother do this to him? Soldiel was no longer to blame for the damage to his soul. His soul was fractured long before he entered the world. He could not believe what he was reading. There were eight kids out there, doomed because of him. What was she thinking? If left intact, he would have killed her. Nacilias and Shoxz were scared to see what the rest of her writings contained. As her familiar, not even Nacilias knew about the Elders. He felt betrayed and hurt.

Alexander pulled his head up from staring at the cover of the journal and walked over to the hot spring and washed his face. With a sigh, he composed himself and opened the door leading into the caverns of the volcano. Thalanidl stood at the end of the hall. She led them to the dining hall. In the center of the room was a twelve-seat table filled with breads, apples, grapes, and roasted potatoes. After their fest was over, King Silverskull escorted the prince back to the Room of Enlightenment. While the prince trained, May was granted lessons with the High Elves.

King Silverskull began with kicking techniques, *Gin*, a circular leap followed by an arcing movement. Next, was *Balan*. A high jump followed by a series of turns and then spins up in the air. *Nyawo* came after, a high-flying strike from the air, which twists the body into a complete circle. After numerous falls, the prince enjoyed himself as he began to get the hang of it. Now, it was time to introduce takedown movements. *Esqui de Bai*, required a scissoring motion of the legs to put the opponent off-balance, forcing them to topple backwards. *Arma co Marte*, was a simple shoulder throw. Evasive techniques followed. *Duvi*, a one-handed cartwheel into a dive roll. *Igni*, required a low dodge, by placing a hand on the ground and scooting away, then converting into a one-handed cartwheel.

Even with a demonstration, the prince could not grasp the concept. Gazing at the king, he tried his hardest to accomplish the moves, but his body was not allowing him to. His energy was depleted, and he needed rest. The day was almost dark, and the prince could not take any more of the intense training. The first part was finally over. With enough rest, he would be ready to pick up again in the morning. He declined to have dinner with the group and returned to his room. His body ached from the physical torture he was exerting. He rested in the hot spring. Fang skipped toward him and jumped into the water beside him. In his tired state, he closed his eyes, and the warmth of the water relaxed him. Peace and relaxation were short-lived as a knock on the door stirred him back to reality. Nacilias entered and noticed the prince was zoning out. He lay as close to the edge as he could without getting wet. The prince rubbed the fox's forehead.

"Nacilias, can these people be trusted?"

The prince's words caught him off guard. "My prince... what do you mean?"

"My sister, King Silverskull, Anri. How do we know they can truly be trusted?"

The worry in his voice concerned the fox. What if he was right? What if no one could be trusted? The journals clouded his mind. Nacilias had faith, "Put your trust in King Silverskull. He has always been a man of honor."

His words alleviated the prince's anxiety. Without Soldiel and Hans guiding him, he was putting his fate in the hands of strangers. No matter who they say they pledged their loyalty to, there was still the thought in the back of his mind.

"Tell me about King Silverskull."

Soldiel's stories were limited with information. Nacilias had to fill in the blanks. Their host was the great grandson of King Habagin, the oldest brother to the prince. After the formation of Seraqus, nine of King Habagin's grandchildren came together to rule. The Empire of Seraqus became their seat of power. King Galatic Darkarrow and his kin went missing after a battle with Eris. After his disappearance, his title was passed on to his son. King Galatic was one of the Mystic Otrant's four children. They were not raised by her, as she left them as infants. Many of her children lived with King Habagin until he was murdered by Eris and Lord Dark Lucus during the Holy War.

They took over his palace and converted it into their base of operations. Tartarus was a marvelous mountain fortress surrounded by

Nightfeather Forest. Before its corruption, it was a gateway to eternal rest in the heavens. It was the one spot on LunaSol where the spiritual energy of the dead resided. Eris poisoned the forest, turning it into a swamp, while Lord Dark Lucus collapsed the mountain, creating a lake of acid. The entrance to Tartarus was submerged, and only a few were given authority to enter. Intruders would dissolve upon contact with the lake. Eris tortured King Habagin until death became a mercy for him. The Wardens of the Dead were no more, and the souls remained trapped on LunaSol wandering the Lands of Goul. His descendants fled the destruction and scattered to the winds.

Alexander felt foolish to call the king's loyalty into question as their hatred for Eris was surely matched. Shoxz was already sleeping by the time the prince got out of the hot spring. He slipped into his robe and went to bed. Fang snuggled in above his pillow as Nacilias found a spot next to him. He revealed to Nacilias that his mother had a journal dedicated to the Mystic Otrant. Its pages were still unread as he could not bring himself to complete the journal she wrote about him. Being able to see through her eyes only made his pain worse. He closed his eyes and drifted away.

Every thought escaped his mind and once again his astral form was awakened. He found himself in the mind of another. The room around him was murky and ominous. It appeared to be a laboratory filled with all sorts of machines that were linked to one another. The man left the lab and walked down a dark corridor filled with goblins and orcs.

"Nathaniel Darkbloom, you have served us greatly. With the help of these machines, the Potuliari we captured will fuel our ultimate weapon."

"Lord Marlusha, it has been an honor to serve you. What is our next move?"

Alexander's heart was crippled to hear the very name of the betrayer. Lord Marlusha finally came into view. The tall and elegant man had long black straight hair and very deep-red eyes. He was dressed in an ornate red and black robe with spiked shoulders. On each sleeve was an embroidered dragon. Nathaniel broke the prince's concentration when he began to speak.

"First, we must deal with King Silverskull and his army. Then they will unleash The Destroyer."

Lord Marlusha planned on burning Forgon Forest to cut off Castle Silverskull. A chuckle escaped his lips as the Divine Lord left the room.

Alexander thought his behavior was rather abnormal but realized that he was not there by accident. His intrusion into the man's mind did not go unnoticed. Nathaniel placed his palm on his forehead and the prince's body materialized.

Alexander was mortified. The being in front of him did not look human. His skin was black, and his blue veins could be seen through his skin. His eyes were red, and his hair was long with many braids. He stood seven feet tall and was very muscular. His clothes were made of snakeskin weaved into his armor. His nails were long and black, and in his palms were two red crystals embedded into his skin.

"Why wait until now to reveal me if you knew I was in there all this time?" questioned the prince.

"Child, you thought you were powerful enough to get into my mind. You are here by invitation. Their plan to revive Lord Nebula is halted until they can find the missing star fragments. Lord Marlusha is close to releasing The Destroyer of Lands. It is coming for that precious Blue Flame and your sister. Prepare yourselves."

Nathaniel confirmed the pixies warning. He felt his mind was tearing in two. All of the prince's memories were unfolding in front of Nathaniel. One of his many gifts included telepathy. He could feel the prince's fear and confusion. From his time with Anagar he recalled 'The Destroyer of Lands' as the fifth Cardinal Deity created to dethrone Hyperion.

Nathaniel's mind showed the prince a glimmer of Lord Marlusha's plan. Lord Nebula's Generals were doing everything in their power to take out the competition. The Blue Flame of Oricale could be used to eradicate magic from existence. It would rip the world to its foundation. Prince Alexander stared into Nathaniel's eyes. *Could he kill him in his astral form? Did he have access to his abilities?* The prince thought to himself as he twirled his right hand.

Nathaniel smiled, "You take advantage of my hospitality. You think you have it in you to kill me."

Nathaniel waved his hand and the prince's astral body tensed up. He dragged his body forward until they were face to face.

Alexander stared into his eyes, frozen. He was not strong enough to resist Nathaniel's abilities.

"Let me go. You are slaughtering innocent people. Why wouldn't I want to kill you."

"Because I know your secret. I know you have one of the three missing star fragments to release Lord Nebula."

No thought was safe while in the presence of a telepath. Nathaniel reassured the prince that his secret was safe with him. Fragile in his state of mind, he wondered why Nathaniel would help him? What did he have to gain from it? The mirror into the telepath's mind was harming the prince. He witnessed an agreement struck. His life for the lives of the Potuliari and Alulim.

Reality began to bend around them. Nathaniel realized the child prince was growing in strength and forcing himself into his thoughts.

"Boy, I suggest you stop before you hurt yourself."

"What am I doing?"

"You are a kitten, I am a Lion. I will devour you. Remember that."

Nathaniel waved his hand and crippled the prince's senses. He could not move.

"The Alulim are a dying breed. The Potuliari are an infection in this world. A breed that should not exist. I am cleaning up this mess."

Nathaniel's eyes darted to the Eclipse Amulet around the prince's neck. Now that the prince was aware of Lord Marlusha's plan he wondered if the prince would agree to a bargain. He would continue to feed the prince information if he agreed to help Nathaniel when asked. Agreeing to his terms relied on blind faith. The favor he requested would come later. There was something about this man that seemed familiar. Alexander knew making a deal like this would backlash against him, but he agreed to the terms. Nathaniel placed his hand toward Alexander, and the red diamond in his palm began to pulsate. The prince's astral form was placed back into his body, and he was finally able to sleep.

The depths of night were overtaken by the radiance of the sun. Day in and day out the High Elves entered Alexander's room to wake him from his slumber. Everyone would gather into the grand dining hall to feast. Training resumed after each meal. The prince continued to work on his techniques until he mastered them. The king stood in amazement. Techniques that would require hours of practice the young prince absorbed in half the time. From basic punches and strikes, like *Benco* to the *Gan* to the *Mei lu de Compas*. Alexander's glory did not stop there; he even mastered advanced fighting stances such as the *Asfixi, Cutel,* and *Cru*.

Living in the castle for a week allowed him to learn quickly. King Silverskull trained him day and night. Capoy was brutal and required extensive body work, but he kept faith. Nathanial Darkbloom's message kept him driven. Being around the king was like having an older brother. During one of their many dinners, May flirted with the gigantic man. She played with her hair and held the king's hand. The prince sensed there was history between the two of them. The topic changed gears as King Silverskull asked the prince about Soldiel and how he was raised. He was more than happy to respond. His childhood was amazing. He described the marvelous mansion he lived in and the many schools he attended, but when the topic changed to friends the prince grew silent. Finally explaining how his friend ended up being a demon and was the reason why Eris was able to find him.

Seeing how the mood changed, the king challenged the prince to a battle to test his strength. Prince Alexander was not ready. He wanted more time, but King Silverskull did not take no for an answer. His surprise attack destroyed the dinner table. King Silverskull was victorious in all their battles.

The tired prince refused to give up. He knew that if the king won in battle, he did not have a chance in the outside world. He anticipated the prince's movements, but the prince knew that he needed to strike quickly. The two began and battled for hours. Prince Alexander found the king's weakness, his own weight. Combining the skills he learned, he played at a combination of moves the last being the *Esqui de Bai*. Silence echoed in the chamber. It could not be possible. The massive warrior was subdued. To his amazement, he was the victor. The king rose from the floor in pure joy. Training was finally over. The king stumbled to his feet as he congratulated the young prince. It was time for a bath and rest.

Fang leaped onto the prince with joy and licked at his sweaty brow. His scales sparked causing the prince to stop walking. Reality warped around him. His head began to beat like a drum and his vision blurred. King Silverskull had already exited the room and noticed the prince was not behind him. He turned to see the prince in pain but before he could re-enter the room the doors slammed shut. His ears pulsated as sound was nullified. Fang's scales caused the crystals around the room to glow. His body shifted and walked toward the center of the room. Eyes scanning the floor until a piece of stone caught his attention. It began to glow. He could see through the stone and saw a staircase beneath it. He bent down and moved the stones until the hidden staircase was revealed.

He descended further into the volcano. It was as if his skin was being ripping off. The extreme heat made it hard to breathe. The Eclipse Amulet ignited, creating a barrier around him. Before him stood a long walkway. Lava waterfalls and streams poured around him. At the end of the walkway was a temple of hardened magma. Ascending the steps, he noticed the massive stone sphere and angelic statues again. He analyzed the statues. The closer he got, Fang's scales glistened. The baby dragon rolled around the floor in pain. The Eclipse Amulet burned at the prince's neck. It shattered, and the emerald dust brushed against one of the statues. The stone exterior fractured and exploded. From the dust, the prisoner expanded her wings and shook it off.

The sublime creature in front of him stood eight feet tall. Her pale, violent hair and purple eyes mesmerized him. Unlike the others, she did not have a sword, but rather a staff made of wood, and at the top was a purple sphere. She wore an armored breastplate that revealed much of her stomach. Her armored kilt had a trail of silk fabric that kissed the floor as she walked. She stood out from the others who were fully armored from head to toe. With the angel released, Fang's pain went away.

"I know that face. You are of her blood."

Confused by her statement, the prince questioned her. "Who?"

"The Empress. Mistress of Secrets. Lady Eileen. You are the one to end it all."

A lump appeared in his throat. He could barely swallow. Hearing him compared to his mother after reading about what she did. He could not stomach it. The beautiful angel was Anystazia. The other two angels were still dormant. The Luna and Sol Amulets were needed to revive them. Anystazia rubbed the stone face of her sister as she gazed toward the prince. His soul was open to her, and she could see into his mind. Nathaniel's face flashed before her eyes.

"You have been touched by the Great Deceiver."

His face squinted and his thoughts changed, allowing her to see more. Nathaniel was the reason for their imprisonment. She tapped the sphere with her staff revealing a hologram within it. The Trinity Angels used the hologram to oversee LunaSol and report back to the Creator.

She held the prince's hand as she explained how his mother was misled. During the Purge when Hyperion began banishing creatures, Nathaniel managed to rip through the void. As an Alulim, he was far older than the gods. Another soul corrupted by the Nebula, unlike Hyperion, he did not want to rule. Merely, end the one thing standing in the Nebula's way: Oricale. His emergence from the void came before her. Falling to LunaSol he lurked in the shadows and observed the Imperial Family and the Divine Lords. Drawn to the Mystic Otrant, he posed as her to get close to Lady Eileen. Without knowing, he infected her and seeded visions of Hyperion's transgressions into her mind using his telepathy.

He used her to strike at the heart of Hyperion's false reality. Confused and unsure, she came to the Mystic Otrant with her dreams. Still posing as her grandchild, Nathaniel kept up the ruse. Luring her away from Hyperion. Lies upon lies flowed from his mouth until Lady Eileen agreed to help him. He instructed her to go to Heaven and seek out a relic. That is where she came into contact with the Tri-Oricale Crystal.

Having touched the obelisk, her connection to Hyperion was fully cut off. She was shielded from him. Oricale noticed the black aura around Lady Eileen. She used her as a pawn to get to Nathaniel. The Keepers found her and Lady Eileen turned them to her cause. That foiled Oricale's plan of dragging Nathaniel out, but she did not stop there. She allowed Lady Eileen to take the obelisk for now.

Nathaniel continued to hide behind the mask of the Mystic Otrant to get close to the relic. He could never get close enough, until one day during a mysterious solar flare, the Trinity Angels noticed an influx of power on LunaSol. Hyperion could not sense it, but they felt it. He ordered them to bring the person to him. It brought them straight to Lady Eileen. They could feel she was influenced by another.

The Pretender grew worried. He needed her to unlock the powers of the crystal. She was its warden. He could not risk the angels interfering. Nathaniel took matters into his own hands. He entered Heaven under the disguise of an angel. When he was able to get close enough to Hyperion, he corrupted his thoughts and made him believe the Trinity Angels were on LunaSol gathering forces to overthrow him. Upon their return to their post, Hyperion ordered their detainment. He used his flame to remove their souls from their body. He shattered a precious gem from the relic room and forged three amulets as keys to their prison. The very amulets that would be passed down to the Royal Families.

He was unaware the gem already housed the spirit of three dragons. By forcing the Trinity Angels into the stone, he bound them together. One could not die while the other survived. It dawned on the prince. Fang survived because Anystazia survived. His realization only made her wonder. She saw inside his mind that Lord Marlusha was coming to burn the forest. Could he have known they were hidden there? If so, that meant, if they destroyed the angelic statues there would be no physical host for the angels to return to and their souls would die inside the gem. This would allow for the dragons to face death in the battlefield.

Anystazia's thoughts made the prince worry. The Destroyer of Lands was coming for his sister. If this was true and they managed to destroy the statues underneath the volcano. He could kill both their dragons in one shot. There was something looming in the prince's mind. She paused as the prince spoke. Alexander revealed that Nathaniel made a cryptic request, and he would call on the prince later. A bargain with Nathaniel was a dangerous thing.

"Little Prince, Nathaniel Darkbloom is very clever, but you will figure out a way to stop him."

The angel urged the prince to hurry to his sister. If the Destroyer of Lands is unleashed and gets its hands on the Blue Flame, it would be a monumental blow to Oricale. As the angel leaned in to kiss the prince on the forehead, she could feel the energy of the star fragment.

"Like mother, like son. You expose yourself to danger. Be wary!"

Even though it held Lord Nebula's light energy, it was a bomb waiting to be set off. Hearing this news caused the prince to wonder if he could use the star fragment against the serpent beast. Anystazia counseled him to keep the stone a secret. If its power was unleashed, it would be a beacon for the enemy, and they would know his location. The prince vowed to return with all three amulets and release them from their prison.

LunaSol and its history were an enigma. The longer the prince was there, he unraveled more stories that he was deprived of growing up. How could the Trinity Angels and the dragons be unlinked? That question remained a mystery. They did not even have that answer. Time was limited, and the angel's body began to fade, but before she parted with the prince, there was one last thing she needed to bestow upon him. It was another relic stolen from Heaven and hidden in the cavern. He was given the Winged Staff of the Eclipse. It was a totem to the gods Apollo, Hermes, and Artemis. A piece of their essence remained in the object. If he had any chance of winning against the Destroyer of Lands, it would be with their guidance.

Once the prince had the staff in hand, the angel returned to stone and the emerald dust compacted again to reform the amulet. He lifted Fang from the floor and placed him on his shoulder. The roars and banging of King Silverskull once again filled the prince's ears. He had to get back before the king broke the door down. He exited the shrine and headed for the door at the edge of the platform. He climbed the stone spiral staircase and lifted his body up through the opening. The staff minimized into a necklace as he placed the stones he removed back into the ground. Grabbing ahold of the necklace, he hid it in his pocket, once the last stone was in place the doors flew open, and everyone piled into the room. They rushed to his side badgering him with questions.

Not knowing who to trust still, the prince thought it was best to keep his visit with the Trinity Angels under wraps. Instead, he faked a vision from the crystals. He divulged that Lord Marlusha was set to release a beast that could destroy them all and was close to breaking through the Black Gates of Martilo so he could have his army take over Seraqus. They planned on burning down the forest before heading to the empire. King Silverskull grabbed the forearm of the prince and helped him get up from the floor. They exited the Room of Enlightenment and into the throne room where the others waited. The prince's training with the king was finally at an end. They rested for the night, but at daybreak they had to return to the Empire of Seraqus.

CHAPTER
17

SISTERS

War was coming, and a dark horizon awaited them. Prince Alexander and his companions feasted with King Silverskull one last time before their voyage back to Princess Ionica. He escorted them to the outskirts of his castle and watched as they disappeared into the shifting trees of Forgon Forest. Preparations were underway. He was not the only one preparing for war.

Lord Marlusha managed to separate John Vader and Lady Phoebe. John was now a prisoner; he sacrificed himself, allowing her to escape. Alone and afraid, she traveled through the inhospitable mountain ranges that separated Sharaa from Northern Salahea and then into Southern Salahea. She sought shelter in the Palace of Otrant. Her arrival came after the defeat of Lord Marlusha's troops. The Council of Otrant were weary of her arrival and what it would mean for their people. She only came for one of them - Amaris. With Potuliari being hunted for their abilities, their only choice was safety in numbers. She also needed her help locating another powerful Potuliari that was rumored to live in a secluded part of Seraqus. Outraged by the request, the council ordered her banishment from court. Amaris would do no such thing. Forced with a terrible decision, she agreed to temporarily abandon her post. The throne was no place for her, but the battlefield was.

Cleopatra and Piers urged her not to forsake them in their time of need. Their palace was infiltrated, and Lord Nebula's forces were mobilizing against them. The broken factions of mankind had to be united against their common enemy. A taste of disdain was left with the council members as they escorted Amaris and Lady Phoebe through the back of the palace. There was a secret cavern that led to Eternal Lake. It was an escape route in the event the palace was ever breached. Hundreds of boats were docked in the river that led from the cavern to the lake. Piers gently kissed Amaris on the cheek as he helped them get into one of the boats. He pushed the boat out and waved farewell to his old friend. The dampness of the cave was no more as the ravaging heat hit their face as the boat glided into the lake. The violent waves of the lake pushed their boat off course. They grabbed ahold of the oars and pushed against the waves until they made their way down the Livera River.

On one side was the mountainous terrain that protected Southern Salahea, and on the other was Seraqus. The open valley was filled with exotic creatures grazing on the lush banks of the river. A pack of young Mangelic Rams recently discovered their horns and were nibbling on the protruding edges as their mothers watched nearby. The beautiful mount was six feet long and ranged in color from white to brown. Four fully grown horns protruded from the top of their skull and curled backwards. The Spotted Deer made sure to stay clear of the territorial beasts. These exotic treasures were a sight to see. The deer were nearly extinct in most parts of LunaSol. Their fur was exclusively used in high society. Their white underbellies accented their green spotted fur. Having four ears helped them steer clear of hunters and bigger animals. The further south they traveled down the river, the closer they came to Forgon Forest. The roots of the Weeping Willows wrapped around one another, creating a bridge above them. The salty mist cascaded against their skin as the boat descended a small waterfall. A garden of blue ocean breeze orchids lined the riverbanks.

Their presence did not go unnoticed. The nymphs watched them closely as they made their way downstream. The dryads shifted between the trees in silence until Lady Phoebe's telekinesis caught a glimpse into one of their minds. The connection was too much for Lady Phoebe. The voices of the forest overwhelmed her, and a telepathic shock wave was released from her body. Amaris was thrown from the boat and found herself swimming to catch up to it. Guided by compassion the nymphs sprinted to her aid. Twisting and turning, the roots of the trees broke free from the dirt and stopped the boat. Three nymphs leaped into the river and brought Amaris to shore. Nymphs were faded memories among the humans. Having nearly drowned in the deep river, she thought her eyes were deceiving her. Her attention shifted, as Lady's Phoebe's moans got lower. She picked herself up from the ground and moved toward the boat. She called out the prince's name, and it startled the nymphs. Amaris glimpsed their reaction.

"Ladies of the Forest, thank you for saving us."

The common tongue was not a language they spoke for thousands of years. They were confused and the blank stare on their faces only made it harder for Amaris. She slowly approached one of the nymphs and hugged her. She resisted at first and then realized she was being thanked. The other nymphs jumped on Amaris and joined in on the hug. After Amaris was set free the nymphs tended to Lady Phoebe. She finally opened her eyes and panicked once she saw what was looking back at her. Amaris calmed her down and explained how she caused the boat to tip over when she lost control of her abilities. Lady Phoebe recalled the voices in her head.

"Dryads!"

"What?" questioned Amaris.

"I fixated on the voice of a dryad. She was talking to the others about Prince Alexander."

The name once again triggered the nymphs. Lady Phoebe asked them what they knew about the prince. The beauties could not communicate with her. She thought if she were able to hear the dryads' thoughts, maybe she would be able to communicate with the nymphs. She focused on their minds and asked the question again. This time she heard them speak.

"The prince was here!"

"How do you know?"

"Weirdly, I can hear their thoughts."

Telepathy was a gift Lady Phoebe discovered early on in her life. She walked into the minds of hundreds of people and learned their secrets and inner thoughts. When she was younger, she tried to communicate with a snake and caused the creature to seize and die. Every time she tried to connect with the animals of LunaSol, they ended up dead. Connecting to the nymph was rather easy. She spoke again to her, and this time the nymph spoke back.

"Prince Alexander came to the forest to train with King Silverskull. Now that it is complete, he is returning to his sister."

Their connection was lost as the nymph began to bleed from her nose. She began to seize, and the forest rumbled with terror. Amaris held the nymph and tried to help her, but it was too late. They cried for their dead sister as her body turned into soil. Their heartbreak summoned their protectors. The trees grumbled and shook with vigor as Aiars emerged to gather the weeping nymphs. Unlike the nymphs, the Aiars were well versed in the common tongue. For centuries they avoided humans, but this time they chose to speak and warned her that invading the minds of animals was harmful and would result in death.

Tears flowed down her eyes as she apologized for the loss of the nymph. She meant no harm. She was excited to learn that the prince was nearby. The Aiars ordered her back to her boat. Amaris stood before Lady Phoebe and signaled her to follow their command. Fighting against the protectors of the forest would end badly for them. Once boarded, the roots unbound and allowed them to leave the forest. The nymph's death weighed on her mind. The gloomy boat ride made Amaris worried about Lady Phoebe's state of mind.

The nearby town of Santaruz was a good place for them to regroup and gather their thoughts over dinner. They pulled the boat up the riverbank and hid it beneath a bunch of shrubs. The town was built at the base of the Zypherion Mountains. Home to hundreds of stonemasons, the influential pearl of the south was desired by many. Monumental towers and homes interwoven into the mountain. The smell of fire and steel danced through the cobbled streets. It was rumored to once be the home of dwarves before the Purge.

Lady Phoebe was following a lead in Sharaa about an area of Seraqus that was home to elves. The rumors were that they raised a Potuliari amongst their ranks. She was said to harness the minerals in the very ground and had extreme telepathic abilities. She was saved from the royals who sought to kill her. Noticing a local tavern was still open and offering delicious items, Amaris and Lady Phoebe decided to check it out. They devoured potatoes and chicken as the guests gawked and grinned at the women. A tavern of greasy men and devious eyes meant very little to the dominant women.

Dining at a proper table was something of a distant memory for Lady Phoebe. Since the death of her adopted parents, she grew accustomed to living off scraps and running from those who wanted to abuse her abilities. Amaris could see this was new to her and wanted her to enjoy it, but her mind was elsewhere. The voices of the tavern filled her head. She was drawn to the thoughts of a miner who was heading back into the mountains for his shift. She caught glimpses of secret tunnels leading to hidden lands. After discussing it with Amaris she convinced him to help them get through the mountains to find this woman. The skies above were dangerous and filled with griffins. Many of the townsfolk went missing when they tried to tame the beasts. The opening into the mountain was massive at first. Once they got into the heart of the mountain, it became narrower. Legends of dwarves kept most of the townsfolk from drilling any deeper. Down a hill they went until they reached what appeared to be an archway sealed up with stones. Runes were carved along the border.

Amaris touched the boulders and could feel a gentle breeze through the cracks. Harnessing the wind from the other side she caused a cave in. Lady Phoebe's telekinesis shifted the boulders, revealing a perfectly carved road. It led to hundreds of sealed off archways. The road twisted and turned with no end in sight until they found refuge in an abandoned town. The marvel was built from steel, unlike the stone and wood buildings seen in Seraqus. Amaris and Lady Phoebe walked through the desolate streets until they came across another opening into the mountain. A thump caught their attention, and as they turned around, the miner was gone. Dwarves began appearing all over, the size of children, with red curly hair nearly covering their body. A select few were battle ready covered in armor with mattocks and crossbows. Two of the dwarves held the miner on the floor as their leader stepped forward.

"You are trespassing."

"We are looking for a Potuliari like ourselves."

The dwarven leader was in disbelief. "You are traitors."

Amaris and Lady Phoebe were perplexed. As one of the dwarves picked up his mattock to kill the miner, his form contorted, revealing a creature comprised of rock and emerald flames. He incinerated the dwarves closest to him and charged at Amaris. Lady Phoebe's powers betrayed her.

His true intentions were hidden from her. She watched as electricity rippled through Amaris' veins and manifested in her hands. She flung a bolt of electricity at the creature, knocking him into one of the nearby houses. The dwarves piled on top of him and chiseled away. Filled with rage, Lady Phoebe waved her hand and flung the dwarves off the creature. Her aura pulsated as she began to crush the creature using her mind. The screams of agony echoed through the mountains as she ripped his exoskeleton apart, only leaving the emerald flames that comprised its insides. The flame released the skeleton of a human before reanimating itself and retreating into the ground.

Amaris' heart was racing, "What was that?"

The dwarven leader examined the hole the creature burned into the ground, "That was a Refam."

The term escaped them. This was their first encounter with a creature like this. They were taken to a tower for safety. It was the palace of the dwarven leader, Asula. They were surprised to learn that it was a woman rather than a man. They soon learned many of the dwarves that they met were women. Their masculine features and hairy bodies fooled them. Asula took them to her private office to look beyond the mountain. The top of the circular tower was filled with floor-to-ceiling windows. The only thing in the room was a desk littered with maps of the roads leading in and out of the mountain, three chairs, and one lamp. Asula tapped her finger on the glass.

"Beyond these mountains is Elven Territory. We were tasked with sealing up all the exits through the mountain to make sure no one ever stumbled into our homes."

"Why would you help us now?"

"That creature knows where we live. If it deceived you into bringing it here. It is no longer safe for us. It will be back with more."

Amaris sat in one of the chairs and questioned Lady Phoebe, "You could not sense the monster?"

Lady Phoebe was left without words. She stared at Asula for answers.

"A Refam is immune to telepathic probes. They are parasites that leech onto the skeletal remains of a human and can shapeshift into the host. It allows them to retain the human's memory. That is how it was able to trick you."

"Why have we never heard of a Refam?" asked Amaris.

"They are newly mutated experiments by Lord Marlusha. My husband went out one day, and it took him two days to return to me. When he returned, I was suspicious. One night a freak thunderstorm erupted over the mountain, and my husband panicked. His body deformed and reformed. My husband was dead. The creature had taken possession of his body to learn about the mountain."

Lady Phoebe sat down next to Amaris as Asula stared out into the valley.

"We interrogated the creature and learned that a scientist working for Lord Marlusha killed one of your kind. Whether it was a man or a woman, we will never know. All we know is that they had the ability to animate inanimate objects. The scientist manipulated its ability and sculpted the Refam, creatures of stone, steel, and lava."

Lady Phoebe banged on the table. "We need to get going. If that thing comes back..."

Asula feared her clan would die if they remained in the mountains. Amaris offered an alternative. With Prince Alexander's return, a new war was brewing. He would need supporters to challenge Lord Nebula. Asula agreed that her clan would be best suited for war. She swore her allegiance to helping the prince and would escort them to the temple. For now, they rested. The dwarven leader brought the two women to an empty house for the night. Four guards were stationed outside for their protection. Lady Phoebe showered and was gifted with spare clothes that Amaris had packed for the trip. She lay on the floor staring at the ceiling as the showerhead turned on again, it was Amaris' turn. Her mind was her enemy. It kept replaying all her mistakes. She was numb. After spending years learning how to control her powers, they were slipping back into chaos again. Her thoughts were silent as she heard another.

A males' voice called to her. It was not the prince's voice. The man screamed out for her to return to the prince, or he would die. Distracted and caught off guard, she allowed the man to connect with her. A shadow with red eyes appeared before her. Nathaniel Darkbloom urged her to protect the prince from a beast that was coming. Lady Phoebe did not trust him. Why did he reach out now? He refused to give her anything more and disconnected from her. Amaris was done showering and walked in on Lady Phoebe in a trance. Her aura lit up again. Amaris shook her until she snapped out of it. She shared her bizarre interaction. Amaris was worried for her. Her powers were unstable. They laid together on the floor until they finally fell asleep.

The following morning, they were awakened by knocks on the door. After getting ready, they traveled down the dwarf road and made it to the clearing. The hidden valley came into sight, but their joy turned into devastation. They were too late. The valley was overrun. The Temple of Light that stood nearby was crumbling. Ships were anchored nearby, and a horde of creatures were seen burning everything to the ground. The dwarf clan rushed through the valley in search of survivors. They were stopped in their tracks as high-pitched screeches from the tai'yne echoed overhead. Creatures born from death; they were once dragons infected with a deadly plague. Their corpses were reanimated using dark magic. They were not alone. Ogres ravaged the land and dug through the rubble. They took their commands from a golden figure mounted on the serpent-faced creature.

Dark Riders could only maintain their humanoid forms so long as they wore their enchanted cloth. As the creature spoke, its voice sounded like shattering glass. A familiar face stood by the ogres as they searched the ruins; the Refam. Whatever they were looking for was not there. The ogres were recalled to their ships as the tai'yne took off into the sky. Enraged, Lady Phoebe rushed toward the fallen temple. All that remained was the marble base. The white marbled columns were reduced to fragments. All the rubble was scattered across the valley.

With a wave of her hand, she levitated the stones on the base and separated them, revealing a hidden chamber. The dwarves stood behind to guard their escape. The two glided down the circular opening with caution. It led to an underground tunnel that was used as an escape route. The tunnel was endless, but once they reached the end of it, an open shaft stood above them. Fresh air filled their lungs as they emerged into a forest. Amaris was blindsided, and she was knocked out. Lady Phoebe paralyzed the residence of the forest with a telepathic blast.

Her abilities had no effect on the High Elves, Sherra and Raejisa that surrounded them. Wards radiated around them. Lady Phoebe called to the dwarves. They rushed through the tunnel and leaped from the opening. The elves were glad to see it was them and not Lord Marlusha's servants. Adorned in blue and green robes with armor over it. Each had ten blades on their belt.

They escorted the travelers to their sanctuary in the heart of Hemino Forest. Untouched by war, giant pandas played with their young. The hoots of the Ptilosis leucotis chimed overhead as a loud bang silenced the entire forest. Trees toppled as a six legged behemoth charged at them to build a nest. Its massive hammerhead horn covered most of its face and eyes. Their armored blue skin faded to gray near its legs. The four-eyed giant stared at the elves as they walked right by them.

The dwarves were excited to see the creatures. Running past them and disregarding their warning, they howled, jumped, and rolled on the ground. Amaris and Lady Phoebe laughed, but the elves were furious. The mammoth-sized beast dropped to their knees and rolled onto their back. The dwarves leaped onto them and rubbed their bellies, shocking the prude onlookers. Asula shared that Hammerhead rhinoceroses were their preferred mount in battle. Before the separation of beasts and humans, the dwarves were their herders. Dwarves picked up mining as a last resort. Once they were done having their fun, they continued along the trail until they came to the mountainside that divided them from Martilo. Its black mountains staining the forest.

In front of them stood a gem in the chaos, a shrine of white marble. Griffin-like columns held up the ceiling. It was covered in jade vines and lavender. Atop a throne of vines stood an old and fragile man. His skin was covered in black moles, and his nails were about six inches long. Amaris noticed his hair was gray and extended down to his forearms. His eyes could barely open to see who was in front of him. The elves tended to his decaying body as they whispered to him. His lips quivered as he spoke.

"Why have you come here?"

Amaris was the first to respond, "Prince Alexander has returned. We too will join him. We have come here to seek help."

"Help? Our temple has been destroyed. We seek refuge in a forest, and you come to us for help."

Lady Phoebe stepped forward, "We mean you no disrespect. Lord Marlusha is hunting Potuliari and we have learned that one resides on these lands. We have come to ask her for help."

"Potuliari or Alulim. Do you know which is which?"

His question only confused them more. What was an Alulim?

"What is an Alulim?" questioned Lady Phoebe.

"Without eyes to see, who wants to know!"

"I am Phoebe."

"And I am Amaris?"

A smile appeared on the man's face as he trembled. He raised his hand as a signal to someone in the distance. Lady Phoebe and Amaris turned to see whom he was signaling. The mysterious woman appeared from the treetop. She was regal and refined. She wore an emerald dress that hugged her body. There were two slits on the front that came up to her knees. The dress connected around her neck with a choker covered in diamonds. Her cape descended from her choker and connected to her wrist with two metal cuffs. Like a princess, she was adorned with a tiara of emerald stones that sat atop her fiery red hair. She walked past Amaris and Lady Phoebe and kneeled in front of the man.

He held her hand as he cried, "Palar, my girl. My three girls are together again. It seems like just yesterday when I found you abandoned and alone."

Amaris and Lady Phoebe looked at one another. What was this man talking about? What did he mean, he found them? They watched the woman stand up and stand beside him. Amaris approached the steps of the shrine but took two steps back as a gray-furred lycanthrope appeared from behind the throne. He wore a navy leather kilt with hidden daggers and a leather sleeveless vest.

"My girls, my son, Lord Zylo likes to make an entrance."

"Sir, we do not know you. Who you are?"

"There is no mistake. Each one of you was lost. Infants abandoned; I found you. You are my children. No matter what family I left you with. I raised you until I couldn't anymore."

Lady Phoebe gasped for air as his words sent chills down her neck. Tears formed in the corner of Amaris' eyes as she stared at him. The dwarves knew exactly who the man was. Asula whispered to Amaris that they were in the presence of a royal. Master Yami Nightfeather, the first-born son of King Habagin Nightfeather and Calista Stormfal. Secrets shrouded their upbringing. Now, they could confront their past and get genuine answers. Master Yami was more than happy to share their connected past.

He was married to Kesia Stormfal, one of the many daughters of Lord Grevis. When Lady Phoebe was found, they had already conceived their first child, Zylo. During a lunar eclipse, he snuck out one night to observe the lycanthropes. The savage beasts violently attacked one another, and Lady Udana intervened. She did not realize that Zylo was hiding nearby and was attacked by one of the creatures. She later found his body and brought him back to Master Yami. Stricken with grief and paranoia that he would succumb to his inner animal; they took him to the elven kingdom ruled by King Gandrago. Elven magic stopped the process, and Zylo became a sentient lycanthrope.

Master Yami confessed that he and Zylo traveled to Sharaa in search of the beast that turned him; instead, the cries of a baby caught their attention. When Lady Phoebe was removed from the lake, a telepathic shock wave twisted the water, creating a whirlpool. Her powers were already manifesting. Master Yami adopted her and raised her until she was three. Lady Phoebe was an Alulim, not a Potuliari. Her lineage transcended time, but she managed to end up in their reality during a meteor shower. Alulim's bore a diamond shaped birthmark. Lady Phoebe had it hidden under her outfit.

Amaris' story was a tragic one as well. Unlike Lady Phoebe's parentage, Master Yami knew Amaris' mother. Queen Hippolyta Moonspark, the daughter of Lord Celeio and Lady Uma. Her marriage to Prince Marteo Dawnrider resulted in three children and years of abuse. A slave to sex, he would often leave the queen's side to sleep with the servants of the palace. Fueled with vengeance, the queen decided to do the same and had an affair with an Alulim by the name of Jean-Paul Brightheart. Knowing that the child would be slaughtered if it remained in the palace, the queen ordered her servants to bring the child to Master Yami. She thought since his wife was barren for many years that he would have no issue raising an orphaned child. Amaris could not believe her ears. She was related to the Pharaoh of Salahea.

Master Yami explained that children born through the union of Alulim and any of the races on LunaSol were deemed Potuliari. It was a word coined by Servilia after Lord Nebula's entombment. There was an uptick in Alulim offspring.

Palar already knew her story and did not care to have it repeated. She too was a Potuliari. After Master Yami found them, he went on to conceive three natural-born children: Imperious, Zello, and Charles. Things changed when a few of the Royal Families issued decrees that Potuliari were abominations and ordered their execution, so he hid them with people he trusted. Amaris was left with the Magnus' who swore an oath to his sister, and Lady Phoebe was left with his servants back in Sharaa. In the end, Amaris' life turned out better than Lady Phoebe. Master Yami's servants abandoned her after she attacked a child in the street using her abilities. She was left to fend for herself and live off scraps. She resented her upbringing and blamed him.

Palar was also telepathic and could sense her anger. She stepped toward Lady Phoebe, "He is not the reason those people mistreated you. He tried to save you!"

"How dare you invade my mind?"

"It wasn't that hard."

The tensions were rising, and a fight between telepathies would level the forest. Amaris grabbed Lady Phoebe's arm and stood in front of her. "You cannot blame her for her feelings. This is a lot to take in at once."

Palar turned her back to Amaris and returned to Master Yami's side.

"You don't think that all of this is too much for him too? He took us in, raised us, and then had to give us back up. You would not be here today if it were not for him."

Amaris agreed with Palar. Deep down inside, so did Lady Phoebe. Master Yami began to cough up blood, causing the elves to secure the shrine. Palar and Lord Zylo stepped away once they started tending to him. Asula slid next to Palar to learn about the attack. She was away on business in the Elven city of Dal'Riv. Lord Marlusha's army came for her at the order of another Alulim, Nathaniel Darkbloom. The ground shook with vigor as Lady Phoebe's breathing increased. Listening to Palar recount what happened and who sent the army made her blood boil. The rocks on the floor levitated, and the trees began to crack. The shadowy figure that came to her tried to get her to leave before she could learn the truth. Lost in her emotions, her abilities became unhinged. The mountainside cracked, the animals ran scared, and the ground began to dissolve.

Amaris could not get Lady Phoebe to snap out of her trance. Her aura was blocking out sound. A telekinetic shock wave pulsated from her aura and crippled the High Elves. Master Yami was unaffected by her abilities. He slowly rose from his throne and gently walked toward her. He held onto her hands and wrapped them around him. Sound returned to the forest, and his shoulder muffled her screaming sobs. She blamed herself for what happened to the temple. She admitted having a run-in with Nathaniel Darkbloom when she was traveling to the Temple of Light. He connected to her telepathically and warned her to find the prince. She assumed it was to distract her from finding Palar and him.

Her blame was unwarranted. They were dealing with a master manipulator. Master Yami never crossed paths with him. Only two people ever challenged him - Lady Eileen and the Mystic Otrant. He learned of Nathaniel's ruthlessness through stories the Mystic Otrant left in her journals. He could not recount how long Nathaniel hid amongst the people. While others mated and sought refuge in this new world, he plotted and schemed. Nathaniel's game was bigger and more intricate than anyone could comprehend.

A puddle of blood began to form near Master Yami's foot. He was bleeding from his lower abdomen. Lord Zylo picked up his father and carried him back to his throne.

"Why is he bleeding?"

"He was stabbed by the Dark Rider."

The blade was drenched in venom and overtook his body. Master Yami's life was near an end. Master Yami held Palar's hand as tears flowed from her eyes. His life was fruitful and plentiful. He made peace with his fate. His journey was over, but theirs was just beginning. He was glad his final moments would be in the presence of his children. Their hearts crumbled at the notion that he thought of them as his own. Amaris fumbled with her thoughts. Nathaniel's plan was foiled for now, but what about next time.

Master Yami warned his adopted daughters to stay clear of Nathaniel. He was up to something dangerous. Their conversation was interrupted as the High Elves prepared for his death.

"My dear children, it seems that I will soon depart from this world. I have ruled as King of Weguard for many centuries, and now I must take my leave. You will be my witnesses. My son, Zylo Nightfeather, Lord of Hemino Forest; you are the future King of Weguard."

The elves rejoiced for his appointment. No one was more deserving. With the Temple of Light destroyed, it was time for him to reunite with those beyond the Zypherion Mountains. Amaris welcomed his company. Prince Alexander could use every ally. The High Elves vowed to rally the elves of Dal'Riv for the coming war. They could no longer remain hidden. A neigh echoed overhead as flapping wings descended through the trees. An elegant, white Pegasus landed near Master Yami and sat beside him. Palar was overjoyed with its arrival. Omega was the king's warhorse. His arrival was a blessing and a curse. Master Yami began to fade into death; he instructed them to leave at once. Lord Zylo mounted Omega and took off toward the dwarven road, while the others traveled by foot. It would be reckless for them to emerge in Santaruz with a horde of dwarves, a Pegasus, and a lycanthrope.

The dwarves had another idea - the sky. The sky above the Zypherion Mountains was filled with griffins. They could be swayed to take them to the Empire of Seraqus with Lady Phoebe's abilities. Ashamed to tell them the truth, she went along with it. The road to the top of the mountain was steep. The blistering winds zoomed past them as they reached the snow-covered peaks. Hundreds of empty nests came into view as they searched for signs of life. Dozens of screeches roared from above as the griffins descended on their prey. The elephant-sized creatures with steel-tipped claws landed nearby with eyes locked on their target. Amaris stared into the clouds and whirled her hands around. The clouds shifted and darkened until a mighty blizzard was summoned.

Blinded by snow, the griffins were unable to move. Lady Phoebe slowly approached one of them. She held out her hand and slowly touched the creature's face. She focused on its mind but had a hard time talking to the creature. Palar could see her struggling. She stood behind Lady Phoebe and slid her hand beside her. Together they were able to take control of the creature, but it did not stop there. All the griffins were now under their control. Amaris twirled into the clouds and dismantled the blizzard. She was shocked to see that the griffins did not react the same way the nymph did. Excited, the dwarves mounted them and zoomed off toward the Empire of Seraqus. Heartbroken by leaving his father behind, Lord Zylo looked back once more before taking off.

Knowing that his son was safe with his adopted sisters, Master Yami drew his last breath. The High Elves prepared for his burial. After digging his grave, they lowered his body into the ground. One elf removed something from her pocket and placed it on his chest. Eris' dark shadow stayed clear of the funeral until the relic was exposed. She approached the shrine and battled her way toward him. Their bodies turned to ash in her fingertips. One elf managed to escape and ran for Dal'Riv. Eris removed the relic from his body and unwrapped it. It was a crystal snowflake.

It was one of the many items from Hyperion's past that were scattered around LunaSol. The elves of Dal'Riv built the Temple of Light around the beautiful gem. They knew it as the Star of Nimah. During the war, the elves had possession of it; they learned it belonged to Hyperion's wife. She was depicted as a tall, exquisite creature with massive wings. Her existence was kept a secret until Lord Nebula was imprisoned. The angels found her held captive in his vault. She was released and took control of the heavens. Her dominance was short-lived, and she was imprisoned once more.

Eris stared at the beautiful snowflake and faded into a mist of darkness.

CHAPTER
18

DEMON OF THE DEEP

With the Star of Nimah now in her possession, the enchantments placed on the Black Gates of Martilo could be destroyed. Thousands of those loyal to Lord Nebula were trapped behind the protective wards. Once the barrier was destroyed, Seraqus would fall to the overwhelming might of Martilo. Eris' dark form appeared before a wall of iron and stone that stretched two hundred and fifty feet long and one hundred feet high. There were two spiral towers at each end engraved with angelic runes. The runes were set ablaze once she approached the gate. The ground around her quaked as the star ignited and began to drain the runes of their energy. With each ward that faded, the trumpets of heaven sung. A devious smirk appeared on Eris' face as the final ward disappeared. She pointed the relic at the impenetrable gate and dismantled it in a massive explosion.

The explosion caught the attention of millions. A plume of dark smoke rose higher than the clouds. Shards of iron plummeted from the sky like bullets raining down on the neighboring cities. The expanding cloud caught Amaris' gaze from the west, even though they were hundreds of miles away. Grabbing ahold of the griffin's fur she guided the creature toward Lady Phoebe's side to inform her. Below were the remnants of war. The ground was scorned with ash and destruction. Lady Phoebe was hit with sharp pain. Her head pulsated and her vision distorted. Her grip on the griffins was weakening, and the creatures flared their wings as they dropped from the sky. Palar tried to regain control over the creatures on her own, but it was too much for her to handle.

Princess Ionica's soldiers watched from below as the creatures fell to their doom. Amaris leaped from her griffin and whirled the air around them to ease the landing. The soldiers secured the intruders. The griffins were unconscious and so was Lady Phoebe. Amaris ordered the soldiers to stand down and retrieve the princess. Her request was denied. She balled up her fist, and electrical sparks flared in her eyes. The soldiers slammed their shields into the ground and drew their weapons. Screaming came from the distance and distracted her. The voice became clearer as it got closer.

Prince Alexander and his companions pushed through the blockade toward Amaris and the others.

"Stop! They are here to help us."

May ordered the soldiers to stand down. The prince was pleased to see that his warning helped them escape. Formalities had to wait. His eyes were drawn to Lady Phoebe's body, and he rushed to her side to lift her to her feet. Her skin was ice cold, and her pulse was weakening. May ordered the guards to take her to the healers. Asula stood at the prince's side and explained to him what happened. He was infuriated by their callousness for the griffins. He approached one of the disabled creatures and rubbed the side of its face. He closed his eyes and whispered to the beast to wake up.

The dwarves were stunned when all the griffin's eyes shot open. They flared their wings and stumbled upright from the floor. Confused by where they were, the creatures screeched and rallied together. Prince Alexander tried to calm them down.

"No one will harm you. You are safe here."

As the prince spoke, Palar watched as the griffins gathered around him and licked him as if they understood what he was saying.

"They respond as if they understand you."

"They do!"

Palar was puzzled by the prince's reaction. He was not like the inhabitants of LunaSol; Ilihi's did not care for the animals. They were seen as a means to an end, but he cared for them, and they cared for him. She noticed only one of his companions was a human and the rest were animals. She studied the prince and his interactions with the Corsac fox and the Unicorn. There was a deeper connection between them. A gentle nudge brought her back to reality when the dwarves told her to follow them. The griffins would remain in the garden.

They boarded a boat to the fortress. The prince was intrigued to see a Pegasus and a Lycanthrope. He engaged Lord Zylo in conversation and soon realized that he was kin. The prince was ecstatic. Palar could not peel her eyes away from the prince. He was nothing like she imagined. The three continents were ruled by Royal Families, and they were all known to be tyrants, especially the Ilihi. They made sure to keep Magnus' and mortals under their thumbs. The boat docked, and Samistha was there to greet them. She escorted them to the palace, but her advances were halted. Anri and her Magnus' were at the palace gates.

"Samistha leave us at once."

Samistha's smile turned into disappointment. Prince Alexander was annoyed with Anri's behavior. He turned to Samistha and apologized. Anri grimaced at the prince and turned to enter the palace. Samistha left his side and returned to her post. The prince was boiling inside with anger. Nacilias urged him to leave it alone, but he refused to allow her to treat Samistha like that.

"Why did you have to speak to her like that?"

Anri paid the prince little mind and continued walking.

She changed the conversation: "Princess Ionica is in deep meditation right now. I will escort you to our guest chambers."

Palar and the others did not appreciate the High Magnus' rudeness but did not want matters to escalate. The prince had enough of her behavior. He pushed past the Magnus' and stopped right in front of her.

"I asked you a question, and you ignored me. I will not ask again."

Anri stared into the prince's eyes, "I have bigger things to worry about than someone's feelings getting hurt."

She walked around the prince, and everyone continued to walk with her in silence until they reached Geyser Hall. May held the prince's hand as she whispered to him.

"Do not let her get to you."

Before Anri could make it to the massive staircase, the prince once again got in her way.

"Little prince, we have pressing matters."

"You will address me correctly. You are not speaking to your servants; you are speaking to the son of Sir Erin and Lady Eileen."

This was the first time he puffed his chest and exerted his authority. Anri's eyes bulged. He was right. Once again, she acted as if he was beneath her station. She apologized and tried to explain, but he did not care about explanations. He demanded that she treat her servants with respect. He would not tolerate her foolishness again. Anri swallowed her pride and nodded her head. The prince stepped aside and allowed her to continue to guide them to their rooms. Palar inquired about Lady Phoebe.

One of the Magnus' revealed that she was in the healing chamber and was under observation. Amaris and Palar wanted to be by her side, but Anri could not allow the room to be contaminated.

They reached the top of the staircase and entered a long corridor. Anri revealed that her frustration was festering because Eris destroyed the Black Gates of Martilo. Lord Nebula's army now could ravage through Seraqus and potentially take over the continent of Weguard.

"How did this happen?" asked Lord Zylo.

"Your father."

The High Magnus had news about his father's burial. It was the first time they received communication from an Elven city. One of Master Yami's servants managed to escape the slaughter and get word across the border. After Lord Zylo and the others left his side, Eris attacked Master Yami's burial. The item in his possession was stolen and used to destroy the Black Gates of Martilo. Palar began to cry, and Amaris held her hand. Lord Zylo punched the wall and cracked the glacier.

"Your father was betrayed. They knew he would have the item close to him."

"What do you know about this item?" questioned Palar.

"Apparently more than any of you."

Anri took them past their rooms and into the library. The black iron gates were engraved with all the phases of the moon. The Magnus' each touched one of the moons, and the center of the door split open and allowed them entry. Three floors of knowledge were preserved on shelves

196

behind glass. Each of the shelves shifted in a circular pattern until a lever was pulled to stop them. They were taken to the back of the library, where there was a statue of an angel. Her name was carved into the bottom: Queen Nimah. She was holding a staff, and Anri pointed to the star at the top of it.

Gazing at the statue caused the prince to tremble. That face. It haunted his dreams.

"I have seen her."

His words caused the room to stir.

"How is that possible?" questioned Anri.

The prince recounted his night terrors growing up. They became more vivid as he got older until one night, he was standing in a damp room and saw her hanging from her wrist in chains. Eris was also hiding away in the corner, watching him. He was paralyzed once more as he stared at the statue. The smell of burning coal filled his lungs. The same smell he encountered when he visited Nathaniel in Lord Marlusha's palace.

'Could she be the angel that was helping them break the runes?' Prince Alexander wondered. He could not fully trust them to reveal what he knew. He kept his mouth shut as Anri pointed to the staff in the angel's hand.

"The Star of Nimah is one of two pieces. It was separated from the rod. It can draw on energy and reuse it. It belonged to the wife of Hyperion. She was once his prisoner in Heaven, but when the angels learned of her existence, they freed her after he was imprisoned."

Palar could sense Anri was withholding something from them. She invaded her mind and learned that Queen Nimah was betrayed by the angels and imprisoned again. She believed she was hidden on LunaSol. The High Magnus was outraged with the telepath; her thoughts were private. With haste, Anri enchanted her mind with barriers to keep Palar from digging any deeper. She confessed that they sent soldiers to find the tomb, but they came back empty-handed.

"Is Eris looking for her too?"

She did not have the answer. If she was looking for Queen Nimah, then that could be devastating for them all. The Magnus' brought forth a massive map of Weguard. Anri pointed to Forgon Forest; it would be the first stop on their campaign to overthrow Princess Ionica. Sweat poured from the prince's brows. The Trinity Angels were vulnerable if Castle Silverskull fell. He wanted to tell Anri, but his jaw locked up. He could not betray their trust. At every turn there was a spy, and he could not trust them with this information.

Palar sensed his sorrow and was not shy of using her powers. She attempted to read the prince's mind, but his amulet ignited and prevented her from hearing his thoughts. She was hit with a crippling pain. Her actions were unacceptable. Lord Zylo urged her to stop before she made matters worse. She was noticed by one of the Magnus'. Shifting his hands he caused Palar to scream out in agony.

The dwarves retaliated against them and drew their weapons. A female Magnus snapped her fingers and froze their weapons in ice. Anri stood there and watched the chaos unfold. Prince Alexander ordered everyone to stop but no one listened. He grabbed the necklace from his pocket and used the energy of the amulet to reanimate it. He was now holding the Winged Staff of the Eclipse. Its presence caused a stir. His own companions wondered how he came to possess it. He lost himself to the chaos once the staff touched his skin. He slammed the bottom of it into the floor undoing the enchantments.

Fang growled at the Magnus. The prince turned his rage toward Anri. He pointed his staff at her and her apprentice jumped in front of her and began to convulse. Blood dripped from her nose and then her ears. A loud scream silenced the chaos in his mind as he heard his mother. Her voice drew closer and closer, telling him to stop. She whispered for him not to fall into depravity. Her gentle voice filled him with relief, and he lost his grip on the staff, causing the Magnus to faint. His staff returned to its normal state. No one realized that Princess Ionica was standing behind them and witnessed the entire dispute. She was shaken to her core. She ordered everyone to their rooms and requested to speak with Anri alone. Lord Zylo lifted the prince over his shoulder and took his leave. The prince secured the necklace in his pocket once more.

"Your majesty, I can explain."

The princess did not want to hear another word from her. She turned around and headed back to the throne room. Anri followed suit until they were out of ears reach.

"What happened back there?"

"The prince is not an Ilihi, but something else entirely."

The princess sat down on the edge of her throne as Anri explained what occurred, her voice shaking as she spoke. Princess Ionica's eyebrows rose a few times when she heard of the prince's abilities. He not only could manipulate water, but he also had the ability to speak with animals and now used a staff to cast spells. The prince was an abnormality. No Ilihi in history had these gifts. Why him? The question burned in her mind. In order to manifest his abilities his emotions had to be triggered. This was harmful for the rest of them. War was upon them, and the prince could lose himself to chaos again and wreak havoc on those closest to him.

"We must keep my brother under control. You will report back to me on his status."

"But your Majesty?"

"Do not say another word. Your service is needed elsewhere. You will serve my brother and report back to me. We need to know what he is and how dangerous he can become."

"What will happen to the boy?"

"We have to wait and see!"

The High Magnus could not believe her ears. What did the princess have in mind? She wanted to be alone with her thoughts. She ordered Anri to check on Lady Phoebe and rest for the night. Anri took her leave and went to the healing chamber; Lady Phoebe was still in stasis. She returned to her room to sleep as war prepared around them. As the stoic princess closed her eyes, fires raged across the land in Forgon Forest. The castle fell. King Silverskull retreated with his people to the empire. The volcano was ignited, cutting off its secrets to those who invaded its walls. The Aiars gathered the helpless and raised the river to flood out those who remained. The only thing that stood in their way were the Shaman Mountains.

The pixies abandoned their village and scattered to the winds. Lord Marlusha's army reached the mountain range. Leading them was a Black Orc, a mutated elf-turned berserker. His purple skin filled with scales. His black soulless eyes focused on destruction. He raised his horn and blew with all his might. The ground cracked and quaked as an enormous mouth opened and swallowed it whole. His troops continued over the rubble toward the empire.

King Silverskull's battalion never made it into the fortress. The furthest they got was the meadow before they were picked apart in the darkness. It provided Lord Marlusha's troops with amble coverage to infiltrate the undetected meadow. King Silverskull was the only one to escape. Surrounding the princess' army on all sides they slowly crept into dismantle her forces but fell into her trap. A goblin scout stepped on a mine and was ripped apart. The mine released a spark of light into the air and created an electrical barrier connecting all the mines together.

The savage creatures pressed forward thinking they could overpower the barrier. Up in flames they went. The sound of beating drums echoed from the distance. The second wave had arrived, this time with a dozen chimeras. These twelve-foot-long beasts were chained to a platform and pulled by trolls. The trolls ripped through the chains with their hammers, unleashing the lion-faced creatures onto their enemy. With every flap of their wings, their peacock tails illuminated the night sky. They dashed over the barrier and ripped the flesh from the soldiers. Arrows were launched into the air, but none could pierce through their red scales. Samistha could see the battle from the docks and rushed to the closest bell tower to sound the alarm, signaling the empire to prepare for war. Hearing the screams, she created her water serpent once more and rushed to assist the others.

Princess Ionica was awoken from her sleep. She was still sitting on her throne when the Imperial Guard came to inform her. Everyone awoke to the loud voices of her soldiers gathering everyone to the princess' throne. Prince Alexander did not move as quickly as the others. He was still gathering his senses. Nacilias and Shoxz pushed him out of bed to get his clothes and his staff. He held onto Shoxz as they made their way to the princess. He was the last to arrive. Anri stood by the princess' side. She was finishing up her speech when they locked eyes on one another. She asked everyone to go into Geyser Hall and wait for her.

"Sister, I must speak with you."

"We are at war; I must attend to my subjects?"

"This attack is going to get a lot worse."

"What do you mean?"

Prince Alexander confessed using the White Witch to explore his abilities. Being able to destroy her soul. Having access to multiple elements and while stumbling through it all he managed to get intel that Lord Marlusha was going to release The Destroyer of Lands. The prince explained the severity of the problem. They needed a plan of action if the beast was on its way.

"Thank you."

The princess held her brother's hand as she pushed through the throne room doors. They walked down the staircase toward Geyser Hall. Everyone was gathered around Lady Phoebe. She looked up at the prince and smiled. He was ecstatic to see her moving around. The soldiers separated and allowed her an audience with the prince and princess. She embraced the prince and apologized for harming the griffins as she did. The prince was most forgiving. He advised her to treat the creatures of this world with respect. Princess Ionica stared at him in disbelief. The creatures of this world meant very little to her. She did not see them as equals, but merely servants. Lady Phoebe could sense the princess' mind was already enchanted to keep her out. She wondered why.

While they spoke, Anri's mind was summoned elsewhere as she heard her name uttered from the battlefield. Samistha lay on the ground injured with blood pouring out of her wounds. She warned her that the barrier had fallen, and their troops were at a disadvantage. The only upside was King Silverskull had managed to survive and take control of the troops. Her warning was repeated to the princess.

"Anri, I need you to gather the others. Imperial Guard, I need you to evacuate the streets and gather those who cannot fight into Saint John Nepomucene's Cathedral. All warriors are expected to head to the outer rim of the empire and prepare for a heavy onslaught. I want the archers ready for an aerial assault as well."

Anri and the Magnus' made their way down the stairs and into the streets as Geyser Hall was shrouded in uproar and cheers. The Imperial Guard left Princess Ionica's side and gathered those in the city that could not battle. Those that remained struggled with a plan to overcome the creature that approached. The Destroyer of Lands was the main objective. No one could think of a way to end a creature. The hour in which the beast was mentioned caused the empire to tremble. Ice shattered from the ceiling and penetrated the ground. Princess Ionica and Prince Alexander could sense a malevolent presence. They rushed through the palace and into the streets of the empire. They made their way to the steps of Saint Isaiah's Courtyard to get a better grasp of the situation. The sun was rising in the east.

Princess Ionica moved toward the courtyard and trembled as she felt the ground beneath her quake in fear. The waves splashed against the exterior wall of the fortress as they rose higher and higher. The serine blue water blackened as the cataclysmic beast penetrated through the surface. Its stone scaly tentacles ripped through the water attacking the highest towers. The crumbling fortress was now a prison. The siren calls of the monstrous creature bellowed through the streets. From the depths of the lake the stone serpent's face emerged. The impact sent a forceful shock wave through the air that fractured the fortress walls. The Imperial Guard rushed to the cracked surfaces in order to repair them before the empire flooded.

Alone in his thoughts, the prince lost his will. Staring at him from a distance were six black piercing eyes. As the serpent's body rose through the water, the three hundred- and five-foot snake towered over the empire. Two sharp protruding tusks lined the sides of its jaw. Gray scales covered the majority of its body, but its hands and head were formed from molted rock. The creature rested its long claws on the surface of the lake studying its prey.

Everyone stared and waited for Princess Ionica to speak. Her stoic glare fell upon them all. "Let's end this!"

Without hesitation, Amaris took off into the sky like a rocket. Electricity manifested in her eyes and radiated around her body. The shimmering sun faded as hurricane clouds swooped in. Lightning crashed down on the empire and loosened the creatures grip around its buildings. Its tentacles were sensitive and retreated into the water. Amaris returned from the sky and landed near the princess.

Before the Destroyer of Lands could regain its grip on the fortress, Lady Phoebe and Palar generated a force field to secure themselves from any more damage. Prince Alexander stood on the steps of the courtyard and watched the beast. Fang was ready to fight. He jumped out of the prince's arms and fluttered around him. A serpent created to kill a god was now here for him. He thought to himself that his birth was a death sentence to everyone who loved him. His thoughts were no longer his own. For the first time he heard the creature speak.

With an earth-shattering roar, the serpent spoke directly to the prince. The princess called to her brother, but he did not listen. The steps of Saint Isaiah's Courtyard led to the exterior gate of the fortress. The prince descended the steps and ordered that the gate be opened. Princess Ionica refused the order and commanded him to return to her side. He would not obey. If the creature did not get what he wanted, everyone would die. Lady Phoebe and Amaris gazed at one another and readied themselves for battle.

"The prince will not do this alone. We are going with him. Palar will hold the force field up once we are outside."

Before the princess could even object, the prince waved his hand, and the gate magically opened. The water of the lake lined up with the final step of the courtyard. Lady Phoebe and Amaris were the first to emerge from the force field. Lord Zylo mounted Omega and Prince Alexander mounted Shoxz. Fearing the creature's tentacles, they flew up into the sky giving them some distance from the water. Dementorol created a whirlwind and floated into the air. Jecxas stepped onto the water and took aim first. He summoned waves and typhoons to attack the great beast. Princess Ionica watched from the courtyard with Shonux and Nacilias at her side. May stared from the steps as Omega got close enough to the creature and launched Lord Zylo onto it. With his metallic claws he ripped through the molten rock. The rock took on a life of its own and attacked back. Amaris glided into the air as sparks radiated throughout her body. She raised her hands into the air and electrified the sky. The massive discharge of energy darkened the sky and jolted back into her body. She launched a massive bolt of lightning at the creature's head. Lord Zylo broke free and jumped onto Omega to retreat.

All their attacks only angered the beast even more. Prince Alexander could hear the creature calling to him. If he did not surrender, everyone would die. Alzamther's tentacles pierced through the waters to grab ahold of the prince, but Shoxz dodged them. Amaris and Lady Phoebe managed to run interference until the prince was safe behind the force field again. Standing on the steps of the courtyard, the prince looked up toward the towering beast. One of Alzamther's tentacles penetrated through the water and jolted toward the prince. Not even the force field could keep him at bay, as his tentacle was inches from his face. Anri stepped closer and her chanting grew louder. The tentacle convulsed and withered away.

She extended her hand to the prince, "We cannot let him win."

Princess Ionica watched as her brother's face lit up. He held onto Anri's hand as she led him away from the steps. He stopped in his tracks and turned to the creature as it screeched out again.

Prince Alexander roared out, "Look out!"

His words were silenced as the creature finally attacked. Jexcas was devoured as the creature dived back into the lake creating a massive tsunami. The massive wave collided with the force field as Palar tried to keep it from caving in. The force field gave out and the water that remained drenched the empire. The prince tried to focus on the creature's thoughts, but he was too late. Alzamther wrapped himself around the foundation of the empire. The monster rose from the depths once more and crushed half of the empire with its claw. Princess Ionica broke down in fear. She trembled and lost all hope. Her brother could not allow her to crumble. He dropped to his knees and tried to comfort her. Their two amulets ignited on contact.

"What was that?" questioned the princess.

"Summon your dragon!" answered the prince.

The fractured princess could not even bring herself to speak while her home was crumbling around her. Anri tried to reason with the princess, but she was deep in her thoughts. Her sadness turned to rage as she was overtaken by emotion. With each hard breath the water quaked. She began to emit a bluish glow. Anri held the prince back as she was lost in the chaos. The princess approached the lake and placed her hand in it. She spun the water around continuously and created a gigantic whirlpool around Alzamther that dragged him back into the water, releasing his grip on the fortress. The prince watched as his sister single handedly took on the Destroyer of Lands. Blast after blast she kept him from getting closer to the empire. She launched three spears of ice that penetrated the creature's torso.

Master Yami's adopted daughters took flight to protect the princess. Her stamina was nearly depleted. Prince Alexander stood on the steps of the courtyard in disappointment. He was no closer to having control over his abilities. His training could not help him in this battle. Once again, filled with hopelessness and despair he began to sink into darkness. In that darkness a voice spoke to him. For the first time he heard Fang telling him to find the Blue Flame. He took off like a bullet through the streets to reach his sister's palace. Upon entering the palace, he noticed it was abandoned. The devastating blow of Alzamther's claw nearly collapsed the entire building. Climbing over debris he made it to the throne room. The obelisk was still intact. He came around to the front and read the words '*Nos Animadverto Totus.*' The Eclipse Amulet began to glow and once again the room was encased in its emerald glow. The emerald glow escaped the oculus and set the sky ablaze. Princess Ionica and the others watched as the emerald glow spiraled into the air and surrounded the entire empire in its majestic glow.

The crystalized obelisk trickled into liquid and a whirlpool appeared in the lake. He jumped into the opening and was once again in the hidden chamber. He made his way to the Blue Flame of Oricale. The room was in ruins. Colossal stones collapsed from the ceiling and lined the floor. The great Sapphire Dragon was a prisoner with nowhere to go. He approached the foot of the flame, and it ignited. The soothing whispers called to him. He rushed to the stairs and walked toward the platform. Prince Alexander's mind was focused on the roars of the battle overhead. The Blue Flame of Oricale broke his concentration when it separated and welcomed him further onto the platform. His amulet and staff ignited. Placing the tip of the staff in the indent on the floor caused the flames to spiral out of control.

The astral energy of Apollo, Artemis, and Hermes were released without a form. The prince took this opportunity to ask them about the Destroyer of Lands.

Apollo was the first to speak, "Alzamther was born from our hatred for Hyperion. In the end it was not enough."

Not even the gods stood a chance against the beast. They laughed at the small boy in front of them. He was foolish to have summoned them. Help would not be given. Prince Alexander argued with the gods to allow him to tap into the staff's power to destroy the creature. Apollo and Hermes refused. Artemis stared at the prince for a while before noticing the amulet.

"What do you have around your neck?"

"Do not concern yourself with my amulet!"

"Feeble child!"

Artemis leaned forward to grab the prince and his amulet ignited the room. The flames in the caldron raged again. The gods glanced at one another as they witnessed his connection to the Blue Flame of Oricale.

"You are the beginning and the end!" muttered Hermes.

"What does that mean?"

"Hermes! Silence," roared Apollo.

"But there is someone we can help," interjected Artemis.

Words were no longer uttered. Apollo and Hermes turned into orbs of light and fluttered around Artemis. With a wave of her hand, she levitated Fang toward her. The prince was paralyzed to do anything. The two orbs entered the dragon causing his scales to spark. Artemis faded and entered the dragon too. Fang dropped into the chasm below. Screaming in fear he dropped to his knees and watched as Fang faded into the flames. He ran from the platform toward the side of the opening. Narsacil finally moved her position, causing the room to quake. The chunks of rocks that collapsed on her shifted and slid off. She stared at the prince as he screamed into the flames. A massive quake cracked the floor around him. Narsacil grabbed the prince with her claw before he could fall in. The floor was caving in. A massive emerald claw jolted out and then another. What once was a baby dragon was now a fully grown behemoth, twice the size of the Sapphire Dragon.

Fang was adorned with a collar of emeralds embedded into his skin. Gilled ears flared on the side of his head. His horns were over two feet long and resembled withered trees. One massive emerald was seated on his forehead, between his horns. His scales sparked with electricity as he dragged himself up. Once freed, his massive wings expanded, nearly smashing Narsacil in the face. The room was crowded. The massive Emerald Dragon lowered his body to the floor. Prince Alexander jumped from the Sapphire Dragon's claw and rushed to his back. The Blue Flame of Oricale ordered them to collapse the cavern over the meteor. It was their only way out. Once seated on his back, Fang and Narsacil blasted a hole in the ceiling and swam to the surface.

On the surface, Alzamther slammed Princess Ionica into the lake, causing her amulet to ignite. From its depths rose Narsacil with the princess on her back. The mighty dragon attacked the Destroyer of Lands. Fang pierced the lake like a bullet. His dragon fire burned through his scales and inflicted pain. Narsacil's frigid ice breath blinded the beast. The prince tried to summon water from the lake to aid the dragons, but he kept getting in Fang's way. Fang's teeth ripped at the creature's throat. He released his hold on the serpent as Narsacil swooped down from the sky and drove the creature back into the water. The others raced back to the courtyard steps to protect the fortress. Nothing could keep the Destroyer of Lands down for too long. He shot up from the water with his mouth open, ready to devour Narsacil. The dragon was caught off guard, but she managed to dodge the beast with minor scars, but the princess fell to her doom. The prince jumped from Fang to save his sister. He twisted and turned the air around him and flew through the sky toward her. He held onto her and glided her down to the surface of the lake.

She dipped her hand into the water, creating a glacier for them to stand on. Puzzled by his actions, she turned to her brother. "You used the wind to glide us down?"

Prince Alexander stared at her confused.

"You can manipulate water, earth, and now air."

Stunned by his sister's comments, he looked away in fear. Realizing his sorrow, she rushed toward him and embraced him. She kissed his cheek and cracked the glacier, pushing his side toward the shore far away from the empire, while the dragons kept the serpent occupied. As she approached the steps, Lady Phoebe greeted her. Witnessing the prince's gifts and how he was more in tune with nature than anyone realized, stirred up a plan in her to kill the creature. All beings of nature have a spiritual tether connecting them. If they could exploit Alzamther's tether, then maybe he could be undone. Staring at the beast, it dawned on Amaris that he was created of molten rock. To destroy him, they would need to separate his head.

Hearing Amaris' idea, inspired Palar. Aside from her telekinetic abilities, she could manipulate rock. Amaris needed to district the beast. She took off into the sky and twirled the air around her, creating tornados. This allowed the dragons to flee to the meadow as the storm raged around them. They ripped through Lord Marlusha's army in no time. Lady Phoebe blasted the serpent with fire, distracting him while Palar landed on his head. As powerful as she was, she could not put a dent in the rock. Faith disappeared as Alzamther's claw slammed Lady Phoebe into the water, her body heralding toward the deep abyss. Princess Ionica stopped her onslaught and dived into the water to save her.

Lady Phoebe could feel her life slipping away. It was hopeless for them to even think they could face a creature so powerful that even the gods feared. She thought back on her life as her lifeless body sank to the depths of the lake. Images of everything she had accomplished filled her mind and heart. The memories of helping those in need, the memories of saving countless lives, and even the memories of seeing the man who saved her life as a child – these were the things that kept her alive.

Her fire was far from extinguished. She would soon know what it was to be an Alulim. Just as she did when she was a child, she let out a mighty scream that rippled through the water. She was encased in a telepathic blanket of energy. Princess Ionica raced through the water to reach her in time, but what she found waiting for her blew her mind. Lady Phoebe's body released uncontrollable amounts of energy that shot her back to the surface of the lake. As she emerged, her body unleashed telepathic energy unlike the world had ever seen. Mist rose from the lake and covered the surface. Her aura was extremely hot. Princess Ionica rose from the water to gaze at the marvelous creature in all her glory. With every step, her aura pulsated and burned brighter.

Alzamther attacked Lady Phoebe, but her telekinetic powers were too much for him to handle. His tentacle dissolved to dust as it got close to her. His claw was next. He drove it down to crush her, but the force of her aura pulled away at the very minerals in his hand and crippled him. Her body glowed with the power of the radiant sun. Having caused damage to the Forest Spirits with her telepathy, she charged her telepathic power onto the great beast. With every thought he cried out in agonizing pain. Alzamther tried to move toward Lady Phoebe, but Princess Ionica created a funnel around the great beast while Palar generated magnetic fields to stop it from moving. They sealed Alzamther's fate.

With all their strength, Palar and Princess Ionica joined forces to throw Alzamther back once more. As the creature managed to rise again, Lady Phoebe's body pulsated with extreme heat. She levitated into the air, and like a bomb, she released all her energy with one clap. The others rushed away from the blast as it ricocheted. Alzamther's entire body quaked, and in the blink of an eye he exploded. The extreme force threw everyone back and wrapped their entire lake in a thick cloud of dust.

PART V - BATTLE FOR THE STONES

CHAPTER
19

AFTERMATH

Horror and dread prevailed today. The smallest fragment of hope was now a flickering light in obscurity. Seraqus, one of the four major countries of Weguard had fallen. Soon Salahea and Sharaa would meet the same fate. The thick plume could be seen from hundreds of miles away. At the edge of Forgon Forest, the Aiars gathered and watched as the dust storm scattered ash across the land. The fall of the empire signaled doom for them all. Many of them died trying to save the forest from burning. The lush green ocean of trees was reduced to the size of a lake. Those that remained gathered at their most sacred spot, the ruined city of Forgon.

It was encased by the thick vines of the forest. At the epicenter was a colossal Pinus Longaeva. Withered stone roads, half-crumbled buildings, uprooted tree roots, and faceless marble statues told the story of a long-lost metropolis. All sorts of creatures made the ruins their home. Puddles of rainwater pooled in the dried wells. Young centaurs drank from the water as their elders tended to the wounded creatures. Giant scops owls flocked to the colossal tree and swirled around it.

The Aiar twisted and thrusted itself against the floor, ripping its deep-seated roots from the ground, cracking the temple walls it grew above. Fargo, the Father of the Forest, cared deeply for the Royal Family until they abandoned them and were exiled. As he watched his children gather, the memory of his imprisonment surfaced. No recorded history, only scars.

Masters of whispers and secrets, they became the queens' eyes and ears until the unfortunate day when Hyperion descended upon their city.

Excited to see their creator, they failed to see his true intention. With a snap of his fingers, the humans burst like ballons, and their skeletons disintegrated into dust. Running for their lives, the Aiars lost their footing as he waved his hand, and the ground swallowed their feet. Their roars for help were silenced as he took their voices.

Fargo begged for answers, but the last words from his God were, "You are all traitors!"

Those words still rang in his ears. Death was truly a luxury. His creator gave them no explanation as to why they were discarded. Centuries of imprisonment tortured the mind. Seeing the world change around him, and being forced to watch, made him bitter. His imprisonment only made him more connected to the world. His roots allowed him to see and feel over far distances. With the prince's return, he followed his movements. Armies were being raised in support of his return. Lord Nebula would pay. Forgo sent an envoy to find Narnarie and request an audience.

The centaurs rallied to his call. The Aiars rejoiced at his decision. Fargo's attention diverted as he could no longer feel the prince. Plunging his arm into the ground, he could feel the vibrations of nature. Every heartbeat in the Empire rang in his ears except for one. He scanned for him as the citizens went silent, but a slight exhale caught his attention. The prince was still alive.

The grainy sand rubbed against the prince's face as he came to. A loud buzzing sound hummed in his ear. As he struggled to lift himself from the floor, he noticed thousands of soldier's unconscious. The thick clouds of debris was toxic. Each breath he took made it harder for him to stay awake. He managed to mutter for help. The air soon cleared as a whirlwind expanded around him. He was not alone, Dementorol vacuumed the air around them and condensed the toxic fumes into an air bubble. The Ilihi noticed the prince and rushed over to him. He drew the toxins from his lungs and added them to the bubble.

"Take shallow breaths."

Prince Alexander could finally breathe without choking. Standing up straight, he surveyed the land. Dismembered bodies soaked the ground with gallons of blood. Lord Marlusha's army had retreated or joined the soldiers already in death. The prince shifted through the bodies until he made it to the shoreline. Samistha's lifeless body floated in the shallow water. The lake and the empire were still encased in a dust cloud. Dementorol floated above the lake and contorted the air around the empire, creating another air bubble of toxic dust. The prince could see the smoking towers and ruins of the glorious fortress. The Ilihi returned to his side and merged the remains into one. He compressed it until it was the size of a marble in his palm. He placed it into his pocket as he wrapped his hands around the prince's waist and flew toward the steps of Saint Isaiah's Courtyard.

Princess Ionica and the others slowly came to. Alzamther's damage was extensive and brutal. The devastating blow nearly leveled the entire fortress. Everyone was wounded and in excruciating pain. Princess Ionica wanted to assess the destruction. The pillars and stones that once comprised many of the buildings lay in ruin. Omega carried her on his saddle as the others made their way on foot to the palace walls. Prince Alexander could feel his energy depleting and could no longer stand on his own two feet. The dragons were nowhere to be seen. Before he could hit the ground, Lord Zylo grabbed him and held him up as they walked. Lady Phoebe was the most fatigued of them all. She could barely speak as the others held her up and escorted her to the palace.

The palace was barely left standing. Some of the walls remained intact, but the majority of the ceiling was caved in. Shonux moved the rubble from the princess' path. She led everyone toward the throne room. As they entered, the princess found Anri and Jecxas recuperating. The High Magnus was overjoyed to see her princess in one piece.

Anri approached the princess. "Our wounds will heal, but this attack was a mere ruse."

"Speak. What do you mean?" questioned the princess.

"This attack was to distract us from their true target...Mercure Tower."

Anri and the princess locked eyes. They knew exactly what he was after. The color of the prince's face faded. He knew the tower was more than meets the eye as well, but did his sister know what the tower was intended for?

"Is he after the weapons within the tower?" inquired the prince.

His voice silenced the room. Everyone slowly turned to him with a look of dread on their faces.

"What do you know about the tower?" questioned Anri.

"Our mother wrote about them in one of her journals."

The look of confusion on her face only deepened the divide in the room.

"What journals?"

The prince dug into his bookbag and pulled out one of his mother's journals. Seeing his name on the cover caused the princess to cry. It was her mother's handwriting. She grabbed the journal and tried to read it, but to her surprise, the pages were blank.

"Is this a cruel joke?"

Enraged, she tossed the book to the ground. Angered by her actions, the prince pushed past her and grabbed the book from the floor.

"How dare you throw mom's journal on the ground!"

"Are you demented? There is nothing in it!"

Her words only caused more anger to stir in the young prince. As he flipped through the pages, he could see each page filled with words.

To prove his point, he read a passage to his sister. She was outraged that yet again he would feel the need to keep a secret from her. The others stood by and watched as they argued back and forth. The prince got the final word.

"How can I trust you, when I barely know you?"

His words cut deeper than a blade. They were family. She was his older sister. Why could he not bring himself to trust her? Just as he lost himself to his emotions, so did she. A chill crept through the room. The temperature dropped, and everyone began to quiver. Frost appeared on the iced walls, creating a thicker layer. The air quality in the room became unbearable. Anri tried to stop the princess from killing them all, but she was wrapped in a blanket of blind rage.

Jecxas intervened and ripped open the throne room doors, allowing the air from the outside to enter. With each breath the princess took, the air around her grew colder. Anri had no choice but to use magic against her.

"*Spavati!*"

The princess collapsed into her arms. She was extremely hot to the touch. She presented symptoms of a fever. Dementorol rushed her to the healing chamber along with Lady Phoebe. With the princess out of commission, the prince was finally able to explain how he stumbled upon the journals in the Hall of Records hidden beneath his parents' fortress. Each journal had a title for a specific person. He was scared to share them with anyone.

"I never meant to hurt her."

"Your sister is stubborn and will hopefully come around. Our main objective is to get to the Island of Mercure and protect the tower."

Anri explained that Mercure was inhabited by tribal women. They were skilled in combat and loyal to no one. The Jasha as they were known could help them locate the tower. It was built within a maze of mountains. Before the shifting of the world, it was once a part of the super continent Anahata.

Alexander, in his weakened state, needed rest. His friends were all exhausted as well and were in no shape to travel. Anri ordered the Magnus to rotate each of them into the healing chamber. In the morning, they would reconvene and formulate a plan. The Imperial Guard shifted through the rubble, allowing access to the living quarters. Many of the rooms were destroyed, but the Magnus' were able to make them suitable for the night, until more attention could be given to them.

Once the room was empty, Dementorol and Anri met in secret. He removed the marble from his pocket, revealing it as the remains of the dust and minerals from Alzamther's explosion. Anri ordered him to have the minerals tested and to begin gene splicing. If everything went according to plan, the princess would be able to recreate the creature. The two exited the throne room and Anri went to check on the healing chamber.

The last two remaining were Alexander and Lord Zylo. They sat on the edge of the bed, and the prince shared the journals with him: the Mystic Otrant, Ro, Asphera, Servilia, and lastly Alexander. He opened the journal with his name and to his surprise Lord Zylo could see what was written. He allowed him to read the portion of his mother's journey to Mercure Tower. Learning what the prince knew only caused his mind to stir.

"Something doesn't seem right. When you told your sister that you knew what Lord Marlusha was after, she seemed surprised by your answer. I think there is something else in that tower."

Before he could say more, a Magnus knocked on the door. On their way to the healing chamber, they passed Palar and Amaris. Lord Zylo whispered to them to meet up in the prince's room. As they entered the healing chamber, the room was frigid and circular, and in the center of the room was a pond of lavender water that ran into seven submerged tubs in the ground. Lady Phoebe and the princess were still in their tubs. Alexander and Lord Zylo removed their clothes and submerged into theirs. The Magnus began to chant her spells, and within seconds they were unconscious. Minutes turned into hours, and the only one to awaken was Lord Zylo. He dried himself off as he watched the prince stir in his sleep.

Anagar's voice echoed in his mind. Flashes of the desert sand ripped him from his dreams. He exited the tub and dried off quickly. The princess and Lady Phoebe were still too unstable to be moved. They were escorted back to their room where the others were waiting in hiding. Lord Zylo asked the prince to recount the story he read in his mother's journal.

The others were still confused.

"Lord Marlusha is not after the weapons. From your mother's journal, I believe the rumors are true..."

Amaris knew exactly what he was referring to.

"Lord Zylo, do not say another word."

Amaris stepped toward the door. Palar could sense she wanted to say something. She connected them telepathically.

"Every word we speak is being recorded in the ice sheets. The water is enchanted to retain memories. We cannot risk any more traitors out maneuvering us. We will keep this between us."

Everyone was in accord. They left for their separate rooms and turned down for the night. As they slept, Princess Ionica finally awoke. In her naked state, she refused any assistance from her attendee. She exited the healing chamber and slowly approached her throne room as if possessed. In the dead of night, she sat on her throne and waited for the sun to rise.

The princess was surrounded by voices. Nightmares called to her from the deep. Jealousy, rage, and hatred filled her heart. Life was better without her brother. Since his arrival, everything was crumbling around her. For the first time in years, in her trance-like state, she heard her mother's voice.

"Do not fall prey to his call!"

The further her thoughts went, her mother's voice slipped away. The Nebula fed on her emotions and called to her. In the end, her soul was marked. Just as the nightmare voices came, so they went. She regained her senses and awoke on her throne, covered in healed scars. Her eyes were drawn to the dark corners of the room. Shadows danced and taunted her. Distorted faces appeared and disappeared. Closing her eyes only forced her to hear a cold whisper on her neck.

"Enough!"

Her aura jolted out a cloud of frost that encased the room. When she opened her eyes again the shadows were gone. Red eyes stared at her from behind the obelisk as she placed her face in her hands.

"Do not worry, princess, I am here for you!"

She picked up her face, and what stood before her was a mutation. Four red piercing eyes, no mouth, and two small horns stared at her. As the creature came out of hiding, she noticed its goat-like legs. Its arms dragged on the floor, and its knuckles were bent, allowing it to walk.

"I will not go down easily!"

"I am not here to attack you. I am here to help you. Your sisters have big plans for your brother."

"Sisters?"

Lowering her guard, she allowed the creature to speak. It's pheromones spell-bound the princess.

"I was attacked in the Forgon Forest by Asphera. She has a lot to say."

Intrigued by her statement, she agreed to work with her. "New friend, what should I call you?"

"Amira!"

The sun was slowly rising overhead. Soon, the guards would come looking for her. Amira retreated to the shadows and disappeared. The light glistened against her naked skin. She retreated through a secret passage that stood behind her throne, leading into her bed chamber. The massive room lay in ruins. Her gowns were all scattered across the floor. A massive hole stood where the bed once was. She gathered her clothes from the floor and chose a pair of turquoise harem pants with slits up to the pelvis and a halter crop top that crisscrossed in the front and back and put it on. The healed scars on her body remained visible. As she rubbed her arm, she winced from the memory. Her hands slowly dropped to her stomach, and then she stopped and wiped her eyes.

The pain was unbearable. Taking in a deep breath she pressed on. She grabbed a pair of white boots and returned to her throne. By this time, distant voices and rumblings from outside her door caught her attention. The guards were awake and heading to their post. She exited the room and walked toward Anri's chambers. She could hear chatter from within and proceeded to knock. Surprised by her visit, Anri tried to keep the princess outside of her door. Forcing her way in, she noticed no one else was in the room. Anri was practicing magic. A salt circle and runes were drawn on the floor. In secret she was working on a spell to see into the prince's mind and bypass the telepathic block. She could not tell the princess what she was doing, or she would risk being put to death.

"I have need of your gifts. Come with me."

Anri followed her back into the throne room. With the princess' memory foggy, she could not recall how she ended up naked on her throne. Using her magic, Anri tried to probe her mind, but there was a fracture. The princess winced again. She heard her mother's voice once more. It was faint and she was crying for help.

"Do you hear her?"

Anri was puzzled by the princess' behavior. "Who?"

"My mom."

Fearing the princess was losing her mind. She grabbed ahold of her face. Chanting and humming, she managed to calm the princess down enough to see into her mind. Anri was assaulted by a wave of darkness.

"Your mind is fighting me."

The princess stared at Anri in distress.

"What did you see?"

"Darkness."

The princess was annoyed. She was done experimenting with Anri. She ordered her guards to summon her brother and his companions. Everyone piled into her throne room to discuss the towers. She confessed that there were no weapons of value inside the towers, but there were stones housed within each of the Elemental Towers. The Divine Lords built them after an ancient plague nearly wiped out the Ilihi. The plague was trapped inside the stones.

"He is going to kill us all," mumbled the prince.

"We may be able to stop him," replied the princess.

The princess and Anri glared at one another. The princess continued on to explain that within Mercure Tower was the Water Stone. During a cosmic storm, meteorites fell from the sky. It was the second time Ilihi encountered space debris. The minerals seeped into the land and unleashed a plague. The Divine Lords sought out the source and learned it originated from the Elemental Diamonds; four beautiful crystals that sprouted from the ground the same day the Divine Lords were born. These diamonds were anchors created by Hyperion. Unlike the Divine Lords who were born from their respected elements, their descendants could only channel their elements by drawing energy from the natural world. The Elemental Diamonds would allow the Ilihi to draw on that energy.

She further explained how the Royal Family issued a decree to minimize the exposure while the Divine Lords investigated. The infection grew from beneath the diamonds and took out half of the world's population. Lady Eileen appeared before Hyperion and pleaded for his help. Even God could not stop the plague, but there was a way to contain it. She was given four holy relics; the Divine Lords channeled their energy through it and drew the plague from the Elemental Diamonds into each object. The relics were separated and hidden within the towers. If Lord Marlusha was to weaponize them, he would unleash a global pandemic.

"It's starting to make sense now," whispered the prince.

"What is?" questioned Anri.

The prince once again let his tongue slip. He had no choice but to tell them what he knew. He explained astral projecting into Nathaniel Darkbloom's mind and learned that their mission to awakening Lord Nebula was halted because they were missing star fragments, so they were pivoting. Thats why the Destroyer of Lands was unleashed. It was a ploy to buy themselves time.

The room was quiet. Their faces spoke volumes. Rage manifested from the princess. Screams and curses across the room shattered everyone's attention. He could not get in a word edgewise. As her voice got louder the ice walls began to crack. Her tone infuriated the prince. He roared out to his sister to silence herself.

"You may be the Ruler of this empire, but you are not my mother."

219

His words only made the room gasp. They could not believe the response he uttered. He approached his sister and reminded her that she may be older than him, but she did not control him.

"Have you not once considered that by me telling you what I hear and see could jeopardize everything. We have no idea who is friend or foe, especially with the recent traitor in your court, but you expect me to open myself up when I barely know any of you."

The princess opened her mouth to speak, but he silenced her again. He explained Anagar's warning and expressed that he was sorry that his actions were keeping them apart, but he felt in the end it would save them all. The prince's tone escalated as his emotions got the best of him. He could not stand to have his sister lose faith in him and question his motives. He knew his intentions were pure, even if the others doubted him. They merely wanted someone to blame and needed a scapegoat. Anri walked over to aid the princess as tears cascaded down her cheeks. The fear of another great war consumed their souls. As the princess wept, the High Magnus instructed the prince to gather his emotions and calm down.

"This is not the time to deal with such nonsense. This matter calls for a strategic plan. Rebuilding our empire takes precedent, but at the same time so does keeping the Elemental Towers safe."

Princess Ionica could not deal with two tragedies at once. Her empire was crumbling beneath her feet while Lord Marlusha launched a coordinated attack. She could not abandon them in their hour of need. She instructed her brother to handle the invasion. As a future ruler he needed to prove himself. The princess would oversee the reconstruction of her empire.

Prince Alexander could hear the disappointment in his sister's voice. Instead of talking it through, she internalized it. He knew they were counting on him, and the eyes of the world were watching. A deal done in the dark nearly cost him his sister. The lives of many were at risk and the young prince was emotionally defeated. He regretted listening to Anagar and Nathaniel Darkbloom. Hopefully, he would learn the meaning of trust.

"Ionica...sister...I know I cannot take you away from your duties, but we must work together to stop Lord Marlusha."

She let a smile escape from the corner of her mouth, "I understand you are worried about who you can trust. Anri will join you."

Hearing her name split her in two. Before she refused to let her train the prince, now she was more than happy to let her go. Worried about her decision, she tried to speak, but Princess Ionica reassured her that she needed her amongst his ranks. With an embrace she whispered to her that she needed a spy to report back on his movements. Her loyalty was tested; spying on a royal was one thing, but the heir to the throne was another.

Seeing her hesitation, the princess promoted the High Magnus to High Chancellor. The newly deemed High Chancellor could not help but cry for joy. The celebrations came to an end when the princess ordered her servants to return to their post. Shonux, Dementorol, Jecxas, and May took their leave while she spoke with those that remained.

Upon her throne, her body was battling against her, and the pain was unbearable. The clouds shifted overhead blocking sunlight from entering the oculus. The lake below stood in perfect harmony with the crystal obelisk.

"This voyage will be dangerous. The Island of Mercure is a territory most people would not dare to voyage to. The tower is protected by magic as old as our realm."

Glancing at his sister he noticed she was trying to keep minimal eye contact with him. Filled with guilt, he turned and opened the frozen doors. His emotions were written on his face. He let her down and felt he could never redeem himself. Turning and looking back at her she gazed over to him with a blank stare on her face – a stare that slipped from disappointment to numbness. Grabbing both handles he sealed the gates behind him. The ghost of war took a toll on the prince's heart. He blamed himself for the destruction of the empire. He regretted coming back. He was in no shape to handle what came next. His faith was shattered, and his mind was raddled.

Anri could sense the worry on the young prince's mind. She watched him as he stood in deep thought. Silence. All were silent as they headed toward the docks, like walking to the guillotine.

"What is done is done. No need to dwell on it."

Anri's words were ignored.

Her compassion exuded tenfold, but he could not bring himself to warm up to her. Climbing out of the dark spiral hole was harder than one thought. The High Chancellor saw his face change and she slowly grabbed his hand. Pity was for the weak. They needed strength...unity.

The docks of the fortress were no more; all that remained was floating rubble. To their surprise, Asla and a few of the dwarves were still alive. They avoided the Imperial Guard after the battle. After the battle, Fang was seen flying off to tend to his wounds. Narsacil flew overhead screeching as she looked for a place to rest. The dwarves were caught up to speed on the plan, but they would not partake. If another war was approaching, they needed to rally others. Asla vowed to seek out her dwarven kin and return with fighters. She held out her hand to the prince and shook his.

The prince and Nacilias mounted Shoxz, while Anri and Lord Zylo mounted Omega. Amaris, Palar, and Lady Phoebe requested to stay behind. An eye on the princess was warranted.

CHAPTER
20

WATER STONE

Making their way through the sky, they climbed until they pushed past the clouds. West was their destination. The atmosphere changed as they approached the edge of the continent. Descending, Shoxz clipped the water with its wing. The misty air from the Sea of Forgiveness - a vast and magnificent piece of art splashed against their faces. A squadron of giant oceanic manta rays jumped around them the further they got from land. Shoxz pulled up to avoid their deadly stinger. Following the path of the sea creatures led them to the shores of Mercure.

Covered in a thick fog, they proceeded with caution. Once the outer layer was breached, the beautiful island could be seen. They dismounted onto the moist sand and noticed a ridge with beautiful plant life. As the waves attacked the shores, the smell of salt water was overbearing. The mainland of the island was three feet above the sand. The outline was covered in red barberry and pink queen. Pushing himself over the landing, the prince was met with tragedy; countless Jasha were murdered. Only one remained; a statuesque woman appeared from the tree line. She wore a pink bra that was wrapped around her neck and connected to a hood. As she jumped out of the tree, they noticed her silk pink pants with ties around the ankles. Her feet were covered in a cloth-like sandal.

"This is as far as you go!"

Blood stained her lips. Her hand trembled. Her left eyebrow was cut. She barely had any fight left in her. Prince Alexander lifted his hands in front of himself, showing that he came in peace. She took a step forward and collapsed into his arms.

"Help me!"

"What is your name?"

"Sora..."

Placing her on the floor, the prince ripped a piece of her pants off. He applied pressure to her ribs to stop the bleeding. She was the last of her kin. The Jasha were slaughtered by a monster leading a battalion of Lord Marlusha's servants.

"How far have they gotten?" questioned the prince.

They were already too late. The Temple of Zephyrus had fallen and soon Mercure Tower. Anri healed her fractured bones and internal bleeding. In the eyes of a Jasha, a payment was due. Sora would lead them to the tower. With minor pain she still led them across lush grass toward a mountain range. The sun disappeared the closer they got to them. Overhead, a storm was brewing, giving them their name the Mountains of Rain. Sora slightly turned to the side and slid through an opening that was invisible to the eye. Due to their massive size, Shoxz and Omega remained in the rear. Each passageway led them to dozens more.

Sora led them further into the maze. The rain became snow, the deeper they traveled. One final passageway led them into a courtyard of snow. At the center was a massive tower of ice that pierced through the clouds. The snow-covered ground remained untouched by footprints. Anri raised her hand to her chest and faced the palm of her other hand toward the tower.

"*Otkriti.*"

The spell was obsolete. The charms were already dismantled. Anri and the others approached the crystal doors, but it was an ambush. The courtyard came under attack. Omega and Shoxz's wings were bound by shadows. A dark mist swooped down from the surrounding mountains and swirled into a horde of dark servants, concealed in purple robes with the Nebula symbol embroidered on the hood. Prince Alexander and the others were bound in chains of darkness. As they resisted, the chains burned at their flesh. One of the Dark Servants approached the prince and rubbed his finger across the amulet. It ignited to the touch, and like acid, his body collapsed onto itself. Anri laughed as the others cautiously approached to search them. Her chilled laugh froze the chains, allowing her to break free.

Swirling around on the ground, she created a tidal wave from the snow, causing them to lose their balance. With a flick of the wrist, she released the others from their chains. Heavy breathing could be heard from behind her. Blood-lust-driven, Lord Zylo leaped over the High Chancellor and ripped the spinal cord out of one of the Dark Servants. His long tongue licked the blood spatter off his fur. His claws swelled before he sprinted onto another one and dug it into his face. Anri ordered the others to watch her back as she prepared a spell. Dancing and kicking the snow around her, the air grew thick with mist. A song was sung, and a blizzard was summoned. She ordered the orders to huddle together behind her. They were untouched by the storm. Once the blizzard subsided, the Dark Servants were frozen to death.

With the tower already compromised. Sora kicked the massive doors open, revealing a cylindrical room of glaciers. At the center of the room stood a spiral staircase that led to the upper floors. The walls were brimming with carvings. The tower was completely empty. There were no statues, no paintings, not even a table. Where were the weapons the prince heard so much about? The higher they ascended into the tower, Anri began to understand the carvings. Each floor depicted a cosmic event in LunaSol's history. On this floor, it depicted four meteor showers. One depicted the Blue Flame of the Oricale falling, another the elemental plague, but the other two she was unfamiliar with. The first depicted a man and a woman falling from the stars and the last showed a ship falling from the sky onto LunaSol. As they cleared each floor, they encountered none of Lord Marlusha's warriors.

They slowly ascended the final staircase and could hear whispers. Sora lowered herself to the floor and peeked up. To her surprise, there were three powered-blue creatures bound to the floor while multiple Dark Servants paced the room. Prince Alexander stuck his head out fand noticed them kicking at the creatures, trying to get answers out of them. The beasts roared out in pain and then purred to one another for comfort. The invaders sought access to the shrine above the room. The enchantment was impenetrable. The Dark Servants refused to send another scout into the sky to try and breach it. Those that tried were lost to the storm clouds.

The three creatures noticed the prince peeking out. Without a word, Lord Zylo leaped over him and ripped away at a nearby Dark Servant. Anri enchanted the ice beneath their feet and created spikes to pierce through the bodies of those remaining. Prince Alexander and Sora unchained the massive beasts and helped them up. They descended the staircase to seek refuge, but the creatures led them to the back of the tower. On the third floor, one of the beasts pointed to the wall and opened a passageway into a hidden chamber carved into the mountain. The dark and ominous corridor led them to a massive cavern filled with water from the nearby sea. The damp environment made it extremely cold for everyone except for the creatures. Each of them nursed their wounds as the others recuperated. Anri and the others gawked at the creatures as they were not indigenous and interrogated them.

Yoin was their home, but Earth was their ancestral birthplace. The name confused half the room but fascinated those who knew of its existence. The three yeti brothers fought against Hyperion in the Imperial War on Earth and witnessed the death of their god - Oceanus. To preserve his knowledge, they escaped with the help of Baru, one of the Cardinal Deities. The yetis lived their lives out on Yoin until the destruction of the universe. The biggest of the three, Giohuyre, shared that it was like the blink of an eye, and they were back. No one knew of the existence of Hyperion's new universe, until Lady Udana stumbled into theirs.

The smallest, Selrettry, revealed that Lady Udana traveled into Yoin with Lord Grevis' help. He confided in her when he became aware of the portals. After building his temples over them, he sent troops into each, but none returned. She would not allow him to send any more civilians to their death. While he slept, she stepped into the vortex and found herself surrounded by a blizzard of ice and snow. Weaving her hands, she disrupted the storm and set it at ease. From a distance, a massive, four-eyed white wolf attacked her. His paw flung her into a nearby pile of snow. The beast leaped over to her, ready to feast, but she created a ball of ice around her. His teeth pierced the sphere, but she managed to blind him with a tidal wave of snow. The battle lasted hours until she harnessed the full potential of her powers. Her spirit radiated with Oceanus' aura, and this caused the Lord of Yoin to halt his attack.

The third brother, Awcoup, explained that Lord Baru was unable to communicate with her, so he summoned them since they could speak the common tongue. Lady Udana stood for years with them on Yoin, studying about the past. When she returned to LunaSol, she learned she was only gone for a week. As a gift, Lord Baru allowed them to return with her and serve as counsel. Lady Eileen and Lord Grevis were the first to witness her return, and the prince's mother shielded them from Hyperion's gaze. The yetis were heartbroken to learn that their mistress would not be returning to them. For thousands of years, they waited for her, and when they heard her voice at the door, they were foolish to believe it was her. A Dark Servant spelled her voice to mimic Lady Udana's. They lowered the charms to embrace her but were outnumbered.

Sora sighed.

"If the dark servants were able to make it to the top of the tower, how come they could not reach the shrine above it?"

Her question caused them to chuckle. Selrettry brought forth a small tube of glowing water.

"Without the Water of Life, they will never gain access."

The Water of Life was rumored to be the very water Hyperion used to give life to humans. It was kept in a vial for safe keeping. One of his many relics that were stolen from Heaven. Lady Udana enchanted it to become a key for the tower. While distracted, Sora revealed her true intentions and tossed three grenades in front of the yetis, blasting everyone back. The Water of Life was tossed into the air, allowing her to grab it and escape back through the cavern into the tower.

Sora made her way back to the top to find the entrance to the shrine, while the others tried to regain consciousness. Lord Zylo was the first to stir, as a raucous sound echoed his ears. The shrine was breached. Prince Alexander gathered all his strength to get up from the muddy floor and make it to the opening in the cavern. In pain, they all stumbled to make it to the final room but were too late. At the center of the room a staircase descended to the shrine above. At the foot of the staircase was a circular carving of a cloaked figure with his hands holding the relic.

Anri ascended the staircase, and her worst nightmare was realized. Sora's burnt body stood at the foot of the shrine, while the lifeless bodies of countless Dark Servants tainted the pool of water from Lady Eileen's journal. The altar where the Water Stone was rumored to rest was empty. A bleeding female elf tried to hold herself up. The seductive elf caused a stir amongst the group. An Elf of the Twilight, a rare species of elf that was spoken about in legends. Her skin was an alice blue with eyes as black as night. Her hair and eyebrows were white. Prince Alexander turned his face in embarrassment as he noticed her body was nearly exposed. Her breasts were covered in a chained bra, and she wore a purple loincloth.

"I see Lord Marlusha sent more of you. I will not go down so easily."

Anri stepped forward. "We are here at the request of Princess Ionica. We are here to help."

The elf laughed, "Help?"

The battle was already over. What could they do to help? Blood continued to trickle down her arms as she staggered toward them.

"You are too late!"

She fell onto Nacilias. The prince lifted her up to lay her across his lap. Anri used her magic to tend to her wounds. She purified the water from the pool for her to drink from it as the yetis stacked up the dead bodies into a corner. Zaos, as she was known, fought to keep her eyes open.

"What happened here?" questioned the prince.

Using blood magic, she placed her bloody palm on the floor and drew a rune. She chanted beneath her breath, and the water from the pool animated. Sora's betrayal played out right before their eyes. Zaos was seated on the top step of the shrine. Sora approached with Dark Servants at her back, demanding the Water Stone. Tapping her finger on the closest pillar, initiated a lockdown protocol. Shimmering runes appeared on each of the pillars. Perched on the top of the shrine was a statue of a coiled, four-winged serpent. Lightning crackled down and shattered the statue, unleashing the stone's protector. Many of the Dark Servants were either sliced through by its dagger-tipped tail or burned to ashes by its blue flame. As the first group fell, others came, but this time they came prepared. A figure cloaked in shadows approached the massive beast holding a stone of their own. It was as if the very air went stale. The stone weakened the beast, until inevitably, they captured it. It affected Zaos' powers as well. She fought through them, but the closer she got to the stone, the weaker it made her. Her speed fell, and so did she. Sora was able to remove the Water Stone from its altar, and in the end, she was betrayed as well. The cloaked figure incinerated her.

Torment clenched the prince's heart. Every step he took forward was ten steps back. He fled Earth because he was in danger, and now, here he went chasing after it. Zaos fell asleep in his lap as Anri, and Lord Zylo inspected the shrine. Anri used her own spells to uncover the tower's secrets. The altar of the stone radiated with magical properties.

"There is spiritual energy still lingering."

Anri weaved her hands around the altar.

"*In morte et in vita; prope te vocamus.*

Ignotae spiritus incoepit."

(*In death and in life; we call you near.*

Spirit of the unknown reappear.)

A thick fog of blue astral energy swept through the shrine. A sliver of it took the form of a tall, blue-skinned man, with long black hair. They stood before a dead god, Aegir, God of the Oceans. His life was bound to the Water Stone, a giant Eastern Murex that he once used to control the oceans. Like many of the gods that Hyperion slaughtered, their essence remained in many of their tools. The Divine Lords used the souls of the gods to bind the plague inside. The god paced around them as they talked. He touched the ash marks on the shrine.

"Auressela!"

"What?" questioned Anri.

"What happened to the protector?"

"Gone!" replied Zaos as she rose from the floor and stared into Aegir's eyes.

Zaos had gained enough strength to finally talk. She was furious with the god. His spirit was bound to the stone and to the shrine. He was the last line of defense and allowed the Dark Servants to imprison a Titan.

Lord Zylo quickly turned to her, "A Titan?"

Aegir explained that the Titans first appeared during the Purge. An era when thousands of creatures were rounded up by the angels and placed in secluded areas since they were devouring humanity. During the second meteor shower, the bodies of the Titans fell from the sky. The angels were too preoccupied with the Purge, so the Divine Lords intervened and secured them. The Titans were made of geo-technical matter, which dated back millennia. Three Titans were called upon to protect the shrines from danger and bound to the towers.

Prince Alexander turned to Zaos, "Can you tell us anything about the stone they had?"

"I have only ever felt energy like that once before. From the Nebula. The stone feeds on the darkest parts of your soul until there is none left."

Aegir's form began to fade. Anri's magic could not sustain him anymore. Aegir cautioned the prince to stay as far away from the stone as possible. It would be his undoing. Nacilias looked up at the prince in fear. What did Aegir know about the prince?

With one stone down, they needed to secure the others, but Mercure was still under siege. They could not leave without liberating the Temple of Zephyrus. Zaos agreed to show them the way. She summoned two tiger hook swords and ordered the others back into the tower. The staircase rose and sealed the outer shrine. The yetis carefully lifted the Water of Life and handed it to the prince for safekeeping. As they made their way back into the Mountains of Rain, Zaos led them to a fork in the road. Turning left, they came upon a dead end.

Overhead, the screams of carnage could be heard. Lord Zylo's eyes darkened with the moon rising. His fur spiked as his claws protruded from his hands. He scaled the mountainside as the prince mounted Shoxz with Nacilias and Anri and Zaos mounted Omega. The massive lycanthrope ascended the clouds with vengeance. He leaped onto the temple balcony, where archers were waiting for them. He was shot in the leg but bit the head off the shooter. The balcony wrapped around the summit of the mountain. Five archways led into the heart of the temple. Each pillar was carved into Pegasus' standing on their hindlegs.

Before Omega could land, Zaos leaped off and dug her swords into the head of another warrior. Their battalion dismounted to aid the monks fighting. Prince Alexander searched for his necklace. Once in hand, he pressed the center button, and it popped out into a full-blown staff. Without relying on the elements or spells, he battled his way through Dark Servants.

The temple floors were covered in massive pillows and silk sheets. The atmosphere seemed rather intimate prior to the assault, but now everything was covered in blood or body parts. The prince was caught by surprise as a group of frayjains joined them. Their talons ripped through enemy flesh as they swooped down from the sky. The monks retreated before their head monk. A man adorned in green robes with brown jewels. His sleeveless robe stopped short of his knees. In one hand he held a massive hammer and in the other an arm of armor. Gong was a well renowned Magnus and served Lord Grevis' daughter, Madam Argia, until she was overthrown by her sister.

Dark Servants were dropping like flies. The few that remained retreated deep into the mountain temple. Anri walked over to Prince Alexander and the others and escorted them inside as they awaited news from the head monk. Lord Zylo wiped the blood off his fur as he approached the others.

Two frayjains approached; the golden frayjain spoke first, "We ask that you follow us to the ruin room."

Entering the temple only confirmed the prince's suspicions; dozens of naked bodies lined the floor. They were not ready for the ambush. Gong confessed they were preparing to celebrate the Lunar Rite; once the full moon was at its peak the monks would have sex with Ilihi and draw on their energy to grow in strength. At the center of the temple stood a chamber that appeared to be crumbling. Golden tiles still held the circular ceiling up. At the center of the room was a platform with a broken archway, like the archway the prince appeared through at the Temple of Notus. The remaining Dark Servants surrounded the ruins of the Western Gate. Four creatures were chained to a nearby stone. Gong gestured for them to hide behind the pillars that were scattered around the room. The two frayjains drew their weapons as they jetted behind the pillars stalking their prey. Gong drew his hammer from his belt, revealing himself to the enemy. He spun his hammer, and it expanded. Without consulting the others, he sprinted at them but was rebounded by a force field.

Laughing at his failed attempt, the Dark Servants removed their hoods, revealing themselves. Gong recognized his kin. They bore a blood mark on their forehead. The symbol of the Nebula. They surrounded the archway and held one palm toward it and raised their other hand into the sky as they chanted:

> "*Od sjevera do juga na istok kroz Zapada; otvoriti vrata koji je bio blagoslovljen.*"
> (*From the North to South to the East through the West; open the gate that was once blessed.*)

Near the group of captured creatures stood a cyan-colored stone reflecting energy off it to sustain the force field. Anri moved closer to the stone and used every magical spell she could think of on it, but she realized it was Serendibite - an agent that could withstand magic. The forcefield began to shatter as the ruin gate rebuilt itself. A massive wave of energy expanded from it and lashed out across the room generating a dust storm. Using it for cover, the Dark Servants entered the gate.

Gong rushed to rescue his imprisoned servants. The portal began to flicker. It was closing. The prince, Nacilias, and Shoxz left the others behind as they rushed in. The blinding light faded to destruction. They stood on a platform with a massive gate on one end. The floor was covered in scorch marks, and the bodies of the corrupted monks bled out onto the floor. The guardian of the gate was a Hagerod, a sheep-like humanoid with the torso of a horse. The prince tried to help the creature to its feet, but its wounds were poisoned.

Malifa was another of his sister's familiars. The amulet glistened as he approached her. She ripped a key off her neck and handed it to the prince.

"Do not allow them access to Yoin."

Upon touching the prince's flesh, the key marked his skin. Malifa collapsed, and the life in her eyes faded. The key levitated and floated toward the locked gateway. As it entered the keyhole, the runes around the archway ignited and tossed everyone back. The blinding light faded, and a valley of snow could be seen within it. Snow trickled in covering half of the platform. From a distance a dark shadow grew and grew until Baru appeared. His majestic four yellow eyes glared down at the prince. Shaking off the snow, he revealed a blue strip descending from his neck down to his tail and four blue stripes on his stomach. His paws were massive and could crush a house. Mist escaped his nose as he inhaled the prince's scent.

"Lord of Yoin, I am Prince Alexander Whitespear. Lord Marlusha grows closer to reviving Lord Nebula. Will you stand with me for the coming war?"

The massive, four-eyed wolf used his nose to push the prince. In doing so, he noticed the amulet around his neck.

"Your sister gave up her familiars to protect our realms from danger. Now, you summon me to fight your war?"

"This is not just my war. He will come for your worlds once he is done with this one."

Baru was a proud beast, but he knew it was inevitable. Hiding behind wards and portals would not stop darkness from creeping into his world. He agreed to come to the prince's aid when summoned.

Behind the prince, a tear unfolded between the worlds. Gong appeared; accompanied by two unicorns, one with a magnificent orange mane and the other with a bewitching black mane. Solaris' orange mane flicked with flames. Its white body blended in with the snow. Nefania's purple body radiated dark energy as it walked. Lord Grevis found them in Nightfeather Forest; their mother was near death as she pushed them out of her womb. He saved their lives and raised them. Solaris could light up a darkened room, and Nefania could darken it. Gong believed the mother was infected by the Nebula and altered the creature's biology. With Malifa's death, an opportunity arose. Solaris and Nefania would take her place as guardians.

Gong watched as Baru turned and left. He grabbed the prince by his forearm.

"What did you do? The Cardinal Deities were entombed for their safety."

"Baru has agreed to help fight against Lord Nebula."

Gong was confused. He stared into the winter wasteland and then back at the prince.

"Let us take our leave of Vordaris."

It triggered the prince. Anagar's vision. Vordaris was a planet from the original Solis System before Hyperion's remaking of the universe; now it was a waypoint into different realms.

As they returned to their realm, Gong confessed, "The gateways were raised centuries ago to prevent the creatures below from ever entering the other realms."

He escorted them back into the ruin room. Dozens of monks and Frayjains bowed as they gazed upon the prince. Two massive birds, Massio Eagles, stood at the back of the room. They once guarded the treasures of the gods. Lord Grevis adored them and bred them. They were massive beasts with a twenty-foot wingspan and a height of eight feet tall. Lord Zylo stared at the creatures as he passed them and followed the others down a corridor. They were being led to the Room of Gravity, a massive planetarium. Unlike the entrance with its five archways into the temple, this side had a massive opening. From it, all of Mercure could be seen. They were at the highest point of the mountain.

In the center of the room was a massive replica of their solar system. Nine planets - Dramadear, Vectis, LunaSol, Martoris, Bodaris, Jupario,

Oceanis, Platonis, and Glace - all rotated around the burning star, Sol. Everything was so primitive on LunaSol, but the technology used to build the machine was centuries ahead of its time. As they examined the planetarium, Gong explained its purpose. Lord Grevis first used it to study the cosmic storm that appeared every ten thousand years. It ravaged the planets and made them uninhabitable. LunaSol seemed to be the only planet life continued to thrive on. He found it odd and made a discovery that could have gotten him killed. Reporting it to Hyperion only made matters worse. His research was halted at the command of his creator. Lord Grevis found a gash in the universe.

Lord Grevis wrote a journal and left it behind in Gong's care. The text described how the cosmic storm was a result of the massive destruction of the previous universe. It tore through the fabric of reality, creating the gash. The storm grows more powerful every time it comes. If the storm builds enough force and breaks through the gash; all of reality can crash upon itself. They were left in charge of making sure each realm remained safe and keeping all the creatures in their own realms.

Lord Grevis was the first to encounter a being from another realm. During one of his astrological studies, he stumbled upon a bloodbath. Countless Hagerods were slaughtered and drained of their blood. He tracked down a rip in reality and came across a group of vampirics. Lord Zylo growled at their mention, sworn emeries of the lycanthropes. They were created on Earth and imprisoned on Vordaris. Immortal creatures that survived on blood. Their bite could kill a lycanthrope and vice versa.

Drail's bedtime stories fluttered into the prince's mind. One of his earliest stories was about a war between the vampirics and the lycanthropes. It got out of control that the gods had to intervene. Gong laughed as the prince shared his story.

"Dear boy, there is so much more to that."

Gong's statement caused the prince to squint his eyes. What did he mean by that? Gong stared into the prince's eyes; he was not going to get an answer out of him even if he asked. Turning from the conversation, he walked to the balcony and gazed out into the sky. The moon was at its apex. The ritual was ruined. Anri and Lord Zylo walked out to the balcony to comfort him. The prince was the last to exit. He sat on one of the pillows and stared up at the stars.

"What happened to the vampirics?" questioned the prince, shattering the silence.

"Hyperion cleaned it up!" responded Gong.

Lord Grevis never saw them again. The rips were magically patched up. It would not last. If the cosmic storm raged, the tears would continue to appear. Gong believed the attack on Mercure Tower was connected to it somehow. Lord Grevis hid his research from Lord Marlusha because he grew infatuated with the gash in the universe. It became an obsession of his. Lord Marlusha could easily release Lord Nebula, just by tracking down the keys to his prison. Why go after the Elemental Plague? The prince did not see the connection. Gong's ranting confused him. With the Water Stone in Lord Marlusha's possession, he would go for the Earth Stone next.

A knock at the door forced all of them to turn. Two Frayjains approached the chattering group. Gong gestured for the two Frayjains to proceed and stand at his side.

"Ultra, what news do you have?"

"Our troops have gotten word that Lord Marlusha's servants have divided their legions. They are taking the Water Stone to the Black Kingdom, and some have made their way to the great gate that divides Seraqus and Salahea."

"Poepe, I see you have a scroll in your hand. What news?"

"The Pharaoh of Salahea requests an audience with the prince. He has sent this request to every kingdom across the three continents in the hopes that word would draw you out."

"I do not trust the pharaoh." Gong let slip.

"I cannot refuse his invitation. If this can get me closer to the Earth Stone, then I must go."

Anri and Lord Zylo glanced over at one another. Prince Alexander could not turn away from this. He needed to follow them into Salahea. The prince's conviction and determination shocked the room. The child that once feared the worst was now ready to take on Lord Marlusha and bring him to justice. His path was now becoming clear. Salahea was their target.

CHAPTER
21

GAEATONIC GUARDIAN

No one would be travelling tonight. Every bone in their body ached. A bath was much needed. Ultra and Poepe escorted the prince and his companions out of the planetarium and into the lower levels of the temple. The prince's room had a view of Mercure Tower. The glistening tower sparkled in moonlight. Monks came into the room and drew a bath for him. They removed the prince's clothes and scrubbed him from head to toe. He was given a green, cotton robe to sleep in. Nacilias and Shoxz were also catered to and washed. Anri and the others were treated with the same hospitality. The monks departed; gentle silks caressed their bodies as they turned in for the night. Shoxz slept at the base of the bed on the floor. Nacilias cuddled next to the prince.

Whispering winds eased their pain and guided them into slumber. In the land of dreams, no one was truly at rest. Hot desert sand grazed the prince's cheek, forcing his eyes open. He was no longer in the Temple of Zephyrus but standing in a bazaar. War and famine consumed the desert city. Children ran scared, trying to gather food from the floor. Blood flowed through the streets like a river. Where there once stood buildings, now there was rubble. Combing the streets, the prince found himself at the center of the city, staring at a man from a distance. His vision was clouded by a sandstorm. He was able to get a glimpse of him, augmented with parts of his body comprised of geotechnology. The cries of pain and devastation shattered the dream into shards of glass. Prince Alexander awoke in a cold sweat. Nacilias was still nuzzled next to him. He rubbed his head and turned over to go back to sleep. This time he was unbothered by dreams.

Night faded to dawn, and the sounds of beating drums startled them awake. Light was just barely peaking over the mountains. The monks were gathering for prayer. They knocked on the prince's door and were welcomed in. The prince was given new clothes to change into, beige shorts and a hooded vest. Just as before, they undressed the prince and dressed him. Fingerless gloves were placed over his hands and boots on his feet. The monks combed argan oil through the prince's golden blond hair. They were the last to be escorted into the ruin room.

It was as if the battle from the night before never happened. From floor to ceiling, the room was covered in a variety of silks. Pillowed beds across the floor. Candelabras were lit, and incense was burning. The prince watched as Gong and his fellow monks chanted and drummed away. Once their morning ritual concluded, Gong led them through a corridor to a limestone bridge that connected the temple to a bird sanctuary on a nearby peak. Hundreds of Massio Eagles nested in their perches. Shoxz and Omega were too exhausted still from battle to fly; Silverbeak and Blackthorn would usher them to the outer rim of Salahea. Each of the creatures had baskets as saddles.

Gong bid them adieu as they settled into the baskets, and the gigantic beast soared into the sky. Northeast, they flew back to the shores of Mercure. Covering more ground, they were already over the Sea of Forgiveness. Prince Alexander took this time to read his mother's journal.

The Elders continued to pressure Lady Eileen to allow them to harness the prince's power, but she refused. Hyperion would kill them all if he knew what they were planning. Any misstep could harm them. They needed to keep up appearances. The Elders took a sample of the child's blood and were ordered to work on a cure, while Lady Udana and her traveled back to Venus Tower. Upon their return, they were met with resistance; soldiers of Lord Celeio were lined up ready to attack. Enchantments kept them covered from Hyperion's gaze, but what they found was unsettling. The armored warriors bore a painted sigil that was unfamiliar to Lady Udana. Lady Eileen was disgusted; she knew the sigil very well. Lord Celeio had aligned himself with Hyperion's third wife, Gaea. The allure of her relics must have enticed him.

The soldiers detained them until their commander arrived. Prince Dacus-Nexus, eldest son of Pharaoh Kimhairo, grandson of Lord Celeio. No one outside of the Divine Lords and the Royal Family was supposed to know about the towers. This compromised their entire plan and left them vulnerable. The prince demanded that Lady Eileen drop the enchantments on the tower, but she refused. Prince Dacus-Nexus cracked his whip at her, an act of treason. The prince ordered his soldiers to take them into custody. His actions were foolish; even outnumbered she could hold her own against them. The soldiers were defeated, and the prince's mouth, hands, and feet were bound to prevent him from channeling the terrain.

With the prince in custody for treason, the scandal would catch the attention of Hyperion. She would deliver the prince to his father herself. The smell of saltwater soon faded. The prince closed the journal and peered over the head of Silverbeak. From the distance, a colossal quartzite wall divided Salahea and Seraqus. The two birds screeched as they descended to the valley below. A herd of Bull Mooses were startled and stampeded toward the wall. Their bronze-colored fur sparkled in the light as their gray-colored horns collided with one another as they raced past each other. The prince and the others dismounted, allowing the Massio Eagles to fly off.

The battalion made their way over the hill and bore witness to the interminable vision of greatness. The massive quartzite wall stood as a totem of the past; carvings depicted an endless war. The massive structure shimmered in the sun's glare. The prince was transfixed on the Gates of Salahea. His concentration on the images of the Holy War was broken as Anri and Lord Zylo raced down the hill in a panic. Zaos raced after them with Omega on her tail.

Shoxz pushed the prince and told him to hurry up, because she could sense something was wrong. As Prince Alexander moved closer to the enormous wall, he noticed that the gate was open and on the other side stood an endless desert. As far as the eye could see, all the soldiers were turned into stone. One lonely soldier stood inches away from them.

Anri panicked, "Kilmao, what have they done to you?"

Lord Zylo interjected, "Who is this person?"

He was one of Princess Ionica's generals and a skilled swordsman. Zaos came around the High Chancellor to examine the body. The aroma of Elven magic sparked her senses. The work of a Pandemonium Elf. Sniffing the statue, she was able to pinpoint the curse. A form of dark magic called Gorwenchi: if the victim stared into the caster's eyes, they would turn to stone. The curse could be undone, Zaos gathered sand from beyond the gate and requested a drop of blood from the prince. He extended his hand to her, but Anri slapped it away. This type of magic was dark and malevolent.

As an Elf of the Twilight, she could practice the Arcane Doctrines and Nexus Disciplines. Practices cultivated by humans and their covens. Dragons were the first magic wielders and passed their knowledge onto a select group of humans before they were enslaved and hidden away. Those that did not fall into Hyperion's slumber taught the Fae. Those who follow the path of virtue access the Arcane Doctrines and those who followed the Nebula practice the Nexus Disciplines. Many tried to master both, but it ended in death. The darkness was too tempting; only the Elves of the Twilight were lucky enough to master both without succumbing to it.

Zaos slit her hand and placed her blood in a vial. She did the same to the prince and placed it in the vial and mixed the sand in as well. The mixture of their blood caused a reaction. The sand absorbed it and spiraled out of control. The vial vibrated in her hand and exploded. She blew the residue onto the statue, causing it to crack.

Zaos muttered, "*Ambrazsis.*"

She kicked Kilmao in the chest and flung his body out of his prison. He was gasping for air. His stone tomb nearly suffocated him. Anri's judgment was written all over her face. She was displeased. Kilmao was safe, but the fate of his troops was grim. They were stuck in stone longer. Each body she removed was already dead. The swordsman urged her to stop. The Pandemonium Elf and her troops were plotting to kill the pharaoh's sister before stealing the stone. There was an abandoned city nearby where they could take refuge for the night before traveling into the heart of Salahea. A sharp pain took over the prince's shoulder. His vision faded, and his dream resurfaced. The countless bodies. Deep blue eyes stared at him through the sandstorm. Why now? What was the importance of this vision? Lord Zylo noticed the prince was not engaged in their conversation. He shook him out of his trance.

"Are you okay?"

Prince Alexander replied, "Something's wrong. The place we are going..."

"It is haunted by the sins of the past," interjected Zaos.

Her answer was followed by her turning her back to them.

Going to Salahea without Fang was a bad idea. The prince worried about him. Since leaving the empire, there wasn't any sight of him on their voyage. He asked Kilmao for a favor as the swordsman was heading for the Empire of Seraqus. He asked for him to request a search party be sent out for Fang. The swordsman agreed and left their side. Anri mounted Omega, and the prince mounted Shoxz. Once through, Kilmao closed the gate behind them. A vast sea of sand stood before them. Dry wind brushed against their cheeks. In the distance, swirling ash danced over the dunes. Tracking through the hot terrain was not easy. There was no clear road leading to any town or city. For miles they continued east with the sun on their backs with an insatiable thirst for water. Salahea was a boiling pot. The heat was too much for Prince Alexander. His body quaked with agony. His sweat drenched his amulet, causing it to ignite. An emerald glow overtook the valley and then retreated to the prince. For a while they waited to see what would happen, but there was nothing but heavy silence.

The scorching sand shifted beneath their feet. As they stared out into the desert, the whistling sand rattled like a snake in the distance. In seconds, they were staring at a bizarre sandstorm approaching. Zaos and Anri came together to enchant a barrier around them. The storm was upon them. At first it sounded like raindrops hitting the roof of a house, but through the sand they could see lightning. This storm was not natural. The sand continued to pummel the barrier like a drum. Two ruby-colored eyes stared at them through the sand. Four protruding fangs appeared as it rushed at them. A serpent composed of sand attempted to crush the barrier in its teeth. It jolted them through the sky and launched them deeper into the storm. It continued to come for them until Zaos and Anri decided to fight back.

The barrier needed to fall. As it came down, the others dug themselves into the sand in a group, as Zaos was the first to attack. The serpent opened its mouth and tried to devour her, but she held the creature's fangs back with her hands and feet. "*Fizieren!*" Sparks of electricity shifted up Zaos' spine and cascaded across her body. The electricity swirled through the creature, crystalizing it. Anri slowed the creature down by slowing the flow of time around it. Zaos was unphased by her magic and broke free. She summoned her weapons and sliced through the sand creature, shattering it to pieces. Anri, in a fit of rage, swirled the glass pieces around her, creating a tornado, and as she screamed out, flung the shards in every direction, dismantling the storm.

Out of the chaos rose a crumbling, ruined city, with dozens of stone temples, passages, and statues. Mountains of sand pressed against each side in an attempt to reclaim it. The remnants of war were written everywhere. As they walked through each corridor, the wind whistled and shifted the stones. The ghost of the past was talking to them. The city had been undisturbed by outsiders. Many of the inscriptions on the stone were faded. There was no sign of animal life either. Each corridor became a maze. The deeper into the city they went, the prince felt a presence following them. Its energy seemed familiar. They had finally arrived at the center of the city.

The smell of burnt flesh filled the prince's nose. Flashes of his dream resurfaced in his mind. His amulet was getting hot around his neck and began to glow. No one else noticed they were too busy looking around. Staring at its glow made his vision blurry. Once it stopped, he rubbed his eyes, and they began to deceive him. Flickers of light, in the silhouette of a person stood there watching them. The prince's stares forced the abnormality to retreat to an abandoned building. The ceiling was caving in. Dampness was in the air. The deeper he went, he noticed there was a staircase that led into a dark and ominous basement. He followed it deeper into the ground until he came upon a massive cavern. Torches were lit all around, but the prince's eye was drawn to the center of the room. Towering more than four hundred feet was a geo technological pyramid. The closer he got to it; he noticed two others stood nearby. They were mostly silver with green accents. They pulsed like heartbeats to the touch. He cleared off some of the ash and noticed there were inscriptions etched all over.

It was like a force of nature; the energy he sensed earlier was now massive. It was all around him. He turned from the pyramids and noticed multiple figures of light watching him.

"Stand back. I do not want to hurt you."

His warning held a little bite. The sparkles of light continued to walk toward him. Fearing for his safety, the amulet ignited and generated a force field around him. The silhouetted figures were paralyzed by the emerald glow. The sparkles of light began to take shape and revealed six hooded figures in tawny garments with elaborate pleats and golden beadwork. Each had an armored, chest plate weaved into the fabrics for protection. Their hoods drew his attention the most; they resembled the hoods worn by the Magnus' that helped Eris kill Hans. Using their tattooed hands, they removed their hoods. He noticed runes mixed in with a few images. The faces of the two Magnus were not among them. The salt-and-pepper-haired woman who stood in front of him smiled and bowed her head. She seemed harmless. Prince Alexander rubbed his hand over the amulet, and the force field came down.

"Grab him already."

The prince locked eyes with the woman. She was a warrior by appearance. Her armored breastplate revealed her stomach and arms, while her kilt showed off her muscular legs. She wore a fur cloak and a horse diadem on her forehead. In one hand she held a golden spear and in the other a shield. Rather than wearing shoes on her feet, she had belted sandals.

"No, he is the prince."

The woman stood aside as a mysterious man approached. From head to toe, he was covered in a snakeskin suit. His face was covered with a golden helmet that connected to a collar plate of gold with blue accents. The plate connected to a black and gold cape that seemed to camouflage against other objects. His hague blue and black robes were held together at the waist by three interlocking leather belts. Unlike the female warrior, he wore black boots to cover his feet.

"Traitors! All of you. What do the Gaeatonic Guardians want with me?"

The room broke out in awe. How could he know who they were? Their mission was secret; their name only was known to those within their group. What knowledge did he possess? The older woman approached the prince and held his hands.

"Child, we have much to discuss. I am Queen Ishuzuya, one of Lord Celeio's widows; you have much to learn."

Could she be trusted? The Gaeatonic Guardians served another god. Lord Celeio was dead for centuries, and now his widow turned up in hiding. Why? They headed toward a tunnel that led further underground. Sulfur filled the air as they came upon an old temple structure carved into

243

bedrock. The Temple of Terra was a haven in times of need. Weg was once the kingdom of Terra Firma, and through this temple, many tunnels connected to the smaller kingdoms under their dominion. Queen Ishuzuya shared the story of the temple as she walked to her throne. Lit torches gave life to the spectacular images carved into the wall depicting the Gaeatonic Guardians fighting a war. Collapsing pillars barely held the ceiling in place. Sand fell with the pressure from above. The queen approached a small pyramid-like throne in the center of the room and took her seat.

"How is all this still here? I saw this place burned to the ground?"

"You saw?" questioned the queen.

"Speak up! The queen asked you a question."

The prince turned to see who was barking orders. A man with blue hair and pale skin crossed his arms and puffed his chest. The others had darker skin. His robes were white and blue. A full-length cloak trailed behind him. He had padded shoulders with embroidered golden trimmings, cuffed wrists, and a raised collar. On his forehead was a shimmering crystal connected to a head chain hidden in his hair.

The prince could not reveal his vision. Queen Ishuzuya stared into his eyes. Glimpses of the tablet reflected back at her.

"You saw him, didn't you?"

The queen's question forced the prince to nod his head yes. That face. His blue skin. His augmented body. It was not something he could forget. She revealed he was the progenitor, the one from which Oricale was replicated. Born from the blood of the First Ones and Titans. The First Ones kept him preserved in stasis. After Lord Nebula's imprisonment, the world saw stability for a time. Until he descended from the void and brought destruction in his wake. His sole mission was to consume the lives of the Alulim that escaped the void and their offspring - the Potuliari. Killing them off wasn't enough for him. He turned his attention to the Ilihi. Their blood threatened him. The pyramids were built to destroy anyone with Ilihi blood. Before he could activate them, the Gaeatonic Guardians fought against him.

"How did you survive?

"Ancient magic!" interjected the man with the helmet.

They did not fight alone, The Elders, the rebel aliens that Lady Udana helped, also joined their cause. Combining their forces, they were able to seal him away after he destroyed the kingdom. The prince was amazed to hear the mention of the Elders. Why would they help these traitors? Each of the Gaeatonic Guardians lined up and introduced themselves.

The man wearing the golden helmet was Fatei. The blue haired man was Alexi. The woman with the spear was Destiny. To her right, the prince's eyes were drawn deeply to the man with a lightning bolt scar on his eye. His chest and abdomen were exposed to the world. He marveled over his great physique, lusting over him. By appearance alone, he was no more than seventeen years old. The prince tried not to stare too long, but his eyes could not resist true beauty. He introduced himself as Mahadi and kissed the prince's hand. The prince locked eyes with him and could not help but smile. The man was stunning, causing the prince to blush.

Mahadi pushed a wooden wheelchair toward the prince with a blind woman seated. Her eyes were covered with a white cloth to protect them. Seated on her white, curly head was a beautiful piece of art – a crown with three stallions. A beauty unmatched by any in the room. She also wore armor – a metallic corset, depicting legions of angels surrounding an archway. Her legs were covered in snakeskin material. Norn, as the others called her, was the deadliest of all.

Many of their faces were different from those in his vision, but they held the Gaeatonic items.

"What do you know of our ranks?"

Queen Izhuzuya tried to scan his mind for answers, but her magic was silenced. The amulet ignited upon her intrusion.

"That will not work on me."

Alone, the prince was rather cocky, but he was not ready for Mahadi. The young man approached and gently touched his hand. A spark of lust radiated through his body. His eyes lingered on his muscle lines. The light of the amulet faded, allowing him a glimpse into his mind. The Tablet of Anagar came into view. Mahadi tried to dig further but was thrown out.

"You were in the presence of Anagar!"

The prince removed his hand from Mahadi's. He allowed him to slip in when his guard was down. Fearing the man read too much, he ordered the queen to allow him to leave and find his companions. Queen Ishuzuya refused.

"Anagar, he is the one showing you the past. This is not good. His visions are not always reliable."

245

His head was spinning. What game was this woman playing at? Prince Alexander backed away from her. He held onto his amulet, ready to attack, but she tried to ease the tension in the room.

"My prince, what did you see exactly."

Prince Alexander revealed seeing Lord Celeio betray his mother and had his Magnus' perform a ritual to prove their loyalty to Gaea and were rewarded with the golden items in their possession.

"You saw the original Gaeatonic Guardians. We were not there during that time. We did not get dragged into this mess until far later."

"Mess!"

The prince was in the presence of fallen angels. Before becoming Gaeatonic Guardians, the six of them were once Nyhpalim, they oversaw the Solaris Angels. Their fall from grace was not by choice. After their fall they came into Lord Celeio's service. They were forced into the Gaeatonic Guardians after many of their members were killed.

"How did you fall?"

After the abnormalities and time fluxes began appearing all over LunaSol, Hyperion retreated to the far corners of the Universe to study the Tarsem. The Nyhpalim were left in charge of the Heavens. A shadow infiltrated the citadel and made its way into the Relic Room. Inside was an antler crown carved from a tree. By the time the Nyhpalim arrived, the shadow had broken off a piece of it and attacked them. The shadow stabbed each of them. The crown belonged to Gaea; through their blood the figure bound them to her service. Only after her resurrection would they be free.

Torturous pain overtook their bodies. Crying for help, they summoned Hyperion from the furthest reaches of space. No amount of pleading could get him to see reason. Cursed with fear he would not allow them to speak. In his eyes the Nyhpalim were traitors. Using the Flame of Aterma, he tried to burn them from existence, but it failed. He resorted to clipping their wings and flung them to LunaSol with no memory of their past lives, or so he thought. Lord Celeio found them wandering the desert and brought them to safety in his palace. He fell in love with Ishuzuya after years of service and enlisted them into his council. The other members converted to their cause.

The prince felt sorry for them. Who was this shadowy figure? Was it Eris? In his mind, she was the first to control the shadows. He allowed his thoughts to manifest.

"Why did Eris want to unleash Gaea?"

The guardians laughed.

"Who said anything about Eris?" laughed Alexi.

Sand fell from the ceiling, landing on the prince's hair. Shaking off the residue, he looked down at the floor. Hopeless. At every turn, there was someone else trying to gain power through his death. None of Soldiel's stories depicted other villains, but apparently his sister, Asphera Bloodmoor, was more sinister than Eris. Marked by the Nebula rather than Satan, she was the first to channel dark magic. Lady Eileen found her in the aftermath of the second meteor strike amongst the broken shards barely breathing. Over time, her wounds healed, but her purpose was clouded. Corrupted and blinded, she trained under Nathaniel Darkbloom.

Prince Alexander grimaced. Nathaniel was rotten to the core. His motives were never to help the prince. Since the beginning, he has been working on hidden agendas to destroy him and LunaSol. Queen Ishuzuya could sense the prince already had his own interaction with the Great Deceiver. Their mission to turn the Nympalim into Gaea's puppets was just the start. Hyperion's hand was forced, and he unleashed the Horseman of Pestilence. Thousands of Magnus' and Mortals began dying off. Asphera placed herself in jeopardy; being a Magnus, she was at risk of infection. She sought to rectify her mistake. Stealing a feather from the horseman and combining its energy with a nebula shard, she was able to create the Elemental Plague that tore the world in two. It was not a natural disease like the Divine Lords thought. Hyperion would never confess it began with him. The Elemental Stones bound the Horseman of Pestilence.

Lord Marlusha's plan was finally starting to make sense. This massive plague cross infected three major groups. He had to find the remaining stones and stop him. He gripped the straps of his bookbag. The journals. All he could think about was his mother's journals. One was named after her.

If the Elemental Plague played a huge role in shaping LunaSol, why did Soldiel keep it out of his stories? Fatei could feel the prince's concern. It was a lot of history to take in at once. His fragile mind needed time to wrap his head around it. Ever since the prince's return, darkness resurfaced in troves. Unholiness spread across the land, bringing war. It was fate that the prince stumbled into their chamber. Learning about the true connection to Gaea could only help weed through Anagar's visions, but what about Saturos? What role did he have to play in this?

"I saw something else. Someone else."

"Who?"

Prince Alexander revealed he witnessed Saturos being presented. Norn gripped onto her wheelchair. Knowing about the child was even more dangerous. What he saw was the day Saturos was cast from Heaven. Long before they were. A baby left in the desert sands to be eaten. Lord Celeio's Magnus' felt the godly presence and he investigated it. No one knows why he was cast out of Heaven, but while on LunaSol he was unaware of his parentage. The Divine Lord saw it as a blessing to groom a divine child.

The prince's presence in the temple did not go unnoticed. Each of the relics held by the guardians vibrated with a low hymn. Queen Ishuzuya watched from her throne, as the other guardians began to act unusually. They circled the prince like stalking prey.

"What are you doing?"

None of them spoke a word. Their eyes were dilated. Possessed by their relics they attacked the prince and forced him into submission. He was imprisoned in Gaea's Eye. Her symbol appeared beneath his feet and a force-field of golden energy wrapped around him. The force of its energy kept the queen from rising from her throne.

"You are hers now!" they roared in a trance.

The Gaeatonic Guardians were no longer in control of their actions. They circled the prince and chanted. The force of his cries and roars from the depths reached the surface. The incantation had begun, and no one could break the circle. Emerald light erupted from the amulet and created a barrier around him. Nacilias and Shoxz sniffed out the prince and followed his scent further into the cavern. Rumbling through the tunnels signaled that his friends were getting closer. Anri was the first to race into the temple. Blood formed in the prince's eyes as the chanting grew louder. Lord Zylo attacked the barrier but was electrified and sent flying into one of the statues. Shoxz and Omega tried to attack those circling the prince but collapsed under the immense energy. Anri tried to use her magic to enter the barrier, but it held strong and kept her out.

Queen Ishuzuya was able to get her footing.

"ENOUGH!"

Summoning all her strength, she shattered the symbol beneath the prince and flung all the Gaeatonic Guardians' back. Prince Alexander was numb. It was eating at his soul. The queen rushed to his side. She could not remove her hands from him. She examined his eyes and could see sparks of emerald and gold. Gaea tried to force her way into him. The energy of Oricale was fighting back. His body levitated into the air as his aura glowed with fury. The prince's soul was rejecting Gaea's hold. The Gaeatonic Eye appeared on his forehead and electrified him. The surge of energy took over the room. The two powers were fighting for control over his body. Everyone sought shelter from the storm. The monumental power exuded from the prince nearly wiped out the room. As the dust settled, the prince was left standing. Gaea did not prevail this time.

The Gaeatonic Guardians were sick to their stomachs. Gaea's influence over them was stronger than initially thought. Anri would not allow them anywhere near the prince. Shoxz and Omega helped Lord Zylo up. Destiny walked over to an underground river behind Queen Ishuzuya's throne and brought them some water. The prince did not hold them responsible for their actions. Anri and the others did not have all the facts. Anri examined their faces and was at a loss for words. She recognized the queen. For centuries, she was presumed dead. Anri was the only one to bow. The others did not respect her authority.

Chaos raged around them as the prince's companions argued with the Gaeatonic Guardians. The prince knew he had to step in. He expressed gratitude to the queen for saving his life from Gaea's parasitic attack. With their connection to her, he could not risk being around them anymore. Information was critical at this point. Knowing how the plague was created and what the stones housed, only made their objective more vital. Having the queen's counsel would be invaluable, but the longer he strayed from their mission, the closer Lord Nebula came to power. He filled Anri and the others in as Queen Ishuzuya warded the minds of her guardians from Gaea's meddling.

She hugged the prince.

"I pray for your safety. Your mother would be proud."

He held back his tears. Pride. What a word? All his life he felt like an outcast and was never good enough. At every turn, he was arguing with his sister. What would she find pride in? A small smile escaped his lips. His dark thoughts faded. He held onto the queen and questioned her about the

249

sand serpent. The Pandemonium Elf was clever. It was her doing. Stumbling into Weg would keep them occupied and allow her to get further ahead. Mahadi touched one of the pillars and closed his eyes. The sand above shifted and became his sight. Her trail was leading her to the Kingdom of Salahea. Lucky for the prince, the temple connected to its outskirts.

In his mother's journals, she spoke about Prince Dacus-Nexus. What connection did he have to this pandemonium elf? Were they being led into an ambush? Anri could see the anxiety written on his face. The prince would be meeting Pharaoh Atemu-Nacus, son of Pharaoh Kimhairo. He was now the ruler of Salahea. Just as he thought he was putting the pieces of the puzzle together; the puzzle only grew bigger. The prince was sworn to secrecy. If Salahea learned that the queen and her servants were still alive, it could cause a revolt. They agreed to her terms and were shown to one of the passageways beyond the stream. It was a straight shot to the kingdom.

Mahadi stopped the prince from leaving. Their bodies nearly touching. Lips just at a distance from each other.

"Promise me we will see each other again."

Quivering lip. He forced himself to swallow.

"We will."

Mahadi's soft gentle skin caressed his own as they embraced. His warm breath against the side of his neck entranced him. The prince pulled away as he noticed Anri staring at him. The tunnel continued as far as the eye could see. It came to an end as the passage was blocked by dozens of boulders. Anri tried to move the boulders with her magic, but it caused the ground to quake. They feared any sudden movements would cause a cave in. Zaos' magic was stronger; with a tap of her hand; the boulders floated backwards into a massive cavern. An old torn bridge remained intact, hovering over a lake of lava. Her concentration was shattered by the extreme heat and the boulders fell into the lake sending up streams of lava into the air.

Nacilias was the first brave soul to walk across. Anri and Zaos crossed together, followed by Omega and Shoxz. Lastly, Prince Alexander and Lord Zylo took their time to cross, fearing they might fall into the pit of lava. As the last of them crossed the bridge, they began their ascent. Nacilias led them up the stone staircase until they reached their exit. Lord Zylo maneuvered to the front and was able to push it up and over, exposing them to the dead of night. He jumped up out of the hole and helped lead everyone else out. It was a tight squeeze for Omega and Shoxz, but they managed to escape unharmed.

Starlight illuminated the world in a blanket. Camp was set up underneath a group of trees resting on the outskirts of the kingdom. The night air filled their lungs with scratchy sand. As the cool breeze allowed them some peace to rest for the night.

CHAPTER
22

BLOOD OF MY BLOOD

The rising sun boiled the desert sand. The fabric of the tent was nearly see-through. Crouching soldiers circled the perimeter. Anri stirred from her sleep and slowly exited her tent with her hands up. Lord Zylo ripped through his causing the soldiers to draw their weapons.

"We are here at the Pharaoh's request. Please put down your weapons."

One of the warriors asked, "State your name?"

"I am High Chancellor Anri of the Empire of Seraqus."

Another one of the warriors spoke out against Anri, "The Pharaoh is not meeting with anyone. A formal request must be placed through his council, and it will take about two weeks for them to grant you an audience."

"We are here at his request!"

"Be gone!"

"There are traitors amongst his ranks. We must get to the pharaoh."

His words only elevated emotions. Omega and Shoxz flapped their wings, causing the warriors to stumble back. Lord Zylo hunched his back, showing off his massive teeth. One bite from this carnivorous beast could turn them. They knew not to get too close. Prince Alexander could not allow Lord Zylo to kill innocents. He pushed past them and urged the High Guard to listen. In the struggle to get through, his amulet ignited. They dropped to their knees and pleaded for forgiveness. He could not believe the terror his amulet inflicted upon them. The prince urged them to announce their arrival to the pharaoh.

The General of the High Guard ordered his soldiers back to their post. He yelled up to the watchtowers and ordered them to open the gates. The guards blew their fierce horns, signaling the delegation's arrival. The enormous stone gate slowly cracked open; dust shot out from the center. As the view behind the gate became clearer, the prince's excitement turned to exasperation. The smell of fecal matter, urine, and a variety of putrid smells lingered through the streets. Children begging for money, naked with scars all over their body. As they moved through the second ring, he noticed woman with elegant dresses walking by without a care in the world. The customs of Salahea were very different than Seraqus. As they continued further through the city, the prince noticed a young boy steal a piece of bread from a stand and was nearly beaten to death by a group of men for not being a resident in that ring. That was the final straw. He broke away from the others and ran to the boy's aid.

"Leave him alone!"

They scurried from the floor and drew their hidden knives from their garments. The High Guard ran toward the prince and secured the scene. The men were taken into custody. The prince demanded to know why the citizens of Salahea were living in such conditions. Baffled by the prince's reaction, they chose not to answer him. He needed to address his concerns with the pharaoh and his council. It took everything within the prince not to explode. The emerald light of his amulet flickered with each breath. Anri grabbed his hand and grabbed his face.

"Not here. Not now!"

He was outraged to see people being treated like insects. First his sister and how she viewed the animals of this world, and now the pharaoh. He could not sit by and watch this tragedy continue to unfold. As they continued down the streets, whispers of an emerald dragon caught his attention. Noble women in their wine-colored robes adorned with gold lingered in an alleyway purchasing slaves watched as the prince approached.

"Where did you hear about the emerald dragon?"

Realizing who he was, the women bowed and finished up their business.

"The dragon was seen flying over the desert."

This was good news. Fang was alive and well. He was not too far. With Zaos and Anri's help, they could use a locator spell to find him once this business with the pharaoh was concluded. After his outburst, they were escorted toward another stone gate. This layer of the kingdom was heavily guarded. The floor trembled as the doors opened, revealing monumental statues of gold. They lined the walkway toward a spectacular staircase. Dozens of people paraded about talking to one another. The prince bit his lip; those within these walls had the luxury of impeccable robes, while those outside, were burning in the sun with rags.

Salahea was nothing more than tyranny and oppression. He could not stomach the thought of being there any longer. Before he could tell the others, he wanted to leave, they were approached by a slender woman. She wore a veil that widened and spread below her shoulders. A cloth mask covered her nose and mouth. The prince stared into her amber-colored eyes. She was covered in a rosewood-colored sleeveless dress that stopped at her ankles. The bottom was like a sarong with golden accents depicting hieroglyphics. Unlike the civilians, she had golden sandals and ornate jewelry. She was another servant of Gaea, as she flaunted the Gaeatonic Eye on her jewelry.

She did not speak a word to the General and his soldiers. She just waved her hand dismissing them.

"I will take it from here!"

Without a peep, the warriors returned to their post.

"Allow me to introduce myself; I am High Magnus Atenzu. The pharaoh is ready to receive you. Please follow me!"

They followed her up the grand staircase and into the palace. It was shaped like a pyramid. The corridor was enormous, and the light from the outside faded the deeper they went. Torches lit their path as they got further in. The palace consisted of tiles, limestone, and metal. Beautiful sculptures and wall fixtures depicted Salahea's rich history. Atenzu stopped as they arrived in the throne room. Below them, in the center of the square room, was a pyramid throne. Four steps led down to the throne. The floor was covered in bronze and painted tiles. There were three additional doors leading out of the room. Two directly on each side of the throne and one behind it. They each had four steps leading down onto the platform. Cauldrons of fire illuminated the luxurious view. Six memorial statues with offerings were elevated in the corners with narrower steps leading to them. One honored Lord Celeio and another Queen Ishuzuya.

As they marveled over the architecture, Atenzu stood near the pharaoh's throne. The prince's inner rage manifested again as he noticed the Gaeatonic Eye on the closed door at the back of the room. Clenching his fist, Shoxz brushed against him. He rubbed her mane until his attention was drawn once again to the door. It opened, and the room was flooded with the pharaoh's servants. They bowed as the Pharaoh entered after them. The pharaoh was smaller in stature, like the prince. He wore a headdress with Gaea's symbol and a necklace as well. His honey-colored skin was on display as he approached with no shirt on. An embroidered belt held his half-pleated kilt up. With each step he took, his servants made way for him to get to his throne. His jade-colored eyes locked onto the prince, staring aggressively at him from the crowd.

Once on the throne, the entire room dropped to their knees and bowed. The prince was the only one who did not. Atenzu was mortified at the lack of respect.

"Bow before the pharaoh."

"No!"

"Bow now, or you will receive sixty lashes."

The prince slowly turned his head, "Lay a hand on me and I will have you gutted."

The room grew savage. Trying to intimidate the prince, the Magnus' began pushing against him. Anri and the others surrounded their prince in his defense.

"I will not bow to a man who allows his people to starve and die of disease. I do not respect tyrannical rulers."

The room went silent. Speaking against the pharaoh was unwise. He rose from his seat and slowly descended the throne and walked toward the prince.

"Why do you spew these allegations."

Atenzu interjected, "Do not pay mind to them, Pharaoh. They have come here to spread lies."

Anri was furious with Atenzu. "High Magnus, you will remember your place. You stand before a royal. It would be wise to watch your tongue."

Atenzu's eyes widened. Growing tired of the pleasantries, the prince blurted out his true feelings.

"Pharaoh, while you are in here enjoying the comforts of fine living, your people are dying. Starving. The living conditions outside are horrible. You cannot be so blind?"

The pharaoh was appalled by the prince's allegations. Could it hold weight? Were his servants not reporting back the truth? For thousands of years, the true power of Salahea rested in the hands of the Magnus'. His powers were limited. The pharaoh was a political figurehead that they reported to. As he stood inches from the prince he observed his face. There were no markers indicating he was lying.

The Magnus' could see the pharaoh was going to cave. Atenzu interrupted, "Pharaoh, you cannot believe him?"

The pharaoh responded, "But I do."

He ordered all of his servants out of the room while he spoke with the prince and his companions. The Magnus' did as they were told, allowing them to speak in private. Gruesome detail after gruesome detail filled the pharaoh with dread. Did his father face the same misguided counsel? The pharaoh wondered what travesties he inherited. He could not listen anymore. The Magnus' reported a prosperous kingdom, but it was all a lie. He called for an emergency summit.

"It has been brought to my attention that the kingdom is not doing as well as I was led to believe."

The room was filled with fear. The pharaoh scanned the room and noticed two of his High Magnus' were missing. He ordered Atenzu to retrieve them. She left his side in search of them and returned with two men; their dark purple robes caught Nacilias' eye. The prince turned to see what his friend was growling at and noticed them as well. He drew his staff and blasted the two men behind her.

"You declare war in my house?"

Pharaoh Atemu-Nacus roared out against the prince. Before he could attack the prince, the prince waved his hand, forcing the pharaoh into his throne.

"You summoned me here while you are conspiring with traitors. You're Gaeatonic Guardians and their loyalty is to Gaea, not you. These men are working with Eris and tried to have me killed at the Shrine of Glory."

The two High Magnus' rose from the floor and belted out in anger, "How dare you attack us?"

"You are the reason Hans is DEAD!!"

No one was prepared for what came next. Flooded by pain and hate, he was blinded by emotion. The fires within the cauldrons intensified. The ground trembled at the sheer force of energy radiating from his body. The wind from the outside flooded the room and surrounded him in a funnel of dust. The ground and ceiling cracked under the extreme pressure. Anri and the others slowly backed away from the prince as his power dramatically increased. A massive explosion of wind threw everyone back. The two Magnus' tried to escape through one of the doors, but with a wave of his hand, the prince raised the limestone floor, sealing off the exits.

Under the pressure of the wind, no one could move. The pharaoh tried to stand but was in excruciating pain. Atenzu lowered her head to the ground and whispered, "*Vjet huric.*" She lifted her head and opened her mouth. Sucking in the air, she was able to channel the wind around her and shield the pharaoh in a bubble of air. Anri tried with all her might to communicate with the prince. His mind was too clouded to listen to reason. She was able to drag herself close to him and grab his hand.

"Stop this. Think about your mother."

At that moment, she caught a glimpse of him. Even in his altered state, his mother still had an impact on him. He opened his eyes and was surrounded by darkness. He could hear Anri's faint voice calling out to him. Each step he took forward, his foot was covered by a dark liquid. It became thicker as he tried to run. He began to sink into the liquid. The pain in his heart grew, causing the wind to intensify. Anri could barely breathe. She held onto his hand and cried for him to come back to them. As he continued to sink into the darkness, he heard his mother calling to him. She grabbed him by his hand and pulled him from the liquid.

"You cannot fall into depravity. Stop this! Fight back!"

"Help me!"

The prince's eyes shot open. He was released from his emotions, and the elements around him simmered down. His eyes locked onto Hans' killers.

"I will kill them."

Prince Alexander moved away from Anri and Lord Zylo. He began to approach the throne where all the Magnus' were. Pharaoh Atemu-Nacus gazed into the prince's eyes and saw hurt. Even as Pharaoh, he could not refuse him. Something inside of him believed the prince. He called for the two Magnus' to come before him.

"Heishini and Akmadin, you are being accused of treason and murder. These allegations are serious. What do you have to say for yourselves?"

"The prince is mistaken," explained Akmadin.

"See this for what it is - a ploy to take over," roared Heishini.

"This is going to end now."

The pharaoh ordered Atenzu to uncover the truth. Before the other Magnus' could move, she froze everyone in place. She used the Eye of Gaea to read their minds. She lifted her arm to her core and summoned an amber stone from her armband. The stone levitated into the air and spun in place. She entered their minds and saw Prince Alexander was telling the truth. She tried to dig deeper. Their minds were shrouded in shadow. As the shadows parted, she was able to see the truth. They tortured countless citizens and servants, turning them against the pharaoh. She saw a pact of blood between them and Eris. As she dug deeper it became harder for her to see, but she was able to glimpse Venus Tower. Their true mission was still not complete. Atenzu returned the stone back into the armband.

"Traitors."

The prince's accusations were in fact the pharaoh's nightmare. Atenzu recounted her visions and ordered the pharaoh to execute them.

"Since their inception into the High Council they have been plotting your downfall. They are the reason the outer city is dying. They are the cause of devastation in our country!"

With their secret out, they had to escape. Heishini evaporated into a cloud of mist. Akmadin disappeared, but he reappeared near the Magnus' and attacked them. He stomped on the ground, shattering the area around him, and flung the shards at the prince and his companions. Anri dissolved them with a spell and ordered the others to seek cover behind one of the statues. One of the Magnus' brought forth a sapphire encrusted shield and slammed it into the ground, creating an energy field around them. Another summoned blue fire into his hands and attacked Akmadin, tossing him against the wall. Two others tried to apprehend him, but his body turned to dust.

The pharaoh roared out as he reappeared behind a small, blind, fragile girl. He gripped her by the neck and disappeared again.

"Sister!"

He cursed and screamed at his subjects for their incompetence. It was their job to advise him of threats. They allowed evil to influence their ranks and cloud their judgments. He could no longer hide behind blindness and false leadership. The pharaoh kept rambling and repeating that now they had the key. Prince Alexander tried to get him to come back to his senses. He wanted to know why they would kidnap her and why he kept rambling about her being a key.

"They are going to kill her!" The pharaoh gripped his chest. He could no longer trust his servants. He turned to the prince for his help. Princess Toa became blind because of their older brother, Prince Dacus - Nexus. He tried to kill them and take over Salahea. Lady Eileen found him trying to break into Venus Tower. After he was brought to the kingdom to face his crimes, she learned about the poisoning. Every healer tried to save the princess, but none were successful. Lady Eileen was able to heal her, but it caused a rift between her and Lord Celeio. They never spoke again. After Dacus' betrayal, Lord Celeio used the princess' blood as the key to the tower.

Anri was consumed by the devastating information.

"This is what happens when children play at rulers."

Her words sparked heads to turn.

"Anri, what has gotten into you?" questioned the prince.

"A child is going to die for the sins of her grandfather. The Divine Lords plotted to kill Hyperion and never saw it through. They got themselves killed and left us with children running the world. This is a travesty."

One of the pharaoh's High Magnus' tried to silence her. A goddess among women, towering at six feet. Unlike the others, she did not wear a mask or headdress. Atop her hair was a sun crown embedded into her dreads. They twisted alongside her face, covered her ears, and cascaded down her chest. She had a sun painted on her forehead and white dots along her eyebrows. Around her neck was an embroidered black and gold collar with three strands of cloth that connected to her off-the-shoulder dress. The entire thing was black and gold. Her ribs were exposed as the dress revealed two thigh-high slits and alligator skin pants underneath. She had armbands and leg bands that reached her knees.

Anri did not take kindly to being subdued. The beautiful Nefertiti was brought to her knees in excruciating pain as Anri rubbed her index finger and thumb together. The pharaoh's servants rallied against her, but her power was even more powerful than all of them combined. She waved her hand and clenched it in place, immobilizing them.

"This is an act of war."

The pharaoh reminded Anri that she was a servant of Seraqus and within his dominion. This angered her even further. Prince Alexander tried to step in, but Lord Zylo held him back. Anri slowly ascended the steps of his throne.

"I am no one's servant. I am the granddaughter of Lady Udana."

Prince Alexander and the others were enthralled; not even Lord Zylo saw that one coming. The pharaoh fell back into his seat. In his lifetime he believed to have met all of Lady Udana's descendants, but apparently this one escaped his memory. The pharaoh's mother, Amatila Moonspark was a granddaughter of Lady Udana as well. Amatila was the daughter of Sir Gabriel Whitespear and Trinity Moonspark, which made the pharaoh and the prince kin. The prince was stunned. The prince watched as the pharaoh questioned Anri about her lineage, but she refused to speak about it any further. The laws of LunaSol were archaic; the children of the Royal Family had unlimited authority in any country that hosted them. The same law applied for the children of the Divine Lords. As for their descendants, the further removed they were, the more limited their authority became in the presence of one another. Since Anri and the pharaoh's mother were both grandchildren of Lady Udana, they held the same authority, so that meant while in her presence, she held more dominion than him in his own kingdom. Prince Alexander approached her and whispered into her ear to stand down. This was not the way. She did as commanded – hand shaking, sweat drenching her face. Her head was clouded by emotions.

The Magnus' were guided by fear and retreated from the room, all except one. Blue flames appeared around his fingertips as he approached her.

"I am not of noble blood, but I will not allow anyone to threaten my pharaoh. Compose yourself."

261

"Saturos, to my side," ordered the pharaoh.

The strands of fate intertwined and led them to him. He stood out from the others. His skin was pale ivory with sapphire eyes and choppy brown hair. His high collared, asymmetrical, ankle lengthened vest had a circle cut out, exposing his muscular chest. The fabric blended black and gold with accents of blue. On top of his white sheer pants was a kilt held together by three royal blue belts. There was a holster on each side for his swords.

Saturos turned to the prince and kissed him on the cheek. Alexander inhaled his scent: lavender, and rosemary. For people exposed to the extreme sunlight and desert sand, they did not smell musty. The prince held onto his upper arms and noticed two gold bands were wrapped around them. He stepped on the prince's foot with his gold and blue leather boots.

"Apologies, my prince."

The prince was silent. He was in awe, being near a godling. Saturos noticed he was making him uncomfortable and stepped back to give him space. He turned to Anri and watched as she apologized for being baited by her emotions and not only verbally attacking but physically attacking his servants. The pharaoh accepted her apology. He wanted nothing more than to fight alongside another descendant of the Divine Lords, but he could not leave his people to be slaughtered by traitors. Reclaiming his kingdom from the grip of fear and mistrust was his goal. Prince Alexander could not deny the pharaoh's duty.

"Thank you, my prince."

Time was of the essence, but the prince needed time to regain his strength after nearly ripping the room in two. The pharaoh escorted them to the healing chambers to replenish their energy before tracking down his missing sister. This war was turning for the worse. Lord Nebula's legions were gaining ground, and his forces were growing by the day. Saturos could not resist this moment. His heart was drawn to the prince. He was a shadow amongst the souls within the pharaoh's court. He could not miss out on a chance to separate himself from the rest. He offered to be the prince's guide. The pharaoh agreed and allowed him to travel with Prince Alexander to retrieve his sister.

The prince's companions did not agree with allowing Saturos to join their ranks. Feelings of uncertainty resonated amongst them. Prince

Alexander had his own reserves as well; knowing he was the son of the god that wanted him dead. He was no closer to mastering his abilities, and with him close, he could observe him. A decision was made. While Saturos prepared for the voyage, the others soaked in a hot spring deep beneath the pyramid. They were alone, and the prince was finally able to speak with Anri.

"That was some secret you kept from us. Does my sister know?"

"No."

"Why?"

Anri's history dazzled the prince. She was the daughter of Sir Amos Darkarrow and Madam Argia Stormfal. Sir Amos was the prince and princess' older brother, making her their niece. Amos was also the grandfather of King Silverskull, but the king's mother was not Argia, but rather the Mystic Otrant. Her father had two wives; from the Mystic Otrant he had four children, and from Madam Argia he had three.

"If you are my niece, why would you tell the pharaoh you were a descendant of Lady Udana only?"

Anri played with the water as she tried to get her words together. She was a descendant of Lady Udana and Lord Grevis through her mother. Madam Argia and Sir Amos were having issues in their marriage, and she separated from him. She created her own kingdom but later found out she was pregnant. Anri's birth was kept a secret from the other royals because she was the first to be born with magic. Magic was a learned or stolen trait depending on the user. Fearing a coup was coming, she could not risk anyone learning about her. Madam Argia was betrayed by her own sister and murdered. Anri was taken in by servants and protected until she was old enough.

Pain was written all over her face. For too long she held onto this secret, and it finally felt good to let it all out. Tears formed at the corner of her eyes, and as she finally took a breath, it all came out, an uncontrollable cry. The prince watched as she sobbed; he slowly maneuvered to her and squeezed her. She embraced the prince and continued to cry as the others watched. Anri was not ready to speak upon her mother's death any further. Seeing how his sister reacted to the secrets he kept from her; he could only imagine how much rage she would have against someone who was by her side for longer.

Her secret was safe with them. Seizing upon the moment, the prince took the opportunity to let the others in on something he was keeping close to his heart. He revealed that Eris was not the first person to try and kill his mother. The news startled the others. No one seemed to know about it. Voices eclipsed their own as the pharaoh's servants entered with new clothing for them. Each of them exited the spring and dried off. As the prince dried off, the pharaoh's servants dressed him. A beautiful black and blue silk vest went over the prince's head. It was sleeveless with golden shoulder plates. The vest was cut into an upside-down V-shape and stopped at his knees. After his bottom half was dry, he put on black and gold pants and tucked them into knee-high boots. One of the servants placed a golden band on his upper arm and two blue ribbons on his wrist as a symbol of good luck.

Saturos appeared at the entrance of the spring and led them back to the throne room. The pharaoh hugged the prince and Anri. He thanked them for trying to locate his sister. A group of soldiers escorted them to the fortified wall surrounding the palace. The High Guard separated the stones, allowing them access to the city streets. They stared at the prince in utter disgust. Their loyalties were clearly not with the pharaoh, but with someone else. Lord Zylo noticed the same and watched their movements as they made their way to the rim of the city.

CHAPTER

23

SHRINE OF DRAGONS

Dead carcasses lingered in the desert sand. Vultures strayed in the air, hovering over their prey. It had been three days since they embarked on their voyage to the tower, leaving behind the dark stain of the kingdom. Their eyes felt like they were melting into the backs of their heads. The roof of their mouths felt like leather. Sunlight was the enemy, stabbing at their skin, making their flesh unbearable to the touch. To reach the tower, they would need to travel through the Forest of Dragons. It was another day's journey on foot.

Lord Zylo's fur was very damp. Anri's face was flushed, and the prince seemed to be hit the hardest of them all. He could barely stand on his own two feet. Omega tried to shelter Anri with his wings, while Shoxz did the same for the prince and Nacilias. Zaos seemed to be the only one not affected by the extreme, unnatural heat. As an Elf of the Twilight, she was not bound to emotions such as empathy or sadness. Most of her emotions were turned off like a switch. In that moment, she could sense the toll it was taking on everyone. Their auras were depleting rapidly. Zaos grabbed a handful of sand and tossed it into the air as she spoke the words,

'*Zazistos Elementum.*' The sand twisted and turned and became a blanket around them. The sun's piercing light burned away all life in the desert. Saturos threw himself on the floor to rest his feet. They rested in the blanket of sand before pressing forward. The prince took the opportunity to read more of his mother's journal.

Lady Udana and Lady Eileen returned to the Kingdom of Salahea with their prisoner. Upon their arrival, they were met with resistance and hostility. Lord Celeio was not there to receive them, but rather his son, Pharaoh Kimhairo. He ordered the release of his son, but Lady Eileen refused him. She wanted to speak in private. The pharaoh declined to receive her. His wife, Amatila Moonspark, pleaded with him to think about his decision. Not receiving her grandmothers would be unwise. Against his own judgment, he allowed them in.

Lady Eileen explained why he was bound and gagged. The pharaoh was mortified. He confessed that two of his children had fallen ill, and Lord Celeio was seeking help. Her arrival at his gates, with his son, only caused his paranoia to increase. As the pharaoh spoke with Lady Eileen, Lady Udana went to check on the children. She flushed their system with healing water and extracted a fragment of poison from Atemu-Nacus, but the princess was nearly gone. The poison was the same used on Lady Eileen. Enraged, the prince closed the book. Only someone close to his mother and the pharaoh could have done it.

Zaos could see he was upset by what he was reading. Tucking the book back into his bag he turned to Lord Zylo.

"The pharaoh and his sister were poisoned by the same substance as my mother."

Saturos sat across from them, listening, sharpening his swords. The prince pondered over the thought circling in his mind. Could Amatila have poisoned his mother and her children? She was her granddaughter and could gain access to her. Taking a shot in the dark, he asked Saturos about her. Saturos lived in the palace since birth. He knew Amatila. She was a stunning beauty just like any of Lady Udana's children. She was calm and regal. She was the voice of reason in the chaos. Her presence was missed at court.

"Could she have poisoned us?"

Saturos laughed. During the trial of Prince Dacus-Nexus, he confessed to poisoning his brother and sister. There was no mention of his

266

mother falling ill to the same poison. There was no evidence to point to Amatila. Something did not sit right with the prince. If he truly poisoned his brother and sister, who did he get it from? For now, his questions had to wait. They rested a while before continuing further south. A massive hill of sand stood between them and the rest of the desert. As they reached the top, they witnessed a dry-land forest below. The prince slid down the sand, shattering Zaos' charm. They followed suit. Extravagant and enchanted with life, the outer rim of the forest showed signs of heat damage, but as their eyes dug deeper, the trees and plants seemed to thrive with life.

Lord Zylo seemed hesitant to enter, as the dead trees around him told another story. He could sense the dangers that awaited them. He smelled the surroundings, inhaling the trees and plants. One exotic tree exuded an aroma that numbed the senses and dilated his pupils. Zaos could feel the magic taking over his body. She raced to his aid and tackled him to the ground.

"That Wiliwili is hexed. It will subject you to your basic animal desires."

The beauty of the forest was a smoke screen for the darker dangers within. Saturos used his sword to cut through the bushes and make a path for them. As they progressed further, they noticed a huge difference. The scorching sun was like a distant memory. Zaos twirled her finger in the air.

"There is old magic here."

It kept the trees and plants alive in the Forest of Dragons. Anri touched the trees, and a chill went up her spine. The trees were communicating with one another. A massive Ginkgo biloba stood out from the rest. Anri placed her hands on it and was shocked to see a nymph standing in front of her. Its beautiful green skin covered with a dress of flowers tried to communicate with her, to no avail. With each word she spoke, the wind danced around her. Their connection was broken by Saturos' touch. They moved away from the bewitched tree and further into the forest. Lord Zylo's nose inhaled a stench from a mile away. An enemy was approaching. The prince and the others followed him as he led them away from the danger. They stumbled upon a pack of dire wolves hunting near a stream. Carcasses of black foxes stood at their feet. Zylo's civilized ways went out the window. His body contorted, and he was now on all fours. His razor-sharp claws extended, and his fangs were salivating. His howl had no effect on the dire wolves.

It did catch the attention of a deadlier beast. A deeper, fearsome roar from the belly of the forest overshadowed his howl. Trees flung into the air, as two colossal dragon-like creatures approached. One of the beasts grabbed a dire wolf by the tail and swallowed it whole. The pack disbursed before any more would fall prey to their hunger. Standing at a whopping ten feet tall, muscular, and agile, they stared down at the prince and the others with one thing in mind. Food. Nacilias trembled at the presence of the Dragoons.

Dragoons were older than LunaSol itself. When Chaos ruled, he hunted dragons for sport and stole their eggs. Experimenting on the embryo took centuries to master. Born into slavery was a hybrid beast, more aggressive and agile. Covered in sharp scales with razor claws, these beasts were destructive and untamable. Many were unable to fly as they were born without wings; they relied on their speed, since they walked upright on their hindlegs. Nacilias slid into the grass near the young prince in fear. The massive creatures wore battle armor and held axes and war hammers in their hands.

Their serpentine eyes locked onto the prince's amulet. The ground shifted as one of them jumped into the stream. Like a ghost, Zaos pushed her way to the front, and with the wave of her hands she whispered the words, '*Trapiz Gregoda*.' The roots from the Ginkgo biloba sprung to life and bound the mighty creatures. Lord Zylo questioned them, but they refused to speak. The prince slowly walked around the others, catching the eye of the leader.

"You!"

The tree roots snapped as he broke free and tried to grab the prince. Zaos used her magic to tighten the roots around their throats. The prince could see their pain even if they refused to acknowledge it.

"I am Prince Alexander. By order of Pharaoh Atemu-Nacus, we are journeying to Venus Tower. His sister has been kidnapped."

The dragoon who stood closest to the prince broke free from the roots and tried to attack him. Zaos muttered, "*Schmerz*" and in seconds the beast dropped to his knees in agonizing pain. She slowly approached the beast and waved her hand, casting another spell. '*Landsam Ansteigen*' escaped her lips, and the creature slowly rose to his feet. She kept the creature's body immobilized, only allowing his head to move.

"Try it again and I will set your brain on fire."

268

Zaos' words struck fear in everyone.

Prince Alexander moved toward them, "We are not here to cause you harm. We seek passage. The princess is in danger."

The green-scale warrior closest to Lord Zylo shook his head in agreement to help. Zaos released the roots from his throat. Their assistance came with a condition: an audience with the Council of Seven. The amulet around the prince's neck was valuable to them. Rahu, as he was known, was released from his prison with a simple word, '*Loslassen*.' Zaos' spell retracted the roots back into the ground.

Rahu led them down the stream. The deeper they went, the more constricted the sunlight became. At the mouth of the stream was a hidden pond. Inside were astonishing fish covered in bioluminescent algae. Behind the pond stood the steps of a massive shrine covered in purple Wisteria vines. The golden step pyramid was a jewel. They ascended into a grand corridor covered in images of magnificent dragons.

They were escorted past the sculpture into the council meeting room. At the far end of the room stood a massive dragon skull. Countless candles burned, and offerings were nestled beneath the totem. Seven limestone thrones stood empty. Rahu roared, signaling the others. Confused and scared, the prince stood close to Lord Zylo and Zaos. Distant rumbling from up above caught Saturos' attention. There was an upper chamber with entrances. Seven massive dragoons soared down into the room. All stood a towering ten feet tall, apart from their leader. He towered slightly over the rest. Deep-set purple scales shimmered as he spoke.

"You are in the presence of Master Zu. Rahu and Pelua, explain yourselves. Why have you brought outsiders here?"

Rahu bowed and then rose from the floor to speak.

"This boy claims he is the lost prince-Alexander."

Rage exploded amongst the dragoons. They were led to believe the child was dead, and now an insect of a boy shows up claiming to be their herald. Master Zu could not help but stare at the prince. The dragoons demanded to examine the child. Zaos and Lord Zylo stepped aside.

To the far right sat an older one. His hair, whiter than the others, and his scales, duller. He shouted, "Look at his neck!"

The amulet was tucked into his shirt. Master Zu's long, scaly nail lifted it out, revealing the Eclipse Amulet. It was all the proof they needed. Their golden pupils lit up with intrigue. The primal beasts were fixated on the emerald gem. Zaos grew worried for the prince, but her paranoia was put at ease when the dragoons lowered themselves to the ground and bowed.

Saturos' patience was growing thin. He did not have time for idle conversation. "Master Zu, we must get to Venus Tower."

The council disregarded his comments. They had other plans for the prince.

"Walk with me, child!"

Master Zu and the other dragoons escorted the prince back into the foyer. There was a mural with a hidden lever. The dragoon placed his foot on it, and the floor descended into the ground. A spiral staircase led them into the belly of the temple. He confessed that the Shrine of Dragons was not built by any native to LunaSol but by a group of refugees from the stars.

"The Elders!"

Scatha, a yellow dragoon trailing behind them, turned the prince around with her claw.

"Forbidden knowledge! How do you know their names?"

Zaos lifted her hand, but stopped in her tracks as she heard the prince respond.

"My mother wrote about them in her journals."

Scatha's eyes lit up with amazement.

They were led down a corridor filled with purple bell vines. The heart-shaped leaves and dark, purple-shaped flowers dangled from their thread-like stems. The room was dark and bleak. In the center of the room was a mechanical structure commissioned by his mother. It was like the planetarium within the Temple of Zephyrus. The room was cylindrical, and there were countless dragon eggs preserved in wall pockets. The massive beasts surrounded a hole in the floor. Master Zu pressed a lever, and the rest of the machine rose from the depths. The prince was distracted by the colossal door at the far end of the cavern. Carved from molten rock, depicting a three-headed dragon.

He separated from the others and touched the door. Smorgol, a brown-scaled dragoon followed him. Seeing the intrigue in the prince's eyes, he explained. The cavern was built by the Elders as the last stronghold for dragons. Hyperion was gone, the destroyer from the sky was placed to rest, but the dragons were dying, and their cause of death was going unnoticed. The Elders intervened and created a backdoor into Magna Dragonis by using the machine and a celestial event. Countless dragons were saved and escaped LunaSol. By saving them, the royals sought retribution for their betrayal. Before their banishment, the Elders configured the machine to perform another function, separating the Royal Dragons from the Trinity Angels. It was the Elders last attempt at correcting a wrong. It would only work with all three amulets.

Smorgol was called to order. Leaving the prince's side, he returned to Master Zu. As the prince turned from the door, it felt as if someone was breathing down his neck. He turned quickly and heard a whisper through the crack. He could barely make out what was said. '*Journals.*' What did his mother's journals have to do with anything?

The prince was called to the machine. Anri saw the scared look on his face. Pale and sweating. She approached him and ran a cloth over his forehead. Casting a spell under her breath, she was able to hear the whisper. She turned to him and grabbed his hand.

"The prince is in danger!"

Master Zu was alarmed by her statement. Her fear manifested. The dragoons, Typhon and Sirrush attacked Zaos and Lord Zylo, while Ryujin sank his fangs into Master Zu. Smorgol ordered the prince to seek safety. Anri rushed him back through the corridor only to find lifeless dragoons littering the staircase. A river of blood flowed down from the opening above. As the prince tiptoed around the bodies, he noticed the deep gashes. The dragoons turned on one another. Peering through the opening, they watched as the massive creatures ripped through each other. Their movements seemed orchestrated. None of them defended themselves from the blows. Anri waved her hands and murmured, " *Velze.*" A wave of energy radiated across the room. revealing a purple mist swirling around their heads. A curse. Each of the creatures were forced to fight against their will to the death. Her heartbeat began to sing in her ears. Her breaths grew rapidly. All her formal training did not prepare her for this. Without hesitation, she plunged her hand into the open carcass of a dragoon. She ripped out its heart and used its blood to draw a circle of runes around her.

The swirling clouds of mist turned red. Their attention was now on her. The prince's amulet would not work within the temple. Zaos and Lord Zylo were making their way up the spiral staircase when they heard the

271

prince scream for help. Anri could not complete the spell trying to hold the dragoons at bay. As the Elf of the Twilight rose from the opening, she was covered in blood, chanting in her native tongue. Forcing the creatures into submission, she allowed Anri to continue her spell. Drawing a line of blood down her nose and across her cheek bones, she clenched the heart in her hands. The blood ignited, and her pupils darkened. It was insatiable. Dark energy flowed through her veins for the first time. Flicking her tongue against her teeth, sending out a massive scream across the room, she shattered the curse. The individual strands of mist bound together, forming the silhouette of a woman before fading into the ground.

"What just happened?"

Anri turned to the prince, eyes still blackened, raising her hand toward him. Zaos intervened and placed her entire hand over her face. A taste of black magic was enough to drive anyone insane. As an Elf of the Twilight, she could see the darkness taking over. She drew the dark energy out and fed off it. Lord Zylo held Anri in his arms as she slowly came to her senses. The injured dragoons gathered their dead and tended to their wounds. Saturos and the others finally emerged from below. Master Zu was injured, but Smorgol was still in one piece. He dragged his master into the Council Chamber and placed him on his throne.

"Answers? We need answers now!"

Master Zu sought answers from his remaining council, but no one could explain what happened.

"A curse!"

The prince's words alarmed them. No one has seen them in centuries. The last visitor they had was his mother. Could she? The thought crossed Master Zu's mind and made him angry. His anger was set at ease when Anri revealed the true assailant.

"Asphera."

Her shade appeared after the curse was lifted and retreated. It was marked with residue of the Nebula.

"Poisoning Lady Eileen wasn't enough for her. She came for us as well."

"What did you just say?" questioned the prince.

Master Zu's words revealed the truth behind his mother's poisoning. It was after Prince Dacus-Nexus' trial, she came to visit him. He was not master of the shrine at that time, but merely a servant to Alzamir, a fearsome crystal dragon. Lady Eileen was surprised to see the dragon was unaffected by Hyperion's enchantment. Alzamir's abilities were unlike any of his kin. Just by her standing in his presence, he felt death calling to her. Her body was compromised and would not recover. Using his dragon breath, he was able to see into her soul and pinpoint the moment she was poisoned by her daughter. Gasping for air, the prince nearly fainted. How could she? What did she have to gain?

Lady Eileen entrusted Alzamir with a secret. During a meteor storm, Asphera was found amongst the rubble, scarred with pieces of shards embedded into her skin. Unbeknownst to her, her daughter would become a servant to the Nebula. Asphera was the first to study dark magic and cloaked herself from the sight of Hyperion. She trained in secret, and one day Lady Eileen confronted her. Asphera knew all about her mother's betrayal of Hyperion and her plans to destroy him. Mutual destruction was ensured. To avoid it, they forged a truce.

The pact between mother and daughter was broken. He did not know what the pact entailed. Under false pretenses, Asphera was brought to the shrine. She believed her mother was going to ask for her help taking down Hyperion. Betrayed by her emotions, she fell into her mother's trap. The Mystic Otrant stood in waiting with Alzamir. Combining their efforts, Asphera was killed, or so they thought.

"Something is not right about this! Why place a curse on the dragoons? Why, upon the prince's arrival, would it activate? Did she have foresight? What if she planned to be captured from the beginning to make sure this moment happened?"

"This took careful planning. A calculated attack!" responded Zaos.

"It wouldn't be the first time one of my sisters had a plan to kill me. Eris was able to corrupt a demon in my world to steal my blood and open the portal back to LunaSol."

Saturos grew impatient. These schemes further distanced him from his princess. He urged the prince to see beyond this attack. The longer they remained in the shrine, the closer the princess was to death. Anri and Zaos did not agree with Saturos, but the prince did. His life would always be in danger. He could not stomach letting the princess die while he was distracted. Upon exiting the temple, starlight covered the forest. They could not travel into the darkness. They were offered shelter for the night.

The vacant room was sterile. Zaos whipped her hands around, and with a snap, she created beds for everyone. Anri placed protective wards around the room. Everyone slowly began to doze off, and the prince was left staring at the ceiling: a carving of a three-headed dragon leading an army of dragons against a woman and her dragons. His eyes began to feel heavy, and he slowly closed them. Everything went dark, until he heard steps. The vibrations from the ground lit up his eyes. At first, the prince was puzzled, but then his thoughts subsided when he heard voices.

"Princess Toa, we will not harm you. You are the key. Help us and we will spare your life." Prince Alexander recognized Heishini's voice.

"I will never."

Heishini laughed and slapped her. "I will smear your blood all over the door if I have to."

Prince Alexander awoke from his nightmare and noticed Zaos standing over him.

"My prince, what is wrong?"

"The princess is still alive. I saw her."

"My prince, we mustn't wake the others. They need their rest. Today has been draining, and tomorrow they will be ready for battle. Rest easy, and I will wake you in the morning." Zaos waved her hands over the prince's eyes as she spoke the words, '*Schlafen.*'

The spell kept his mind asleep and warded from traveling outside his body. Nacilias' tongue woke him. Anri was standing over him, holding out her hand. He was led to the bathing chamber; he was the last of them to get ready. While he bathed, the others spoke with Master Zu in the throne room.

"You will be escorted to the western parts of our forest. From there, you will travel into the desert once more. Head west and you will find Evergreen Forest and within – Venus Tower."

Nacilias waited outside the throne room for the prince. Turning the corner, he startled the Corsac fox. The prince was gifted with a cream snakeskin tunic, and burgundy snakeskin tights. The tunic had three slits at the hip: two down the side and one down the butt. His sleeves were tucked into dragon-scale wristbands, and around his waist was a belt made of the same material - a gift from the dragoons to protect against the heat.

Prince Alexander and his companions were escorted to the front of the shrine. They were led through the untamed and seductive beauty of the forest. Dozens of red pandas caught his attention as they moved across the trees. Lord Zylo could hear the chirping of Palm cockatoos overhead, making their way to the edge of the forest. Anri witnessed a beautiful sight, as hundreds of Leadbeater cockatoos flew through the trees singing a stunning tune. The soft-textured white and salmon-pink plumage and large, bright red and yellow crest of this amazing bird filled their eyes with lights. War and destruction had consumed most of the world but still produced such amazing creatures to accent it with life.

The beauty of the forest was soon overturned. Dry air and the desert heat consumed more of the forest. The dragoons parted ways with the prince as Saturos led them back into the hot desert sands. Zaos grabbed sand from the floor and cloaked them in shade, allowing them to make the trip without feeling the effects of the heat. For as far as the naked eye could see, all that remained was a sea of shifting sands. Stumbling to the top of a hill of sand, Zaos spoke, "We are here!"

"This is not a forest," interjected Anri.

Zaos shouted, "*Fata Morgana!*"

The hill of sand rumbled, and in seconds the sand dematerialized right before their eyes, and in its place was Evergreen Forest. Saturos took two steps forward and was thrown back by a force field. Lord Zylo grabbed him by his cloak before he could tumble down the hill. He ran his nail across the surface, generating sparks.

Saturos reapproached the barrier. Looking at the palm of his left hand he uttered, "*Oganji.*" His hands ignited with blue flames. He blasted the force field covering half of the dome. Unleashing his fury on the barrier only drained him of his energy. Not even a dent was left when the flames subsided. His chest fluttered up and down as he struggled in the heat to catch his breath.

Saturos unclipped his sword from his waistband and spun it around as he roared, "*Antene.*" The gem on the handle glowed as he pierced through the barrier. The flame sent a trail of cracks throughout until the entire thing shattered. As the flaming shards rained down, the tantalizing forest stood exquisitely in the background.

CHAPTER
24

EARTH STONE

Saturos' fire magic was remarkable.

"We need to watch out for that one," growled Nacilias.

Prince Alexander could no longer keep his secret. Each of the visions he witnessed in the tablet he confessed. Anri watched as the prince spoke softly to his companion. Knowing her orders, she approached them to eavesdrop. Prince Alexander believed in her and confided in her as well. For the sake of the world, Anri demanded that they release Saturos from their battalion. If he were to find out he was one of Hyperion's heirs, what would stop him from trying to take over and killing the royals. Aside from Anri and Nacilias, the prince chose silence. He would not repeat it again; he needed time to think.

Saturos watched them from afar. Their behavior was strange. The glances back and forth. He knew they were talking about him. Idle gossip would not deter him from finding the princess. Being familiar with the forest's defenses, Saturos took the lead. A forest that once stirred with life, stood quiet. Birds that once sang a distant melody were now muzzled. Staring into the distance, his eyes watched as the gnarled roots and twisted branches began to move. Trees, ancient and timeless, ripped through the ground and dragged Nacilias and Shoxz away through the dense bushes.

The prince tried to chase after them, but Zaos placed her hand on his chest before he could pass her. "Something is coming!"

Growls and cat-like eyes appeared from the bushes. Saturos spun his sword around and stared at the eyes watching them. The creatures slowly protruded from the bushes, revealing themselves as white tigers. He lowered his guard, welcoming the guardians of the forest, but he learned the hard way. One of the tigers lunged at him. Zaos immobilized the beast and flung it into a tree, while she magically controlled the others.

Anri gazed into their eyes and noticed a parasitic creature. She ordered Zaos to reduce the pain she was inflicting on them, so she could try and remove the parasite. Anri moved closer to one of them. She placed her hand on the creature's head.

"*Ući.*" As the words escaped her lips, her body convulsed, and the color in her eyes faded to black. The parasite latched onto Anri, and the veins in her hands began to darken, and her skin decayed. Seeing her pain, the prince ripped her away. "I was close to freeing them. Why did you intervene?"

Her frustration was misplaced. He grabbed her hands and showed her the damage her spell was doing. It was too risky. The spell work had the traces of Heishini written all over it. Saturos examined them. Anri knew the only thing that could counter such magic was drawing from Oricale. She had to act. Closing her eyes, she began to hum. The High Chancellor continued her melody as Zaos snapped her fingers and shouted, "*Spavati,*" placing the beasts into a deep sleep. Sparks of emerald energy flicked from her fingertips. Anri levitated from the ground, as she chanted.

"**Stella magna vitae nunc dicam.**
Dividite metu conturbata animarum.
Saltem in lumine suo; et cessare hoc mundo
impium dictitans dedecus."
(*Great Star of Life, I call you here.*
Divide these souls that have been darkened in fear.
Allow only light to remain in its place; and rid
this world of this unholy disgrace.)

Loud, savage noises roared through the clouds. Lightning poured down and devastated the forest. Everyone ran for cover as Anri descended and forced each of their mouths open. She drew the black toxin from them

278

and into her palms. Overwhelmed by the power, blood formed at the corners of her eyes. Saturos and Zaos rushed to her aid but were thrown back. The darkness surrounded her and chipped away at her aura. Saturos swung his sword around, calling upon the Gaeatonic Eye. The handle of his sword ignited. He eradicated the toxin. Anri's aura was flickering as she nearly collapsed. She kept whispering '*the Nebula.*' Zaos enchanted the trees and bent them to her will, creating a carriage. She placed Anri within it and attached it to Omega. The prince entered the carriage to watch over her as the others stood guard outside and walked the rest of the way looking for Nacilias and Shoxz.

The vine marks led them past the rich wildlife; a family of wolverines hunted for food as the mating screams of the black-and-white colobuses vibrated through the trees as they swung through the branches. Their path was blocked by a herd of bongos making their way across. The largest of the forest antelopes pushed each other as they saw the group staring at them. Once the path was cleared, they pushed on and finally made it to the edge of the forest, only to be disappointed.

"Where is Venus Tower?" questioned Prince Alexander.

"Right in front of us." Zaos explained.

"I don't see anything?" questioned Saturos.

"It is covered in dark magic. Multiple layers. They cannot see out, and we cannot see in. Twisted magic. We, Elves of the Twilight, are trained to sense spells and ways to counter them."

Zaos approached the invisible barrier and blew on it. Her breath rippled across the surface as she muttered, "*Ufdeck.*" The first barrier fell. She was able to get a better sense of the secondary one. Holding her hands into the sky, she began to chant.

"**Kräfte von Licht und Dunkelheit; entfesseln
Sie Ihre große Macht. Lassen Sie Ihre Energie
durch mich fließen, so dass ich zerstören kann
mein Feind.**"

(*Powers of dark and light; unleash your great might.
Allow your energy to flow through me, so that
I may destroy my enemy.*)

A dark mist appeared on her hands. The darkness was acidic. It ate away at it and spread like wildfire. As the barrier faded, a thick layer of fog became visible.

Saturos' placed his index and middle fingers together on both hands and growled, "*Vatostri*."

Fire enveloped his fingers. He sliced the barrier, allowing them to have a clear visual of what was going on. The High Magnus' were still trying to gain access to the tower. Saturos tried to advance, but Zaos' hand stopped him. She lifted a leaf from the floor and sent it flying toward the barrier. As it got closer, it turned to ash.

Saturos would have exploded if he walked through it. Zaos called for the prince's assistance. The amulet around his neck would protect him as it did when Gaea tried to invade his body. She enchanted his aura, so as he entered the barrier, it would shatter. She placed her hands on his head as she mumbled, "*Schützen*." Prince Alexander felt a strange sensation overcoming his entire body. He slowly moved toward the barrier, fearing the worst. As he drew closer, the aura around him began to burn. He could feel pain, but it was mild. Zaos instructed him to place his hands on the barrier. His touch burned away the dark magic, causing the barrier to crack. Saturos waited impatiently as the barrier imploded.

A hoard of creatures awaited them in the valley leading to the tower. The sandstone beauty was covered in jade vines and clematis. A grand staircase led to a masonic tiled platform where Heishini and Akmadin were still attempting to gain access to the tower. The explosion caught their attention, forcing them to imprison the princess, while they led a counterattack against the intruders. Saturos rushed to the front to defend the prince. Akmadin succeeded in prolonging their advances by creating a wall of thorny roses. Using his flaming sword, he sliced through them.

Prince Alexander and the others raced toward Heishini, but he sent them flying back with a wave of his hand. Zaos waved her hands and detached the carriage from Omega. The underbelly of the carriage opened and gently lowered Anri's weakened body to the ground. Still controlling the carriage, she sent it hurtling toward the corrupted beasts. With a snap of her fingers, the carriage exploded, and the shards injured those adjacent to it. Shoxz and Nacilias were hanging upside down from a tree. The prince raced toward them and grabbed ahold of the vines. Focusing on their release, the vines turned to ash. Nacilias tumbled to the ground, as Shoxz flapped her wings and took off into the sky. Soaring overhead were carnivorous griffins. Cupping their wings, they descended and attacked Shoxz and Omega.

Two leopards circled the prince as Nacilias snarled at them. Lord Zylo roared out to beware of the leopard's bite because they were filled with venom. Prince Alexander summoned his staff and attacked the leopard. Using the tip as a spear, he gouged the beast. Omega and Shoxz trampled the griffins, only leaving the Magnus'. Akmadin was out matched in strength. Zaos was able to get close enough to him to block his access to magic.

Saturos placed his sword into the ground in front of Akmadin. He rubbed the sapphire stone on the handle as he spoke the words, "*Sjel deleg*," the Gaeatonic Eye appeared. Blue flames erupted from his hands and encased his sword. It spiraled down toward the floor and jolted toward Akmadin. The flames consumed him, and all that was left were his robes and his weapon. The flames jolted back into the sword, and the Gaeatonic Eye faded. Heishini glared at them from a distance in fear, but he would not go down without a fight. He was more powerful than his counterpart.

Heishini's staff exuded a frequency that stirred Anri from her slumber. Zaos noticed her and helped her up from the ground. The runes on the handle confirmed he had a relic imbued with Oricale's touch. It was drawing on negative energy. While he was distracted, the princess managed to free herself and tried to run past him as he was throwing fireballs at the prince and his companions. The Magnus grabbed her by her hair and threw her against the gate. The impact illuminated the entire tower and the vines that sealed the door shut, untangled. The protective charms were no more. Heishini's staff encased the entire valley in a paralyzing blanket of black fog. Minutes turned into hours before the prince was able to wake up. He pulled himself up from the ground and dragged himself to the others.

The grand entrance was open. Time was the enemy now. Saturos led the others beyond the tower gates, only to find themselves in a maze of sand. The staircases were constantly changing and disappearing. Zaos seemed to be the only one who made a full recovery. Everyone else still felt dizzy and weak. Dazzling gems and jewels littered the room like a vault. As they cleared each floor, the gems grew. The final room was empty. Statues of Lord Celeio's children stood guard around the room. Pharaoh Kimhairo's statue smiled slightly at Anri. The buzzing noise was back and infected her ears. She crept toward the statue; touching it sent a ripple throughout. She turned to warn the others but found herself grabbed from behind and imprisoned inside. Heishini appeared in her place and imprisoned them in the remaining statues. Princess Toa was placed in the center of the room and pinned to the floor.

"A life for a life. I offer you the princess, for the power of the stone itself."

Beneath the princess, markings began to appear and created the image of the Gaeatonic Eye. The darkness that pinned her to the floor slowly eased up. The markings cascaded over the statues and drained the prisoners of energy. Heishini moved back as the glow intensified and nearly blinded him. Within the statues, they could see the princess in agonizing pain. With each scream, the ceiling opened and allowed them to ascend. The High Chancellor stood surrounded by silence, calling to Oricale for strength. With a single thought she shattered her prison and ripped the others from their tombs as well before they could suffocate.

Zaos and the others were depleted and could not fight. They could barely stand on their own. They refused to let Anri face him alone. They ascended to the top of the tower only to find blood and gore. Heishini was holding the head of an elf in his hands. Zaos screamed out in anger. She cried out uncontrollably for the death of her friend Tisharu, a fellow Elf of the Twilight.

Princess Toa was bound on the steps of the shrine. She was bleeding out from a stab wound. From Saturos' vantage point Heishini was not the one who stabbed her. It had to be the elf. He used her as a shield. She sat on the floor toying with the blood and dirt. Saturos took one step forward causing Princess Toa to react. She pounded the floor and threw him back with a pillar of sand.

"Why are you helping him?" questioned Anri.

"I am protecting you."

Heishini walked around the shrine, chanting as the blood from the Elven head marked the ground. Once his circle was completed, the blood erupted into a golden flame. At the center of the shrine there was a glorious statue. The fabled Elephante; an elephant-humanoid warrior. Adorning its head was a crown and in its hands was the earth stone. Carved to look like a withering tree, the scheelite stone glistened in the burning sun. It was missing a piece. The prince realized the Gaeatonic Guardians were telling the truth. It was the piece Asphera broke and stabbed the Nympalim with.

The traitor positioned the princess in front of the statue. Even though she was blind, she saw the world differently. Through touch, taste and sound she could feel the vibrations from nature which allowed her to see without physically seeing. She placed her hands on its forearms, activating the shrine. Blood poured out of her pores and turned into gold. The statue absorbed it, depleting her life force.

Saturos screamed for her to stop. He felt very vulnerable. Zaos was unhinged by the death of her kin. Anri trembled as the prince lay by her feet in a daze. With the last of her blood drained from her body, she collapsed, giving life to the statue. Heishini removed the earth stone from its hands as its grip loosened. The Magnus vanished in a cloud of shadows as the barrier finally dissolved. Saturos raced for the princess, holding her in his arms, she felt ice cold. Her pupils were unresponsive, and her lips were blue. A single strand of golden blood remained on her cheek.

Anri screamed for Saturos to move, but her voice faded in the background. All he could think about was the princess and how upset the pharaoh would be. His inner voice was silenced as he noticed a glaring shadow standing over him. In the place of the statue was a living, breathing Elephante. Another Titan. Anri and the others raced to the shrine to help Saturos.

"Do not fret, child. This goddess cannot die!"

"Goddess?" questioned the prince.

"Young one, connected you two are."

The creature's words stirred in the prince's mind. Could his mother have gone through with the elder's plans? Could she be one of the vessels anchored to the prince? He turned to the elephante, "What is your name?"

"I am Uyxi!"

"We don't have time for this. My princess is dead. REVIVE HER NOW!"

Prince Alexander shot Saturos a disturbed look. He understood the Elephante. Crying in agony, all he wanted was to save the princess. Uyxi commanded him to draw his sword and place it in the princess' hands and hold onto her. Placing her nose on the princess' forehead, she forced the Gaeatonic Eye to reveal itself. Once connected, they crossed into the princess' mind and were brought before an archway covered in blue Wisteria vines. The prince was familiar with the archway. His own mind had one that allowed him to connect with the spiritual world. A portal opened in the archway, allowing them to cross into a new realm.

What stood before them was an enchanting meadow. The sacred space had a harmonious blend of vibrant colors, soothing sounds, and intoxicating fragrances. It was a living tapestry, painted with an array of wildflowers, soft pink peonies, red poppies, and golden sunflowers. The air was alive with nature's symphony. Birds singing sweetly, their melodies weaving through the gentle hum of bees and the distant flow of the riverbed. There was a single leafless tree in the distance. They proceeded with caution.

As they approached, it began to change shape, taking on the form of a woman, a god; Gaea. Her earthly form resembled the earth stone dramatically. She bore similar traits to the Aiars. Her legs were tree trunks, her skin resembled bark, her forehead had small branches folding backward with long jade vines flowing downward like hair.

Look who we have here. Son of the damned and Son of the whore."

Saturos trembled. He was in the presence of the one who granted them power. He could not faulter.

"Give me back my princess."

Her bark-colored skin changed as she twirled around, and vines spiraled up her skin creating a dress of rose-colored orchids. Towering a stunning ten feet tall, she plopped herself on the floor.

"Asphera promised me a body. I will take what I am owed!"

"What deal did you make with my sister?"

Gaea chuckled as she twirled her fingers in the grass. Her words cut like daggers. Lord Celeio lost faith in Lady Eileen's plan. He thought she was weak and sought to strike first against Hyperion. Asphera exploited that paranoia and convinced him to enact Gaea's revival rite. It came with a price. She needed a body with celestial properties. The Nympalim became her target. She attacked them and forced Hyperion to banish them. Lord Celeio brought them into his service and then married one of them. As his queen she gave him children. Descendants with celestial properties. She poisoned two of his descendants for Gaea to have a host, but once Lady Eileen caught wind of their exploits, she intervened. His mother did, in fact, tie his life to eight others. Princess Toa being one of them. With her in her state of limbo, she had another chance to return. The goddess unleashed her destruction onto the valley. Her rage manifested, and the ground cracked beneath them. Shards jolted into the air and threw Saturos and Prince Alexander around. The goddess' advances did not affect Uyxi.

Uyxi was not alone. Around her neck she wore a necklace of orange iris. A totem for Ki.

"Daughter! You scorn me. Hiding behind a Titan. Face me!"

"I will not allow you to harm my prince. The Imperial Gods have lost. Your reign is over!"

Gaea attacked the elephante and separated the spirit she was protecting. Ki was majestic and beautiful. Hair, thick and filled with orange roses. Deep brown set eyes. She was covered from the neck down in gems and jewels beaded together. Her arms were visible and covered in henna. Her nails - long and sharp like claws. Separated from her host, she grew weaker. Ki and Uyxi battled the goddess. Saturos joined the fight and was able to get close enough to her and pierce her heart.

"Traitor!"

A tear ran down her cheek as she stared into his eyes. Her olive skin turned to tree bark and then to ash as her body hardened. Uyxi severed the bond, allowing them to return to the top of Venus Tower. Gaea's remaining hold on the princess was gone.

The princess was still unconscious. There was still no pulse. Uyxi handed Ki's totem to the prince. A life for a life. She would undo her mother's mistake. Alexander touched Saturos on the shoulder so he could move over. Sitting beside him, he removed the sword from her hands and replaced it with the Iris necklace. Holding the Eclipse Amulet in his hands he called to Oricale. Both necklaces illuminated. The orange glow of the Iris' petals faded to black as Ki's life force was drained. Rejuvenated with life, Princess Toa gasped for air. Saturos held her in his hands, and he cried for joy. Even with the Earth Stone lost, they managed to save a Titan and the princess.

As the others tended to the princess, Uyxi pulled the prince aside.

"This belongs to you!"

The prince was in shock, "What is this gift?"

"The Crown of the God's possesses the souls of Athena, Ares, and Aphrodite. Take it with you on your journey. Seek their wisdom."

As Prince Alexander removed the crown from Uyxi's head, she began to slowly turn to stone. Their enemy was two stones away from succeeding in bringing about the end. With Heishini on the loose, they needed to return to the pharaoh with news of his disappearance. Having traveled from the Kingdom of Salahea to Evergreen Forest, it would be a long journey back. Staring at the princess, Zaos got an idea. Having three Magnus', she recounted a spell that could teleport them. Ripping the vines from the tower, she wrapped them around everyone's waist. With additional vines, she tied everyone together in a circle. She asked the princess to focus on their home as she slowly hummed in the Elven language. The soothing sound sang to the birds who spiraled around them. Each of the birds lit up, and time and space bent around them.

CHAPTER
25

UNLEASHED

Two stones were now in Lord Marlusha's possession. With another victory he celebrated atop the roof of the Black Kingdom. Clouds of ash swirled around the five shrines as Heishini handed him the stone. Its amber glow intensified in the presence of its sister stone. The Burma ruby tiles were covered in volcanic ash and cleared as Lord Marlusha's cloak dragged across the floor. He handed Heishini the stone back and showed him where to place it. As he placed the stone on the pillar, its glow faded, and horror ensued. Stricken with a plague, he could no longer feel his hands. They were glued to the stone. His skin turned gray and his veins black. His skin hardened and then he turned to dust. The Betrayer's menacing laugh echoed through the air.

Losing the Titan would not delay the process. A death was a death, and with his death, the shrine lit up, but something was interfering with its signal. The Lord of Martilo noticed Heishini's staff lingered. Its dark emerald sparks were speaking to the stone. Lord Marlusha attempted to grab it, but it threw him back against the middle altar. The staff vanished, enraging him. His entire body was consumed by flames as he descended through the cracks of the tile and reemerged in his throne room. The boiling cauldrons simmered as dark shadows crept around him. Unwanted guest had arrived; Lord Dark Lucus and Eris appeared.

"I do not have time for your games, foul creatures!"

"We come at the bequest of the Master."

He dug his long nails into the handles of his throne. "He spoke with you!"

Lord Dark Lucus dug his sword into the ground. "How are the preparations going with the weapon?"

"It will be ready!"

Eris chuckled as she glided behind him. "The Master tires of how long it is taking us to find the keys to his tomb. This weapon must work."

Lord Dark Lucus punched the wall. "We do not have time. It is time we let the Uvali loose!"

Lord Marlusha clenched his hand into a fist and punched the throne. His face changed and he could feel an eerie feeling overtaking him. For the first time in his life, fear invaded his soul. He could not believe Eris and Lord Dark Lucus could even suggest this type of recourse. Bringing forth these creatures could jeopardize his plans. Eris agreed with him, but she could not disappoint Lord Nebula. They were under orders to bring him to Tartarus.

Shadow and darkness spiraled around Eris and Lord Dark Lucus and engulfed Lord Marlusha. When the shadows cleared, they were standing in the halls of a gloomy and ominous palace; lit with purple crystals. Angelic statues that once lined the halls crumbled. Hundreds of doorways were covered with mirrors, each depicting events happening all over the world. It was their spy glass to report back everyone's movements. Lord Marlusha glared into one mirror; tombs and statues of those departed could be seen by torchlight. It was the royal crypt. They escorted him to the depths of the palace and into a cavern that contained Lord Nebula's prison.

Lord Marlusha gasped, "So, this is where you have been keeping the Nebula Gate?"

Eris laughed and turned toward Lord Dark Lucus, "Yes. After we stole it from Heaven, we brought it here. Tartarus has been enchanted to keep it hidden from the outside world. No one will ever make it this far to stop us."

Lord Dark Lucus was annoyed by Eris' voice. "That is enough. Lord Nebula wanted Lord Marlusha here for a reason. Bring him forth."

His eyes bulged. Could his master have known the truth? Even in prison, could he know he was being double crossed? Lord Marlusha gazed at the chiseled stone and noticed a few star fragments were already in place. Lord Nebula already had a foothold in this world. The gateway gave him pause. He watched as Eris closed her eyes and manipulated the shadows around her. The shadows flickered and sparked the torches on the wall to light up with flames. Scaling the walls above were hundreds of gargoyles. Their skin a rugged stone gray, flecked with patches of moss. Its wings, vast and leathery. Lord Marlusha gazed into their haunting emerald eyes. Unlike humans with five fingers, each beast had three on each hand with razor-shape claws.

Lord Dark Lucus killed one of them and flung its body to the ground. The shadows lifted the corpse and consumed it. Out of the darkness appeared a white sphere...Its essence...Its soul...Contorting the shadows, she levitated the sphere into the hands of the angelic carving on Lord Nebula's prison. She blasted the sphere with dark energy, causing the prison to react with an unnatural purple glow.

The closer he got to the gate, the harder it became to breathe. An offering was needed to communicate with their master. Snapping his fingers generated a spark of fire. It grew into a string and elevated toward the eyes of the angelic statue before being absorbed. After devouring their offerings the stone stars shattered, becoming crystals. A purple liquid poured from them and formed the cursed Nebula Symbol. Its deep, ominous color pulsated, and the door slowly opened. Frozen in fear, they waited, but nothing happened.

Minutes later, Eris' arm began to tremble, and her eyes glazed over, turning black. She turned to the others, "I am glad to see you all here."

As Eris spoke, her voice paralyzed the room. Lord Marlusha's knees buckled, and he dropped to the floor.

"My liege, it is an honor. How is this possible?"

"Each key that is returned to me allows me to slowly get a foothold in this world. Devouring the souls of dark creatures has allowed my connection to grow."

Lord Dark Lucus could see the dark aura radiating tremendously off Eris. Even in his fragile state, Lord Nebula was incredibly strong. "My Lord, we are doing everything in our power to revive you before the child becomes a threat."

Lord Nebula roared at Lord Dark Lucus to silence himself. He flung his servant onto the wall.

"A threat? You have no idea!"

Lord Dark Lucus tried to get out the word, "Apo...Apolog...Apologies, My Lord."

"The child possesses power that could destabilize my universe. If he is allowed to live, he will be unstoppable."

His servants had disappointed him, and he could not allow such things to go unpunished. Those touched by the Nebula were given extreme strength, and they still could not seem to overpower his enemies. As he opened his mouth, a sonic scream encapsulated the room. Lord Marlusha crunched over in pain. It was as if ice shards were piercing his eyes and ears. Blood poured down. It had the same effect on Lord Dark Lucus. Closing his mouth released them from the pain.

"That is a reminder of what a fraction of my powers can do. Do not fail me again, or I will skin you alive!"

Lord Dark Lucus whispered his plans to unleash the Uvali to appease his master. Their master praised his thinking.

Lord Marlusha rose from the floor. "How will we revive them? They were sealed away by light magic."

"With the Creator's help, of course."

Lord Nebula clapped, "Of course!"

He ordered Lord Dark Lucas to bring him ten pure souls from the vault below them. He vanished into the shadows and returned holding a machine containing ten crystal spheres. As he handed them to Lord Marlusha, he dug his sword into the ground, opening a hole. From the center rose an irregular black monolith. It stood twenty feet tall. At the top of the stone stood the Nebula Symbol surrounded by runes. Depicted underneath it was a withering tree. With a wave of her hand, Eris released the lid from the machine, and the crystal spheres circled her hand. Lord Nebula infected the souls. He channeled all his energy into her palm and blasted the Nebula Symbol. It reacted, and the individual symbols around it lit up. The floating crystals were drawn into the runes. Eris' body released a massive mist of purple shadows as it was sucked back into the Nebula Gate. Lord Dark Lucus was beside her but did not catch her as she fell. He stood in all as pieces of the structure shattered. Each of the runes stopped glowing, and a mist spiraled out of the Nebula Symbol giving new life to the Uvali.

They surrounded Lord Nebula's three generals as the final one took form. Their leader, an octopus-faced creature, stood towering over them. One hand resembled a crab's claw, and the other was comprised of eight tentacles wrapped together to form a hand.

"It is good to be free. Tell us what you need done and it shall be!"

Eris could barely get up from the floor, and Lord Marlusha was too scared to speak. Lord Dark Lucus answered, "Bring us Prince Alexander Whitespear and dispose of those who have come into contact with that abomination."

"It is the will of the Master, and it shall be done."

The other creatures rose from the floor and were escorted out of the room by Lord Dark Lucus. He handed Eris' body to Lord Marlusha. Eris slowly opened her eyes and looked up at the Divine Lord. Tears formed in the corner of her eyes. He helped her to sit on a nearby rock as they awaited Lord Dark Lucus' return.

"This is insane. Those creatures cannot be trusted. They will ruin everything for us," roared Eris.

"How about we take this conversation somewhere else?" interjected Lord Marlusha.

He ignited his cape in flames and twirled it around the others. As the flames subsided, they were once again in the throne room of the Black Kingdom.

"Speak freely; Lord Nebula cannot hear or see into my kingdom."

"So, what is the plan for handling the Uvali?" questioned Eris.

Lord Marlusha chuckled, "We let them worry about finding Prince Alexander, and if they so happen to fall in battle, we will be there to pick up the pieces when they do."

Eris chuckled before fading into the shadows. The Divine Lord was left alone with his thoughts. He could not allow these creatures to upstage him. The foul odor of death was in the air. He called for Nathaniel Darkbloom.

His throne room was bleak and ominous. The paintings of his descendants hung on the walls. The air smelled of coal and ember. Thick, heavy, red curtains closed off the light from the outside world. Torches and fire pits were scattered across the room, illuminating parts of it. Lord Marlusha approached his throne and took a seat, only to see Nathaniel

Darkbloom lurking in the shadows. He inquired as to why he was summoned so abruptly. News of the Uvali altered his plans. With their revival, he would soon outlast his usefulness. He pushed through the throne room doors, passing by countless hooded servants until he reached his bedroom. He slammed the door pacing back and forth. He snapped out of his state and raced to his study. Dozens of books were scattered over his desk. Fixated on finding what he needed, he tossed all the books onto the floor. Beneath them was a box with the Oricale Star engraved on it.

Taking a deep breath, he unlatched the handle and inside was a black crystal that exuded a ruby glow. Upon contact with his skin, he found himself surrounded by darkness. He called out for the prince but heard nothing. His grip around the crystal grew tighter as he focused on the prince and called out to him once more. Silence surrounded him. Gripping the crystal even harder, his eyes flickered, and the Oricale Star appeared to glow a fiery red.

"Prince."

Like a whisper in the wind, his voice tickled his ear. Prince Alexnader and his companions were approaching the Kingdom of Salahea. He heard his name called again, but this time Nathaniel's astral form jolted into the prince's mind. The prince dropped to his knees, and his eyes sealed shut. When he opened them, he was no longer surrounded by friends.

"Where am I?"

"We are in your mind," said a familiar voice.

"Nathaniel! Release me at once."

He snickered at the request. "You need to hear this."

Nathaniel warned the prince of the Uvali. They were formidable. Assassins sent for everyone loyal to the prince. Abominations of Earth, born through the union of Adam, the first man and Lilith, daughter of Hyperion. Their union bore the first demons. Hyperion adored their savagery.

"This is not the first time I have had a run-in with demons."

The prince's response frightened Nathaniel. "How?"

"Apparently, Soldiel killed the gods in my reality, giving rise to three tribes: Elves, demons, and shapeshifters. After centuries of crossbreeding, humans came to be. Eris was able to connect with a demon in my world and find me. Amira St. Clair, she is the reason I am here."

"DEMONS!?"

"You have met a demon," Nathaniel laughed. "In your reality, demons are still alive! This is a recipe for disaster if they find a way into our reality."

"What do you mean?"

"The blurring of reality can cause major damage."

"But even if Amira was to find me here, how does she differ from the Uvali?"

Nathaniel sighed. "They were more powerful than any king or queen of Earth. The gods sent a great flood to wipe them out. They were not easily killed, unlike the rest of Lilith's children. Chaos enlisted the help of a witch, who managed to seal them away in a Nebula Stone the size of a monolith."

Nathaniel confessed this was not the first time they were unleashed. The first time their reign came to an end was at the hands of the Mystic Otrant. She took on the legion of demons and sealed them away. In the process, she nearly lost her life. The prince could see true fear on Nathaniel's face. He was worried about the prince. A jolt shocked the prince as he got closer to the traitor, and it broke their connection. He was once again standing in the desert, inches away from the Kingdom of Salahea. Anri and Nacilias tended to the prince as he slowly came to. He broke the news to them only to set off more alarms. Saturos and Princess Toa were distracted by the strange silence.

The guards were ordered to open the gates, but they were received with treason. Dozens of spears and arrows filled the sky, hurtling down on them. They ran for cover. Prince Alexander's arm was grazed by an arrow. Anri entered the line of fire again, and as a spear came close to her face, she enchanted it and redirected it into the skull of one of the guards. Zaos used her magic to assist in redirecting the arrows and spears. Princess Toa ordered Saturos to stand down. They watched as she approached the gate and punched the massive limestone doors in.

As they entered the city, they saw a war-stricken image. The High Guard was attacking the citizens. Children hung from their feet. Rivers of blood filled the streets. The sounds of women being raped filled their ears. Saturos tore through each of them, adding to the body count. It was a rebellion against the pharaoh. Zaos pulled a spear from the ground and launched it into the head of a man raping a woman. Lord Zylo went into a fit of rage as the body of a little girl lay bleeding on the floor. He intervened and slaughtered countless men as Anri stood back and protected the prince and princess. Saturos led them toward the wall of stone that protected the palace. Traitors heavily guarded it. They drew their swords and charged toward them. Anri walked ahead of the group and flung her arm up. She crushed their lungs from the inside, bringing them all down at once.

Princess Toa could feel their pain. The vibrations of the world ran through her body. Each vibration spoke to her. When the cries of the men faded, she realized they were others mounting an attack. Prince Alexander held her hand and the princess smiled. The princess ordered them to stand behind her. She was a trained fighter but was never allowed to showcase her skills. She slammed her foot into the ground sending a wave of rocks toward the gate. The gate was thrown inward and crippled those behind it. Omega pierced countless warriors with his armored wings, while Shoxz trampled the others to secure the courtyard.

He saw Saturos and Lord Zylo out of the corner of his eye, racing from the outer wall. Anri and Zaos were keeping the High Guard at bay while they made their way toward the palace. There were too many of them. Prince Alexander was punched from the side and fell over. He felt another kick him in the stomach as he turned to look up and saw Lord Zylo leap onto the warrior and bite through his neck. Anri and Zaos were the last to walk into the courtyard. Princess Toa could feel more soldiers heading to the palace. She stomped her foot into the ground again and raised her hands up. The floor trembled as if struck by an earthquake before elevating them above the rest of the city. The soldiers stared and watched below as the grounds of the palace rose twenty feet. The commander ordered them to get grappling hooks so they could climb up to surround them. Saturos incinerated those that remained in the courtyard.

With the courtyard cleared, they proceeded into the palace with caution. Zaos snapped her fingers as she spoke, "*Unsichtbarketit,*" turning them invisible. It allowed them to slip in unseen and observe. The throne room was crawling with the pharaoh's army. General Abu Hamza sat on the pharaoh's throne. A plump olive-skinned man with a Gaeatoinc Eye headdress. His right arm was covered in tattoos down to his fingers.

As they hid behind a pillar, Saturos noticed something odd.

"What is that in his hand?"

Anri peeked around the corner and noticed Heishini's staff. What happened to the High Magnus.

"We must find the pharaoh," whispered the prince.

Princess Toa dug her fingers into the pillar, it allowed her to get a lay of the land. "I can see him."

Her brother was bound and gagged in a cell. He was bleeding from his head and had a gash in his stomach. Consumed by her anger, she punched the pillar, fracturing it and manipulated the shards to rip through the nearby guards.

'*Zeigen*,' as the word was muttered from Anri's lips, the invisibility spell dismantled. Saturos and the others took on those that remained. Lord Zylo was busy feasting on the blood of a soldier that he left the princess unattended. She was surrounded by troops. With her exceptional agility and precision, she outmaneuvered her enemies in the battlefield. She could anticipate their moves and counter them swiftly with powerful strikes. Interchanging between her combat skills and manipulating the earth. She subdued them.

General Abu Hamza was amused. He sat on the throne as he watched his warriors fight for their lives. Blood spilled and stained the floor. A spear sliced at Lord Zylo's leg, causing him to take a knee. He looked over toward Princess Toa, who was also covered in blood. With the last warrior down, they turned their attention onto the general.

Lord Zylo swiftly moved in for the kill, only to be thrown back by the force of the staff. Its power was unpredictable and immense.

"I was an apprentice to Heishini. You thought you could stand a chance against the Dark-Oricale Staff!"

General Abu Hamza approached Princess Toa with his staff radiating with the force of the sun. Lord Zylo ran toward him again, but this time the General pinned him to the floor. The princess slowly backed away from him. Each attempt to manipulate the earth ended in failure. He grabbed her by the neck and placed the top of the staff on her forehead. The princess' eyes shot open, projecting a golden light. It tossed the general back. He slammed the staff into the ground, allowing him to hold on. The staff began to suck the air out of the room. Lord Zylo roared and tried all he could to get up, but it did not work.

The princess was always seen as the weak one. Frail and blind, but the general underestimated her extreme power. The princess peeled away at his skin until the bone was exposed. The staff no longer protected him. While she was in this altered state she resembled Prince Alexander in

295

power. Lord Zylo's body felt little resistance, and he managed to get close enough to break General Abu Hamza's arms and subdue him.

The princess approached them, "You have betrayed our city!"

Princess Toa placed her hands on his face and kissed him on the lips. His cheeks caved in, and his body slowly turned to sand. Lord Zylo could smell the residual energy resonating from the princess. It was as strong as the prince's. She manipulated the earthbound minerals in the human body and killed him. It was an ability not even Lord Celeio was known for.

They noticed the ruby crystal of the Dark-Oricale Staff continued to pulsate as it lingered on the floor. With his claw, Lord Zylo tried to grab it, but it burned through his flesh. The ruby color faded as the prince approached it. He managed to pick it up without feeling pain. With one final flicker the ruby color changed to emerald.

"This must be returned to The All Mother."

While Princess Toa tended to Lord Zylo's hand, the others moved on ahead. Once his hand was tended to, the princess led him into a large corridor with sphinx statues lining the walkway. In the depths of the palace stood the old prisons. Lord Zylo positioned himself in front of the princess as the smell of burning flesh filled his nose. Prison cells were filled with the pharaoh's subjects. His army crucified dozens of them before burning them alive. The scorch marks stained the ceiling mural with black ash, a gory depiction of the war that separated Salahea into four regions. Beneath it was a stockpile of confiscated relics. Lapis lazuli's were placed around them to suppress their magic. Lord Zylo moved the princess behind a pillar before anyone could see them.

Prince Alexander and his companions were captured and kept in a cell. She could not see where the pharaoh was. Her gaze was focused on the Lieutenant. He held Akmadin's staff.

"We need to come up with a plan, princess. We need to free the others. How could he subdue everyone with just one staff?"

"Mind control. If he senses us, we are doomed."

Lord Zylo scaled the pillar and told Princess Toa to take cover. He made his way toward the prison unnoticed. The princess ducked down and touched the floor, absorbing the vibrations, allowing her to see. She opened the ground and jumped into it. Lord Zylo looked toward the pillar and realized she was gone. He jumped down from the ceiling and landed behind the prison. Prince Alexander noticed his friend and tried not to draw attention to them. Beneath the prince, a hole opened, and he fell through. One by one, the princess helped them escape through the sewer system. Another hole appeared next to Lord Zylo, and each of them ascended.

Like shadows, they sliced through the soldiers protecting the cells. One of the soldiers noticed the prisoners had escaped and yelled for the Lieutenant. Zaos waved her hands to enchant him, but Pharaoh Atemu-Nacus used his sickle blade to separate his head from his shoulders. One of his Magnus' used their blood and painted the floor. After igniting the symbols in fire, the staff disappeared. It was returned to the pharaoh's vault.

Princess Toa could feel Prince Alexander's heart racing. Gaea nearly killed her to have possession of her body. He wanted nothing more than to destroy her relics. It only fueled her power.

"I can feel your anger. I promise you we will find a way to deal with Gaea."

"The more you cling to her relics, the more you allow her to have a foothold in this world."

It was a delicate dance the princess had to perform in the eyes of her people. The Gaeatonic Guardians were the true power holding the realm together. Gaea's gifts helped them, and it would take careful planning to get the Magnus' to denounce her and disconnect from each of the items. The princess sought to rid themselves of Gaea's influence, but it would take time.

As the last of the traitors was dealt with, everyone made their way back into the throne room. The soldiers who scaled the wall managed to make it as far as the throne room before realizing the pharaoh was unharmed. They were taken into custody to await a public execution.

A look of disdain crossed the prince's face. The pharaoh noticed it.

"You do not agree with our justice?"

"Justice. What do you know of justice?"

"My prince, stop!" Zaos tapped his hand as she whispered.

"Pharaoh, where I come from, we have laws and systems in place to try people and issue punishments suitable to the crime. Bloodshed is all you know."

"I am truly grateful that you saved my sister, but I am ruler of Salahea. Not you. I will continue to issue out a king's justice."

"When everyone is dead, what will you be the king of then? This is what our enemy thrives on. Destruction. Death. We need to strive to be better. Otherwise, we are just as guilty as they are."

His words, like a thousand cuts, caused the pharaoh to ponder. He was right. His servants misled him, and he was disconnected from his people. How effective of a ruler could he truly be? Nodding his head, he agreed to be better. Looking over at Princess Toa, knowing they were connected by destiny, he could not leave without warning them.

"Ready yourself, my pharaoh; this was just the beginning."

Salahea could no longer hide from the coming war. Nathaniel's warning was met with abhorrence. The prince was echoing the Great Deceiver's propaganda. The Pharaoh could not fathom anyone had the power to release such creatures. The Mystic Otrant ended their reign, but that knowledge faded into history with her disappearance. There were rumors that she left her grimoires to a trusted servant. He was now the overseer of the Temple of Boreas on the Island of Venus. Within the temple there was rumored to be a gigantic library filled with knowledge collected by Lord Grevis from all over the world. The island was captured by legions of Dark Servants seeking entry into the temple. To reach the island, they would need to travel through the desert to Dous Docks.

Watching as the pharaoh and prince spoke, Saturos felt a pinch in his heart. His inner voice called to him. He could not miss out on this voyage. All his life he was confined to the pharaoh's service. Spending a lifetime in the desert and walking in the same halls only made him yearn for adventure. Having traveled with the prince and his companions made him feel like he had purpose. He did not want to lose himself in the background of the Magnus' again.

At first it was a whisper, but no one heard him. Then he spoke in a low voice, but still no one heard him. A nudge in the gut finally got him to speak.

"Pharaoh!"

His words silenced the room.

The prince's eyes darted to Saturos.

"My prince, in our short voyage together, I have witnessed the great bond you share with your companions. Since you have a representative of major factions amongst your team, I would ask permission to travel with you."

He longed for adventure. Since his time in court, he has felt uneasy and alone. Being around the prince made him feel whole. He was not judged, and he felt at home. Looking over at the prince he prayed he would speak on his behalf and welcome him into his service.

The pharaoh would not allow it. Losing three council members in a span of days was crippling. The prince watched as Saturos petitioned the pharaoh and argued his case. There was a knot in his stomach. Anagar showed him Saturos for a reason. He was one of many puzzle pieces on the board. If the prince agreed to let him come, could he risk Gaea taking control of him? Could he allow a potential spy for the pharaoh amongst his ranks? In the end, he needed Saturos close to him.

Prince Alexander stepped forward and seconded Saturos petition. Anri and Zaos disagreed with the prince, but the others believed he would be an asset. Seeing how vigorously the prince advocated for him, the pharaoh left it up to a vote. The council members showed their hands and unanimously agreed for him to dissolve his title and travel to assist the prince. Watching the looks on their faces, the prince saw the hatred they had for Saturos. Could they know about him? No matter the obstacle, each path he followed only brought him closer to his end goal... the destruction of Lord Nebula.

CHAPTER
26

ISLAND OF VENUS

Sleeping in the pharaoh's palace had its perks. Hot water, freshly cooked meals, and cozy beds. The prince, on the other hand, could not sleep. How could his mother bind Toa to him? He needed to know more of the story. As he opened his mother's journal to read, the words faded, as if rejecting him. More mysteries, more puzzles. He was tired of it. He missed his old life when things were simple. He missed Gabriel, his scent, his smile. Thinking of Gabriel triggered memories of Hans and Drail. He was filled with sorrow. Closing his eyes, he prayed for a vision of his mother, yearning to see her again.

It started like all dreams – dark and eerie. Damp walls and trickling water were all he could smell. Slowly walking forward, arms stretched out, feeling on the walls to guide his path. A new smell filled his nose the further he went. Blood. It was everywhere. The buzzing of flies and the smell of open flesh turned his stomach. He stopped only for a moment to settle his stomach, but he heard whispering up ahead. A flicker of light became a bonfire. Bound in chains was a female angel being tortured for information. Her blood drained and collected into tubes.

Her eyes shot open, radiating electricity like a storm cloud. *"Death will have you. Surrender now before you lose everything you love."*

The prince woke up in a puddle of sweat. His pupils dilated and fixated on the woman. It was Queen Nimah. Pulling on the satin sheets, he peered out the window, the sun was rising over the desert sands. The residual smoke of chaos lingered in the air. Nacilias and Shoxz rested, while the prince tiptoed to the open balcony. It appeared the princess returned the palace to its normal altitude, as servants could be seen entering and leaving the palace. A gentle knock at the door caught his attention. A servant of the pharaoh came bearing gifts.

A brand-new saddle for Shoxz and clothes for the prince. The servant showed him to the bathhouse. He was one amongst many. Naked men showered freely in front of each other. Staring down at the floor not to catch anyone's gaze, he found an open stall and showered himself. Flowing cold water cascaded down his skin, releasing his tension. Liquids that appeared to be homemade shampoo and soap were handed to him by the person in the stall next to him. Turning his face, he locked eyes with one of the pharaoh's High Magnus'.

"Do not be shy! We all must bathe. Use these; it will clean off the filth and soften the skin."

"I have never showered in front of others. Sorry."

"Do not fret, we were all virgins at one point."

His words caused the prince to pause. Was he trying to make fun of the prince or light of the situation? He continued to wash himself but tightened up as he noticed the man come over to his stall.

"We were not properly introduced to one another. I am Martis Aran."

The prince turned around uncomfortably and peered down at the naked man's feet and slowly shifted his gaze upward. His penis was in full view. Moving his eyes upward, he noticed his chiseled body. He had a healed wound on his left hip and underneath one of his nipples. The man's green eyes sparkled with a hint of gold. The sides of his head were shaven, but the top nested a ton of black hair, chopped and messy.

"I am Alexander."

As the prince mentioned his name. Everyone in the bathhouse stopped what they were doing and turned to him. Whispers broke out as everyone finished up and made haste to leave. Martis and the prince were the only ones left.

"They fear you. Rumor has it you are the most powerful Ilihi ever born."

Turning around to finish his shower, the prince continued to engage him in conversation. "I don't know what I am."

"You are the Prince of LunaSol. That is what you are."

His words only elevated the prince's fear. What did he know about being a prince? The title was a curse, not a blessing. His mind wandered off as the water hit his face. Martis' hands caressed the prince's skin. He rubbed the soap on the prince's hair and neck. Helpless to move, he stood there in ecstasy. It was the first time he was touched this way, and he enjoyed it. Martis rubbed his shoulders and washed off the soap. The prince took a step forward, trying to create space between them, but Martis grabbed him by his arms and brought him back to him until their skins touched. The prince could feel his damp body against him. The High Magnus kissed his neck and handed him a towel before finally letting go and walking out.

Alone in his thoughts, he smiled. He rinsed off and made his way back to his room with his towel wrapped around his waist. The servants had laid out a pair of tan pants and a shirt. He was given a wrap shawl for the desert heat. As he dressed, he heard another knock on the door. This time it was Martis and another High Magnus, Kepuri. They had one final gift for the prince. It was an armored arm plate; it extended from the shoulder down to the wrist. It was lightweight and had a wrist blade. Embedded into the armor was also a sonic pulse gun. Kepuri was the Master of Arms for the pharaoh and a great inventor. His armory was filled with advanced weapons of war. He came from a family of skilled blacksmiths. He first discovered he was a Magnus when working on a hammer for the previous pharaoh. He mistakenly enchanted it, and when used, it knocked out an adult Brontotherium. Kepuri was also easy on the eyes, and the prince noticed Martis gently grab for his hand after installing the armor on the prince. The two High Magnus' wished the prince luck and exited his room.

It was a revolving door of servants. Another knock at the door called for the prince to come to feast before he departed. A banquet hall filled with food was prepared for the travelers. The pharaoh and his court attended as well. Little to no words were spoken between the prince and the pharaoh. Alexander wanted out of Salahea. Saturos was the first to rise and bid his pharaoh goodbye. Prince Alexander and his companions got ready and departed the palace. Saturos led them into the vast desert oasis toward the pharaoh's road, a stone walkway that connected the kingdom to all those under its dominion.

They traveled northwest on the road for two days. It was nearly covered with sand, so it made it difficult to follow the trail. The statue markers of the previous pharaoh's were crumbling in place. The heat of the sun made it impossible for them to keep their eyes open with all the sweat pouring down. Heat rebounded from the sand and lingered in the air. Prince Alexander mounted Shoxz and rested as they pressed on. Finally, the moon took its place in the sky. Everyone was tired from the long journey and collapsed from dehydration. Falling from Shoxz, the prince landed on a sand dune and gazed up at the glory of the moon. Its silver gleam radiated over them, bestowing comfort on them.

Saturos lowered herself onto the sand and gently blew on it. The ground shook and it began to shift, creating a hut. Lord Zylo helped the fatigued prince into the hut to rest for the night. He was given a few drops of water to wet his lips before falling asleep. He felt more alone than ever. The focus of his thoughts changed. The memory of Drail holding him at night while he wept came to life. Chasing him in the park and tickling him into submission. These dreams caused the young prince to cry as he slumbered.

Night turned into day, and distant roars of chaos startled him awake. Six carnivorous Megistotherium circled the hut, awaiting their prey. These massive hyena-like creatures had razor-sharp teeth that measured a foot long. Zaos, Anri, and Lord Zylo were already outside. In fear, the prince ran outside to lend assistance. The sound of ribs cracking and howling shook his teeth. Saturos' armor was being torn at by one of the creatures. While protecting his face and limbs from being feasted on, it was hard for him to grab his sword. Without thinking, the prince ran for the creature and leaped on top of it. Pressing a release valve, his wrist blade appeared, and he dug it through the creature's head. Anri and Zaos dealt with the others. Drool fell from their mouths as they opened their enormous jaws, revealing two rolls of diamond-shaped teeth. One leaped first at Anri, but with a wave of her hand, the beast went flying into a sand dune. Saturos attacked without warning and slit the throats of two of them. The Megistotherium that the High Chancellor threw back came running toward her, but this time she gripped her hand and was transfixed on the beast. Its feet stumbled, and its fast speed became a stride until it collapsed at her feet and died. Black magic was forbidden in court, but its temptation kept calling to her since she last used it.

As a Magnus, her abilities were unparalleled. Magnus' were taught to be reserved and were limited in their casting under the watchful eye of the Ilihi. Spells that were deemed heresy came naturally to her. She was the first to frighten even Saturos. With a twirl of her hand, she shifted the sands to cover their remains. Zaos smelled blood in the air. It was not from the slaughtered beasts. As the sands shifted, Lord Zylo could be seen limping toward them with deep wounds. He nearly collapsed, but Zaos made it in time and grabbed him. Saturos and the prince assisted and returned him to the hut for healing. The longer his wounds remained open, the more it would attract other Megistotherium. They were kings of the desert and hunted for sport. Zaos tended to his wounds.

Anri's eyes darted to the prince. "This was not a random attack. They were sent to hunt us."

Zaos looked up. "I smelled it too. Elven magic!"

They wanted revenge against the Pandemonium Elf. Acting on impulse is what the enemy wanted. The prince did not want any harm to befall the others. They would not travel until everyone recovered. No one dared challenge him. His annoyance said it all. Allowing his friend to rest, he left the hut and walked to the outskirts of their campgrounds. As far as the eye could see, there was nothing but sand. No end in sight. Omega approached the prince, and the prince leaned on him. The Pegasus had a lot on his mind.

"What's wrong?"

"We need to warn Narnarie. If he is gathering troops to aid you, he is a target for the Uvali. I need to make sure he is safe."

"Protect him!"

Omega placed his wing over the prince, embracing him. Rubbing his soft fur, he gently kissed his forehead before stepping to the side, allowing the Pegasus to take his leave. The golden speck of Omega's armor faded into the distance as the prince turned and returned to the hut. He lay beside Nacilias, petting him for comfort as he dozed off. Flickering images of a mountain shrine covered in thick clouds faded into a majestic overgrown tree protruding from the ground, gleaming from the inside out. A peaceful vision turned chaotic in seconds as the exquisite tree was engulfed in flames. Alexander's screams disintegrated the hut drenching them in sand. Zaos and Anri stared in fright. The prince's eyes sparkled with lightning.

Recounting his vision made the others more nervous about their voyage. Manifesting three abilities at once caused a stir amongst the camp. The prince's powers were unpredictable and getting worse. Zaos saw the look of concern on their faces.

"Maybe a book from the Temple of Boreas can help us understand what you are?"

Her words were like daggers. Alexander perched up his eyebrows in annoyance. "What I am?"

If left unchecked, he could do more harm than good. Saturos opened his mouth to speak, but Zaos interjected.

"Yes. You are an enigma. You speak with animals, control elements, you can even astral project. You have visions and can use magic. There is no one like you besides..."

She stopped abruptly. Her mind raced over her next words. There was only one person who showed similar abilities, Lord Nebula. Arguing about it in the desert would solve nothing.

"Zaos, what were you going to say?" questioned Anri.

"Haven't you wondered why Lord Nebula wants him dead? Why do they have similar abilities?"

Her questions shook them to their core. She was right. No one truly knew the reason Hyperion wanted the prince dead besides the vision he received. Her questions made them even more terrified of him. Zaos hoped the library had something to help them understand his abilities.

"We need to focus on the Pandemonium Elf and not me. What does she want with the tree?"

Lord Zylo lifted himself up as his wounds were finally healed.

"It's a gateway."

Prince Alexander turned to face him as he spoke. What the prince witnessed was the Tree of Life, a deceitful gift to Lord Grevis from Hyperion. After the slaughter of the Hagerod's, Hyperion tried to cover it up. He temporarily closed the portals, but years later they reappeared. This time, Lord Grevis decided to build his temples over their locations and research them. Hyperion grew suspicious of him and tried to force his true intentions to the surface. Gifting him the tree, he promised to share

Heaven's secrets with him if he could unlock the true potential of the tree. The old gods used it to birth new life. The Divine Lord was not a pawn. He used the tree as a conduit for the portal and met the Cardinal Deity - Ewonbi. The tree was in fact a seedling from the Tree of Knowledge, which once resided in the fabled Garden of Eden before finally resting upon the shell of the serpent-tortoise. The seedling houses residual energy from Gaea. For the tree to call out to him, it only solidified Zaos' concerns about the prince.

The prince questioned the vision. Could it be a plow to sidetrack him from finding the remaining stones? Or could it be Gaea trying to connect with Saturos again and turn him to her side? No matter what, he needed to get to the tree. They mounted Lord Zylo's body onto Shoxz and prepared for the journey to the docks. The afternoon sun was setting. A herd of Aepycamelus passed alongside them. Its head was small compared to the rest of its body. It had a very large neck like a giraffe. Its legs were stilt-like and measured at least four feet. Its head was about ten feet above the ground. Saturos praised the creatures as a sign of good fortune. They were always seen grazing near the docks. The sands turned green as they arrived at a patch of grassland surrounding Dous Docks.

Nacilias grew worried. The smell of ash and burnt wood filled the air. Seeing the ocean over the sand dunes, their eyes were drawn to the burning masses. Ships wreaked and sank. Bodies crucified and skinned to the bone. A stunning stone harbor was reduced in seconds. Cries for help echoed over the splashing waves. Zaos and Saturos ran to their aid. Anri jolted her hands toward the ocean. As she weaved her hands in and out, strands of water spewed from the depths and put out the flames. Consumed by her ignorance, the Pandemonium Elf mistakenly left stragglers behind. A few of the ferrymen tended to their captain. His lungs filled with smoke. If he survived the night, his crew vowed to take them to Venus. They prepared for the three-day voyage.

There was an inn on the shore that was still intact. It would house them for the night. An old innkeeper greeted them. Her gray, wavy hair covered most of her face. Anri noticed the yellow in her eyes. As she led them up the stairs, her long nails scrapped the railing. She showed them to their rooms before disappearing into a dark corridor. All slept through the night and were awakened by knocks at the door. The innkeeper woke the prince and his friends to meet the captain in the dining hall for breakfast. The grand table was filled with fruits, breads, and fish.

The innkeeper's generosity was overwhelming. They sat with the captain and his crew and indulged in the food before setting out on their journey. Once the crew finished eating, they left the inn and prepared the ship. Anri and Zaos noticed the innkeeper lurking in the shadows, watching the prince's movements. As they prepared to depart, she was no longer lurking. She was nowhere to be found. Following her gut, she went looking for the innkeeper, only to find her dead body in a broom closet. The wall was covered with Elven wards. The Pandemonium Elf was among them. Anri did not want to alarm the others, but she made sure Saturos and Zaos were aware. They boarded the ship on high alert. The voyage would not be the easiest. The waters of the Sea of Hope were very dangerous, and the creatures beneath the sea were even more dangerous. The prince gazed over the side of the ship and noticed a pod of white-striped dolphins following them. Their fins danced through the waves as they sailed through the ocean, captivating the prince.

He heard his wounded friend moan and moved toward the heart of the ship. They spoke until the sun faded and the moon overtook the sky. The savageness of the sea ensued and ravaged the deck with its waves. The three-day voyage cost them three sailors, but in the end, they found themselves gazing at the mist covered island. The captain anchored the ship a great distance from the actual docks. They offered a smaller boat to the prince to reach the shores. Anri stood close to the prince trying to navigate who the traitor was onboard. They rowed the two wooden boats through the mist and came upon a dock covered in purple marble. At one point it was a beauty, but now it is covered in thick ivy, decaying wood, and crumbling statues. Remnants of the war. Without a sound, they exited the boat and explored the ruins. There was no sign of human life, not even a whisper. A shadow through the mist caused them to regroup.

Saturos pulled out his sword and pointed it at the man. "Do not proceed any further. State your name!"

"I am Hellmeo, Keeper of the Docks of Textile. What business do you have on Venus?"

Hellmeo got closer and noticed they were surrounding a young man. "I know you! Why have you come here? You must leave. They will kill you!"

Zaos slowly approached the old man. "Who?"

Hellmeo pointed at the crew. The mist was enchanted and revealed their identity, Dark Elves. Corrupted by dark magic and soullessness. Their blue veins shimmered through their black skin. Atop their heads were long silver locks braided backwards into a ponytail. Saturos shifted his sword toward them. Anri slowly moved toward Hellmeo. The elves did not attack. They feared the keeper and fled into the shadows. Anri and Hellmeo seemed to know one another. She kissed the old man's ring, and his form changed. A heap of a man, towering a full eight feet and a body carved from stone. He gazed at them with his silver-colored eyes. His battle armor was unscathed and reflected the small rays of light from the sun.

Nacilias noticed his belt and pressed up against Prince Alexander's leg. The prince noticed it as well. The Star of the Oricale. His glove had a metallic version of the star on it with three sharp bladed claws attached to it.

"It feels good to be in my own skin again."

"Wade, you know it was for your own protection. If I did not cloak you, you would have been killed."

Anri and Wade were allies. During the Holy War, he joined their cause and became a spy for the princess. He was an Alulim. Thousands of years before the creation of Earth, Chaos' sister had two children. Her youngest, Tarma gave birth to five children. One being Wade's father. Prince Alexander had already met his brother John when he astral projected in Lady Phoebe's mind. Wade was a teleporter and was one of the few Alulim who sought refuge on Chaos' Earth when the Nebula consumed most of the universe. Before he could be killed, he teleported into an alternative reality where the Nebula was good, but when Lord Nebula was imprisoned, his abilities went haywire and flung him onto LunaSol.

Anri gently grabbed his hand. "Take us to Kemzata."

Wade picked up his rags and covered his newly formed body. He walked over to one of the broken statues and moved it out of the way, revealing a hidden bunker. As they descended, Zaos placed her hands on the stone walls.

"*Imluminite.*"

A trail of fire cascaded along the brick, giving them light. Wade led them to the outskirts of Kemzata. Once topside, he moved quickly, gathering information before returning to them. The city was overrun by dark servants. He was in contact with one of his agents, who agreed to hide them until nightfall.

"We must move quickly. Dark Servants are rummaging through every home and interrogating anyone for knowledge of the temple entrance. Hold hands. I will teleport us to safety."

They gathered into a circle and held hands. Wade pictured a living room and a fireplace. He focused on the image, and when he opened his eyes, his entire body erupted into flames and consumed the others. The flames subsided, and they were no longer out in the open but in a small cottage.

Teleporting took a lot out of them. Some of them had to catch their breath. They felt like they were thrown with a slingshot. The prince was hyperventilating. Nacilias had to jump on him and push him to the ground. He held his head on the prince's chest until he finally stopped. They did not realize they were being watched. Sitting in the corner was a monk. He wore a puffy robe with sparkling blue fur around the collar. Sapphire jewels were embedded into it with silver chains holding each side of the robe together. A single sapphire was placed in the center of his forehead. Under his robes, he wore skintight armor that also had a blue sparkle to it. His pants were oversized and puffed as they got closer to his ankles.

Wade introduced him as Duke. He was once a monk within the Temple of Boreas but was cast out for challenging the current Head Monk for leadership. He wanted the monks to fight back against the Dark Servants rather than hide in the mountains.

The prince remained on the floor. He sat up, and Nacilias laid on his lap. "Duke, why is the Pandemonium Elf going after the tree?"

Duke was chilled to hear that the tree called out to him. He took it as a dark omen. The monks had to be warned.

"Lord Nebula is desperate. His pawns are everywhere and trying to exhaust you. You are right to worry. Your path is being diverted, but for what? To buy time? You speak of the last two stones. Something is holding him back if he seeks to infiltrate the temple. There must be some knowledge within it about the stones that he seeks."

Duke paused as bangs resonated throughout the room. The prince and the others moved away from the sealed door as the bangs became louder. He rushed them into hiding.

"Just a minute!"

He looked back as he approached the door, and everyone rallied together as Zaos recited, "*Unsichtbarkeit.*" They became invisible just in time as he opened the door, and dozens of dark servants piled into the room. They pushed Duke out of the way and searched the house.

"Why have you come barging into my home?"

The Dark Servants did not speak, but a voice of death creaked into the room as they continued searching. Duke's eyes fluttered in dread. A massive, cloaked entity entered his home and set his gaze toward the warrior. The demonic figure's face was hidden behind a golden mask. It wore spiked golden gauntlets that reached its elbow. As it glided over the floor, the wood decayed. The Dark Rider got closer to Duke and fed on his lifeforce. Duke's face turned pale blue. As the creature spoke, it pierced the ears like nails on glass.

"The boy prince is here seeking shelter."

"I have not seen him."

"You lie. Ukna can see it in your eyes."

Ukna took his leave, and the Dark Servants followed suit. They grabbed a hold of Duke and dragged him out, kicking and screaming. Prince Alexander demanded that Zaos drop her spell and allow them to help. She could not refuse him and did what she was told. The prince ran out of the cottage and used the sonic gun in his armor. The malevolent being laughed as his gauntlets absorbed the blast. The enchantment around them was no more.

"Good. You did not disappoint."

"Let him go!"

The prince did not know what he was getting himself into. Anri chased after him and was paralyzed with dread. Dark Riders were powerful wraiths and servants of Lord Dark Lucus. Born from concentrated dark energy, they have no true form. The cloaks that they wore were enchanted to provide them with a silhouette of a form. The gauntlets were enchanted to absorb magic. Even the ground, which they glide upon, withers away. She screamed for the prince to stop his advances. Anri held his arm. He was not ready to face off against a malevolent being. They were soulless, carnivorous beings that feed on human souls. Their safest bet was to flee.

Anri's staff radiated with frost as she blasted the nearby Dark Servants. The others made their way around the prince to shield him. Ukna stared at the prince as chaos erupted around them. Anri's warning went in one ear and out the other. Prince Alexander summoned his Winged Staff of the Eclipse and charged at him. He vanished into shadows and reappeared behind him, clenching the prince's neck. He could not speak. Breathing the cold, toxic air into his lungs nearly caused him to lose consciousness. Calling upon Fang could weaken him even more, but something else called to him. Placing his hand in his pocket, he removed the stone. It radiated a light so powerful; it blasted the Dark Rider into a cabin. Duke roared for the others to run into the Forest of Smoke, while he and Wade kept the Dark Servants from advancing. Shoxz stopped in mid-gallop, allowing the prince to mount her, while the others raced for cover. The prince slowly turned his head to see a cloud of darkness appear right in front of Duke. His heart dropped to his feet as he saw Ukna rip out his heart. Closing his eyes, he leaned forward. Each gallop echoed in his ears as he faded further into the forest. His heart slowed, and tears filled his eyes. Countless lives were lost because of his birth. The world around him faded to nothing. It was just the prince and his thoughts.

The noises of the battle became more and more distant. Shoxz stopped dead in her tracks and cried out in pain. The prince was launched from her back and into the dirt. The forest was not safe. A buzzing sound infected her ears crippling her. Nacilias and Lord Zylo could hear the same noise.

"It's paralyzing!"

Lord Zylo was able to get the words out before passing out on the floor. A thick cloud of fog covered the floor. Zaos and Anri feared that death had overtaken them, but to the touch they were still breathing. Her ears could not sense movement, but as she rubbed her hands over the plants, she could sense vibrations from them. She moved closer to one of the trees and could feel dark magic emitting from it.

"*Zeigen sie mir.*"

Her words revealed a hidden dryad. The beautiful creature was paralyzed. Vines bound her naked body in the heart of the tree. Zaos noticed Prince Alexander slowly rise from the floor, gawking at the pale-faced creature. Zaos touched the vines and could feel the dark magic coursing through it. The Pandemonium Elf was responsible for this.

The prince felt useless. Nothing he did brought them closer to victory. Without Hans or Soldiel to guide him, he felt incompetent. He was leading everyone to their death. Weakened and tired from battle, the prince sat beside the poisoned tree. Zaos used this time to try and figure out what caused the others to fall unconscious.

Sitting in his sorrow, he placed his hands in his pocket and ran the stone fragment in between his fingers. Realizing it could be used as a weapon, he removed the Star of Orion and showed Zaos and Anri. To his surprise, they were unfamiliar with the relic. He divulged it was a gift from a pixie queen he met on his travels. It was one of the fragments needed to revive Lord Nebula. Using it came at a risk now; the Dark Rider was aware he had it. Zaos inspected the stone, but no magical properties were radiating off it. She found it odd. If it contained portions of Lord Nebula's power, why was its aura not exuding it?

Soldiel's stories finally came in handy. His working theory was that the angels were the only ones who could sense it as it was – they who stripped Lord Nebula and stored his powers away. Zaos was inclined to agree, but that still made matters worse; Lord Dark Lucus remained an angel even if corrupted by evil. Anri urged the prince to keep it hidden and not use its power again. It was too risky. He agreed. Zaos went back to focusing on how to help the others wake up. Blackened by the curse, the bark of the tree was rotting. It was a dark and contagious spell. More power than the Pandemonium Elf could muster on her own. Elves of the Twilight were well versed in ancient magics, but this was prohibited even for them. She knew a ritual that would counter the spell.

To combat dark magic, she would need to tap into darker magic. Anri worried it would corrupt her. Without her spell, they were sitting ducks. Wade could not hold the dark rider and his troops back by himself. They needed to gain some distance between them. Zaos ordered them to find three white bellflowers from the Bois dentelle, the blood of three clouded leopards, one black bat flower, and the bark from a giant sequoia tree. Each was native to the forest.

Zaos smiled, "Nature will always produce a remedy to heal itself."

He followed Anri into the fog. Everything in front of them was concealed by its grasp. It created a challenge for them. Anri waved her hands and created an opening in the fog, allowing them to see. There was a tree root visible. She placed her hands on it and could feel the flow of water in it. It was a long shot, but she focused on the water and used the trees to scan for the items. Resorting to another locating tactic, she pressed her hands into the moist ground. Closing her eyes and slowing her breathing, she muttered, "*Az rai calidem.*"

Shifting leaves and crouching footsteps could be heard from far away. Hear ears could hear for miles. The creatures of the forest were using the fog to stalk their prey; a pack of clouded leopards remained hidden from sight.

Prince Alexander tried to communicate with them, but the clouded leopards pounced on them. They were crazed. Their minds were scattered and infected with darkness. Hunger was their source of focus. Anri used the fog and compacted the air and froze their bodies. They picked up the creatures and brought them to Zaos, so she could prepare the ritual. Only one item remained. Staring at the tree where the dryad was imprisoned, she waved her hands, and the roots of the tree formed into three small caldrons. Hidden in her clothes was a small silver blade. Its handle was as black as midnight, but the blade sparkled like starlight. She quickly slit the throats of the three leopards over the caldrons. The prince gasped. Innocent creatures, now dead, for the sake of saving their friends. He tired of sacrificing others for his needs.

Seeing the look on his face, Zaos turned to him. "If we do not do this our friends will die in this forest."

Turning back to her, he sat on the roots of a nearby tree as she continued. Zaos had already cut the bark from the tree was began carving it into a stake. Anri took the prince by the hand and went to look for the black bat flower.

The further into the forest they went, the creepier it became. Rotting trees and fecal matter surrounded them. Half-eaten carcasses hanging from ropes. Streams of black ooze seeping from the trees. The forest was silent. No birds chirping. No insects buzzing. Not even the breaking of a tree branch could be heard. Anri believed it to be darker magic. She took a step forward and activated a trap. Vines shot up from the ground and wrapped around her wrist. Runes were etched into the vines and suppressed her abilities. A massive shadow could be seen in the fog and knocked the prince out cold.

Hours later, when he awoke, he was tied to one of the trees. With his blurred vision he noticed Anri was imprisoned next to him. He tried to wiggle free, but a rugged voice drew his attention.

"It is truly an honor to see you moments before your death, Great Herald."

Sangria-colored eyes stared at them from across the field. Elegant and mesmerizing as they were, they were detached from any form. Swirling around them, the fog shifted, taking on the form of an elf. Dark skin, blue veins pulsating through the skin, and long silver hair. Her breastplate bore a serpent sigil, and her armored tunic tightened around her skin as she walked closer to them.

"Introductions. I am Esve. Glad you finally caught up."

Struggling to break free from his prison, it only tightened the vines around his wrist even more. The Pandemonium Elf reached forward, and the vines holding up Anri detached from the tree and placed her on the floor in front of her. Anri did not struggle; she knew she was going to die. A belt of silver daggers wrapped around the elf's waist. She toyed with them as she pulled Anri's hair back to show off her neck. Kicking and screaming, the prince tried to untangle himself before she could cut her throat. Heart racing, pulse rising, the sounds of the world faded. Rage was his sole focus. Drowned in anger, he let it absorb him. As he screamed, his amulet lit up like a beacon. Sweat from his pores turned into fire, engulfing the vines. Soulless were his eyes as he charged at the elf.

Using her magic, she created a shield of vines. Distracted by the prince, this allowed Anri to get up and make a run for it. Her abilities were still nullified. She turned around and watched as the prince used the fog around him to freeze the vines and then blast through them with flames. The elf dematerialized into the fog, leaving the prince in his altered state. Anri slowly walked toward him as she noticed his blackened eyes. His body was trembling. Remembering a song his mother would sing to the princess; she hummed the tone for him. It seemed to calm him. Humming the song finally settled him. She grabbed his hand and made a run for it. They found themselves in a field of bois dentelles.

There the elf stood in the center of the field. Smiling at them. The fog cleared as she waved her hand revealing even more uprooted vines. She used them to bind them again and tightened them around their necks, taking every breath from them. No matter how powerful the elf was, the prince was relentless. Knowing he could not beat her on his own. He gave in and called on the power of the amulet. Once free from her grip, he grabbed his staff and drove it into the floor. The wave of energy sent Esve flying into a tree.

Three white bellflowers fell from the tree and landed on the floor. Before she could recover, he twirled the staff, and the very vines she conjured bound her to the tree. Her own runes lit up as she tried to use magic. Anri caught her breath as the vines retreated from her back into the ground. She approached the prince and picked up the flowers from the floor and stored them in his bag. Before Anri could say anything, the prince snapped Esve's neck.

Without hesitation, without consulting her, he killed the elf. She looked into his eyes, expecting to see his pupils covered with a dark glaze, but they weren't. On his own accord, he took a life. No words were exchanged on their way back. Starlight sparkled above the trees as the full moon was nearly at its apex. Zaos was in mid-chant as they rushed to her a sweaty mess. Anri handed her the white bellflowers, and the prince handed her the black bat flower. She placed each of the white bellflowers into the blood-filled cauldrons as she chanted, with the flower in her hands.

>**"Herz der Finsternis, meinnen Schrei hören,**
>**brennen in den Nachthimmel. Kräfte der**
>**Erde und der Sonne, rückgängig machen**
>**Magie, die geleistet wurde. Versiegeln das**
>**Schicksal dieses Bösen."**
>
>*(Heart of Darkness, hear my cry, burn in*
>*the night sky. Forces of the ground and*
>*sun, undo your magic, which has been done.*
>*Seal the fate of this evil one.)*

With each word, the blood began to boil and erupted into flames. Fire consumed the bellflowers, and the flower in her hands radiated a deep purple. Ripping the flower apart, she blew it toward the tree, which caused the dryad's eye to shoot open. The vines released her, and her body collapsed onto the floor before turning into petals; in her place was the lifeless body of Esve. Grabbing the stake she carved, she stabbed Esve in the forehead. The cauldrons simmered as the tree absorbed her essence, undoing her curse. Nacilias and the others slowly picked themselves up from the floor. Esve's curse puzzled her, a linking curse could only be used by high-ranking generals in the Elven Court. When elves warred between their tribes, those that were killed would be placed into a tree and cursed. The curse would weaken the collective, allowing one side to best the other.

Esve used a creature of nature rather than an elf, so nature and its animals were affected.

It brought her back to her childhood in Avalon. There were whispers of a book of spells stolen from the royal library that contained spells taught to them by the dragons, which included this curse. She shared her knowledge with Anri. If this book found its way into Lord Dark Lucus' hands, it could be disastrous. The nefarious effects dark magic has on the body would consume her if left unchecked. Even Elves of the Twilight are not immune from its corruption. A fine balance between the light and dark magic allows them the fortitude to challenge both, but the more you dabble in darkness, the easier it is to stray from the light. Weakened from the ritual, Zaos needed rest. She laid at the base of the tree and collected the petals of the dryad. She placed them in a pouch on her belt.

CHAPTER
27

TEMPLE OF BOREAS

Anri glanced over at Lord Zylo, who was busy sniffing the floor. With the curse lifted and the fog clearing, dark servants were closing in on them. Zaos was placed atop Shoxz as they followed a dirt road to a valley at the foot of two mountains. From the distance, they could see a staircase carved between the mountains and an archway carved into it. Grazing in the valley were gorilla's and spotted leopards. They were cautious not to stir them, but once they reached the foot of the staircase, they were confronted by two dragoons camouflaged into the mountain.

Abracas and Ancalagon as they were called were as massive as the dragoons of Salahea. Abracas' gray scales and Ancalagon's brown ones flailed around their neck, as they bellowed. Each held a spiked mace in one hand and a lance in the other. Their gray armor was covered in moss and mud. No one was allowed to pass. The prince pleaded with them, even going so far as to show them the Eclipse Amulet. Esve and the Dark Rider were working together. He would not be far behind them. The two dragoons battled the Dark Rider before and managed to keep him at bay. They called to arms the creatures of the forest. Gorillas, spotted leopards, and Roseate cockatoos raced to the call. Ancalagon stepped aside and allowed the prince and his companions access up the mountain.

As they ascended the steps, the moon began to fade behind a storm of sand. They tried to cover their eyes as they climbed, but it pummeled them.

"*Schutzen.*" Zaos' spell created an aura around them to prevent the sand from blinding them. The storm raged on, trapping the moon from sight. Swirling his sword in a circle, Saturos generated some light with his blue flames. He used it to light their path. The steps were getting narrower the further up they went. To their surprise, they did not reach the temple but stood on a massive platform wedged between the two mountains. Hundreds of skeletons were stacked into corners. On the circular platform stood six massive caldrons burning with blue flames. From above, a vociferous noise devastated their ears and caused the ground to surge beneath their feet. Even the mountain trembled, rocks collapsed onto the platform as a shadowy figure could be seen approaching through the blanket of sand. Everyone gathered as the monstrous creature's four red eyes pierced through the sandstorm. Another great roar cleared the storm, revealing the Mesonic stone lion. Towering over twenty feet tall. Its carapace was silvery-white. Its large, spiked fins descended its back to its flat beaver-like tail. The creature's face was small and compact with a shovel-like chin. Its underbelly was sharp like jagged rocks. As it opened its mouth again to yell, its sharp, jagged teeth vibrated. Lord Zylo nearly fainted. These were creatures of history, native to deserts, thought to be extinct during the Holy War.

"Why would a Mesonic stone lion be here?" questioned Anri.

The beast roared out before anyone could answer.

His words echoed in the prince's mind. He repeated, "This is the end of the line for you."

"I am Prince Alexander. The Temple of Boreas is in danger. Please grant us entry!"

The destructive mammoth of a creature stomped its feet and sent the prince flying back toward Lord Zylo.

Prince Alexander turned to the others. "He will not listen. We must get to the temple."

Saturos stood near one of the cauldrons and felt a strange energy emanating from it. The cauldron itself contained its own magical properties. He took his sword and plunged it into the cauldron, trying to reignite it. With Lord Zylo's help they flipped the cauldron on its side, spilling the charcoal and fire onto the platform. The creature stepped on it and screamed out in pain. Zaos and Anri did the same with the other cauldrons. With each cauldron spilled, they could feel their abilities coming back. The amulet flickered, and as he touched it, he was filled with a strange peace. He felt Fang again for the first time. The Mesonic stone lion charged at them, but a jet of fire blasted its face from the sky. Sparkling emerald scales descended from the clouds, as Fang came into view.

The cowering creature dug into the side of the mountain and embedded its body once more. The sandstorm had subsided, and the clear sky loomed above. Fang scaled the mountain as the others continued their ascent. Reaching the end of the staircase, led them to a rope bridge connecting to another mountain. In the distance, Lord Zylo could see the Temple of Boreas. Saturos stepped onto the bridge and grabbed the rope; instantly he collapsed as a massive surge of electricity rushed through his body. Anri ran to his aid. He was barely breathing, and his body was sizzling. The prince held him in his arms and caressed his face. Emotions ran wild and his sadness turned to rage. More than a dozen frayjains slowly approached them, wielding electrified weapons. Two approached without helmets; one was gray, and the other red. Fang roared out and flared his wings, awaiting the prince's command, but the frayjains attacked first. Fang was forced into the open sky without any support. He managed to incinerate four frayjains but they kept up their attacks. With swiftness, their sharp weapons cut through his scales. Blood fell upon the prince's face. His rage amplified in the presence of the star fragment. He mounted Shoxz and took off to help his dragon. Zaos and Anri enchanted their feet, allowing them to glide through the air and join the fight. Lord Zylo and Nacilias stood behind to protect Saturos.

Fang circled overhead and dove down toward the Frayjains causing them to scatter. Getting close enough, the prince was able to slice through their leader's chainmail, leaving one of them wounded. Zaos and Anri did not get to the prince in time, one of the frayjains had an electrical whip and entangled the prince in it. Shoxz and the prince fell from the sky, but she was able to get her footing before she could hit the ground, but the prince was not so lucky. His body lay broken on the floor. Lord Zylo rushed to his side as a puddle of blood gathered behind his head. With the prince wounded, Fang fell from the sky breaking the mountain peak. Anri and Zaos landed and saw the devastating blow. The red furred frayjain descended from the clouds with a smile on his face. Anri summoned the water from the moist air and manifested a spear. Launching it at him, all she could muster was a simple cut on the cheek. The creature was too fast for her. He snapped his whip once again, but in an instant the prince was standing in front of her, holding the end of the whip around his arm.

Eyes as black as coal. The fury of defeat overtook him. His aura was once again ignited and radiating immense power. His blood slithered back toward him and into his open wounds before they resealed themselves. Wind swirled around him, causing the ground to tremble. Thunder and lightning ravaged the mountain, scaring the frayjains. A pulsating energy erupted from his body, sending the creatures tumbling backwards. As he walked toward them the ground shattered from the vast energy emitted from his aura.

"Stop this madness. You will kill us all!" roared Zaos.

Reasoning with the prince was pointless. Pain and anger were driving his actions. His mind was not his own. He extended his hand to the wounded frayjain and lifted him into the air. The other frayjains tried to fly away, but the prince did not allow it. He extended his other hand in the direction of the fleeing creature and gripped it. Their wings crippled, and they plummeted to the ground. He gripped his hand tighter, causing the warrior to cry in agony as he ripped off his armor. His attention was diverted when a gust of wind blasted him into the mountain. The prince was trapped in the overbearing stream of wind. The frayjains were no longer alone, a monk came to their aid. He wore green robes with golden armor. A man with a bald head and a long gray bread to his stomach. The monk was relentless. Blow after blow, he kept the prince pinned to the rock. He broke through his aura and weakened the prince out of his altered state.

Zaos and Anri watched as the monk approached with another group of frayjains. He studied the prince's face and saw the amulet on the floor nearby.

"Bring them. We will interrogate them inside."

As they crossed the bridge, they noticed the temple was carved out of the mountain. The gray tint of its walls was covered in snow. The temple's vimana reached an elevation of fifty feet. It was square and surmounted by a pyramidal roof. The gopuram were ornate and covered with inscriptions. Anri gazed up at the porches and witnessed countless frayjains standing guard. The pillared halls were illuminated with electricity. Waterfalls poured down from up above deep into the heart of the mountain. Lowe, as the servants of the temple called him, escorted them to the healing chamber. The wounded were laid on beds, and remedies were administered.

The others were taken into another chamber. Tiles of emerald, sapphire, and gold lined in circular patterns. At the center of the room the titles were arranged into the form of a tree. Above it a golden eight-pointed star with three circles. To each side of the walkway were trees carved of emerald showered in a mist of water, enchantments only Zaos could smell. The staircase approaching Lowe's throne had twelve steps. His throne was carved out of emerald, resembling a tree as well. It stood on a circular platform with runes etched around it. He plopped himself down on the throne throwing one leg over the armrest.

"What brings you to my doorstep?"

Zaos replied, "A Dark Rider. His troops followed us into the Forest of Smoke."

"By morning we will disappear. The Temple of Boreas is enchanted by day to remain hidden from the sight of outsiders. Only by night can they see passed the enchantment. Preparations will be made. This temple will not fall."

Anri abruptly interjected, "Lord Marlusha's troops were able to infiltrate the Temple of Zephyrus. What makes you think this place is safe?"

Lowe chuckled and raised his hand, That is all for tonight! Rest easy."

Her worries were dismissed. Each of them was escorted into the healing chamber to rest. Alone with his thoughts, Lowe pressed down on a few of the runes activating a lever. The platform submerged into the mountain, leading into a secret room. An altar stood before him, and swirling overhead was a massive sphere of water at its center. Beneath it was a statue of a swan in midflight with its beak nearly touching the bottom of the sphere. Lowe stood beneath the sphere chanting. Strands of water flowed from the sphere and danced around the chamber.

Upstairs in the healing chamber, the prince stirred in his sleep. A massive tree stood aflame in front of him. Leaves gently falling to the ground around him covering the dead bodies of countless warriors. Shadow twisted and turned, and Lord Dark Lucus appeared, jolting him from his nightmare. Covered in sweat, he looked around, realizing he was in an unfamiliar place. His mind was set at ease as he saw his friends sleeping nearby. The monks ran over to him to check his vitals. The aroma of aloe vera, calendula, and ginseng drifted through the air. The prince noticed he was covered in crushed hops and brushed them off. Before he could get up from the bed, one of the monks sprayed his eyes with a fragrance that placed him back to sleep until morning.

Nacilias' tongue woke the prince, as the fox licked his eyes clean of the medicine. His body felt brand new; the pain was gone. Saturos and the others were already called to court. A new set of clothes and armor were laid out for the prince. Each of the monks took a rag and washed the prince down before putting on his seaweed green pants with a shirt to match. The shirt was a long sleeve with glove extensions. From the waist, the shirt had two side slits with fabric reaching down to his ankles with embroidered trees. The armor placed on him was olive green. First installed were armbands with hidden daggers placed over his shirt. As he stood, the monks placed a sleeveless chest-plate on him. The armor allowed for his neck to breathe but had a high collar and curved above his mid-torso. His leg armor was unlike anything he had seen. It was a wide belt connected to armored plates protecting his side thighs that descended and wrapped around his knees. Lastly, an emerald diadem was placed on his forehead.

The monks exited, leaving the woman healers. Unlike the monks, they wore all white robes and hijabs. The main healer had golden eyes and half of her face tattooed with glyphs. She held out her hand and escorted the prince to the throne room where the others waited. Golden statues and faded glyphs adorned the walls of the throne room. The Master Healer could not enter the room; she left the prince and returned to her chamber. The prince was asked to approach the throne as the others waited near Lowe. The Master Monk stepped on three runes and activated the platform, ascending them to the highest chamber. The chilled air made it hard to breathe as they stepped on sacred ground. Six major archways carved into the side of the mountain allowed for a beautiful view of the mountain range. Howling in the air, the wind whispered their ancient tongue.

Before them stood a chamber with the lushest greenery; vines tightly wound together created a bridge connecting the platform to a marble tholos. At its center stood the glorious Tree of Life, massive and twisted. Its roots danced around the room and out the archways. Nuzzled in the branches above were Black palm cockatoos gawking as the prince approached. Hidden in the tree was a blue Frayjain for its protection. Flashes from his visions clouded his memory. Lowe and the others watched as the prince rubbed his fingers on the bark. Golden sab dripped from the bark and onto the prince's skin. He noticed it absorbed into his skin. His presence caused the birds to stir and swarm around him. Lowe tried to move closer, but the tree would not allow it. Once the birds dispersed, the roots of the tree created a doorway. As the prince stepped through, he was taken to the Realm of the Four Spiritual Gates. He was standing on the platform of the northern gate. Grass covered a thin layer around the base of the platinum gate. Oriental bittersweet wrapped around the outer rim. In every direction he looked, there was no sign of the guardian.

A faint scream could be heard from below. To the east of the platform, a trail of blood led down below. With caution, he approached the side and peered over. Nothing but thick clouds lingered underneath. A barrier rippled across the clouds but flickered as if failing. Another flicker in the barrier and a plum of clouds erupted, and the shockwave threw the prince back. A gigantic white wolf with celeste sparkling fur on his tail and mane leaped onto the platform. The four-eyed beast had multiple bite marks on his body.

"You came."

Prince Alexander stared at the creature. Anagar warned him that the wolf had betrayed his oath. "What were you doing below?"

"We do not have time."

Basasael, the White Artic wolf could no longer stand. Blood was gushing from his wounds.

"I will ask you again. Why did you abandon your post?"

With blood pouring from the side of his mouth, Basasael finally answered. Protecting the gate was all he knew. The silence around him drove him into a deep depression, until the voice from below called to him, promising salvation. With the Herald of LunaSol thought dead, the temptation was too strong. Basasael walked amongst the creatures below until the prince's emergence on the western platform. Their agenda changed once they caught wind of his scent. They were coming for him. The wolf's warning was his last as he embraced death. Without hesitation, the prince ripped off the key from his neck and opened the northern gate. The carvings on the door ignited, and Ewonbi's soul was released. The second of the Cardinal Deities was finally released. The creature was gargantuan. His skin was brown and very aged. Six serpent heads protruded from his shell and soared into the sky. The monumental turtle took up most of the platform. His withered shell was home to a fascinating tree protruding from it. Prince Alexander was but a toy in his eyes. Yellow eyes gazed down at the boy with utter joy. The amulet around his neck was all but confirming his identity.

"Speak child, why have you released me!"

"I had a vision about the tree."

"A trap! We must summon Lowe." Swirling his claw over hidden runes activated the portal to LunaSol. Lowe was not the only one to step forward; Saturos joined him. His presence angered the Cardinal Deity. The great serpent-tortoise ordered the body to be burned. Saturos noticed the bite marks from where he was standing. He slowly walked over to the creature and touched the wounds gently before setting his sword ablaze and piercing the creature's heart. Lowe ordered his servants to take the burning remains from the platform.

Prince Alexander stared at the massive beast as he turned and walked through his gateway. Lowe slowly approached the prince while he was deep in thought. It was time to return to LunaSol. With the death of another guardian, Lowe promoted the blue Frayjain to watch over the gate. Upon their exit, Anri and Zaos stood at the foot of the tree frozen in horror. Its leaves blackened with death. Its bark decayed, withered, and broke apart.

"What is happening?" roared Lowe.

The light of the tree was gone. Lowe ordered everyone to his throne room. The descent down was silent. Everyone was stuck in their own thoughts until the platform secured itself and the room was filled with frayjains. The prince and his companions were taken back to the healing chamber, so Lowe could speak alone with his General. In the healing chamber, the prince took another glance at his mother's journals. Turning the page, he finally saw his mother's writing again. The first line read, Salahea had fallen. Asphera saw to that. Poisoning the pharaoh's children, she sought to destroy alliances and create a divide. Her own daughter breached Heaven to see Gaea released on LunaSol. She tipped Lord Celeio's hand and whispered the Usurper's message, so he could revive her. Poisoning her mother wasn't enough. Her atrocities spanned numerous betrayals unseen. Corrupted by the Nebula, she was working to destroy their utopia. Confronting her would lead to everyone's destruction. Her end goal was the death of Alexander. She knew the truth. His curse.

As he closed the page, his feet took charge and led him away from the others and back to Lowe. Seated on his throne, addressing his servants, he saw the prince among them. With a wave of his hand, he signaled them to leave. Once alone, the prince approached him. He had hundreds of questions for Lowe, like what was Lord Dark Lucus' interest in the temple? What happened between Anagar and his mother, and how could a guardian implant a vision in his mind?

His questions caused Lowe to chuckle. Many of his questions he had the answer, but he felt obligated to remain silent. Staring into the prince's eyes, he realized he could no longer keep Lady Eileen's secrets. Lowe instructed the prince to approach his throne. He pressed a hidden button and brought him to the chamber below. Once again, Lowe found himself in the altar with the floating sphere of water.

"Lord Dark Lucus wants access to this!"

"What is it?"

"Memories. Answers."

What floated above them was the Orb of the Sea. A relic with a singular purpose. It was a prison for memories. One strand reached out to the prince's neck and lifted the Eclipse Amulet into the sky revealing the truth. With the death of the Divine Lords, Lord Marlusha remained with all their secrets. He could not trust Eris and Lord Dark Lucus with his knowledge. He was caught trying to enter Mars Tower by Servilia. He was taken prisoner and brought before a group of Magnus known as the Darkarrow Coven. Using their magic, his memories were extracted, and those deemed dangerous were brought to Lowe for the Orb of the Sea to absorb. This was not the first time the prince heard of the Darkarrow name. He looked over at Lowe and asked who they were. Only silence was returned. Lowe stared into the watery images as he chanted. The water shook and the strands bent and changed. Now, the prince was watching his mother talking to Anagar. She was not yet pregnant with him.

Placing her hand on the tablet, she muttered the question, "Show me what will happen when I conceive my final child." None of the visions played out before him, but he saw the pain on her face. She cried as she held her stomach. Anagar was the reason for many of Lady Eileen's final decisions in life. Turning away from Oricale, she clung to the tablet and his visions. Every day she came to him praying for a vision that would turn the outcome of the war to come. His visions made her paranoid and secluded. The images in the water faded and became dancing strands again.

"None of this makes sense. How could Lord Marlusha have lost his memory if he knew how to locate two stones already?"

"Nathaniel Darkbloom. He knew of Lord Marlusha's run-in with Servilia. He promised to help him regain his memories if they worked together to take down Lord Nebula. Nathaniel wanted Lord Nebula's power. He helped kill members of the Darkarrow Coven to gain certain memories back. We do not know how many, but we thought it important to hide the location of the tower he built here."

The prince turned to Lowe, "At dawn they will come for the temple and its secrets."

"Let them come."

"Lowe, there is something that I need from you."

"Speak it and it is yours!"

Prince Alexander requested access to the Mystic Otrant's grimoires. He confessed the return of the Uvali and their mission to kill anyone the prince encountered. The pharaoh believed her books contained how she imprisoned them. None of her relics remained in the temple. The last of her relics were taken decades ago by her servants. At every turn, the prince faced disappointment. His enemies were growing stronger, and he did not have the resources to defeat them. Lowe's voice faded as he focused on the humming in the water. The image of his mother's face fading in and out striking an idea in him.

"Do you have any of my mother's things?"

"Actually, I do."

His library contained a document written by Lady Eileen. Returning to the throne room, the prince waited while his friends were escorted in. Once again, they traveled through the ceiling, but did not travel to the very top where the tree stood. This time they found themselves in a library. Enchanted bricks protected it from sight; Lowe walked right through the wall and the others did the same. The sight blew their minds. Hundreds of thousands of books were lined up from floor to ceiling. They did not know where to begin.

"What is this place?" questioned Zaos.

"Lord Grevis collected rare books and forbidden knowledge from all over the world. When Hyperion placed the ancient creatures to rest, Lord Grevis kept records of them here. The documents you seek is in a glass case in the center of this room."

As the prince approached the podium, he was enraged. "Is this a trick? There's nothing written on these."

"Read the sign, prince."

Quietly he read, "Only the touch of the Herald will show the truth of his birth."

The room shook with vigor. War was knocking. The frayjains below sounded the horns of battle. Placing his hand on the glass revealed it was enchanted. The image of the Oricale Star encircled by three rings appeared. Within each ring there were runes. He turned the first circle to the left, then the middle circle to the right, and the final circle to the left. It spun faster, and the glass levitated into the air, allowing the prince to grab the document. Foolishly, he cut himself, but in doing so his blood drifted across the page. Written in blood was the sentence: *Child of the divine, born from mortal womb, cursed to end his reign...* Before the rest of the sentence could be read, the page was set ablaze with shadow lightning. Lowe was quick and summoned his axe and launched it into the emptiness of the room. The axe pinned Lord Dark Lucus onto a bookshelf.

"Clever man," his voice caused the atmosphere in the room to change.

"You are not welcome here."

"Where is Lord Marlusha's memory being kept, and I shall be on my way?"

"You are in no position to negotiate."

Lord Dark Lucus flared his wings, and a mist of shadows consumed the room. He faded into the darkness, cackling. His voice echoed around them. Zaos and Lowe attacked first, but he was too quick for them. Each fell to his sword. Lord Zylo stood guard of the prince as Anri used her staff to blind the angel and restore light to the room. She held him back as they gathered the wounded and raced to the throne to return to the lower levels. As they descended, they could hear the screams of the monks. Lord Zylo could not wait for the platform to touch down, he leaped off it once he saw the room was overrun with Dark Servants. Saturos climbed on Shoxz and charged into battle. How could they have passed their defenses? The prince noticed the Dark Servants were fighting to gain access to the main door. He watched as they used the mirrors as an access point.

"Shatter the mirrors!"

The monks heard the prince yell as they turned to see what he was pointing at. Lowe and Zaos in their weakened state, were taken to shelter by the few monks left in the throne room. The frayjains saw the injured and protected them as they made their way to the healing chamber. With two of their fighters out of commission, the others charged into battle. Ukna was at the lead, Saturos picked up a sword that lay on the floor and launched it at him. The prince whistled, and when he turned to face him, the sword pierced him and pinned him to the wall. Bellowing cries of pain tortured the ears of those in the room. It crippled and blinded those nearby as blood poured from their tear ducts. Wounded and infuriated, he vanished into the shadows and appeared near Nacilias.

Immobilized from the pain, he grabbed the little fox by his tail and hung him upside down. The prince's eyes expanded with terror as he watched Ukna raise his friend into the air.

"Those who serve Prince Alexander shall die."

He felt helpless. Hans' fate clouded his mind. He took a couple steps forward toward Ukna, but he vanished into darkness and reappeared near the entrance of the temple. In one hand he held Nacilias and in the other he held a spear carved from a Nebula stone. He used the back of the spear to unlatch the doors and allow the others to enter. The prince took slow breaths as he witnessed the Dark Rider thrust Nacilias into the ground and drive the spear into his head. The room slowed down as the light in Nacilias' eyes faded. Ukna smiled at the prince. Death once again embraced him like an old friend. He could not fight back the tears. His veins pulsated with vengeance and fury. The prince's amulet shook and oscillated with energy. Its energy flowed into Orion's Star, triggering the prince to reveal it. He did not see he was being led into a trap. Unleashing his rage onto the room left him vulnerable. The shock wave decimated the Dark Servants, but Ukna managed to launch his spear toward the prince, missing his heart by an inch and blasted a hole through his shoulder. The burst of energy from the prince burned through the Dark Rider's cloak killing him. Anri scurried to his aid and yelled for the others to take the prince and run. Saturos and Lord Zylo picked the prince up and ran to Shoxz. Staring at the scorch marks on the floor, her hand trembled. It was the first time anyone had killed their kind. Anri helped the wounded Frayjains retreat.

While the battle had turned for the worse, Lowe and Zaos gathered enough strength to return to the fight. Lowe asked Zaos to accompany him to stop Lord Dark Lucus from attaining their most prized possession. Returning to the throne room they used the platform to descend into the heart of the mountain. Lord Dark Lucus had already forced his way in. He stood beneath the floating sphere with his sword above his head, draining it of memories. Zaos attacked, only to distract him while Lowe saved the Orb of the Sea. The corrupt angel was extremely powerful, and in her current state she could not keep up with him. Lowe activated the defenses of the shrine, and it allowed her to escape before he could impale her with his sword. The Orb of the Sea compressed itself down to the side of a golf ball and crystalized upon touch. Lowe handed it to Zaos for safe keeping. Stone Sentries descended from their post on the walls and held Lord Dark Lucus at bay while Lowe and Zaos escaped. They returned to the battle only to witness the carnage.

The temple had fallen. Holding on for dear life, the bloody prince's healing factor did not kick in. Saturos tried to cauterize the wound. They needed to get to Fang, but the emerald dragon was already gone. He was being tended to in a secure location since falling into the mountainside. Lowe called for his Massio Eagle, Halo, to transport them to where he was being kept. As they flew away, Anri watched as Lord Dark Lucus appeared behind Lowe. He summoned a scythe and split Lowe's body down the middle.

The prince, barely conscious, was ashamed and filled with regret. He lost a dear friend of his, he lost a supporter, and he lost the Temple of Boreas. The prince was scared by this defeat. Halo took them to the nearest outpost, the Shrine of the North Wind to recover in secret. His arrival startled the sect of monks occupying the shrine. In Halo's claw there was a hidden letter from Lowe. As the monks read it, they dropped to their knees to pray. One remained standing. Unlike the others, she escorted them inside. They would remain under her care until the prince recovered.

PART VI – RETRIBUTION

CHAPTER
28

RECOVERY

The mixture of echinacea, valerian, and ashwagandha filled the air. Heavy-eyed, the prince tried to focus on where he was. Incense burning all around him as he laid on a stone altar. Slowly turning his head, he observed a woman covered in golden silks chanting on her knees. Her eyes caught his and she called to her sisters. In that brief second, he remembered. Reliving the moment, the pain in his shoulder came back. His screams tore through the monks sending them tumbling. Exerting all that energy depleted him. The call of darkness sang to him. He was standing in a black lake staring up at the stars above.

"Alexander?"

That voice. His heart started palpitating. He was scared to look down. Once again, he heard his name called. Lowering his head their gazes met. Those gentle eyes, that starlight smile.

"Gabriel?"

Running through the lake the two embraced once another. Gabriel leaned in and kissed him on the mouth. Lost in lust, the prince gripped him by the waist pulling him in, so their bodies rubbed against each other. For a split second he caught himself.

"Where are we?"

Another voice from the shadows spoke, "The Astral Plane!"

It couldn't be. How was she here? The prince thought he would never see Gabriel again, but now Amira. He turned to the left and watched as she approached. She wasn't the girl he remembered. She had embraced her demonic form. Her face, pale white with no mouth, two slits for a nose and four red piercing eyes. Two jagged curled horns atop her head. Blood-red hair and goatlike legs. Her arms dragged on the floor with bent knuckles.

Amira was trailing him. Keeping to the shadows and watching his every move since she arrived in LunaSol. Her powers were weakening by the day. She wanted the prince to send her home.

"Amira, I have no clue how to return home."

"Your sister tricked me and now I am stuck here."

Prince Alexander walked over to the crying creature. Even after her betrayal he still felt sorry for her. He prayed to go home one day, but he still needed to save LunaSol. It was a wild idea. Lifting her face, their eyes locked.

"Help me and we can try and find a way back home."

"Lies. Why would you help me?"

There was something still good inside Amira, even after all she did. He could not see her die.

"Amira, trust me!"

His words caused Gabriel to collapse to the floor in pain. His memory was crippled. It was hard for him to focus. There was something off. The longer he stared at him, flashes of distortion ravaged his mind.

"What is happening to me."

"Amira end this. You are torturing him."

"This is not my doing."

"ENOUGHHHHHHHHHH." Roared out the prince.

His echo shattered the illusion around him revealing a pack of winged skeletons - Exceaios. They were the remains of angelic warriors imbued with dark magic and reanimated. In their chest, pumping as a heart was a sphere of magic. Each held a staff carved from bones with a yellow sphere at the top and a scythe at the bottom. Latching eyes with Amira, two of the exceaios subdued her. Alexander watched as they bound Amira and Gabriel. They were not working alone.

"I see, I am not the only one who sensed you here. Good to see you again, Amira."

"You said he would be mine."

"I will kill you before I let you hurt him," yelled out Gabriel.

"Little lover, your diluted blood..."

As Eris got closer to him, she inhaled his scent. He radiated divine energy. She inhaled him once more and her eyes lit up.

"Eris, we had a deal."

"Silence, you beast, our terms have changed."

"I will not forget this."

Eris grew exasperated with Amira's threats. She looked over to the Exceaios closest to the demon and gave it a slight nod. The creature flipped over its staff and sliced through Amira's astral form. She vowed not to harm the prince and his companion. She needed him to listen. The longer he was in this state, he was a beacon to forces seen and unseen. Eris was using the exceaios to jam the signal to keep him safe while he recovered.

"Why are you helping me?"

"I have plans for you, but first we must return this young boy home. Your energies are bound together. You drew him here without even knowing. Fascinating!"

Prince Alexander watched as Eris studied Gabriel and pulled out a piece of his hair.

"Get away from me!"

"You have no idea how powerful you are."

Her words stirred in the prince. What power could he possess? Descendants of the Creed of Lykos were mere mortals. The ones that protected him on the mountain had to rely on weapons. Alexander stared into his eyes as Gabriel mumbled, "Find a way back to me!" The exceaios holding Gabriel placed the yellow sphere in his staff onto his forehead and his astral form evaporated. Alexander cried out. Eris promised no harm befell the boy. He would awaken in his own world. She held her brother up and smiled. It was the first time he had seen peace in her eyes. He trusted her words. Without warning, Eris dug her claw-like nail into his mind and shocked him back to the physical plane.

It was faint this time, the chanting of the monks. The aroma of verbena and henbane lingered on his skin. Fluttering his eyes to clear the fog he noticed he was tied down with mistletoe. The Sister Monks stopped their chanting and rushed to get the others. The prince sat up in pain as the women tended to him. Shoxz was the first to grace the chamber followed by Lord Zylo, Anri, Zaos, and Saturos. Six months had gone by since the devastating death of Nacilias and Lowe. The monks drove Lord Dark Lucus and his army out of the Tempe of Boreas, but at a great cost. During this time, his companions took advantage and trained. Lord Zylo and Saturos were taken and taught Quinfi; an ancient fighting form that drew influence from dance and close quarter fighting to disarm and cripple an opponent. As fragile and old as Lord Grevis was, he taught all his servants this technique. It was the first in LunaSol.

Sitting on the edge of the healing table the prince tried to focus his sight. It was still blurry and was hard for him to stand. Carved out of the temple wall was a massive elephant head. Its tusks were used to hold wind chimes while its trunk stood directly over the prince exuding fragrances. Zaos gently held the prince's hand as he stumbled to his feet.

"Where is Fang?"

The Sister Monks took the prince to the breeding grounds of the Massio Eagles. Fang soared in the skies above and trained with them too, learning evasion maneuvers. Cold, rough tiles brushed against his bare feet as they crossed the mountain path returning to the Temple of Boreas. Since the prince's injury, the enemy was radio silent. It was as if they had vanished.

Hope was not lost. Zaos managed to see a few of Lord Marlusha's memories. One place stood out the most: the Island of Mars. Its rugged, desert terrain was unlike any other with its red-colored sands and towers of basalt. With the prince's injury, he could not handle diving into a battle head on. The Sister Monks wrapped his arm and shoulder up and secured it in flexible armor. They were given traditional clothes native to the temple. Each outfit was custom to fit its host. The prince was given a green jacket with no sleeves and a hood with golden trimming along with yellow parachute pants. Once armed, restocked, and fed, they were led to a flat mountaintop where the Massio Eagles rested. Perched highest above the other's was Halo, black feathered with golden tips. Its claws could rip through a fully grown woolly mammoth. Adored on its head was a helmet visor. Seeing them approach, Halo lowered itself, allowing the monks to place a saddle on its back.

Fang descended and landed near the prince; he too had a new saddle. Once mounted, they took off into the sky. Heading east, the air was light and cool with the rays of the sun beaming down. The waters beneath them were calm and tamed. A squadron of giant manta rays were swimming beneath them. It was mating session, thousands jumped out of the water and splashed back down. Tranquil creatures, free of war. One piece of nature untouched by destruction. The longer he leaned against the saddle the more pressure he placed on his wound. Flickers of Nacilias' death flashed before his eyes.

He could no longer hold back his tears. Six months of being trapped in the shadows. Six months of recovery. Six months of being inoperable. He watched as the others laughed on Halo's saddle. He couldn't hear their words, but he felt so isolated. His mother and father were dead because of him. Soldiel died protecting him. No one could avoid death's touch. Not even Hans and Nacilias.

He tapped Fang on the side and rubbed his scales. Fang looked back at him. His eyes could see the pain in his soul. Prince Alexander wanted to be with the others, telling stories, laughing. He called on Halo, Fang glided below him. Flinging down a roped ladder, the prince pulled himself up to the others. He sat there and watched as Fang faded into the clouds, it was hunting time. While the others were busy listening to Saturos' story about his upbringing, Lord Zylo spoke with the prince.

"Since your arrival, we have not had the pleasure of talking one-on-one."

"I know. With everything going on, I haven't gotten the chance to know you."

"What better time than the present."

Lord Zylo was more than happy to share his memories. Being the first grandchild of Sir Erin and Lady Eileen was the most pampered position. Growing up he was the most fearless child, putting himself in danger at every turn. When his grandfather was given the position of Warden of the Dead, they moved to Nightfeather Forest. As a child, he snuck out into the forest with a friend while the moon was at its apex. It was mating season for the lycanthropes, and he wanted to see them for the first time. As creatures of the night, they were a rarity. He stumbled on a branch causing them to stir. Running for his life he was inches from the separation of the forest and his palace, when the world around him went black.

339

Lord Zylo could not move with blood gushing from his body. Riddled with bite marks. His friend, fearing the wrath of his father, left him there alone. Hours had gone by before he heard his name being screamed. His mother, Kesia Stormfal came running in her navy night gown. Screaming for help, his father and his three brothers came out. They brought him into the palace to tend to his wounds. He survived that night, only to fall prey to the curse the following month. Lycanthropes were savage creatures and once in their primal form there was no coming back. While in transition, Master Yami sought assistance from his brother Magister Ro. Hyperion had already placed many of the creatures into their slumber, but Magister Ro was placed in charge of their locations.

He brought them to the Elven King, Gandrago who was one of the few that withstood Hyperion's slumber curse. Zaos recalled the moment that beautiful child was brought before the king. As an Elf of the Twilight, they were sworn protectors to the Elven Ruler at that time. Eight highly trained assassins as wards and healers. Zaos was an apprentice and a rising star. Betrothed to Prince Exceleis, son of the king. A witness to the entire experience. The Elves of the Twilight were responsible for keeping the curse from taking full control of his humanity. Lord Zylo was grateful to be alive.

Reliving that memory hurt Zaos. Becoming a steward of the Elemental Tower meant leaving everything behind. She lost her husband and father-in-law to the Holy War, but more importantly she left her son behind. Before disembarking back home, Magister Ro met in secret with Queen Inyanga. Zaos watched as they conspired to ally themselves against Hyperion. His brother seized the moment to whisper Lady Eileen's plans to those who were wronged by the Creator. His mother's rebellion began with a web of whispers. Having heard of Magister Ro's involvement peaked the prince's curiosity. He took this opportunity to reach into his bag and take out his mother's journals. Unwrapping them only revealed blank pages. Their words were not ready to reveal themselves to him. Only his journal. Another entry unraveled before his eyes.

With Salahea no longer an ally to the crown, Lady Eileen needed to find alternative ways of building her battalion. The pregnancy had weakened her, but knowing the Nebula was now in play, she sought assistance from the Elders. Anchoring her child to other unsuspecting children weighed heavy on her. Having already done it to Princess Toa, it cost her a kingdom, what else would it cost her?

Asphera's poison had done enough damage. Even if she made it through childbirth, her death would come surely after. She felt like a failure. Putting all her children on the line for one. Lady Eileen made a choice that day. Seven more lives for the life of one.

"How could she do that?" Saturos questioned.

Prince Alexander realized he had read the entry out loud. Focusing on the sky above, he exhaled sharply, "To keep me from dying."

Saturos could see the pain in his eyes. This was the first time he heard about the journals. Nacilias was the prince's confidant. He shared every entry with him and Shoxz. He needed to trust the others more now than ever. Seeing the judgment in his eyes, the prince decided to ask about his past?

Saturos' eyebrows flared. His upbringing was clouded in mystery. He was abandoned as a baby, raised by Lord Celeio, trained to be a High Magnus, and was one of the few surviving people since the second greatest genocide in LunaSol history.

"You faced off against Alealam?" questioned the prince.

"How did you know that name?"

"I've seen him."

Alealam, descended from the skies after a cosmic storm long after Lord Nebula was imprisoned. He came in search of his fallen Alulim and their children, the Potuliari. Saturos was much older than Anri. Anri was a mere child when Alealam came to power. The father of the races was disgusted with the dilution of his bloodline. The Gaeatonic Guardians, with the help of the Elders, were able to defeat Alealam and trap him in his own machine.

"How can you tell the difference between an Alulim and a Potuliari? questioned Anri.

"They have a diamond-shaped birthmark," interjected Lord Zylo.

The others looked at him with confusion. Lord Zylo revealed that Master Yami told them about the difference before he died. Lady Phoebe was an Alulim and Amaris and Palar were Potuliari.

"Wait you have met one?" asked Saturos.

The prince laughed, "I guess I know a few!"

341

He gleamed into the prince's eyes and felt a connection to him. They exchanged slight smiles before turning away from one another. Halo's screech signaled they were nearing their destination. Waves crashing upon red sand. Basalt towers as far as the naked eye can see. As they descended, Halo had to readjust as volcanic geysers sprung toxic gas into the air. After clearing the toxic fumes, they were able to make a landing.

Zaos dismounted Halo with haste. She dug her hand into the floor, picking up sand and whirled it around.

"This is the Smokey Valley."

Even though Halo was a gift to the prince, having him around would only draw attention to them. He commanded Halo to return to the Temple of Boreas with haste. The Massio Eagle took off into the sky leaving them. Fang stood guard in the sky as Halo zoomed past him. Fang too would keep his distance. The sun was slowly setting, and they could not be caught out in the open at night. Zaos led them further into the desert as if she was familiar with the terrain. It was as if the Orb of the Sea implanted the memory within her.

"Our direction is east. We must head to Phecda."

The desert went from hot to extreme cold as night fell upon them. Shifting winds tossed the grainy pieces of sand over their faces. As they climbed the sand dunes, Zaos stopped them. Below were breeding grounds. She squatted on the sand and watched as the creatures ran into each other screaming and roaring. There were hundreds of beasts mating, Lava Turtles. They towered over an average giraffe and had molten lava shells on their backs with liquefied magma pouring out of the air ducts as they ram into one another. He noticed the creatures had six legs that allowed them to run on the sand fast. Lava erupted from their shells and set ablaze the sand. The creatures continued in their ritual mating, while they managed to creep away slowly not to anger any of the lava turtles. They continued to the outskirts of the desert where they could see the towering stonewall of Phecda.

Soldiers guarded the outer wall. Sneaking in was nearly impossible. They set up camp and placed protective charms around it so they could rest 'til morning. The young prince slowly curled into a ball and faded into his dreams. He was once again surrounded by darkness. Standing in a black liquid. Staring at him from a distance were deep seeded purple eyes. A skeletal hand appeared and pointed downward. He sank into the liquid and awoke to fire and death surrounding him. The sun was nearly blocked out by the moon and the air stunk of putrid, rotting flesh. Zaos and Anri's bodies were ripped apart. Saturos was crucified upside down, while Lord Zylo was on his knees, decapitated. He awoke from his nightmare covered in sweat. He gazed at friends and cried out in silence. He was terrified of losing them.

Anri was still up and saw the trembling prince. She was standing at the edge of the campsite staring at the watchtowers. She called for him to come stand with her. Phecda had changed over the years. Once a city thriving with merchants and blacksmiths, now hidden behind stone. Each of the watchtowers were patrolled by Fire Ilihi. Any movement close to their post was set ablaze. The tortured screams of those trying to escape the city could be heard from the distance. Piles of burning corpses littered the open desert.

"My mother could have ended this before it ever began. Now, I'm left to fight someone else's war."

"Don't say that."

Storming off into the night, he left the protection of the campsite and returned to the breeding pit. Many of them moved on, but a few still lingered. Their long necks and curved sharp peaks reminded him of a bird. Scaley skin with boils of molten lava down their necks. Marveling over them, he watched as the last of creatures finished mating and went on their way. Sitting alone with his thoughts, the world seemed silent. Closing his eyes, he called out into the darkness. He was once again standing in black liquid. Whispers filled his ears, paralyzing him. The voices of the world amplified around him. Crying babies, secret lovers, murder plots. Each voice unique, but uncontrollable. Focusing on his own thoughts, he screamed out loud, silencing the world, but shattered the ceiling. The darkness around him cracked and flurried down to the ground as specks of snowflakes. In its place danced a multitude of colors.

He was staring at the universe amplified. Witnessing the birth of planets, supernovas, and galaxies colliding. Reaching up his body levitated into the celestial abyss. Cosmic dust danced around him, converting his physical form into astral energy. The higher he was taken the more chaos was unleashed around him until he stopped moving. He was staring at the scar in the fabric of reality. It was oozing out unimaginable amounts of energy. Placing his hand on the tear, sucked him in and launched him through a black hole. Keeping his eyes closed the entire way, he was relieved once he was stationary again. As his eye lids opened, he smiled.

"Home."

Two great landmasses Laurasia and Gondwana came into view as he descended. He was taken to a small cottage in the jungle mountains of Gondwana. Walking through the wall he entered a lightly dimmed room. Gabriel laid shirtless in bed. His sheets barely covered his body. His torso and the top of his pubes exposed. The prince was bashful. His heart was racing. Neither had seen each other in such a state. Curious he approached and gently touched his arm. Gliding his fingertips to his face. The moonlight cascaded through the window, illuminating his purple aura.

Caressing his face allowed him to look into Gabriel's mind. A dream. Rather an exotic dream. Alexander was not ready for what he saw. Gabriel sitting on a locker room bench moaning. A face between his legs and someone behind him kissing on his neck. The scene played out before him as more guys entered the locker room naked. He was in ecstasy. Alexander could feel it. Their breathing and heartbeats were in unison. The boy between his legs continued to move his head up and down causing Gabriel to throw his head back and meet the other boy with a kiss. Alexander watched as the guys showered. Water falling over their curves, trickling down to their feet. It was an unsettling feeling seeing such a dream. Even though the prince was attracted to guys, he was more reserved. Gabriel caught a glimpse of the prince from the corner of his eye. He was embarrassed and tried to suppress the pleasure. He pushed the guys off him, but it was too late. Alexander stared at him with disappointment and phased out of his mind.

Alexander was startled. Amira had tracked him down once again. She quickly grabbed a blade and attacked the prince. They wrestled for it until she kicked him in the face, causing him to lose focus and get angry. The world around him distorted and they were once again in his mind floating amongst galaxies. Amira watched in awe. While distracted, the prince glided away from her trying to run. Floating through the cosmic dust he finally reached the separation. Seeing the black liquid floor again he reached out and fell from the sky. Amira was not far behind. She jumped down from the sky and landed on her feet.

"I will kill you."

"You can try."

Amira dashed at the prince. She was quick with the blade and managed to cut him. Cutting him only made matters worse. His rage became a force of its own. His eyes turned black and the liquid around him shifted and transformed into a faceless four-armed angel. It attacked Amira, separating her from the prince. She crouched onto the floor and bit her finger. Using her blood, she drew a sigil that allowed her to escape back to her reality. The angelic warrior turned to the prince, in fear he tried to run from the creature, but as he reached out his hands became liquid spears and pierced the prince's hands. The dark liquid absorbed into the prince, shocking him out of the astral plane.

"My prince, I was looking all over for you."

Anri came looking for him. She could see the paleness on his face. The smell of blood was fresh in the air. It was not a dream. Amira really cut him. He held his arm while Anri wrapped it up until they could return to the campsite, filling her in on the way. Disarming the charms woke the others. Zaos stared at the prince with terror. What could she see that the others didn't. She raised the charms again, while keeping her eyes on the prince. Zaos and Anri worked on his wound as he cried out in pain. Each of his cries shifted the sands beneath them. His powers were amplified beyond measure. Anri left to grab some herbs, leaving Zaos alone with him.

She grabbed a wet rag and placed it in his mouth. She restrained his arms and legs. With a needle she pricked her hand and with her blood she drew a sigil on his forehead. It allowed her to gain access to his mind. She was standing in the black liquid. As an intruder the liquid attacked. It took on the form of the angelic warrior again, but this time it spoke.

"Leave my master's mind."

Zaos was kicked out of the astral plane and was standing over the prince again. The black liquid was something archaic and poisonous. It was unlike any source she had touched or learned about. She was forced to place the prince into a slumber for his own safety. Anri returned and saw the prince restraint and asleep. She disagreed with Zaos' methods. They were harmful. The prince was not a pawn in anyone's political games, let alone fearmongering. She revealed the prince was not alone in his head. There was a parasite they needed to dissect. The locals have healers that

345

could assist. Zaos exited the prince's tent, leaving Anri by his side to watch him. The fear remained with her. The prince was compromised.

CHAPTER
29

FIRE STONE

Sweat dripped down her cheek as she awoke to bizarre noises coming from outside her tent. Zaos peeked out to see a stampede of lava turtles. The heat from their shells made it nearly impossible to breathe. The faint light of the sun was rising from the east. She called on Anri to gather the others. The beasts were migrating through Volcanic Valley, heading north. The protective charms around the campsite were damaging their shells as they scraped against it. It was the only thing securing them from being trampled under their feet. One of the lava turtles hit the barrier so hard it cut off a chunk of its shell causing it to ooze out lava. The screams drew the attention of the watch towers. They had to leave now.

Prince Alexander was the last to awaken. His head was throbbing. He had no memory of arriving in the valley. As the last of the lava turtles passed them, Zaos urged the others to stay close to her. Troops were dispatched to check out the commotion. She was going to cause a sandstorm to mask their steps. Lowering their protective charms would draw them closer, she had to wait until the storm was on top of them. Everyone gathered as she used Blood Magic. Slicing her hand, her drops of blood hit the ground. As she chanted, the sand absorbed the blood triggering a small pulse through the air. At the edge of the desert where the ocean meets the land, a massive gust of wind picked up obscuring the picturesque scene. The storm drew closer causing the troops to abandon their reconnaissance mission and return to the city. With the gathering storm overhead, Zaos finally dropped the charms, and they ran for the wall.

Keeping their faces covered they walked against the wall until Anri stopped in her tracks. They would not be able to get through the front gate without setting off alarms. She could feel water on the opposite side of the wall. Like a manmade lake. Lord Zylo carved out one of the stones and slowly removed it. Water poured out of it. Anri used her staff to draw the water back in. He continued to carve out more stones with Saturos, creating a way in. As they stepped into the lake, Anri shifted the water around them creating a sphere for them to breathe in. Zaos snapped her fingers, and the stones filled the empty hole. The sandstorm continued to rage overhead, as they slowly rose from the water.

Prince Alexander nearly threw up. Dozens of naked women and men were chained to wooden crosses. Blood pouring from open wounds. Their eyes carved out. Their piercing cries echoed in the storm as the sand grazed against their scars. Zaos tried to quell the storm, but it was not easily extinguished. The prince stared at the bodies in disbelief; tortured, abandoned. How could his family allow this to happen? Dark thoughts surfaced. The images he had of his family were torn apart by disgust. This impression of grace and devotion to their people was nothing more than a ruse to stay in power. What truly separated the royals from Lord Nebula? They maintained their status through oppression. Both ruled with an iron fist. They even enforced the separation of classes. The prince wanted no parts of it. Anger fueled his powers. He watched as his veins blackened and he summoned his staff.

Driving it into the ground he drew in the storm. Swirling twisters touched upon the sand. Anri moved toward the prince and warned him not to draw attention.

"I will bury this city in the dirt!"

Anri saw the poison in him spreading. She turned to Zaos. The colorless look on her face said it all. She knew. His actions came with consequences, the attention of the slave master's drew upon them. Smart in their response, they placed weapons in the hands of their slaves and ordered them to kill the prince and his companions. For each dead body, freedom was offered. Chained at the neck, naked, and covered in filth, the slaves raced toward them. The prince ordered no bloodshed, just disarmament. With each slave fallen, Saturos gathered them to escape through the lake. Their impromptu rescue turned into a trap. The slave master's weren't the only ones inhabiting the city; Dark Servants were in control. Zaos and Anri tried to use their magic, but it had no effect on them. Lord Zylo rushed at one of them, as he drew closer, he began to convulse and collapsed at their feet. A Dark Servant withdrew a black stone from his garments.

Prince Alexander was the last to fall. He used the twisters to kill as many slave masters as possible before he finally blacked out. They were gagged and chained. Saturos could hear the slaves pleading for their lives. Even in a daze he managed to watch as they were slaughtered and thrown into the lake as an example to the others. Hoods were placed over their faces as they were dragged through the city. The faint cries of torture around them. He counted each step until they reached their destination. Three hundred and seven. For a city rumored to be over a thousand acres. They did not travel far.

Each was separated from the collective and thrown into dark rooms. Their hoods were removed, but their shackles remained. Unlike the others, Anri's hands were suspended above her head. Every time she attempted to cast a spell, the runes on her shackles lit up and drained her energy. Focusing on escape, she allowed her senses to become dull. She was not alone. In the corner of the room, stood a cloaked figure. A Dark Rider, a brother of Ukna. As it spoke, the room chilled.

"How did my brother die!"

Anri stared into the shadows, her eyes barely focusing.

The shifting creature moved in closer. Being up close to the creature terrified her. Urine streamed down her legs as her body quaked. The golden cloth that encompassed its body had an opening in the mouth. Its mouth had three rows of razorsharp teeth. Each Dark Rider was a General and commanded their own armies under the direction of Lord Dark Lucus. Anri was a prisoner of Ku'ka, one of the most dangerous amongst them. Revered for its methods of torture and extraction of secrets. Each of the Dark Riders wore a crown of obsidian that mimicked the Nine Kings of LunaSol. While in suspension, Ku'ka ripped away at Anri's clothes. Closing her eyes, she tried to silence the pain and drifted away. First, she felt one finger and then another enter her vagina. She cringed, only making Ku'ka laugh. He forced more fingers into her until she started to bleed.

Nearby, there was a rack of tools, on the rack was a mason jar. It was placed underneath her to catch the blood. As it dripped out of her, the Dark Rider's attention was drawn to another weapon, silver spiked armbands as thin as wire. Anri's screams echoed through the halls. With each movement, the spikes dug deeper into her flesh.

"I will ask one final time, tell me how my brother died."

Anri refused to speak. Her silence was met with pain. A punch in the face, then one to the ribs, and then another to her vagina. Shaking uncontrollably with her legs dangling from the air. Her toes barely scraped the floor. The session was interrupted by a knock on the door. One of the slave masters came with news about Lord Marlusha. Prince Alexander's spectacle not only drew their attention, but his as well. A ship with his sigil was seen heading toward Mars.

"I will get answers from one of them. Keep an eye on this one."

Ku'ka left the room to interrogate one of the others. The slave master stood at the door, lusting over Anri's naked body. Without warning, she felt him inside her. Defiling her. His hands were caressing her curves. Anri tried to fight back, but she was so weak. Flashes of her mother screaming for help filled her mind. The sounds of her cries as she watched her handmaidens beaten and raped in front of her. Memories buried for centuries resurfaced. The High Chanceller bottled her emotions. For days she was tortured and raped. Sometimes multiple times a day. Her restraint only entertained the Dark Rider. It took pleasure in her prolonged pain. During one of her rapes, she felt the man's body maneuvering her, and she finally struck back. She managed to get her legs around his neck and snapped it. Using her toes, she dug into his pockets to find a key. With the shackles removed, she dropped to the floor and laid on top of the slaver. Each breath compressed her ribs and caused discomfort. She dragged herself off the slaver and put on his clothes. Before exiting the room, she grabbed the weapons from the tool rack. She slowly left the room surveilling each corner.

For years, Anri relied heavily on her staff for magical support, but this time she had to dig deep inside. Casting verbal spells came easy to her. Unspoken magic was harder. Silencing her insecurities, she felt connected to her magical spark for the first time in ages. It pulsated in her with renewed purpose. As her fingertips gently touched the walls, she could map out the area in her mind. She arrived at another cell. The voice of two slavers could be heard. With her fingers, she touched the cold steel of the door and continued in a circular motion and then a straight line down to the bottom. Pressing her hand forward, she walked through the door. One of the captors was in the middle of plucking Shoxz feathers off. Anri made quick work of them. Placing her hand over her mouth and swiping down, she removed their ability to speak. She flung an axe at one, slicing through the front of his head, while she dug a blade into the eye of the other.

Shoxz was released from her chains. She was barely touched. Only a few of her feathers were ripped out and stored in a jar of liquid. Continuing down the hall, they came upon two rooms across from one another. Each without slavers. Shoxz kicked one of the doors open to find Lord Zylo chained in iron. Blood-soaked and in a fetal position. A beast that was once covered in fur was nearly shaven to the skin. The closer Anri got to him, she noticed they had cut out his eye. She dissolved the chains to dust and helped him to his feet. Shoxz had enough strength to carry him. She removed the clothing of the two men. Covering Lord Zylo with one.

Across from him was Saturos. He was stripped naked and was bound to a wooden cross. He was positioned to face the wood itself. His back was filled with lash marks. Anri liquified the iron door and turned it into a sword before killing the slavers. After removing his chains, Saturos was not in bad shape. He had endured the torture and was ready to give it back. Taking the clothes from Anri, he got dressed, and they made their way back into the corridor. Each corridor was empty. The final two rooms were side by side. One Dark Servant stood guard. Anri removed her clothing and began to hum. She turned the corner and locked eyes with the guard. He was enthralled by her body. With each step closer, he took a piece of clothing off. She pushed him down into his chair and straddled him. With a dagger in one hand hidden behind her back as their lips met, she sliced his throat.

Voices from the distance released her from her trance. Ku'ka was nearby. Liquefying the steal door again, she crafted lightweight armor for Lord Zylo. Unlike the other cells, this one was a trap. Seven guards stood watch as Anri entered. Zaos was hanging from her feet. Her hands were bound in shackles behind her back. Before the guards could scream for help, she opened her mouth and sucked in. The room was restrained of sound, so long as she held her breath. The others could not enter the room without breaking her spell. They entered the other cell where the prince was.

Each of the Dark Servants circled around her ready to pounce. She took a step back and could feel blood dripping down her legs. Touching the blood with one hand she rubbed it in her hand. As they piled on top of her, she marked each of them. The struggle subsided. One by one they released her. With her blood on them, she controlled them. Releasing the air in her mouth, the sound in the room returned. She whispered to the Dark Servants to release Zaos.

Unlike the others, Zaos was untouched by torture. With Zaos freed, they exited the cell. Saturos and the others were still inside the other cell. The door was slightly ajar. She ordered one of the Dark Servants to open it. As he did, she noticed her companions on the floor. One of the Dark Servants pointed to dozens of stones hanging from the ceiling. Nebula shards. The Dark Servants entered the room and took them down. They could not crush the stones without alarming Ku'ka and the others. They slowly lowered the prince, who was also untouched by torture. As they exited the room, there was a slaver staring at them from the edge of the hall. Locking eyes on Saturos, he quickly turned and ran.

"The prisoners are escaping!"

Time was of the essence. They rushed back to Zaos' cell. Zaos placed her hands on the wall and uttered, "*zu Staub.*" The wall dissolved into dust, revealing an abundant forest on the other side. Anri ordered the marked Dark Servants to kill as many of her enemies as possible to allow them to escape.

Once everyone was cleared, Zaos waved her hands and muttered, "*Wieder aufbauen!*" The dust on the floor reconstructed itself and sealed up the opening. The sound of horns echoed above them. Dozens of archers took aim, causing them to scatter. The thick tree branches caught most of the flying arrows as they ran into the Forest of Flames. No one was injured. The deeper they ran the trees became more brittle. They came upon a pile of decaying trees to rest. Zaos was consumed with hysteria. Saturos tried to calm her down, but she was losing her mind. A groggy prince awoke to the screams. Anri stepped closer and grabbed her hands. The Elf of the Twilight was indeed tortured. She was carrying a parasite: Gugokinsee. It was lodged in the back of her neck. The centipede-like creature attached itself to the brain steam and was used to collect memories.

Zaos fought back against Anri, knowing she was going to try and take out the creature. Zaos flung Saturos against a tree and crippled Lord Zylo with a scream. The prince watched from the corner, with a malevolent look in his eyes. He watched as the Magnus challenged the elf. As powerful as Zaos was, Anri managed to hold her own. The prince grew bored of their fight. He finally intervened. He slowly approached Zaos as if she were a dog. He held out one hand toward her while whistling. She continued to stare into his eyes until she was on her knees in a submissive pose.

"You are welcome." The prince said as he passed Anri to return to his seat on one of the trees. Shocked by his actions, she gawked at the prince, frightened by his demeanor. Anri grabbed one of Zaos' blades and cut out the creature. It had not fully latched onto her brain steam yet. Draining it of its blood, she placed it in a vial. She set the corpse on fire to prevent the Dark Servants from trying to gain memories from it. Zaos remained unconscious as the others regrouped. Anri tended to everyone's wounds, but the prince refused to be touched. His actions gave her pause. He slipped away to explore the abandoned forest. Black rivers of necrosis flowed in between the surviving trees. Those that survived were on their way toward death. Putrid pus, oozed across the darkening bark. The further into the forest he went, the stench of rot filled his lungs.

A massive boulder idly stood in the distance. As he approached, he noticed it moved, and two golden eyes locked onto him. He slowly stepped back as the boulder shifted, revealing a Dragoon. The creature roared, but the prince was unphased by it. Saturos and Anri heard the noise and looked around for the prince. Finally realizing he had slipped away; they gathered their things and ran toward the noise. The floor quaked with every footstep. It was not alone. Two more dragoons appeared through the rotting trees. Unlike the Council of Dragoons, their features were more serpentine than dragon. With their slender neck and faces. The leader of the pack had eight curved horns protruding from its head, its mouth was more beak-like than reptile. Its armor was burned into its scales. At the end of each of its horns were golden rings. Its forest-green scales and amber underside sparkled as it moved.

Saturos and the others finally reached the prince. Two of the dragoons were butchered, and their corpses laid at his feet. His hands filled with blood as the leader stood beside him on its knees.

"Glad you could arrive!"

"What madness is this?" questioned Anri.

"Madness? No, on the contrary, this is retribution."

Prince Alexander's eyes had blackened. His veins were protruding and darkening as well. The poison of the Nebula was changing him. Anri tried to get close to him, but the energy he was emitting was intense. His aura was perverted and amplified beyond recognition. Saturos drew his blade, only enraging the prince. With a stare, the sword was forced out of his hand and into the prince's. Saturos took a step forward and his feet were cemented to the ground. The prince opened his mouth and dislodged this jaw. He unleashed a paralyzing scream that knocked out everyone. Anri was the last to fall.

The cold grass touched her cheek like a gentle kiss. She was enthralled by the darkness. Sinking into it, she emerged on the other side. For the first time, she transcended the physical realm and stood before Oricale. The grass was replaced by a wet, damp floor. A pyramid of emerald and steel stood before her. Behind it, the veil of reality was shattered like shards of glass spinning in a circle. Through it an emerald light could be seen. Its pulsating sound drew the High Chancellor up the steel steps to the altar. Within it was a mantel shaped like a hand. In its palm was a three-inch emerald pendant. The necklace of the gem resembled tree branches. Carved into the necklace were runes in Oricale's native tongue.

The gem whispered to her. "Take it. You will need it."

Anri grabbed the pendant and placed it on her neck. Flashes of her past filled her mind's eye. She watched as her mother and aunt argued. Her aunt had the same black veins as the prince. The vision faded.

Oricale spoke, "Your aunt could not be saved from its poison, but the prince can."

Anri was released from the spiritual plane. The sounds of the natural world returned to her ears. Her eyes were covered, but she could hear the rolling of wheels. They were on a wagon.

"This one is stirring. Remove her blindfold."

The light of the sun was fading. Anri was surrounded by Dark Servants. Everyone was tied up except for the prince. He was sitting at the front of the wagon with the dragoon. They were led to volcanic tunnels in the sand. They were home to the lava turtles.

The prisoners were removed from the wagon. They were hung by their wrist on a post. Anri's eyes locked onto the prince; he was talking with the dragoon. He addressed her as Kryst. She was pointing at a beast in the distance. It was a Panthos, a panther-like creature the size of a rhino. Its underside lined with protruding red-orange scales that get superheated when angered. Its spiked tail covered in the same. If dislodged, it had the same impact as a landmine if it touched the floor. The only time their scales were stabilized was when they were swimming in lava pools. Panthos' normally hunt alone. They were feasting on the corpses of a lava turtle.

Prince Alexander and Kryst were preparing to receive guests. Anri noticed the floor began to decay and a cold frost sweep through the valley. Looking down to the side she saw Ku'ka and the slavers.

"Settle in friends. This is going to be historic."

Saturos and Lord Zylo began to stir. Their blindfolds were removed. Anri tried to warn them, but her words were taken from her. The air in the field choked the life out of her. A side effect of the panthos'. The creature approached her from below. Its fangs protruding with saliva, ready to rip her to shreds. The scales on its neck rattling as they heated up. Slowing down her breath she stopped herself from passing out. The prince called to the creature to return to his side.

Prince Alexander ripped out a rib bone from one of the carcasses. "Friends! Today we gather here to rejoice in the ultimate return of Lord Nebula. I offer to you the Star of Orion."

Anri and the others looked on in horror. What was he doing? How could he have betrayed them?

"In order to activate the final key, blood must be shed upon it. This forest was once home to the rarest of Hyperion's creations, the Unicorn. Creatures of pure light. Embedded with the flame of God. Those that remain are hidden. Shoxz's blood is all we need to recharge the final key."

Saturos and the others screamed and cursed the prince. They fought against their chains for freedom. Shoxz was dragged forward and pinned to the floor. With the bone of the dragoon, the prince began scrapping off her horn. She screamed out in pain. Her horn glowing like the radiant sun, blinding all of those who gazed upon it. With each strike, a wave of energy cracked the ground around them. Ku'ka approached the prince from behind and picked up the residue of the horn. Removing a Nebula Shard from its cloak, Ku'ka took the rib from the prince and molded all three together to create a blade. It was marvelous. A combination of purple and white light dancing together. Positioning himself in front of her, he could see the tears in her eyes. He was surrounded by chanting. Ku'ka stood nearby watching the prince from a distance ready to strike if he failed, while Anri and the others pleaded with him.

Flashes of emerald light distorted Anri's vision. The voice of Oricale called to her to stop him. A technique only ever used once to secure her safety; Anri closed her eyes and grabbed tightly onto her shackles. Restraints, made to negate magic; she siphoned its power. Once depleted of its energy, she broke free and dropped to the ground. Ku'ka took one step toward her and saw the emerald light in her eyes. She waved her hand and banished him back to Lord Dark Lucus' side. The slavers and Dark Servants attacked her, but with each spell, she prospered against them.

By this time, Zaos had regained her strength. Anri drew on the energy of their shackles and ripped them off. Fused with residue of the Nebula Shards, her veins began to darken as well. She ordered the others to subdue the prince while she removed the darkness from within him.

"You will never succeed. The gateway will open."

"I release you of this poison!"

Anri placed her hands on the prince's forehead and mouth. A massive wave of energy exploded from his aura and black liquid shot out of his mouth and nose. The pendant drew out the darkness from her as well. A limp prince collapsed onto the floor, as the liquid took shape. Zaos and the others fought those that remained, but the shade of the prince was too strong. He managed to slice Shoxz with the blade. Her blood spilled onto the ground and the Star of Orion. In doing so he left himself open. Anri ripped the shade apart. The Star of Orion was gone.

Anri and Zaos stood over Shoxz as she bled out. The wound was infected. Her horn pulsated with a blinding light. Lord Zylo and Saturos managed to scare the panthos' into the tunnels, but that only led to even more chaos. With Shoxz's blood soaking into the ground, the ground began to crack. Her blood soaked into the tunnels below causing the panthos' and the lava turtles to fight and reignite the volcanoes below. In doing so, the tower was revealed. A monstrous spire pushed through a broken mountain. Each of the tunnels collapsed, sealing in the creatures below. The air in the field grew staler and toxic. The rosewood-colored stones of the tower emitted heat unlike any other. Anri and Zaos tended to Shoxz as Lord Zylo and Saturos examined the entrance of Mars Tower.

No amount of magic could clean up the wound. It was infected. The wound was black, and the white skin began to corrode into purple. Shoxz tried to call out to the prince. As he lay on the floor next to her, she nudged him with her nose. She dragged herself closer to him and placed her head on his. Her tears burned his flesh and cleansed him. His eyes shot open, and he screamed in fear. He held his friend and kissed her face. Shoxz forgave him, he was not in control of his actions. She was ready to embrace death. As she took her final breath, her eyes dilated, and she went limp in his arms. Anri and Zaos watched as the prince sobbed over the loss of his friend. Another casualty of war.

He refused to see his friend die. He moved to the open wound and placed his hands over it. He screamed at the top of his lungs. No amount of anger could bring her back. Calling the great Oricale, he pleaded with her. Anri's pendant shook and glowed. She gripped it so he could not see its reaction to him. His own amulet had lost its glow. His pleading came to an end as he witnessed the grass around her body begin to decay. Shoxz was absorbing the life energy of the grass. Her fur was now completely purple. Her mane was a mixture of white and purple, even her horn. Her eyes shot open, and she stumbled to her feet.

"What did you do?"

"I could not lose you."

"I have lost my purity."

The prince stared at his friend in confusion. Rather than fixing his mess, he made a bigger one. Shoxz flared her wings revealing shades of purple. Frustrated by the prince's actions she took off into the forest. The prince tried to follow.

"Leave her be. You have done enough for today."

Zaos held the prince by his arm as he turned to look at her.

"I will not abandon my friend."

Anri interjected, "Prince, the tower has revealed itself with her blood. We need to get to the stone before Lord Marlusha or Lord Dark Lucus do."

Zaos led them to the foot of the tower. Two dragon statues formed a staircase leading to a massive black-iron door. Lord Zylo caught a whiff in the air and turned back toward the valley.

"We are no longer alone."

The Dark Servants that retreated came back with an army. Lit torches and drums of war resonated through the forest. Prince Alexander watched as they assembled. Trumpets sounded and a path was cleared, Eris rode in on a Mystic Moose. Its pale white creamy skin glowed with starlight. The blue stripes and dots on its body shimmered in the moonlight with each step it took. Its neck and ankles were lined with blue fur. Protruding from its head were three-foot, diamond antlers. She was not alone. To her side was Jenna. The sight of the two of them ignited the prince's rage. Zaos stood at his side and could see his arm tremoring. She stepped forward.

"I will only offer you this once. Leave with your lives. Otherwise, my blades will be the last thing you remember."

Jenna laughed. "Bring me her hands. Another piece of elf to add to my collection."

Baiting the elf, she rubbed her hands on the head of the death moose she rode in on. The tips of her fingers were covered Elven bones filed down finely into claws. She leaped from the moose and her belt jingled. Each loop on her belt had a ring. Twelve loops. Twelve rings. Each ring belonged to her brethren. She looked down at her ring, three pearls held together by a band of diamonds. They were only gifted to trusted members of King Oberon's court in Avalon.

It was hidden from wanderers. Zaos could sense a high pitch noise resonating from them. Consumed by mania, Zaos disappeared and reappeared in from of her. She punched her in the chest and sent her flying into her troops. Eris cackled as the soldiers attacked. Zaos drew ten darts from her cloak and made quick work of the Dark Servants surrounding her. Lord Zylo snarled at a group advancing on the steps. His lightweight armor allowed him to keep his speed.

Eris watched the chaos unfold. Jenna got up from the ground. Her assault on the elf was unreserved as her flames burnt through her own troops. Saturos and Anri stood guard of the steps while the prince faded away into the background. He was fixated on the door. Its iron forged together to depict a story. Unicorns slaughtered and their blood used to curse the land. Used to hide the tower from sight. At its center there was an indent big enough for him to put his hand through. Saturos turned and saw what the prince was doing and grabbed his arm.

"What are you thinking? This could be a trap."

He was still woozy from being possessed by his shade. Staring into Saturos' eyes, he heard a whisper.

"*Alexander.*"

The voice was soft, calming, and chilling. At first, he thought it was his mother, but then it spoke again.

"*You need a spark to open the gate.*" He quickly realized Eris was in his head. He shot her a glance and she gently twirled her hands at him like a wave. "*Use Jenna.*" Once again, her voice echoed in his mind. Anri could see the look of worry on his face.

"Tell me, what's troubling you?"

"She is in my head!" he replied.

Anri gripped her staff and dragged it across the floor igniting the crystal at the top. She raised it above her head creating a barrier around the steps. Eris' voice went silent. Anri called for Lord Zylo and Zaos to retreat, as the battalion was overwhelming them. Zaos did not make it in time. From the shadows, a pair of Exceaios' appeared and subdued her. Saturos grew tired of sitting on the sidelines.

"*Vat'ren bivi.*" He created a whip of flames and sliced at their reanimated bones. He drew the fire in his hands toward his mouth and blew at it, creating a lion. The beast charged at the skeletal beings allowing him to pick up Zaos and return her to the barrier.

Jenna tailed him and was inches away from grabbing him. She stood on the outside of the barrier banging and cursing them all. Ascending the steps, he placed Zaos on her feet. Groggy, she managed to stand on her own.

Prince Alexander whispered to them, "Jenna is our way in."

"How do you know that?" questioned Saturos.

"My sister."

They all turned their faces and watched as Eris smiled from the distance. The double agent brought the one thing they needed to open the gate. Not once did she interfere in the fighting. She could have easily taken them if she wanted. There was something else brewing in her mind. With one final act of betrayal, she raised her hands as if shooting an arrow from a bow. An arrow comprised of shadow, lunged into Jenna's arm, causing her to fall. At that moment, Anri opened a fraction of the barrier and Saturos and Lord Zylo grabbed her and knocked her unconscious. The barrier closed before any of her soldiers could slip through.

Jenna was taken to the gate, and her arm was placed inside. The gears in the door began to turn. The noise woke her up and she tried to free herself. With her free arm she tried to blast them with flames, but it only caused the opening to tighten around her arm. She cried out for Eris' assistance. To keep up appearances she intervened. Arrow after arrow she launched at the barrier, cloaking it in shadows. The barrier dissolved. Eris slowly walked up the steps cautiously.

"We do not have much time."

Jenna's eyes widened.

"A true bitch and traitor. My father will kill you whore," she roared.

Eris warned them the door would only open with her death. She was the blood of Lord Marlusha. None of them could do it. Eris laughed. It wasn't up for debate. She did it herself. Before anyone could move, she crafted a spear comprised of shadows and pierced Jenna's heart. Removing the weapon, she dropped the barrier and fell to the ground.

As the shadows faded, the army saw Eris on the floor and their commander dead. Battle cries roared through the crowd as they rushed the steps. Zaos enchanted the dragon staircase to fight. Arrows and spears were launched toward them. Anri redirected them. While they were occupied Eris made her move on the prince. She grabbed a blade and brought the prince to his knees. Big mistake. Hidden in his hand was the blade he used on Shoxz. He stabbed her. He looked into her eyes as she lay on top of him.

She whispered, "Thank you!"

Eris faded into the shadows. With their commanders gone, the troops retreated. Jenna's blood soaked her clothes. Her blood was sucked up by the gate, leaving only a carcass behind. As the gate opened, Zaos ripped the rings from Jenna's belt and tossed her body aside as she entered the tower with the others. The prince was in all as he admired the interior. Lord Marlusha's reign was depicted on the walls. It held stunning treasures; rubies, diamonds, sapphires, and golden trinkets piled on top of each other. Like the other towers, there were staircases leading to the floor above.

Unlike the others, these had archways formed into dragon skulls leading to each staircase.

Anri noticed the prince had continued without them. Once they tended to the injured, they followed suit. Each floor they ascended was abandoned. No relics, no paintings, no sign of life. Clearing each floor, they finally caught up to the prince. He was standing on the final floor. In front of him was a statue carved out of volcanic rock. It was an angel. There was something familiar about it. Scanning the sculpture, it finally dawned on him.

"Hyperion?" questioned the prince.

"The Usurper right before our eyes. Uncanny." responded Zaos.

"Why keep a statue of him here?" inquired Anri.

"As a reminder. There is an inscription on the lower backside of the statue," interjected Saturos who was examining it.

Descendant of Chaos, one of seven. Born of light. Sculptor of mankind. Traitor of life and freedom. Father of Fire. As the inscription was recited, a rumbling could be heard from below. The floor sealed up. The walls opened and lava poured in. Everyone jumped onto the statue for safety. Spells had no effect on it. It continued to rise until the base of the statue was covered in it. The stone absorbed the lava and reanimated. Once the lava was completely absorbed, everyone dismounted from the statue.

"My children if you are hearing this that means, I have truly lost my way. I created this statue to house my last memories before the Nebula took control. Its power is seductive, destructive, and corrupting. I murdered my entire family for power. We were gods. It repaid me by taking my child. Satan's rebellion to expose me nearly succeeded, but I saw to silence him. Nothing pure can come from that cosmic parasite. Fate has intervened and created a way to stop me. The child, the curse, my undoing. Protect him at all costs."

Those words, repeated in his mother's journals. There was so much of his parents past that he knew nothing about. His mother's journals were the closest thing he had to her history. Did she ever come across this statue? How did Lord Marlusha get ahold of this statue? Only more questions trifled with his mind. The statue shifted its wings and encased its body. In doing so, it triggered the gears in the room to unlock the shrine atop the tower. A staircase descended from the ceiling. Zaos approached first, twirling magical energy into her fingers. Saturos was next, then the prince. Anri trailed behind to cover them.

Hoping to see a shrine, they only saw steps leading up to a throne. Four male statues on bended knee were holding plates on their heads with flames. They surrounded the base of the throne. Seated atop was a male elf. Extending from the back of the throne was a crystal pillar. Embedded two feet above his head was the Fire Stone. Zaos locked eyes with the elf. She screamed with excitement and ran to embrace him. Adamar, another Elf of the Twilight and younger brother to Zaos.

Adamar's appearance was different than his sister's. His eyes were white with black pupils. His skin was a mixture of purple and black. On his forehead was a tattoo of a crescent moon facing downward. He had tribal tattoos under his eyes, around his cheeks, and on his nose. In the moonlight, the markings had a bluish glow on them. His pointed ears had three diamond studded earrings on each. Sprouted from his head were horns curled backward, mainly covered underneath his white hair. In one hand he had a two-sided sword with blades shaped like crescent moons. In the other, was a staff of blue iron. At the head was a pearl the size of a baseball. Attached to it were two crescent moons.

Taking a step forward he vanished and reappeared, staring into the prince's eyes. Zaos ordered everyone to stand down. Adamar tilted his head and smiled.

"The child of wonders! I never thought I would see you in my lifetime."

"Nice to meet you."

"I smell the touch on you."

"Touch?"

Adamar stepped away and walked toward his sister. Both placed their foreheads together and closed their eyes.

"It is so good to see you brother."

Adamar turned back to the prince. He explained he could smell the stench of the Nebula on him. It still lingered. He ordered the others to get away from the prince. His laughter caught them by surprise. Anri watched as the veins near his eyes blackened. As he spoke, it was as if five voices were speaking through him. The last remnants of the black liquid seeped from his skin and reformed into Eris before the prince collapsed.

She was not herself. Sweat dripped from her forehead. Her scar was growing. With a flick of the wrist, she covered the area in a dark fog.

Saturos roared out, "*Izvu va'uci.*" He drew on the flames from the statues to generate a reflective barrier around them. Eris' laugh echoed around them.

"I will not harm you. I am just here for the stone."

Adamar raised his hand and shouted, "*Un'dizi,*" drawing the fog into his hand and crystalizing it. Eris was seated upon his throne watching them.

"Do your worst."

Zaos launched spells at her only to hear Adamar scream in opposition. The statues were spellbound to defend the throne. Saturos crippled one of them by taking out its legs. It crumbled as it hit the ground. Lord Zylo and Anri teamed together to take out another while Eris made her way to the stone. She destroyed the pillar, allowing the stone to fall into her hands. Staring at the stone caused overwhelming. Screaming with agony, she dropped it. The stone bounced off each step until it reached the bottom of the landing and cracked. An immense wave of energy shattered the guardians.

Adamar appeared behind her, "I will never let you take the Fire Stone!" He grabbed her by her hair and dug his fingers into her wound. With his other hand he dug his nail into her eye. Eris cried out in pain and caught the prince's attention. The world around the prince was spinning. Anri saw him slowly opening his eyes. She lifted him from the floor, and he could see the stone.

"*Brother, I must return with the stone.*"

As if under her spell, the prince got up from the floor and waved his head to the left. Adamar's body was flung from the throne across the floor of the tower. Zaos saw the prince and Eris staring at one another. The Fire Stone ignited. It was comprised of pink tourmaline and carved into a serpent. Grabbing ahold of it, she vanished in a cloud of darkness.

How could he be this blind? Staring at the ground he realized the liquid had oozed out of the stone. Each stone had a spirit connected to it. As the prince touched it, it was devastatingly hot. As he stood there, he felt the presence licking from his neck to his ear and whispering to him.

Like a siren call, he repeated its words, "*Dimittam vestri navitas.*"

A massive quake overtook the tower. Gears turned and lava flowed. The throne exploded as a spire of lava shot into the sky and jolted down. Zaos and the others were too late. The prince was encased. He realized he wasn't burning. Lowering his arms, he noticed he was still alive. The lava around him hardened. Only a pool of liquid lava remained in front of him. It bubbled up taking on the form of a woman.

"I am Chantico, Goddess of Fire. You have freed me from my prison."

"Prison?"

Chantico laughed, "The Betrayer stole my fire and sought to give it to a sapling like Lord Marlusha. I have waited for this day; I am going to end his legacy."

The prince was terrified. In her naked glory she had rings and chains connecting both of her nipples. She wore a feathered serpent headdress. Chains and rubies adorned her waist like a skirt. Her feathered armbands and sandals were also adorned with rubies. Each of her nails were sharp and imbued with gold. Placing her hand on the ground she summoned a geyser of lava. The tower forcibly shook with vigor. The ground below trembled at the tremendous might of the old goddess. The Forest of Flames was completely obliterated. The Volcanic Valley was reactivated, and the geysers rushed with lava.

As she reshaped the island, Saturos sliced at the outer shell allowing them to see inside. Chantico was consumed by the lava and disappeared. Zaos' pointed ears drew her attention beyond the surface of the planet. The goddess was causing a shift in the Mazso Plate and forced the underwater volcanoes between the Island of Mars and Sharaa to ignite. In seconds, thousands of volcanoes changed the layout of the world. The water that once separated them was now gone and a new land bridge connected the two.

CHAPTER
30

OLD ENEMIES

Chantico's devastation was unending. Her wrath unraveling by the minute. The surface of Mars boiled, and the sea of lava killed anything in its path. What didn't die instantly, suffocated from the toxic plumes. Zaos created a barrier around them to help them breathe until they could get off the island. Without Shoxz, they were stranded. The prince tried to use the amulet to call for Fang.

On the sidelines, the prince watched as the others devised a strategy. Keeping his distance, he feared betraying them again; he was a prisoner of his thoughts. He had lost the last friend he had. Those that surrounded him were loyal to another. He could not fully trust them, but on the flipside, he did not give them any reason to trust him either. He was touched by the Nebula. A savior turned pawn. A failure. Lord Nebula was now closer to revival. Whatever sliver of hope they thought they had, was gone.

What would the princess think? Something else she would blame him for. Carrying secrets kept his family divided from the beginning. If she knew the secrets their mother kept, she wouldn't pass judgement so quickly. He tugged at the handle of his bookbag. His eyes shot open. His journals. He rummaged through it franticly, they were stuck at the bottom, without titles. Only to his touch did they reappear. He grabbed the journal with his name. Before he could open it, his attention was drawn to Anri's screams.

Looking up at her, she was running toward him whaling her arms. Seeing fear in her eyes, he noticed she was looking beyond him. He turned to see a lava turtle busting through the floor. The creature was inches away from the prince. Its massive jaw open, jagged rocks for teeth, and a pool of lava seeping out burning through the floor. The ground collapsed around them. Its thoughts were beyond the prince's ability to speak with it. When he tried to communicate with it there was static feedback.

The creature stomped around as if getting ready to stampede. It opened its mouth again, but this time the prince noticed something hanging from its tooth. Against the advice of his companions, he moved toward the beast, it did not recognize him as a threat and allowed him to get closer. Reaching into its mouth, he was able to dislodge the object. It was a vial filled with black liquid. It began to react to the prince's bag. He reached in and grabbed the Water of Life. The vials connected at the hilt and became one. The two liquids entangled one another. Staring at them closer they appeared like children dancing with one another.

"What is it?" questioned Anri.

"You hold his children," responded Zaos.

Her answer confused the prince. "What children?"

Zaos touched the prince on the shoulder and grabbed the vial. Within it were the children of Chaos. His first two. Life and Death themselves. After Hyperion killed Chaos, he made sure to remove his most formidable relatives. He liquefied them and stored them in these vials.

"We may have a way to defeat him."

Her words were interrupted as screeching echoed through the clouds. Next, appeared a set of wings flapping away the toxins. It was Fang. He was roosting on the spiked mountains surrounding Sharaa. Mounting Fang first, he then ordered the others to climb atop and hold onto something. Before they could be incinerated, the emerald dragon lifted from the floor and took off toward the ocean.

The vast ocean steamed with a layer of volcanic smoke. They were still far from clearing the aftermath. Lord Zylo reserved himself to silence, while the others spoke. He replayed the torture he endured. His fur being shaved down. He was poked and pried for answers. Even though Zaos' spells healed his outside wounds, those scars were still potent. He stared over at the prince who was also lost in thought.

Since his arrival he has been unraveling the world rather than saving it. Were the royals correct to move on without him? He stared back at Lord Zylo.

Lord Zylo's negative self-talk was diminished by the voice of his grandfather. King Habagin doted on his mother. He loved his brothers and sisters. Even in the end when Eris murdered him, he forgave her. Family had to come first. He watched as the prince removed his mother's journal.

It was time to finally read what else she wrote about him. He flipped through the pages until new words appeared. In her last days, Lady Eileen turned to Lord Marlusha. Enemy of thy enemy. She had seen a glimpse of the future. He would betray her family, but from that betrayal she saw a way forward. There was no way of stopping Lord Nebula from returning, but there was a way of putting an end to him. The Queen of Nations turned over the cache of weapons to Lord Marlusha so he could build a universal splicer - a machine capable of ripping open the universe. It would allow the Elders to return to the void and retrieve a relic capable of destroying the Nebula. The other Divine Lords could never know. She planted the idea of stealing the Elemental Stones as a power source.

Before the day of her death, she stole all the plans for the towers and gave them to Lord Marlusha. She drew up plans on how to use the Elemental Stones to reactivate the plague. She was willing to risk everything to stop Lord Nebula. It was the final page of her journal. His world was turned upside down. To think, in her last days she betrayed her own people. What did she see in the future that caused her to end all her fighting?

Saturos' voice cut through his thoughts. They were near Salahea. They were able to reach Dous Docks. The sandy shore was covered in construction. The pharaoh's banners and troops were stationed around the docks. The inn was still operational. Fang landed, and they were greeted by High Magnus Kishib and his platoon.

"My prince! We were not expecting your arrival back in Salahea."

"We need a place to rest and then we are heading to Seraqus."

"We will have tents made up for you."

The High Magnus escorted them into their tents to rest. Food was delivered. They were not allowed to roam around the camp. Guards were posted outside each tent. Their actions caused concern. The prince was separated from the others. Anri and Zaos in one, Saturos and Lord Zylo in another. While the prince was bathing, Kishib entered the room. Golden bracelets adorned his wrist up to his elbow. He wore a plastron necklace of a snake. His robes were unlike the others. It clipped together on one shoulder with a golden pendant and crossed down his chest to his belt. The prince was still unaware that Kishib was watching him.

"We need to speak!"

His voice caused the prince to cover himself with the soapy water in the steal tub.

"Why are you here?"

"A warning."

"Speak."

Kishib took a seat next to the prince while he was in the tub. He grabbed a cloth and bathed him. "There are whispers. Your sister. She is making moves that will affect us all."

The prince looked into his amber eyes. "Tell me more."

The princess was carrying out her own operation behind her brother's back. Since his arrival, she has been rallying the nations for support. In each of her letters, she mentioned the instability of the prince. She was planning a vote of 'No Confidence' to de-title the prince and call for the removal of Lord Zylo's title so she could take control of Weguard. His sister's motives were clear. Greed drove her to betray her brother. She was harboring resentment about their argument. He wanted to confront her, but Kishib ordered that he not. If she was truly attempting an insurgence, the prince would need to catch her in the act and expose her.

Kishib dried off the prince and allowed him to get dressed.

"The pharaoh will not take sides in this. Warring between the royals will only move the pendulum to Lord Nebula's side. Put an end to this."

The prince foolishly nodded his head in agreement. Kishib exited the prince's tent and returned to his own. The prince put on his night shirt and laid on his cot for the night. The cool breeze blew through the tent. Allowing him to fall asleep. It was the first time in a while he slept without interruptions.

While the prince slept, Kishib sat in a chair staring at a mirror. A ripple against the glass created a portal allowing Eris to walk through. The High Magnus bowed.

"Is it done?"

Eris turned to the mirror, sealing the portal. Gazing at her reflection the scar was growing. The infection decayed the skin. To the touch it burned with the fury of hell. Kishib approached from behind and slowly removed her garments. On a nearby table was a bowl with ointment. Grabbing a wooden stick, he picked some of it up and rubbed it on the wound. As she winced, he slowly placed his arm around her waist. Standing behind her, he embraced her. Moving her hair to the side he kissed her neck until he reached her shoulder. Moving his hand downward he began to entice her. With both hands she gripped the mirror in ecstasy. It was ages since she orgasmed.

Kishib was one of her three lovers. He reminded her of her first love. His face glided across her memory, cutting off her enjoyment. She pushed off his wet fingers and walked away from him. Still naked she stood in the middle of the room.

"Do you believe this child will end Lord Nebula?"

Kishib was afraid to answer. He knew Eris' rage all too well. Their last encounter did not end well. After the pharaoh learned that she had infiltrated his court, she took it out on him. He did not provide her with any warning. His silence was enough of an answer.

"Make sure he gets to her safely. Lord Nebula's most dangerous assassins are coming for them all."

Returning to his side, she kissed him on the cheek. He stood there frozen without words as she moved toward the mirror. Stepping back into her dress, she turned back and whispered she loved him before vanishing into the mirror. What game was she playing at? Was it worth betraying Lord Nebula? Waving his hand, he turned out the candles. The waves brushing against the sand called to his ears. He threw himself on a massive cot and stared at the ceiling of his tent. He wished to hold Eris while he slept.

As children they played together when she visited the palace. His parents were servants of Lord Celeio at the time. His father was on his council and his mother, a handmaiden to the queen. Every time she visited, he would show her around the garden. Before the pharaoh's father came to rule, there was a luscious garden of apple trees, mango trees, and gorgeous fruits. Exotic flowers and scents to die for. It was her favor spot in all the palace. They bathed in the fountain covered in bougainvillea.

As she got older, she became more distant from him until she stopped showing up to see him altogether. They reunited during the birth of Prince Alexander. Pharaoh Kimhairo and his council arrived at the palace with gifts. Many royals completed the pilgrimage to pay their respects. Kishib was inducted into the council after his father's death. With the royals all awaiting the anticipated news of the prince's birth, he slipped away to find Eris. He found her in the catacombs of the fortress, shrouded in shadows arguing with an unknown figure. Whatever it was commanding her to do, she could not go through with it.

Her concentration was broken as she heard footsteps behind her. She turned to see his face dropping her guard. The shadow entered her nose clouding her eyes in a purple fog. She grabbed him by his neck, her nails growing, ripping through his skin. Like a marionette, she was not in control. Her voice, deep, raspy, and chilled as she spoke. Escaping her lips was a crippling mist. In one ear she whispered her command.

"Kill my parents."

Eris touched his face, transforming him into her doppelgänger. Kishib was a prisoner in his own body. With the transformation complete, they went their separate ways. Eris continued further into the catacombs toward her father's vault, while Kishib hid in the shadows until the dead of night. Wearing Eris' face, he slipped into their bedchamber and jumpstarted the Holy War.

Since then, they have been connected. Intertwined in a secret concealed from even those with omnipotent sight. He loved her. Blind love. At least knowing, she fought against her orders to kill her own family; he would rather have blood on his hands than hers. Rubbing his hand against his chest aroused him. Every memory of Eris and him flooded his mind as he pleasured himself until completion. Allowing him to close his eyes and sleep.

Eris peered through from the other side of the mirror. From the safety of Tartarus, she had a looking glass with worldwide access. Waving her hand, she cleared the image, and the glass turned black. Death lingered in the air. Torturous screams resonated through the corridors amplifying the amethyst crystals all around the palace. Clearing each floor, she descended into the basement. Lord Dark Lucus and the Uvali were discussing plans to ambush the royals across all three continents. One remained elusive - Prince Adam. No one had seen him in years.

"Flush him out of hiding."

Eris' words stirred in the chamber.

"How will we do that?" echoed one of the voices.

"Let's make it a reunion. The princess knows where her brother is. We force her to send the little prince after him.

"How will you force her hand?" echoed another voice.

"Leave it up to me."

The Uvali agreed. Eris glanced over at Lord Dark Lucus with disdain. She would do anything to distance herself from Tartarus. Eris took her leave once more. This time she approached a frosted mirror. Tapping her finger at its center, activated it, allowing her to travel through.

While Eris worked in the shadows, Prince Alexander stirred to wake up. Since arriving in LunaSol the night terrors began to dwindle as he embraced his astral projection abilities. Sleep was a luxury so long as he remained inside his own body. Getting rest without interruption was invigorating without having to take those poisonous pills growing up.

He tossed and turned. He opened his legs and felt nothing. Nacilias always slept at the foot of the bed next to his feet. Turning his face to his left, he expected to see Shoxz's face on the pillow next to him. She liked to sleep with her head next to his. The pit in his stomach returned. His nightmare was not over. He wanted to reverse time. He wanted his life to be simple again when he was still living with Drail. He wished he never came to LunaSol.

"Your Majesty." Soldiers stood outside of his tent awaiting entry. The prince called them in as he got out of bed searching for his clothes. While he slept, his clothing was taken and washed. One had them folded in his arms, while the other had a new set of clothes. Placing his old clothes on the bed, the soldier approached the prince, requesting permission to dress him. Consenting, the soldier took off his nightshirt. Grabbing a vase, he sunk it into a barrel to collect water. Using a rag, he dipped it into the vase and washed off the prince before dressing him. He stepped into a green bodysuit that zipped in the back. He sat on the edge of the bed and stuck his feet in a pair of knee-high black boots.

Kishib watched from the entrance of the tent. He was holding armor in his hands. The prince looked over at him.

"Stop gawking and come in!"

"Leave us." The soldiers bowed their heads to the prince and walked out of his tent. "I bring you one final gift."

On display, he held a chest plate adorned with green and blue peacock feathers. Emeralds and sapphires were embedded into the feathers; upon touch, the feathers were as sharp as blades. In the back of his mind, he wanted to tell the prince he was wearing his father's armor, but it would open the door to questions he was not ready to answer.

"Your friends are awake. They are waiting for you."

The prince stood up and passed Kishib; before leaving the tent, he caught a whiff of something familiar. He turned back and stood by his side.

"What is that scent?"

His question caused the High Magnus to panic. Could his primal senses be that good that he smelled his sister. He quashed his curiosity and diverted the subject.

"You must take your leave soon."

Sweat formed at his brows. Lower lip quivering. His non-verbal reactions only made the prince even more suspicious. A quiet laugh bolted from his lips. Stepping out of his tent, he raised his arm toward his eyes. Salahea's boiling sun made it hard to breathe. Kishib's hand touched the prince's lips and placed a black mouthguard. It opened his lungs, allowing him to breathe. Kissing his hand, the High Magnus took his leave from the prince. Zaos and Saturos could be seen walking on the beach together. A gentle tap on his shoulder broke his concentration. It was Anri. She came bearing news. Lord Zylo slipped away in the middle of the night. Their battalion was withering away. Kishib and his servants gave them barrels of wine, boxes filled with bread, meat, and fruits. Fang was fitted with a bigger saddle. Once mounted, Kishib and the prince hugged once more.

The prince grabbed a hold of the rope and climbed aboard. Once he settled in, Fang took off into the sky again. The sand below danced with beauty, shifting from small dunes to nearly the size of buildings. He crossed over the divide and headed toward the Empire. Crossing near Eternal Lake, he swirled down toward the reconstruction below. The devastation caused by the Destroyer of Lands was nearly repaired. The palace was bigger. Fang was able to land in the courtyard. High Magnus' flooded the courtyard to greet them. The Royal Guard was sent to grab the gifts atop the saddle.

Princess Ionica summoned them all to court with haste. The throne room that they once knew was no more. The massive obelisk that stood in the center of the room was gone. A star-like monograph now covered the center of the floor. It was isolated and darker. The northern part of the monograph led to a circular platform with five steps. Like an image of perfection, the princess was seated in a teal caped dress, with a high slit up the thigh. Her feet settled in high heels with chains and sapphires. Even her choker had sapphires. Falling off her shoulder was a sheer double sash with splatters of blue. Ice vambraces covered her wrist. She was not wearing her crown. Under her hood she wore what appeared to be a helmet without its face covering. The sides of the helmet stopped on her cheek bones. It too was adorned with sapphires.

At her feet laid Dementorol and Jecxas like pets, chained to one another. Anri stepped forward. "What is this, my princess?"

"Trophies."

"This is how you treat your subjects?" questioned the prince.

"They are traitors. Guards! Take them away."

The two Ilihi were working with someone from Valhalla. She intercepted communication between them. The princess looked around and noticed people were missing. She inquired about those missing. She saw her question caused the prince to shiver. Saturos came to the prince's side and held his hand in comfort.

"Nacilias was murdered. Shoxz is gone. Lord Zylo left us when we arrived in Salahea."

Princess Ionica's mouth dropped. Frost escaped her fingertips. Tears cascaded down her cheeks. Was this a show? She cried as if she had lost a loved one. Knowing she was planning to usurp him; he showed little emotion toward her.

"I know this is extremely hard. Those traitors will pay for what she has done. We shall have a feast in the honor of all those who have been taken by this horrible war."

As they turned to follow the princess to the dining hall, the prince noticed his armor growing tight around him. His vision clouded. He clawed at his neck. Banging on his chest plate caught the attention of the others. Princess Ionica screamed for the others. Anri and Saturos saw the prince lying on the floor paralyzed in such disquietude. It was spellbound. Another traitor in the pharaoh's guard. The stones on his armor shattered and a black ooze crept out and flowed into his body. Darkness filled his eyes. Saturos moved away from him as the ground cracked. The prince's aura crippled the others. His body ascended from the floor.

Zaos could feel the darkness taking over the prince. His aura grew and forbade anyone from getting closer to him. Princess Ionica tried a different approach. She diluted the floor beneath the prince and summoned strands of water from the opening as she sang to him. The water wrapped him in a cocoon allowing the princess to get close and freeze him in it.

"Princess...what have you done!" stuttered the High Chancellor.

"It was for his own protection and ours."

"This is treason!" roared Zaos.

Her words echoed in the princess' ears. "Treason." She repeated it multiple times, before lashing out. "Spineless elf. You dare question me."

Snapping her fingers, the ice beneath Zaos' feet climbed up her legs, immobilizing her. Turning her gaze to Saturos, he drew his sword. "Do not create enemies out of us. Stand down!"

Anri stood between them, "Enough. Do you not realize the poison in the prince is corrupting us all."

The princess looked down at his tomb. The darkness was feeding on their negative thoughts. Snapping her fingers, she released Zaos.

The dark ooze ravaged the prison, trying to set itself free. It reentered the prince causing him to spasm. Unable to free itself, it ate away at the prince. Anri noticed the princess was hyperventilating uncontrollably. Her abilities manifested without cause. Frost appeared on her hands and shot across the room. The temperature dropped dramatically. Anri intervened and held the princess' hands to avoid causing damage to the palace or even killing someone. Her fingertips were blue.

Anri sang to her, calming her spirit. The frost around them glistened with each note. The princess stumbled with her thoughts. She recalled something. Something that could heal the prince. She ordered the Royal Guard to bring Amaris to her.

As she entered the throne room, she quickly noticed the frozen tomb. Zaos stood next to it as its protector. She was concerned when she did not see the prince.

"Princess, you summoned me?"

"We have a matter of importance."

Her words only raised more alarms. Amaris listened to the princess as she explained what happened to the prince. She looked down at the tomb and could see he was spasming inside. The princess believed that the Palace of Otrant could help heal the prince.

"Amaris, I would not ask if it wasn't important."

"Princess, that sacred water is prohibited."

"If he does not have access to it. He will die and his blood will be on your hands."

The princess' tone changed. She was no longer asking for help. She demanded that Amaris take the prince to be healed as if she was a mere servant. While the prince and his companions were searching for the stones, she lived with the princess and her subjects. She was not one to take no for an answer. She kept the Potuliari at a distance while the empire was being rebuilt. The princess was not aware she was descendant from three of the four Divine Lords. Amaris agreed to take the prince to the Palace of Otrant.

The Shrine of Visions was never meant for humans to bathe in its waters. The water was enchanted by the Mystic Otrant. She used it to heal the creatures of this world. She refused to allow humans to contaminate it. It was once a massive pond, but most of the water dried up and what was left was placed in the shrine. Amaris had to convince the Council of Otrant to allow her access into the shrine. Without their blessing, the prince could die. The poison in him continued to attack the tomb and then retreat back into his body. Anri enchanted the tomb to levitate and followed Amaris out into the courtyard.

CHAPTER
31

PALACE OF OTRANT

"What was that all about?"

The High Chancellor was mortified. For the first time, she broke her vow and read the princess' mind. The hatred, the schemes, the trips to Valhalla for political purposes. She was turning into someone unrecognizable. Saturos could see the fear in her eyes.

"The princess is turning. Is she not?" questioned Zaos.

"There is a darkness in her I never felt before."

"We must save the prince!" replied Zaos.

Fang stood in the courtyard puzzled by the prince's tomb. He flared his wings and screeched in anger. Zaos tried to calm him, but he lifted off into the sky and took off.

"What now?" questioned Saturos.

"We fly!" Amaris replied.

Amaris glided into the air awaiting the others. Zaos enchanted her cloak and turned them into wings. Anri enchanted her staff and straddled it like a witch's broom. Saturos enchanted his boots to fly. Each took off after Amaris as the tomb floated behind them.

Anri replayed the visions in her mind when she invaded the princess' thoughts. Staring down at her hands, she noticed sparks of magic flickering at her fingertips. When she looked to the side, the part of the tomb closest to her grew darker. The parasite was feeding on her energy.

Zaos pushed away from it. The further it got; the further the dark ooze retreated into the prince. Their enchantments began to fade, the closer they got to the forest. Zaos could hear the songs. The songs of the dryads and the nymphs could only be heard by primitive creatures. The trees danced to their hymns and echoed their curse into the air, keeping anyone from flying overhead.

Night was settling in, and the forest danced in the breeze. Zaos felt its ancient magic. A nasty buzzing sound filled her ears. The forest rejected them. Anri noticed runes carved into the bark of the trees on the outer rim of the forest. He grabbed his sword and dug it into the ground. The gem on the handle lit up and drew on the magic from the forest. The barrier cracked, allowing them to bypass the forest's defenses. Once inside, Zaos could hear the trees screaming to one another.

It was like a symphony of pain. They triggered an alarm. They continued through the forest and found their path blocked by a massive warrior. He placed the tip of his blade inches from Zaos' neck. Saturos drew this sword as well. She did not take kindly to threats and grabbed the sharp end of the blade and electrified it with a spell. It backfired and stunned her. Anri pleaded with him.

"King Silverskull, we mean you no harm. My name is High Chancellor Anri, this here is Zaos, Amaris and Saturos. We are on our way to the Palace of Otrant to save the prince."

"What a surprise, I just caught a trespasser in this neck of the woods earlier."

High Elves appeared behind him with iron chains and Lord Zylo bound.

"What is the meaning of this?" demanded Anri.

"The princess demanded his capture."

"That is Lord Zylo, son of Master Yami."

King Silverskull explained that the princess sent a note to all the royals demanding that they renounce him as a Royal and take him prisoner if caught. Princess Ionica charged him and Master Yami with conspiracy to willfully conceal a dangerous relic that allowed Lord Marlusha's army to storm over Seraqus. Lord Zylo confessed it was the reason he left them in Salahea. He overheard the High Magnus' troops discussing it.

King Silverskull showed them the note. Zaos demanded his release. The princess had no authority to declare them enemies of the nation. The king refused to disobey orders. Anri would not allow him to take Lord Zylo into custody. She explained what she saw in the princess' mind. The princess was compromised. They needed Lord Zylo by their side to save the prince.

King Silverskull agreed. He released Lord Zylo. The princess would have his head if she found out he has possession of him and let him go. As they spoke the breeze shifted the leaves. Rose vines crept around the prince's tomb. Saturos noticed and rushed toward it, but he was too late. Amaris saw the roses burst and their petals danced and took the form of nymphs. The creatures circled the prince while the others watched. Amaris recognized them from her trip downstream. They could sense his agony. The poison coursing through his veins was not from the Nebula, as they sung, the ooze retreated. Their songs were angelic in nature. The blood of a Dark Angel fed on his soul. The prince was stable for the moment. The nymphs released the vines that held him in place. Amaris guided it to the others. The nymphs danced around her and laughed before returning to their natural state.

King Silverskull escorted them through the forest until they reached Taruz, a town of treehouses with a population of less than three hundred people. A merchant town known for selling herbs and remedies for the sick. It was a great outpost for spotting an army. From the treehouses they had a clear line of sight to the Bridge of Sand that separated Seraqus from Southern Salahea. The ground was filled with poisonous plants and bushes, making it harder for travelers. The only way up was to climb the hanging ropes to each platform. Entering the town was easy, but to gain access to the bridge would be harder. The merchants watched in awe as King Silverskull took them to the edge of the forest.

The lushest green trees were withering away. Southern Salahea was ruthless, the desert sand consumed portions of the forest as the winds pummeled them from the north. Placing his sword against the barrier, he allowed them to cross over. His loyalty was to the prince. He would never allow the princess to usurp the throne. The sand bridge that they expected was not there, but rather two Mesonic stone lion statues. As they approached, they could see a massive trench below that appeared endless. Zaos cautiously advanced toward the statues. A magical frequency was radiating from them. She tossed a rock between them toward the other side and in seconds it was vaporized by an invisible force.

Her focus was taken off the bridge as she heard something overhead. The sun blackened, as Shoxz descended from the sky. Without the prince it was hard to communicate with her. Zaos used her magic to retrace her steps. After abandoning them she sought the remaining Unicorns, but their breeding grounds were uninhabitable. She toured the outskirts of Northern Salahea and witnessed Kishib and his army rebuilding the docks. His warriors were not loyal to the royals. The adornments placed on their armor were filled with angelic blood. It enhanced protection from heavy onslaught. They were preparing for war.

Shoxz was surprised to see the prince incapacitated. The poison running through him was like the scent in Kishib's soldiers. Amaris needed to get him to the healing pool. The bridge only appeared twice a day - when the sun rose and set. Southern Salahea was mostly comprised of prison camps for those who betrayed the pharaoh. His Magnus' enchanted a barrier to keep those prisoners from escaping.

Saturos looked at the others, he found a place to rest until sunset. Amaris stood watch as the others rested. She gazed at the colossal black mountains acres away that cast their shadows over a great distance. The devilish mountains worried her. It gave her an uneasy feeling. Her attention was drawn to the floating tomb of Prince Alexander. She could sense his pain. It was consuming his very soul.

Anri scared Amaris as she drew closer. The pair spoke about the Shrine of Visions and the magical properties it contained. Anri could sense that she was not comfortable telling her the whole story.

"There is something else inside the Palace of Otrant?"

Amaris smiled at Anri, "The power of infinite light!"

The statuesque woman was very cryptic and captivating. Anri knew the subject would not go any further, so she placed herself next to Shoxz and waited for the sunset. Amaris was alone by the massive gorge between the two countries. She could feel the presence of another.

"Who are you?"

"I have come to warn you. If you save this boy, you will doom us all" uttered the mysterious figure.

Turning to see who it was, she caught a glimpse of his red eyes in the shadows.

"Nathaniel, is it?"

"In the flesh."

The dark cloud circled vigorously before finally taking form. Nathaniel Darkbloom slightly bowed and smiled at Amaris, gazing at her beauty. She slapped him and whispered for him to leave. He laughed at her spunk. Amaris was no match for him, and she knew that too. He did not want to fight. His warning was true. The Palace of Otrant was in danger. If she healed him, the secrets of the palace would fall into enemy hands.

"That child is a plague on us all."

His words infuriated her, as she turned, he was gone. Amaris thought it was her imagination. The thought ate away at her soul. She could not allow the prince to die. Her heart was torn. Bringing him into her palace could mean the end of everything. The cool air brushed against her cheek. Her mind no longer focused on the evil words spoken by a traitor.

Once he departed, the bridge materialized. Amaris called for the others to hurry. They only had a limited amount of time to cross. Zaos was the last to cross. She was disoriented. There was a loud buzzing in her ears. Trying to focus on the walkway she noticed she was getting extremely hot. Her hands shaking as she tried to take another step forward. Whispers pierced her brain like daggers. The barrier was rejecting her entry. Her bioluminescent veins danced as the blood pumped through her, forcing her aura to become visible. Like a leech the barrier drew on it. An aurora dazzled the bridge, turning her aura into a weapon. It ruptured and flung her onto the barrier. Like a bee caught in a spider's web. Their window of opportunity was closing. Amaris had to act fast.

She took a deep breath and slowly placed her hand on it. Sparks of electricity raced from her body through the barrier, causing an opening. Zaos' body collapsed through it. Amaris yelled at the others to grab her. Lord Zylo sprinted for her and tossed her over his shoulder and made his way into the wasteland. Anri guided the prince's tomb away from the barrier before Amaris released her hold on it. The dry desert breeze filled their lungs. Sand danced in the air and brushed against their flesh. Saturos' body was nearly concealed in sand.

"What just happened?" questioned Saturos.

"Her magic. Her dark magic to be precise. That barrier was erected to keep prisoners of war from escaping this dungeon.
It saw her as a threat," answered Amaris.

Lord Zylo called her bluff.

"If the barrier keeps dark magic from entering or exiting, how did Lord Marlusha's troops get access?"

"We do not know how they got in. That is still being investigated."

Anri sensed the barrier was doing more than just trying to keep her out. Amaris was not forthcoming with answers. Anri feared that Zaos' life would be in danger if she crossed back through it. Her thought faded as the tomb of the prince shook with ferocity. If the prince was not cured in time, he could become Lord Nebula's pawn. The journey across the desert sand took three days. They took shelter in the neighboring City of Sand.

Fortified by twenty-foot-tall walls carved out of harden sand. The guards allowed Amaris and her companions entry. The city was a prominent host for greengrocers. There were aisles of cabbage, beets, turnips, papyrus roots, and lotus on each side. Fragrant smells lingered around them as Earth Ilihi's greeted them. They were taken further into the city and passed aisles of raisins, olives, and apples. Amaris was given a pineapple and a coconut to try by one of the greengrocers. The pineapple was sweet and delectable. She could not resist eating the entire thing as they made their way to the inn to eat and rest.

The inn was nothing compared to the comfort of Northern Salahea. There were no beds, rather, mats on the floor for them to sleep. The windows were tiny and only a dry breeze graced the room. Sweat poured down their faces as they slept the night away.

Saturos could not rest, his mind kept replaying his encounter with Gaea. She called him '*son of the damned*.' What did she know about his parentage? He wanted answers, but he knew by summoning her through his sword it would allow her to control him. He settled down and left it alone. He closed his eyes and drifted away.

A night's rest was what they needed. Daybreak came and Amaris led them back into the scorching desert. A deadly terrain of mountains separated them from their destination. Beyond the mountain path stood Otrant Lake. It's black and still waters separated for Amaris and the others. The cobble stone road beneath the lake led them to the gates of the palace. Blue Magnus' adorned in their sapphire robes, stood guard as they approached. Anri grew rather uneasy around them, more so, when she noticed a sigil of a waxing, full, and waning moon etched into their chest-plate.

Traitors. Thieves. Murders. Her eyes darted back and forth as she fixated on their armor. Suppressed memories resurfaced. The laughter of a child playing at the foot of their mother's throne. Soldiers posted at every corner. Her mother's name being called out, "*Madam Argia*." A man appearing as the General of the soldiers called to her as he delivered terrifying news. Her pale skin sparkled in the morning light. She stared into her alluring blue eyes as the world around her continued. The young Anri saw the sparkle of life in her mother's eyes turn to fear as loud bangs erupted throughout her throne room.

Madam Argia grabbed the young Anri and gave her to the General. She kissed her on her forehead and ordered him to take her to safety. She sent him into a hidden chamber beneath her throne, but before she could seal it up Anri caught a glimpse of her mother being betrayed. Her own soldiers allowed Magnus' to storm the throne room. Madam Argia was too ill to stand against them. Even in her state, she managed to send many of them to their death, but they ultimately killed her. The traitors proudly wore the sigil of her mother's sister Queen Elizabeth, the kin slayer.

Queen Elizabeth was long dead, but her followers still wore a traitor's sigil with pride. She could not avenge her mother until the prince was safe, but until then she proceeded with caution. Amaris requested that they step aside and allow them access. The Palace of Otrant was grand. Sapphire marble lined the walls and glistened in the light. Caldrons of fire filled the room and danced as Amaris and the others made their way deeper into the depths of the palace. Steps carved out of molten rock led them into a crystal sanctuary. The room was filled with shallow water with a singular walkway of stones leading to a shrine. Marble and crystal fused together to form the pillars. A pool of sparkling water sat at its center.

Guarding the shrine was one of the Council Members, Piers. Unlike the soldier's uniform, he wore tribal clothing. Deep wools and furs adorned with runes. A glance exchanged between him and Anri. Her face, her eyes. He knew them.

"You, I know you!" His excitement got the better of him. Piers and Anri were cousins. His grandmother, Queen Mora Stormfal was the sister of Madam Argia. His father, Master Mukomo Dawnrider was her sworn General. He kept Anri safe as a child and raised her until one night she vanished.

Transfixed on her, he could not articulate his words. He could not even focus on Amaris' words as she spoke to him about the prince's illness. She needed to bypass the council's permission. Anri was all he could concentrate on. She was thought long dead. As a child he knew her as Anristasia. Distracted by his thoughts, he just nodded and allowed Amaris to submerge the prince's tomb into the holy water. When placed into the shrine the water bubbled. The ice melted and the prince's body spasmed.

Piers stood back as a geyser from the shrine shot up into the air and solidified. Within was the prince, arms extended, and feet pointed toward the ground. His aura vibrated with the ice causing the shrine to illuminate. The giant diamonds protruding from the walls magnified the intensity. The vibrations turned into screams, burning through their minds.

Piers slammed his shield into the floor creating a barrier around them nullifying the sound outside. The shield only made matters worse as it vibrated the intensity of the sound in front of the spire causing it to shatter. As it shattered, the prince's eyes shot open, soulless, and black, he stared through them with a malevolent smile on his face. His body slowly descended into the water corrupting it as the dark ooze drained from his pores. It was like acid, burning through the shrine and taking over the water surrounding it. The putrid bile disintegrated anything it touched. Nathaniel's prediction rang true. Amaris' heartbeat rippled in her ears as the room around her spun. The palace had to be cleared up. Piers shook her abrasively and brought her back to reality.

"I will hold it off for as long as I can. GO NOW!"

Without a second thought she raced from the depths of the palace and sounded the evacuation alarms. Piers tried to have the others leave as well, but Anri would not leave the prince's side. Piers and the others watched as the black liquid rose from the water and took form.

"It is finally good to be rid of that body."

Piers shivered in fear. Lord Dark Lucus' shade stood before them. Shades were physical manifestations of their host, holding the same strength and powers of the original. For it to be used the host had to be nearby. This shade traveled far from its host. Doing so should have caused unbearable pain. Even for a corrupted angel, he was extremely resilient. Piers was rattled by his presence.

"Give me Nimah's Pendant and you all shall remain unharmed."

Anri trembled at the mere mention of the pendant. Piers noticed that she knew what he was asking for. He liquefied himself and jolted into the air. He sprung toward the exit, but his escape was short lived. Amaris appeared from the doorway and blasted him with electricity, sending him flying back into the shrine.

"We must contain him."

Lord Dark Lucus' shadow rose from its liquefied state and unleashed an attack onto Piers and Anri. Piers was able to block the attack with his shield, but Anri was thrown back into a nearby boulder. She rose from the debris and made her way to the shrine. No one tried to stop her; they knew better than to get in her way. She cleared her mind and took a deep breath. The water around her pulsated and lit up the room. Lord Dark Lucus' shadow extended his arm toward her, and his fingers became strands of darkness. As they approached, her eyes bolted open, and the Oricale Star pulsated with rage.

She dodged the attack and generated spells using emerald lights. She sliced at the creature sending pieces of it all over the cavern. Piers realized that the creature was weak against the power of Oricale. He removed his Oricale Shield from his back and slammed it into the ground. The symbols on his shield were set ablaze and blasted the shadow with emerald lights. The shadow was badly injured and retreated to the shrine once more. He entered Prince Alexander's body before anyone could stop him. The prince rose from the shrine and laughed at their failed attempts.

"Too bad you cannot harm me while I am in this meatsuit."

Before Prince Alexander could attack, Zaos' body reacted. She waved her hand causing Prince Alexander to drop to his knees.

Lord Zylo roared at Zaos, "You will kill him."

Zaos did not answer. The Elf of the Twilight was no longer in control of her actions. She approached the paralyzed boy, "I will not allow you to get ahold of the pendant." Zaos clenched her hand, and the prince could not breathe. He grasped for air, but she clenched tighter. Anri and the others tried to stop her, but they were stopped dead in their tracks. No one was able to move. Something was not right. She got closer to the shrine and submerged the prince in the water. Anri and Piers could see her aura radiating with power that rivaled even the prince. She chanted in the angelic language causing the room to stir. Zaos was possessed.

"Puterea luminii exprimate strălucească pe
tine. Eliberați acest rău în fața mea. Legați-l
în stralucire vreodată și permite energiei
prințului să curgă."

(*The power of light, cast your shine on thee.*
Release this evil in front of me. Bind it in your
ever glow and allow the prince's energy to flow.)

The cavern shook with intensity. The prince whimpered as his aura became visible. Strands of water levitated from the shrine and slowly surrounded him. It entered his mouth, ears, and eyes. The remaining dark liquid was sucked out of his body and was swallowed by the water. His lifeless body collapsed into the pond. The water that sucked out the ooze levitated over the shrine. Zaos approached it and it altered its form. She was able to remove Prince Alexander's body from the shrine, but the darkness had other plans.

Lord Dark Lucus' dark energy was not easily defeated. In its present state it still had extreme power. The darkness merged with the water and took on the demonic angel's form once more. His fingers expanded into sharp claws as he pointed at the Elf of the Twilight.

"I can sense Queen Nimah's energy flowing through you, but that will not be enough to defeat me."

Anri's nightmare was revealed. The mysterious figure inhabiting Zaos was none other than the mother of all angels. Angels could not inhabit the body of another unless they were allowed in. Zaos did not allow the angel access into her body, so how could she have taken control of her? Anri did not want the angel's help. The angels wanted nothing to do with the child. If she was here to help, it meant only one thing. She had her own agenda. Piers tried to break through Zaos' immobility spell, but it was too powerful. Amaris could not focus long enough to generate electricity. Zaos' amplified power was overbearing. Lord Dark Lucus' new form blasted the four pillars of the Shrine of Visions and caused the cavern to cringe.

Lord Dark Lucus had taken control of the shrine's magic and infected it. The crystal pillars discolored and turned purple. Zaos attacked his new form, but he reinstated the barrier to keep her out and it flung her into the cavern wall. Piers screamed out for Zaos to release her hold on them. They could help her defeat him and prevent the pendant from being found.

Zaos turned and looked at him, "She will not let me release you."

She stood and watched as Lord Dark Lucus blasted the center of the shrine and dismantled pool. Beneath it was a hidden chamber. Rising from the opening was the statue of Queen Nimah holding her staff, wings flared, with the pendant around her neck. Before he could place his hands on it, he saw Zaos' aura explode.

"That pendant will never leave here!" She placed her hands on the floor decimating the floor around her. In her eyes, the pendant was more valuable than the life of the prince. If Lord Nebula got his hands on it, it would surely turn the tide of the war. Zaos was too preoccupied to continue to suppress the others.

Amaris felt herself slowly regaining control of her body. Fixated on killing Lord Dark Lucus, she doomed them all. Her energy was far too vast to contain within the elf, it ripped through the cavern, allowing Lord Dark Lucus to bolt through an opening in the ceiling. With the pendant out of reach, Zaos crumbled under the extreme energy dissipating from her body. Anri spellbound the prince's body and dragged him to her. Piers and the others raced to one another before they could be crushed. He raised his shield and created a barrier.

Zaos could not move. Anri tried to use her magic in the barrier, but it was nullified. She screamed and banged on it as the cavern became their grave. Boulders fell around them, imprisoning them. Watching her lips, she mouthed, "I am sorry," as a mammoth boulder crushed her. Each of them bellowed out a horrifying screech as the room crumbled around them and everything finally went dark.

CHAPTER
32

BROTHER VS BROTHER

Dust and debris settled on the cavern floor. To the east, the ground caved in, opening a direct view to the outside world, allowing the sun's rays to dance across the shattered crystals. Piers' shield managed to keep them alive, but the barrier was weakening. Anri shifted herself around Piers and enchanted her hands to levitate the boulders. Blood stained the rocks around her. Corpses of those who did not escape in time filled the room like a tomb. A stream of water jetted through a crack in the wall, slowly filling the room up. What was left of the palace could be seen through the ceiling. Everything was still caving in. If they did not move quickly the ceiling would collapse again, this time trapping them for good.

The others bolted to safety, but Anri searched through the rubble for Zaos. Amaris tried to stop her, but she was not going to leave her friend behind. She combed through the wreckage, stopping to see her hand between two rocks. Pushing the others aside she saw her friend lifeless, blood on her mouth, leg twisted and out of place, and a massive crack in the back of her skull with blood. "Damnit!" was all she could get out. Holding her in her arms as she cried. Saturos rushed to her side and held her too. Piers was surprised that her body was still intact. Elves were immortal creatures. There was no afterlife for them. When they died in battle, their bodies returned to the earth. Zaos was something different.

389

Piers could smell magic still radiating off her body. Lifting her from the ground, Anri summoned strands of the water in the cavern and forced it into Zaos' mouth. Singing as the water flowed through her, she preserved her with a spell.

The ground above began to shift and fall through the ceiling. Lord Zylo grabbed Zaos and flung her over his shoulder. Making their way through the ruins, the walls were marked with human ash. Skeletons lingered on the floor. The floor beneath them shifted and tilted. Running and sliding they followed Amaris into the council chamber. The wall facing the exterior mountains had a massive hole in it. They crawled out and jumped for safety as the remaining structure sank into the ground.

Amaris stared at the devastation, "What have I done?"

"Sister, this is not on you," replied Piers.

"They will never forgive me."

Piers rubbed her shoulder and escorted everyone further away from the sinkhole. There was a trail of blood leading into the mountains. Beneath their shadowy peaks was a temple. It was where the pharaoh brought his prisoners and interrogated them before sending them to one of his many prisons. It was now their sanctuary. Sentinels comprised of red granite, guarded the colossal entrance. Everything was carved from the same stone like one big mural. The injured lined the floor while others tended to their wounds. Turning a corner, they found themselves walking down a long corridor with paintings of dragons fighting one another, humans using them as mounts to wage war against Magnus'. Piers led them to a golden door with the beautiful Mystic Otrant carved into it.

With all his strength he pushed open the doors. Purple petals twirled across the floor. Stationed in the center of the room stood a one-hundred-foot Wisteria tree. Its roots manipulated and formed into thrones for the council to sit. There were no windows. No natural light. Only cauldrons of fire to illuminate the room. Overhead in the shadows where the flames could not reach, a slither and hissing sound echoed. Their protector lingered in the shadows. Three hooded figures occupied three of the five seats.

"Look what you have done!"

"Kera, this is not the time," roared Piers.

"You now speak for us?" interjected one of the hooded figures.

"Odin, I will not say it again. We have news," bellowed Piers.

"Take your seat."

Amaris and Piers took their seats and introduced Anri and the others to the council members: Cleopatra, Kera, and Odin. Before long, they were screaming at each other. Amaris tried to speak, but they silenced her. Odin wanted their heads on a pike. Kera wanted them bound and gagged and ransomed back to Princess Ionica for money to rebuild their palace. Disgusted with the words, Anri tried again to speak. Cleopatra scolded her, ordering her to silence herself. She had no authority in this chamber. Piers stood up from his seat to quell the fighting, but Anri exploded.

"What the fuck is wrong with you?"

Her tone shook the room.

"Calm down Anri," whispered Saturos.

"You are more concerned about your palace than the life of the prince?"

The council demanded her silence.

"Hold your tongue, or I will cut it out," roared Odin.

Prince Alexander was very weak, his eyes barely open. He tried to apologize for the pendant being stolen, but Odin stunned the prince with magic, stopping his advances.

"Traitor," roared Saturos drawing his sword.

"I will rip you apart," growled Lord Zylo as his claws grew.

Piers and Amaris urged everyone to stop before matters got out of hand. Odin clenched his hands, causing the prince to drop to his knees as blood formed in his mouth. Attacking the prince was an act of war. Cleopatra rose from her seat and waved her hand at Anri, sending her flying into a nearby pillar.

"Nooooo," screamed Piers as he ran to her aid. Whispering to her, "Cousin let me help you up."

Anri looked into his eyes, her childhood memories of him at court filled her mind. Laughter and training in the orchid garden. It was like old times, him helping her up from the floor after falling. She caressed his face.

"Sorry for what I am about to do!"

Kera rose from her throne and demanded everyone lower their weapons. With each word spoken, a chill crossed the room. The flames in the cauldron dissipated, causing the creature above to stir. Zaos' body was lying on the floor. Odin unclenched his hand, turning his attention to the

Magnus. Anri reached a point of no return. Her anger manifested tenfold. The small chill caused by Kera was nothing compared to hers. As she walked the floor around her frosted over. Her aura manifested and her fingers sparked with energy.

"I am Anristasia, daughter of Madam Argia, granddaughter of Lord Grevis and Lady Udana and the High Chancellor of Seraqus. I will not be bested by a group of bitches and a mule."

Kera flared her arms and placed a barrier between Anri and themselves. Anri jolted one arm toward Kera causing her to bleed from her ears. With her other hand she forced Cleopatra to her knees. A song escaped her lips entrancing Odin to pull out his own dagger and place it on his neck. Piers and Amaris pleaded with Anri to stop. She was done being pushed around like a peasant. She had their attention now. Kera broke through Anri's spell and launched daggers of ice at her. With a twirl of her fingers, she launched them toward the ceiling, angering the beast. Slithering from the shadows, a basilisk lowered its head inches from the tree. The frill around its neck and down its spine vibrated. Two of its six legs touched down in the chamber.

Lord Zylo stared at the monster, "We are fucked!"

Anri released the council from her spell and turned her attention to their guard dog. Amaris ended the battle before it could begin. Supercharging her body with electricity caused the beast to slither back into the shadows.

"Are we done bolstering."

Saturos urged them to listen. Amaris explained how the prince was poisoned and brought to the temple to be healed. They did not realize what was truly inside of him. Amaris apologized for not coming to them before using the shrine. She revealed Queen Nimah took control of Zaos body.

Kera and Odin looked at Amaris and Piers.

"How could she possess an Elf of the Twilight? They are immune to possession."

The Council of Otrant turned to see the body of Prince Alexander rising from the floor. His movements were still weak.

"Her relics."

Prince Alexander revealed while Lord Dark Lucus was inside him he had access to his memories. Queen Nimah was their prisoner. Her relics contained pieces of her soul, and they were collecting them to get her back to full force. Since Zaos was close to the pendant it nullified her abilities and made her susceptible to possession. Queen Nimah is trying to fight back. She does not want to help them. Queen Nimah is the final piece to unleash hell on their world.

The anger in the room subsided for a moment. The mere mention of the Angelic Mother's name frightened everyone. Kera rose from her throne and descended toward Prince Alexander. She extended her hand to the prince and when he grabbed it, she walked him over to Zaos. He watched as she leaned over the elf and placed her forehead on her chest. Queen Nimah's energy was keeping her alive. There was no way of knowing for how long.

Odin and the others were not equipped to heal her. If they could get her back to the empire maybe the High Magnus' could bring her back. All this talk was draining on the prince. Amaris wanted him to rest and regain his strength. He had been through enough today. She escorted them into a cavern that would serve as their room until they were ready for the journey ahead.

Piers escorted Anri to a deeper cave to speak in private. He was excited to see she survived all these years in hiding. Anri voiced disdain for them to allow traitors amongst their ranks. Upon her elaboration, Piers tried to convince her they weren't traitors, but deserters. After the death of her mother, Queen Elizabeth's realm was met with a civil war. Her own soldiers betrayed her and served her up to Eris. Anri's hatred had festered for years. She pleaded with Piers to be careful. Everyone turned in for the night.

The following morning Kera sought an audience with them. Kera apologized for their behavior, as it was out of line and the prince had every right to be furious with them. But on the contrary, he understood their fear. They were escorted out of the cavern and across Otrant Lake.

Prince Alexander got an eerie feeling as he was crossing the lake. The lake was familiar to him. The world around him flashed away. His mother's sweet aroma filled his nose. She passed him and approached the lake with two young children. She was holding the princess' hand and holding a baby in her arms. His name escaped her lips - *Adam.* The young prince shook off the memory. The vision still made no sense to him. He was still a long way from understanding his gifts.

Time escaped him and he was left behind. He ran to catch up with the others. Four days passed and Amaris led them back to the barrier. Anri and the others rested for the night and once the sun began to rise, she ordered everyone to cross the bridge.

Zaos' body reacted to the barrier. It would not let her through. The prince ran back for her. They were minutes from the bridge collapsing. Anri rushed to the barrier. She placed her hands on it and could feel the wave of energy in rippling through the air. The prince dragged Zaos to the barrier. The closer she was to it, the barrier reacted. Voices whispered to him. On the other side Amaris could hear them. The souls of the damned. She trembled; it was the first time she actually heard them. Those who died in the Salahean prisons were offered up to reinforce the barrier.

His amulet reacted to the whispers. Strands of light escaped from the gem and latched onto the barrier. It ripped a hole in it. Sparks of chaotic energy ripped apart every atom revealing parts of the astral plane. Thousands of souls were cast about, stuck in the chaotic surge of energy. Prince Alexander's hands were covered in emerald lights. He held the cracking sparks together. With one final roar, the tear was sealed, and the souls were let loose. Zaos' body reacted and her chest lit up with the fury of a thousand suns absorbing each of the lingering souls.

Saturos rushed past Anri and grabbed Zaos. The bridge was collapsing, but her body felt like a thousand bricks. Her body convulsed on the floor swinging her from side to side. They stood by and watched as her body finally stopped. Her eyes flung open and were completely glazed over. Her left eye was white, and her right eye was black. The color finally reappeared in her eyes as she gasped for air. She grabbed Anri and Saturos and embraced them with all her might. She ran to the prince and Lord Zylo and jumped on them. Zaos was so happy to be back. Shoxz approached her and licked her face.

They were relieved to see her in perfect health again. It only lasted for a fleeting moment, as her cheer turned to horror. With her memories back she did not want to alarm them, but they needed to return to Princess Ionica. She had information that the Royal Family had to hear. She told everyone to hold hands. Shoxz stood in the middle of them as she teleported them back to the Empire of Seraqus. Everyone was consumed by light, and they reappeared in the courtyard of the palace. Her abilities were growing.

The Royal Guard rushed at them to secure the intruders, but they realized who they were. They were escorted into the palace and taken to

Princess Ionica's throne room. The princess was the only one there. When Princess Ionica's eyes locked on Prince Alexander she cried with joy. She raced from her throne and embraced him. Through destruction and chaos, she found peace in her brother's arms.

"I am so glad you are alive."

Prince Alexander continued to remain civil, knowing she was plotting to usurp him.

"Sister, the Palace of Otrant has been destroyed."

She gripped her amulet and reached to her side for Anri's support. Anri returned her to her throne to sit and gather her thoughts.

"Sister, Queen Nimah has haunted my dreams since I was child. We need to rescue her."

With the princess seated, Zaos continued.

"Queen Nimah has a bigger plan in store for this world. It involves the Royal Family. It will take the three of you to end Lord Marlusha's reign."

Saturos was furious. Queen Nimah was a traitor and handed the enemy something that could potentially destroy them. He could not believe Zaos felt pity for the angel. Elves despised angels. They turned their back on mankind and refused to help aid in the wars since Lord Nebula's demise. In his eyes death was befitting to their kind. His gut was arguing with him. Zaos was omitting much more, and he knew it. He could see through her words. As she spoke it was as if her mouth was enchanted with a spell. Each word radiated a glow only his eyes could see. He raised his sword to her demanding answers. The room turned from silent to tumultuous. The prince and princess roared for him to lower his weapon, but he refused. His anger could not be maintained. Saturos noticed Anri and Lord Zylo approaching, so he grabbed Zaos by her hair and held his sword to her neck.

"She is not telling us the truth. There is more to this story. I can feel it!"

Zaos could have easily disarmed him, but she indulged his curiosity. Jolting her hand to her chest, she enchanted Saturos and froze him in place. She released herself from his grip and turned toward him.

"Clever boy! The elf is in here somewhere, but I still have use of her for now."

Princess Ionica and the others rallied to attack, but Zaos waved her finger clicking her tongue against her mouth multiple times in a way to discourage them from trying.

"If anything happens to me, the elf dies."

"Release her at once," demanded Lord Zylo.

"When I get what I want."

"And what is that?" questioned the princess.

"The princeling is right. I called out to him. I need you and your younger brothers to free me. In return, I will destroy Lord Nebula for you."

"Is that all?" responded Prince Alexander.

"No, I also want you to abdicate the throne."

Princess Ionica glared at the prince; with a dark smirk on her face, it was a blessing in disguise. Whatever reservations she had in the beginning about delegitimizing her brother, was now out the window. With Queen Nimah's ultimatum, it would be easier for her to take control. Saturos tried to overcome the enchantments, but she was too strong.

"Embrace me," whispered a tiny voice in his head.

Saturos closed his eyes and appeared on the astral plane. Standing before him was Gaea in all her glory. She revealed the truth about his birth, her pact with Asphera, and her mission to dethrone Hyperion and place her son on the throne. Saturos was in awe learning about his parentage. Her words were like opium. She seduced him to her side. He finally broke through Zaos' charm and slit her throat. She was unphased by his actions. The open skin stitched itself up. She headbutted him and with her agile strength, she disarmed him and forced him to his knees. Planting a kiss on his lips, she caused him to foam at the mouth and pass out.

Princess Ionica and Prince Alexander were devastated.

"He was a bastard meddling in affairs beyond his control," hissed Zaos.

Anri tried to communicate with the princess using charms, but even as Zaos was engaging the prince, she shot down each spell without even looking. Zaos vowed to return him to his normal state only if they agreed to find Prince Adam. Princess Ionica agreed it was long overdue. It was time the entire family was back together.

The princess was keeping tabs on him. He was last seen heading towards Sol Mountain. Prince Alexander was excited to finally meet his brother. Princess Ionica would only join them after he was found. Zaos released Saturos from his paralyzed state. Dazed and confused, he turned his anger toward the prince and princess. He understood how deviant Queen Nimah was. Without hesitation, he grabbed ahold of his sword.

"Think twice before you do anything stupid," roared Anri.

"I know the truth now." Staring at the prince he continued, "you knew all along who I was. Gaea showed me. You kept me close just to see if I would be a danger to you; faked your kindness. You do not deserve to sit on the throne."

"Saturos I wanted to tell you, but I couldn't," replied Alexander.

"Saturos, you will hold your tongue," ordered the princess.

"I have been silent for far too long."

"Saturos, I meant you no harm," interjected the prince.

You were more concerned about me than this Usurper. We have seen the letters your envoys carry. Lord Zylo and the prince would rather stay silent than call you out for what you really are!"

Princess Ionica looked at her brother. Her mouth dropped to the floor with embarrassment. She stumbled to get the words out, but the sapphire gem on Saturos' handle exploded, engulfing the room in flames. A gentle rumble from below turned into a massive tsunami of quakes. Princess Ionica wielded the water from the floor to crystallize around him. She could not hold Gaea's extreme power back.

"We need the Oricale!" roared the prince.

Princess Ionica, Anri, and the prince called to her. The floor of the room rumbled. Even though the cavern was sealed off they could still feel her power vibrating through the ground. Her energy vaporized any lingering fragments of Queen Nimah from Zaos' body. She could not do the same for Saturos. He fully embraced Gaea.

"You think the Primordial Mother can stop me. I have rooted myself into this world just like her. My influence grows by the day. You have manipulated your last pawn. It is time for my son, my heir, to sit on the throne."

"If you go down this road, you will fail," roared Anri.

"Enough!"

Saturos attacked the prince. Encasing his fist in flames he punched the prince in the chest but was thrown back. The prince blasted him with an overwhelming amount of emerald light, burning through his armor, leaving only his naked body on the floor. In excruciating pain, he lifted himself up and dug his sword into the ground. Blue flames erupted from the sapphire gem and engulfed him. He was no longer in the room. Gaea was now in control of his mind. She would do whatever she could to come to power. Oricale warned them of the danger that would come with Saturos claiming the throne.

Time was of the essence. Losing a valuable ally in their fight against Lord Nebula was devastating. It was a race for the throne. Sol Mountain was not far from the empire. Princess Ionica led them into the courtyard once more. Prince Alexander and Lord Zylo mounted Shoxz, while Anri and Zaos held hands.

"Brother," the word escaped the princess' lips. Turning to look at her, his face was devastated. "I am truly sorry."

Her words held little weight. She was only apologizing because she got caught. Turning his head, he patted Shoxz on her leg. She took off into the night sky with him and Lord Zylo mounted on her, and the two spellcasters were shrouded in water and vanished. They zoomed through the air for hours over the barren terrain on the outskirts of Sol Mountain. She descended through the air and was bombarded by a flock of griffins. They appeared out of nowhere. Lord Zylo plummeted to the ground as one of the beasts managed to grab the prince. Shoxz crash landed too. She managed to keep her eyes on the griffin and saw the direction it was headed.

The dirt around Lord Zylo twisted and turned and Zaos reappeared. The water from a nearby creek overflowed onto the land and rematerialized into Anri.

"What happened?" questioned Zaos.

"We were ambushed. They took the prince," responded Lord Zylo.

Shoxz's mane flared, and her purple skin radiated in the light. She shook off the dirt and galloped into the sky after them, leaving the others behind. Countless griffins swooped down like bullets trying to stop her. Zaos and Anri used their collective magic and launched Lord Zylo into the air. He dug his claws into one of the creatures, sending it soaring into the sky. His claws were dug into muscle, he forced the beast to fly the course he wanted by applying pressure in certain areas.

A peak could be seen through the herd of griffins. Thousands spiraling around it in unison. Shoxz lost visual of the prince. Cupping her wings she dived down and trampled over a few of them behind her. Anri and Zaos could not manipulate any of them. Magic concealed their minds. Seeing the peak on the horizon, Anri jumped back into the creek summoning a wave to glide her further down. Zaos falling behind enchanted her feet to run as fast as a cheetah. The one Lord Zylo was riding on tried to shake him off. He dug his claws deeper into it. Another griffin dove down toward Shoxz and slashed her with its claws, breaking through her skin. Shoxz collapsed onto a rock. Lord Zylo pulled out his claws and dug it into the head of the griffin, sending it plummeting into the ground.

Shoxz' wounds were very deep and infected. Their claws were dripping in toxins. Anri examined the corpse of the griffin and noticed a draconite rune burned into his flesh. The rune was meant to prevent mind control. Whoever placed it on the griffin was prepared for visitors. They continued the journey on foot. Staring overhead the screeches of the griffins could be heard. There were thousands of them.

Anri summoned the water from the creek. She launched ice shards into the air piercing their wings. A hand full of them plunged to the ground. Lord Zylo ripped out their hearts in one false swoop and raced for the others nearby to clear a path. Anri used the last remains of the water and created a barrier around them. Zaos tapped into her darkness. Calling on the souls of the damned, she ordered Anri to drop the barrier. Converting the water into a hammer, she pummeled the nearby griffins. Closing her eyes and using hand gestures in a circular motion, Zaos focused on the griffins. She could hear their breath in her ears. Finishing the circular motion, she closed her hands in the middle of her chest and opened her eyes. The noise was gone and like raindrops they fell from the sky, decorating the dirt with their corpses.

Her aura radiated with darkness. The floor decayed with a single step. Her power was unimaginable. No one alive could bring down thousands of creatures with a single spell. As Zaos tried to settle down her powers, Anri tended to Shoxz, her left wing was broken. Lord Zylo would remain with her and tend to the wounds. He dislodged her bone and popped it back in place. Using the plant life near the creek he created a paste to seal the wound. Zaos and Anri continued up the mountain. Its red and orange clay mixture was soft to the touch. The trail was narrow and jagged. They kept close to the wall as they continued upward. Anri stared down at the destruction left behind. The breeze scattered plucked feathers about. The mountain terrain was very difficult for them to climb. The peak was flat and filled with the residue of volcanic ash. In the center stood a golden shrine of extraordinary beauty. Eight pillars held up a massive dome with an oculus in the center. The pillars each depicted an intense battle amongst the dragons.

Zaos scanned the peak for signs of life, but they were the only ones there. Out of the corner of her eye, she noticed the prince's body tied to one of the pillars. He was unconscious. She cautiously approached the shrine, not realizing she was being watched. Hidden behind the pillar was a woman wielding daggered, fighting fans. She struck the elf down jamming her pressure points.

"Stand down, Prince Adam wants to speak to his brother alone."

Anri had a look of distain for the woman. The others could tell she knew who she was. Many warriors in Seraqus envied her reputation. A vixen who bedded the warrior prince. She was now his personal guard. No man in Weguard was a match for her.

"Katara, stand down. I will not ask again!"

Anri's attention was drawn to the shrine once more. A shadow ascended from the hole in the center of it. He demanded that everyone make their exit, or he would rain fire down from the sky. Anri was appalled when she realized it was Prince Adam.

"I will take it from here."

She urged the prince to reconsider his actions and the repercussions that would follow. Zaos lay on the floor gathering her strength and fighting against paralysis, regaining movement to stand up.

"We are not leaving without the prince," roared Lord Zylo.

The prince's attitude was unwarranted. Anri could not figure out why he was acting this way toward them. This was a child she raised and trained, but he was not the man that left the empire all those years ago. Zaos tried to use magic, but Prince Adam's amulet glowed.

"Your magic does not work here."

His actions brought into question his allegiance. Was this jealousy? Was he falling into darkness like his sister? She did not trust this version of the prince. They tried as hard as they could to use their powers, but every attempt ended in failure.

Prince Adam pulled out his sword from his waistband and gave it to Zaos. He challenged her to battle. If she won, he would give her Prince Alexander, but if she lost, he would feed her to his dragon. The elf tried to decline, but she had no other alternative. He engaged her and sliced her arm. Blood gushed down and scorched the earth. He was a skilled warrior. The amulet gave him an advantage. Zaos was trapped at the edge of the mountain. She flipped over his head, but while in midflight he grabbed her by her leg and slapped her to the floor. Prince Adam was more agile than she thought. It was as if he was trained by the elves themselves. He knew her moves before she made them. His sword was filled with her blood. Zaos stared at Prince Alexander and called to him. His amulet lit up and Prince Adam scowled. The light from his amulet devastated the sky and cast its glow upon the peak.

He struggled against his restraints. Whispering for Fang's help. The light in his eyes faded. He was no longer in control of his body. His restraints dissolved and with a wave of his arm, his brother's sword was flung into a rock. His aura once again was radiating extreme energy. The clouds above spiraled and turned and touched down on the valley below. Dozens of tornados ravaged the terrain around them.

Prince Adam called for his beast. From the depths of the shrine, soared Maxsimo, the ruby dragon. Scales of ruby, claws of iron, with a massive golden stone on its chest. It opened its mouth to consume Prince Alexander, but the screams of Fang could be heard overhead. Turning his eyes to the sky, the beast went after the emerald dragon.

"Maxsimo, no, return," screamed Prince Adam.

Flames erupted overhead and the dragons danced around each other as they fought. Katara raced toward Prince Adam to protect him. Prince Alexander shot her a gaze that immobilized her. She gasped for air and clawed at her neck. Her face grew pale, as if the prince was sucking the life out of her. Prince Adam begged his brother to show mercy. He meant no harm to them.

"Please, stop this. I just wanted to see your angelic state. I placed a draconite rune on your neck to block your power and you still overcame it."

Anri and the others were shocked. Angelic State? What did Prince Adam know about the prince's altered state? Prince Adam's plea fell on death ears. Prince Alexander's anger exploded and nearly threw everyone off the mountain. The storm grew worse. Balls of hail the size of lions rained down from the sky. The prince was not able to control his powers when forced into this state. Prince Alexander elongated his arm and slowly

401

lowered his hand causing Prince Adam to drop to his knees. If the prince continued down this path, he would implode the mountain. Anri had to stop him. She called for the assistance of Oricale. The Star of the Oricale allowed her to move against the wind currents and get closer to the prince. Her palms glowed with the star's energy.

"My prince, I know you are in there. Come back to us."

"STOP THIS!!!" cried Prince Adam.

Anri rushed toward Alexander and jerked his arm, bringing him closer to her. She placed her palm on the prince's forehead, but it cost her dearly. Prince Alexander burned through her flesh causing her to plunge to the floor. Prince Adam was released from his torment long enough to get Maxsimo's attention. The massive beast landed near the shrine and covered the mountaintop in fire.

Prince Alexander bathed in its flame. Now that he was preoccupied, Prince Adam yanked the Sol Amulet from his neck and pointed it toward the Eclipse Amulet. The gems harmonized. Fang loomed overhead as a dust cloud picked up and surrounded the peak. The prince's angelic state was stabilized, the darkness in his eyes faded and he was once again himself. Anri grabbed ahold of him, even though she was in excruciating pain. Prince Adam begged for forgiveness. He did not mean for his brother to get hurt. His foolish antics could have killed them all.

Prince Adam had known for a while that his mother synched Alexander's life force to others. There were rumors in foreign lands of individuals with special gifts outside the norm. He witnessed it once before in a warrior in Atlantis. He was beaten so badly that his eyes glazed over, and he leveled the entire city. He remembered reading one of his mother's letters talking about Alexander. A child born to wield every element, every magic force, every primal energy. A child so powerful, he was a threat to space and time. If able to control his abilities he could even rival Oricale.

Hearing from Prince Adam about Prince Alexander's potential only made them worry more. Should he truly be the next ruler? Was Princess Ionica right to fear what he would do? Anri gawked at him while she played with her fingers. Sitting down as he recuperated; he caught his brother up to speed. Silence was shared between the two of them. No one knew what to say next. Fang landed nearby and rested as he licked his wounds. Katara tended to Prince Adam's wounds as he spoke with his brother. The pieces were finally coming together.

CHAPTER

33

TRAINING DAY

Prince Alexander yearned for the day to finally see his brother. Seeing him brought so much glee. By appearances, they did not appear related. Prince Adam had straight, brown hair. The right side of his hair was cut to shoulder length, while the left side reached his stomach and was tied together by a ruby pin. His brother's look was very refined. Clean shaven with an olive tone complexion. His eyes were not green like his younger brother, but hazel. Prince Adam was physically fit and was not wearing normal armor. The red tunic he wore was made from impenetrable fibers. It had golden embroidered trimmings around the collar and down to his midsection. A silk black belt was wrapped around his core with the embroidered Sol symbol. A cape hung over his right side with a chain connected to his left. His pants were light gray and tucked into his black leather boots.

His ruby dragon was more impressive. His face and underbelly were sparkling. Aside from the golden stone on his chest he had three rubies on his forehead leading to his crown of horns. Fang did a number on him. His wings had bite marks on them. One of his legs had a gash. Fang also suffered some damage. He had a bite mark on his neck. Maxsimo came close to taking a chunk out of him.

With the runes down, Zaos and Anri were able to practice magic. Lord Zylo and Shoxz made it to the peak. As they rested, Zaos and Anri tended to all the wounds. After the prince was done gawking over his brother, Anri wanted a private audience with them.

"Seeing as your plan failed. What next?"

"The plan remains the same. My brother must learn how to control his angelic state. It is a defense mechanism designed to empower him with Hyperion's skills and knowledge. Rumors have it the angels have this ability. It's like a hive mind."

"How do we do that?"

"By having him train with Gods."

There were no gods in LunaSol. Had he gone mad? Anri urged him to come to his senses. They needed to return to the princess and stop Lord Marlusha from getting the remaining stones. Prince Adam disagreed. The young herald served no purpose unless he fully understood his abilities. What good would come of him at the towers if he could not defend them.

Prince Adam was heading for Mt. Olympia. It started as a vault for Hyperion's relics, but it became a space for them to experiment using them and harnessing their power for newer weapons. Within the fortress was a chamber used to siphon energy from these relics to speak with the souls of the gods. It was built by Lady Eileen and the Divine Lords to try and get insight into Hyperion when they started their war. The chamber could only be reached with their three amulets.

Anri did not like the fact that she would be leaving the prince. Prince Adam was not reliable and unpredictable. He was reckless and took risks at the expense of others. Anri did not trust him. She agreed to bring the princess to the fortress. Anri kissed Adam on his forehead and mounted Shoxz. Shoxz took her time flying back to the empire with her broken wing.

With Anri gone, Prince Adam approached the chasm in the shrine. He whistled into it and summoned two colossal griffins. They glided through the opening and shot up into the air. Creatures the size of a whale with a wingspan of fifteen feet. Their muscular physique was covered in golden armor with the Sol Emblem etched on it. Zaos and Lord Zylo mounted one, while Katara mounted the other. Prince Adam raced for Maxsimo and mounted him waiting for his brother to mount Fang. Limping over to the emerald dragon, he could see the pain in his face. Fang placed his forehead upon the prince. Gently giving him a kiss. Prince Alexander mounted his saddle and took off into the sky.

The cool breeze of the upper sky hit their face as the griffins pierced the clouds. The beautiful canvas below was captivating and exhilarating. Bull elks roamed the valleys, while massiritis tigers stalked their prey. The greens of the meadows below slowly became a distant dream as they drew closer to Mt. Olympia. The ground was toxic and dead. Decaying trees and the corpses of animals lined the floor. The peak of the monumental mountain could be seen even at such a high altitude.

The fortress was beautiful. Carved into the stone of the mountain. Ten stories high from the platform. Fountains, gardens, and sculptures could be seen on all levels. Prince Alexander noticed a temple separated from the others on a distant peak. The closer he stared at it he swore he saw Amira. As they approached, the griffins descended first then Maxsimo, followed by Fang. The sun was lost in the background as they landed.

"We are standing in Neith's garden," laughed Prince Adam.

Puzzled by his statement the prince raised the question, "Who is Neith?"

"A god, a daughter of Chronos; one of Hyperion's brothers. During their reign they had many names. She was also known as Demeter, Mama Pacha, Cybele, just to name a few."

The gateway leading into the fortress was covered in Asiatic Jasmine. Runes were carved into the floor around the giant door. Each of the sculptures depicted a different god. He rubbed his hand over one of the sculptures that resembled the Gaeatonic Guardian, Mahadi. It was a stunning replica of the man. Mahadi's beauty and charm remained with the prince.

"That is Brahma, a fearsome god, known for geokinesis."

His attention was drawn toward the gateway as it screeched open. Frigid wind escaped the confines of the fortress. Mist glided onto the platform and circled them. From within the darkness came two warriors: fully armored and ready for battle. Prince Adam approached them with an embrace. Their armor was unique and very intricate. One of the men wore purple plated armor with Oricale inscriptions on it. His two shoulder plates were molded into dragon skulls. Metallic whips were compacted into the back of his armor and connected to a compartment in his wrist. Prince

Alexander was puzzled by his eye color; this was the first time he encountered someone with purple eyes.

Prince Adam was preoccupied with the older man; he wore a white and black tunic with armor embedded into the fabric. Alexander's heart sensed danger and his eyes darted to a hidden blade in his wrist. Without hesitation, he summoned his staff. Covered in confusion, Prince Adam tried to stop his brother, only to leave himself wide open. The purple-eyed warrior lunged at the prince and imprisoned him in his whips.

"Lower your weapon or your brother dies!"

"You picked the wrong day to mess with me," hissed Prince Alexander.

Weakened from being forced into his angelic state, he could not fight them on his own. He ordered Fang to burn them off the side of the mountain. The warriors retreated to cover with their prisoner. Zaos couldn't use her magic. The statues were imbued with charms. Once Fang's flames subsided, it allowed Katara and Lord Zylo to get close enough to finally fight. Both were evenly matched against their opponents. Prince Alexander leaped over Lord Zylo and kicked the purple-eyed warrior in the face, causing him to stumble and his whips to loosen around Prince Adam.

With his hands now freed, Prince Adam grabbed a hold of the whips and set them ablaze. Before the flames could reach the armor, the warrior ejected them. His armor was like a machine. He punched his hands forward, and it was as if the whips were replenished with a new cartridge. The old man bested Katara and Zaos and kept Prince Alexander on his toes. In two moves, he managed to separate the prince from his staff. The prince was face down on the floor bleeding. The blood soaked into the ground, Fang and Maxsimo roared as they felt the energy surge.

Prince Adam raced to him and threw himself on top of his brother whispering in his ear, "Stay with me, if you force yourself into your angelic state, you might kill yourself."

Prince Alexander struggled to breathe. The high was exhilarating. Coming out of it was torture. With Prince Adam still on top of him, he reached his hand out and called to the staff. It burned the hands of the old man causing him to drop it. It floated into the hands of the prince. Once returned the energy surge faded.

"Herald of LunaSol, we welcome you!"

The purple-eyed warrior bowed.

"Forgive the theatrics. For anyone to pass the Threshold of Bolborn, they must prove themselves worthy. See!"

As his words faded, the runes on the gateway were no longer glistening. The purple-eyed warrior introduced himself as Limbo and the other Corag. After the introductions, they turned and entered the fortress leaving the sunlight behind. It was big enough for the dragons to follow. On each side of the walkway were columns that towered hundreds of feet tall. The ceiling was covered in faded paintings that depicted the aftermath of the Holy War. Limbo noticed Prince Alexander was staring at the paintings and helped him understand what period he was gazing at. It was during the rebuilding of the world, when the citizens of LunaSol were terrorized by Alealem. He brought about an era of segregation and destruction.

Prince Alexander's gaze went from the ceiling to the center of the room. In the heart of the ancient stone structure, stood a spellbinding door. Untouched by time, comprised of crystal, encased in an iron depiction of three dragons circling one another. All three of their mouths met at the center and formed a keyhole. Limbo and Corag approached the two princes and told them that the energy of the three amulets would unlock the door.

Corag and Limbo prepared the room for the ritual, while they waited for Princess Ionica to arrive. He waved his sword over the floor igniting the carvings hidden in plain sight. A hole in the floor spiraled opened and from it a magnificent golden trident appeared. Sections of the rod were encrusted with coral and embedded with sapphires. There was one big shell on the pitchfork and dozens of gold chains hanging from it. Limbo grabbed the trident as the hole beneath it shrunk in size. A small opening remained, and Limbo placed the bottom of the trident into it releasing water into the carvings.

The prince was surprised to see that when the water settled the trident was held in the hands of a female angel. Three small pillars rose from the floor surrounding the circle. Each of the pillars in the directional points of east, west, and south. The prince was instructed to place his relics on the pillars. Prince Alexander grabbed the Crown of the Gods from his bag and placed it on the southern pillar. Once the souls were drained into the pillar, the fortress gates slammed open. With her grand entrance, Princess Ionica entered on dragon-back with High Chancellor Anri. Her gaze locked onto Prince Adam. She raced to her younger brother and jumped on him. The hug seemed to last a lifetime. Prince Alexander saw her eyes glaze over him, but she still managed to keep her sinister thoughts under wraps.

"I am so glad you are okay."

Limbo interrupted their merriment for the continuation of the ritual. Prince Alexander had another relic that was oozing with God essence. He was brought to the western part of the circle. There was another indent in the pillar. He placed the staff into the opening, causing the water to retract back into the openings. The trident electrified the crown and the staff. The spiritual essence of the gods within them were drawn to the door. The ritual circle served its purpose. The royals approached the crystal door and brought forth their amulets. The three lights entered the opening and unlocked the door.

A white light escaped through the opening and cascaded throughout the room, blinding them. Time stood still. Sound nullified. Then came the voices. Whispers from beyond the grave. Prince Alexander opened his eyes to see the others frozen. It was as if someone touched his hand. He turned to see an astral form enter the chamber. Following behind it, the prince released the room from the enchantment. The door sealed him in.

Dark and damp, the prince found himself slowly edging forward through a narrow corridor. The walls, slick with humidity, reflected a subtle ambient light that glistened faintly. There was an eerie dance of colors guiding the way. Choking the senses, the air was thick with mold and wet stone. The floor, uneven with small puddles, kept the prince unbalanced. Behind the faint dripping sound of water, debating voices could be heard.

The voices subsided as he entered a circular cavern. The only illumination in the room came from a cluster of luminescent blue quartz embedded in the walls and ceiling. The room was covered in an ethereal glow, with shades of azure and violet. The light created an otherworldly atmosphere. Shadows danced and the astral energy flickered like a mesmerizing ballet. The massive crystals above, frozen fragments like starlight in the sky. Even the massive structures could not reach all the corners of the room. Where the light barely reached, darkness reigned supreme, creating pockets of mystery. The caverns ancient silence was broken, its haunting beauty now touched by the outside world. Sound was restored, the closer the prince got. In the center of the room was a golden fountain with black liquid pouring out of the mouths of four horses.

The astral energy was absorbed by the black liquid and reanimated the gods. Six gods stood before him: Hermes, Artemis, Apollo, Athena, Ares, and Aphrodite.

Hermes, youthful and athletic. Strikingly handsome with a lean, muscular physique. Sun-kissed with blue sparkling eyes. Draped over his shoulder a cloak and winged sandals on his feet. Adorned on his head was a petasos, a broad-brimmed travelers' hat, they too had small wings. Sitting on the rim of the fountain, he tapped his caduceus, a staff entwined with two serpents and topped with wings. He locked eyes with the prince.

"Why have you summoned us," roared Hermes.

Artemis, a thing of beauty with her ethereal glow, stood next to him. Her tall athletic frame suggested her prowess as a seasoned hunter. Adorning her cascading black hair was an elegant diadem of crystals. As she blinked, he noticed her striking silver eyes, mirroring the glow of the full moon. Soft, forest green fabrics covered the golden hue of her flawless warm skin. The left side of her body was littered with tribal markings. Her dress was fastened at the shoulders with intricate silver brooches resembling deer's. Draped across her back was a holster of finely crafted arrows and a bow made from the finest wood.

"My brother thought you could show me how to enter my angelic state."

"Let us hear the boy out. He has come a long way."

Apollo's voice traveled. A being so radiant that it commands attention. Just like the others he stood tall. His golden curly hair cascaded down his shoulders in lustrous waves. His eyes, a piercing blue. Gawking at the shadows, the prince got a better view of him. Dressed in robes of pure white and gold, his chiseled features caused the prince to blush. His body was the epitome of beauty, with high cheek bones, a straight nose, and full lips. Atop his head sat a laurel wreath, a crown of flowers.

"Whilst we debate the tiny details, Lord Marlusha moves closer to retrieving all the Elemental Stones."

"Big words for such a tiny boy," laughed Athena.

Ares on the other hand wanted no part, "Let him die!"

These two divine figures bickered like children. Athena, tall and regal. Her silver armor gleamed under the artificial light. Her breastplate bore intricate patterns depicting her countless victories. Her piercing gray eyes scowled at Ares through her magnificent helmet, crowned upon her head with a plume of white horsehair. In one hand she grasped her spear with a tip sharp and deadly and in the other her exquisitely polished shield, emblazoned with the face of a Gorgon.

Ares held hatred for his sister. His frequent curses spoke volumes. In stark contrast, Ares exuded untamed power. Built like a mountain, clad in blood-red armor, battered, and scared, each a mark to the ferocity of his combats. Staring back at Athena with intense eyes, his fiery passion got the best of him as he lunged forward with his sword. Athena in return blocked with her shield. Ares placed his ram-style helmet on.

"Enough! I have come a long way to meet with you. Please listen to me."

They gave the prince the floor. With each tale spoken, no emotion was shown, they were stoic and silent. A decision had to be made, but they were split. Like a child, he toyed with his hands. Aphrodite approached. A strong scent of jasmine filled his nose. Her golden hair cascaded like a waterfall down her back with hundreds of braids tied together. Her eyes, a deep blue, sparkled with wisdom and mischief. Unlike the others, she wore no armor, only pink silks, and golden jewelry.

"I smell them on you. You reek of gods."

Her words held little meaning until the prince realized she could smell Aegir and the others. He offered an explanation, but she brushed it off. Her vote would not change. Hermes called to the fountain to return their forms into their relics, but as he did so, the mountain shook with fury.

"What is happening?" questioned the prince.

"Someone is trying to breech the chamber," responded Ares.

Athena roared, "They sense us."

From the center of the room, cracks slowly appeared, then a forceful explosion tossed everyone back. Two massive hands composed of hardened lava appeared through the debris. The creature slowly became visible as its head and body rose from the floor. Its entire body was made of lava.

"Demon," escaped Ares lips as he gripped his hammer. The damp air was now thick with an acrid scent of sulfur. Each god, embodying a unique power, prepared to engage the monstrous entity.

"The Uvali come for the boy, step aside."

Seeing this monumental creature sent shock waves through the prince's body. He was not prepared to fight a creature that even Nathaniel feared.

Infrite was not a typical Uvali. He was an elemental golem, a beast comprised of the very minerals in the ground. His very essence was lava, he could supercharge volcanic eruptions and decimate civilizations. Infrite flung his arm slamming it on the floor sending the prince flying into the wall.

First was Hermes, God of Travel, who raced around the beast creating gales that entrapped him, attempting to cool its fiery exterior. Beside him stood Ares, God of War, wielding his hammer and sword. With it he hit Infrite, causing him to stumble. He was flanked by Artemis, Goddess of the Hunt, with her arrows covered in poisonous venom. Upon mortals and immortals her arrows may have worked, but on an elemental beast, they sizzled away on contact. She was the first to fall. Half of her arm was burned away by Infrite. She retreated into the black liquid still pouring out of the damaged fountain. Before Apollo could get close enough to the lava beast, he punched a hole through his chest. Another one was consumed by the black liquid. Aphrodite tried her luck, her abilities worked on all sorts of creatures. Love was love. The closer she drew toward Infrite, he lowered his guard. Her seductive words and glares had him under her spell. Athena jumped into the air behind him and drove her spear into his head.

Infrite collapsed forward. His hardened lava liquefied. The prince cheered for their victory, but it was short lived. Lava shot through the cracks again and Infrite took shape once more. Aphrodite was a sitting duck. He wrapped his hand around her head and melted it off. Another body fell and the liquid collected. The fighting drew unwanted attention from others. As the battle continued, Amira used the chaos to sneak into the chamber from below. She had stumbled upon the fortress when Eris banished her from the prince's mind. She found herself walking the corridors studying its secrets.

From the shadows she called to him. She went unnoticed by Infrite and the others. Prince Alexander noticed her lurking.

"How did you get in here?"

"From below, we have to get you out of here."

"I am not going with you."

"You must trust me. He will kill you."

411

Amira grew impatient with the prince. She raced toward him, but Athena's spear was launched right into the wall separating them. Amira turned her face, only to realize she had been caught. Athena sprinted toward her, dropping her guard, and succumbing to Infrite's blow. His massive hands cupped her and boiled her alive. Her screaming pains of agony echoed through the room.

Amira grabbed the prince by the hand and ran for cover as Ares jumped down onto the creature's skull and struck him with his hammer. An after quake rattled the fortress. A forceful one at that. Amaris released the prince's hand.

"Something else is coming."

As she spoke the words, a mighty eruption of lava jolted through the floor, throwing Ares and Infrite back. Hermes floated above watching as the lava took form. Realizing who it was he floated down and bowed before the woman.

"You have come to save us."

Placing her hand on the side of his face, "You will die with the rest of them." She gripped him by his chin. Nails dug in causing him to explode. Another god absorbed by the liquid. As she turned to examine the room, Prince Alexander recognized her as Chantico. Ares roared out a different name, 'Hestia,' a child of Chronos, like his father, Zeus. Ares bolted toward her swinging his hammer but could not land a blow. She was faster.

"While they are distracted, we must go, Alexander. Follow me. I can get you out of here."

The prince could see concern in her eyes. He gave her his hand and followed her toward an opening in the wall, but as they got closer, a boulder of lava hit the opening. Infrite was gaining on them. Amira could not let him harm her ticket out of LunaSol. She enhanced her body so it could be the same size as Infrite. For a younger demon, she was holding her ground, until he began to fight dirty. He liquified his hand and reshaped it into an axe. The blade was still liquified when he sliced it across her chest. She collapsed to the ground, holding her chest in pain as blood poured out.

"I'm sorry for what I did. Your sisters cannot win."

"Sisters?"

The prince shook Amira to wake her up, but she had lost too much blood. Her lungs were suffocating her. The prince grew tired of being tossed around like a doll. This time he was in it alone and was not going to go down without a fight. All his life he was protected and kept out of sight; this time he was going to strike fear in the heart of his enemies.

Prince Alexander hyperventilated. His chest tightened and the world around him faded into darkness. In the shadow he felt Oricale whispering to him. He only stood a chance in his angelic state. In order to control it he had to find a balance between rage and harmony. Striking said balance, required emotional intelligence and self-awareness. Rage was both destructive and transformative. A powerful force, when unchecked, could lead to physical harm. However, it could be a catalyst for change. The key to harnessing such rage, channeling its energy in a controlled manner. Harmony, on the other hand, a state of equilibrium between peace and understanding. Balancing the two involved recognizing and validating one's emotions and channeling them through an outlet.

His rage was triggered by flooded memories of the death of his friends, Soldiel, Hans, and Nacilias. Darkness encroached upon his heart, without hope the prince embraced it. The sorrow of his loss and the fear of failing consumed him. The thought of death ate away at his soul and was the piece of motivation he needed to finally take the next step. There were billions of lives that were depending on him. He was no longer an orphaned boy, but a warrior. So many people gave their lives to protect him. Soldiel's face flashed in his mind. An image of Hans teaching him how to ride a bike or eating properly. Then Gabriel's face. His sweet kiss.

A flicker of light shined in the darkness. It bathed him in its satisfying glow. The light dissolved the darkness and gave him the strength needed to overcome this creature.

"Well look at this turn of events," laughed Chantico.

The prince stood there at the cusp of his metamorphosis, body shimmering, an ethereal aura pulsating with a rhythm of its own. His radiant glow intensified, with the boundless energy of the universe. The air around him humming with a palpable, but almost electric charge. Every movement, still and imbued with grace. His voice spoke with the tone of legions with every breath he drew from the limitless divine energy. In his angelic form, he was a beacon of hope, power, and destruction.

Prince Alexander raced at Infrite and slashed away at the creature with little luck. The hardened magma regenerated after each gash. The beast slammed the prince into the ground. Lava poured from his mouth all over the prince, but his skin was steal-like. Hermes and Ares tried to

413

intervene and Chantico dissolved them back into the black liquid. Infrite flung him into the air before opening his mouth and devouring the prince. Chantico watched as the magma beast collapse and clawed at his stomach. Tearing him apart from the inside was the only way the prince was able to defeat the enemy.

He focused on life and above all, love - the love he shared with his family. Without them he would be incomplete. The prince finally understood what true courage was - facing his fears head on, no matter the outcome. Infrite's stomach exploded, creating an exit. He watched as the creature failed to regenerate himself. Chantico watched him in awe. Amira's body was the last to be consumed by the fountain. Waving his hand at the fractured fountain, he drew on the black liquid. It changed shape in his hand forming a sword. Once solidified it bore symbols for each of the deities it consumed.

The pommel had an owl holding a sun with a spear through it, honoring Athena, Apollo, and Ares. The grip had a stunning stag for Artemis and a swan for Aphrodite. The guard of the sword bore Hermes' wings. Grasping the sword tight in his hand, he looked down at the hilt and right above it was a demonic rune, Amira's name. No matter how much he hated what she did to him, he was glad she brought him back home. A collective voice told him to use the sword to kill the beast. He leaped into the air and drove the sword through Infrite's head. The prince took no pride in killing the Uvali; a task no one had accomplished. He was filled with a sense of relief and liberation. His knees buckled from exhaustion.

Chantico approached the prince from behind.

"Marvelous work. You have tamed the gods and defeated a demon."

"Why are you here?"

"Seeking something that cannot be found."

Her riddles meant nothing. His focus lay with the gaping hole in the floor as it continued to crumble. Chantico picked the prince up from the floor by his neck.

"Stop!"

"You must help me find it."

She placed the palm of her hand on his forehead, sending him into a trance. Seeking to collect a memory from him, she opened herself up to him. The looking glass worked both ways. He jolted into her memories, seeing the demise of the gods. Every ounce of pain they ever endured; he felt. Prince Alexander dropped to his knees as the voices slowly subsided and the visions were no more. His heart raced at unspeakable speeds. Standing in the distance was Chantico gazing at the white nothingness. He approached her and slowly touched her hand. It jolted them into a beautiful scene. They were standing on the shores of a beach, a massive temple in the distance, with sentries guarding its doors. The vision pulled them inside only seconds to see a burning fire before being tossed out.

Chantico lowered the prince to the floor. "I know where I must go."

Her words echoed as she liquified and retreated into the chasm. The room served its purpose. Prince Alexander approached the crystal door, and the iron-forged depictions were more revealing. A massive caldron of fire stood at the center of the gateway. The prince placed his hand on the door and returned to the vision that was robbed from him. He was once again standing near a great flame. The Trinity Angels surrounded it and called it the Flame of Aterna. His vision subsided and he was once again in the chamber. He pushed open the massive doors and was reunited with his brother and sister.

The prince and princess rushed to him. They soon learned that Infrite came to kill him, but he was no more. Limbo was shocked at the news. No person in recorded history knew how to kill a Uvali. These unnatural beings were said to be immortal and now one was dead. He showed them the sword formed by the gods to help him. The prince was lucky to be alive. His body was covered in scars and burns.

He whispered to them, "We need to speak in private!"

Prince Adam requested that Limbo and Corag allow the prince to rest in one of the rooms. Corag went to remove the Crown of the Gods and the Staff of the Eclipse from its location, but it dissolved into dust in his hands. Limbo took it as an omen, a very bad one. He escorted the prince and his family to one of the living quarters. Each room housed two of Prince Alexander's companions, but once Limbo left their presence, they all piled into Prince Alexander's room.

"I have called everyone here because we have a problem. The gods in those relics are dead. Infrite was not the only one who broke into the chamber, Amira and Chantico followed me in."

"There is something else, isn't there?" questioned Katara.

"The gods and Amira forged this sword, which allowed me to kill Infrite. We can use it to destroy the other Uvali. The combined energy of light and darkness."

"That is amazing!" smiled Princess Ionica.

"That is not all, I see it in his eyes," replied Prince Adam.

"What is the Flame of Aterma?"

The silence of the room was telling. No one knew what the prince was talking about. They looked at one another questioning him. This was something that even escaped their memories. Anri was the only one who grimaced at the prince's mention of the flame. She put an end to all the questions.

"It is Hyperion's power source."

Princess Ionica and Prince Adam turned to her as she spoke. Anri was sworn to secrecy by her grandmother. Lady Udana came upon the flame once in Heaven before Hyperion brought it to LunaSol. She had already sided with Lady Eileen to overthrow their creator, so she wanted to learn as much as possible about where he drew his energy from. After studying it she learned the flame was once a man named Orator. Since learning about the Alulim, Anri believed he was one of them. He was a relative of Chaos and welcomed onto Earth to meet his offspring - the gods. He gifted mankind with supernatural knowledge; in doing so he became a threat to Hyperion's plan.

Anri stopped speaking as she recalled the moments she spent with her grandmother. Lady Udana was very passionate about the flame and its power. Prince Adam brought her back to reality as he coughed and grabbed her attention. She continued and explained that Hyperion obliterated him and all that was left was his soul; a blue fiery soul that burst into an enormous flame. Hyperion infused his power with the flame, and it became the burning red flame that it is today. He used the flame to overthrow the other gods to build his new universe. It was hidden within a temple and kept a secret from Lady Eileen and Sir Erin.

Prince Alexander interrupted Anri and told her the flame was in danger. Chantico used him to learn of its location. Everyone found it odd that she used the prince's memories to find it. He never saw it. Anri rubbed the prince's shoulder. There was no one alive that could lead them to the island. It dawned on the High Chancellor. If they could call upon an angel, they would know where he entombed it.

Her words caused a debate in the room.

Prince Alexander muttered, "I know where we can find an angel to help."

No one moved a muscle. They could not even move their eyes to look at him. They stood in shock as they listened to the prince explain his encounter with the Trinity Angels. He swore a vow of secrecy that day to keep the course of fate untainted. The princess festered in her rage but could not show it. The dark thoughts in her mind forbid her to reveal her true intent. This information was valuable and now they knew where they needed to go. It was time they rested and recuperated to see another day. Anri and the others left for their rooms while the Royal Family relaxed with one another. Prince Adam questioned his younger brother about the power within him. He could sense a great deal of restraint over his new gifts. The prince and princess feared the devastation that would follow if he could not gain a grip on it.

PART VII - DARKNESS UNFOLDS

CHAPTER
34

FLAME OF ATERMA

The prince should have been used to waking up in places of mystery and unease, but it was still something he was not accustomed to. The first sensation was the chill that permeated through the air, seeping into his bones even through the thick sheepskin blankets. The walls, clammy to the touch, its ancient stone a testament to the long-standing battle against the ages. The moisture in the air carrying the scent of earth and moss, reminding them of their seclusion, almost alienation, amongst the clouds. In the absence of windows, time was elusive. The halls cloaked in perpetual twilight, illuminated only by flickering cauldrons and occasional lanterns. The elusive lights cast eerie shadows as they danced on the walls. It was as if the fortress itself was alive, breathing, as the crisp air channeled through the halls. Drips of water echoed through the corridors, creating a haunting ballad underscoring their isolation.

Despite the initial apprehension, there was a certain allure. Whispers of forgotten tales and lost treasures. The prince wanted to explore more. Leaving his room he returned to the gigantic crystal door, stirring the dragons from their slumber.

Princess Ionica's mind was restless, she followed the young prince and stood watching from the shadows. She found herself battling bitterness and the sense of love for her brother. The princess could not fathom why he was chosen over her; she was a prodigy at the age of seven. Prince

Alexander was not fit to rule in his current state. She would not allow him to destroy the kingdoms and rules they fought so hard to build over the years. Princess Ionica' hands became frigid as ice. She gripped the wall, turning the stone to ice. She raced to her room, and everything she touched turned to ice. Finally, in her room she was able to sit and try to regain control of her emotions. Her bed turned to ice and the thin sheet of glacier made its way up the walls. Drained and crying, she collapsed onto her bed.

When the princess awoke the next morning, she was mortified. She was distracted from her thoughts by a hand on the door. She could hear Anri calling for her. The princess panicked and tried to thaw the ice, but it was there to stay; she could not undo the damage. Another turn of the knob caused her to lash out and yell at the High Chancellor that she would meet them at the entrance. The princess could not help but cry. Since his arrival, her jealousy has been getting uncontrollable, for years she was the beacon of stability for the kingdoms. A shining light on the hill. Trying to restrain her emotions, she grabbed her white satin gloves from her dress pockets. They seemed to suppress her abilities from manifesting anymore.

She could not risk anyone seeing her in her flustered state. She placed her hand on the door and walked through the ice, appearing in the hallway. With each breath she took the temperature dropped. A frigid chill oozed from her aura wrapping each stone in ice as she walked through the hallway. She stopped midway to gather her thoughts. Flashes of rage entered her mind as she tried to quell her emotions. Finally, her powers seemed to die down as she continued to the Great Hall. She was greeted by her brothers who could see she was frazzled. Very few words were spoken, as they were escorted to Neith's Garden and mounted their dragons.

It was exhilarating and majestic. The thrill of flight, ascending into the sky, the dominant. The rhythmic beating of their dragon's wings propelled them higher and further. The wind rushing past, tugging at their hair and clothes, the landscape transforming from decayed grass into a breathtaking panorama of hills and gardens. Each of their dragons' scales shimmering in the sunlight, casting dazzling reflections below. Gliding against the air current they moved with grace. From this vantage point, the Meadow of Seraqus was once again thriving with life. The borders of the empire were reinforced.

The dragons began their descent, circling before landing with a thud on the castle courtyard. The Royal Guard stood by as the princess descended. Amaris, Lady Pheobe, and Palar stood waiting for them. Prince Adam and Katara were uneasy around them and excused themselves. Zaos found it rude and disrespectful and brought his abrupt exit from court to Prince Alexander's attention. He found it rather odd that his brother was trying to avoid them. He asked Lord Zylo to keep an eye on them. The princess brought them into her throne room for an update.

"What news do you bring us?"

Amaris and the others found the princess' attitude unsettling and unwarranted. Her voice was dry, and she had a tone of disdain for their visit. She did not dwell on it and continued speaking with the princess. After the restoration of the empire, they found themselves near the Sea of Hope. Before Amaris could continue, the princess interrupted her.

"Can we move this along?"

Now the entire room was taken aback by the princess' rudeness. Lady Phoebe could see Amaris' frustration building, so she stepped in. While inside Mt. Olympia the Sea of Hope was hit by an unnatural earthquake. When they went to explore the damage, they spotted an unrecorded island. When they landed, there was a single pillar with angelic carvings on it. The island. It was what Chantico was looking for. They no longer needed to seek out the Trinity Angels, the earthquake revealed where they needed to go. Prince Alexander stepped forward with his thought.

Anri agreed that they needed to depart for the island before Chantico could do any more damage. She turned to the princess awaiting a response but noticed her faceless expression. The princess was not herself. Something was troubling her. Prince Alexander called for the room. He asked for Anri to get his brother.

"Sister, what is going on. You lashed out at your friends and now you are not even paying attention to something that could potentially harm us all."

Prince Adam slowly entered the room as he observed the conversation. His younger brother was screaming at his sister. Princess Ionica's knees were buckling. Adam's emotions were taking over. He could not think clearly.

"ENOUGH. You have no idea what it is to rule an empire. Let her be."

Before Alexander could get a word in edge wise, Adam screamed at him to leave the room. Alexander watched as Adam approached their sister. Rubbing her shoulders and kissing her forehead. Their odd behavior was enough for him. He felt like an outsider with them. Their relationship and closeness bothered him. They seemed to give him the cold shoulder. He stormed out of the room and into the courtyard where everyone was waiting. He took matters into his own hands. If his sister was unwilling to listen, she didn't need to weigh in on his next move. He mounted Fang and ordered the others to show him where they found the island. Lady Phoebe agreed to go with him. Amaris and Palar would not interfere. Anri advised against it and told him to wait until she spoke with the princess.

Prince Alexander refused to do so and took off. The High Chancellor ran as quickly as she could to get the princess, but as she approached the throne room, she was disturbed by the sounds that came from it. The princess and prince were engaged in matters of lust. She could not stomach the idea of brother and sister engaged in such acts. With a wave of her hand, she silenced the sounds. If anyone were to pass and hear, the princess would be subjected to idle gossip.

Anri raced back to the courtyard and mounted Shoxz.

"We must catch up."

Zaos was excited to try out her new magic. She grabbed a feather from Shoxz and crushed it in her hand and burned it as she chanted. She blew the ashes into Lord Zylo's eyes. He was caught by surprise and clawed at his eyes, unaware of the transformation around him. His body grew until he even outgrew Prince Adam's griffins. Four massive wings sprouted out of his back and fluttered in the air. He was thrilled to have wings even though they were not permanent. Zaos and Lady Phoebe mounted Lord Zylo, while Anri mounted Shoxz. They made their way west to the Sea of Hope.

Soaring over the vast body of water, the rhythmic hum of the waves provided comfort. The deep blue waters stretched endlessly in every direction; its surface occasionally broken by the playful dancing of orcas. The horizon, a world away, a hazy line where sky meets sea. A kiss between them, blending the boundaries between air and water, a display of nature's artistry. Lady Phoebe noticed an unexpected sight, a distant haze. A thick blanket of fog clinging to the surface of the water, swirling mysteriously around the silhouette of an island. The island's presence was both inviting and forbidding, a tantalizing promise of secrets. As the island grew larger in view, details began to emerge - a moist sandy shore, lush greenery, and a singular pillar in the distance. Its foggy shroud, a testament to the ages, beckoned them to venture further.

As they landed, Lord Zylo returned to his normal state. The fog was thick; in order to stay together they held hands as they maneuvered through it. The prince's amulet reacted. The white clouds around them separated and retreated to the sea. The small island was desolate; the only thing the naked eye could see was the small pillar. It was protruding from the center of the grass. Fang stood behind as the others continued. Anri grew faint the closer she got to the pillar. Its energy was more ancient than anything she felt before. It was a land marker. Prince Alexander stared at them and was able to read it.

"Only the light of the maker can bring forth the light of the blessed."

Prince Alexander recited the message and saw the carvings change.

"Those who wish to gaze upon the flame must let loose the fire."

The perplexing message stumped them. What fire must be set free? No one could answer the riddle. They spent hours trying to decipher the message. It dawned on Lord Zylo after nearly a dozen failed attempts that maybe if fire was offered to the pillar, it would reveal another clue. Lady Phoebe twirled her hand and created fire in her palm. She presented it to the pillar and the message remained the same. She flung the fire at the pillar as her frustration escalated. It circled the pillar and spun out of control. The fire was launched into eight directions creating a circle. The area engulfed by the flames crumbled away.

They raced for the outskirts of the epicenter and watched as a circular stone temple, ancient and weathered, emerged from the earth. Summoned by unseen forces. This once-buried marvel stood amidst a landscape of shifting soil and scattered grass. The air became thick with the scent of damp earth. Vines clung to the base as if nature was reluctant to relinquish its hold on this forgotten relic. The structure's circular design, intricate and harmonious, each limestone meticulously carved and placed. Four towers guarded each of its corners. Sunlight brought to life the carvings telling tales of forgotten deities and wars. Atop the temple stood a statue of Hyperion in his prime; twelve wings, fully armored, and a mask covering his scared face. His arms were crossed, and two axes held across his chest.

The entrance was grand, a massive archway with four dormant, Golden Sentinels guarding its entrance. At the base of the stairs were two mantles with griffins perched on top of them and at Hyperion's feet there was another. They were mummified in stone and as the prince approached them, they reanimated. The rock crumbled around them, and they descended on the valley screeching at the intruders. The griffins had armored wings and talons. Each of them had three tails and resembled the feathers of a peacock. The biggest of the three stood on its hind-legs and towered over all of them. The other two charged at the prince.

Zaos, with her ethereal grace and keen senses, moved with a fluid elegance that seemed to make her invisible to her surroundings as she headed toward one of the griffins and grabbed it by its beak. She used it to launch it into the air and slam it into the ground. Beside her, Lord Zylo, a towering figure of raw power and primal ferocity, crouched low, muscles rippling beneath his fur; eyes fixated on the other griffin. He pounced on the other predator. Prince Alexander took out the last griffin. He exuded an air of nobility and courage.

The prince stood over the dead corpse in a white hooded robe, adorned with a beaked tip, reminiscent of a bird of prey. The robe itself is intricately detailed with purple accents and embroidered patterns. Beneath the robe is a fitted long-sleeved tunic, which provides mobility and an extra layer of protection. On his forearms he had leather vambraces. His left vambrace concealed a hidden blade, ready to be deployed with precision. A purple sash wrapped around his waist served as an accessory pouch to carry smaller weapons. The ensemble was rounded out with a belt adorned with the Oricale Star and leather boots to match.

Lady Phoebe and Anri approached the temple slowly. The first line of defense was taken out, but they were in store for much worse. The golden sentinels were on the move. The behemoths slowly removed themselves from the walls and made their way across the valley. Anri stood back as Lady Phoebe wrapped herself in flames. The air crackled with tension as she wreathed in flames that danced like twisted serpents. Her every gesture sending waves of searing fire through the air, bouncing off the stone guardians. They pounded their mighty fist into the ground, sending shockwaves through the battlefield.

Zaos waved her hand, sending boulders flying toward one of the Sentinels. Their combined effects could not stop the sentinel's advancements. Anri summoned streams of razor-sharp water slicing through the air. It made contact. It sliced through their armor leaving cracks. One of the giant warriors flung a tree pinning her leg. The mighty roar of Fang bellowed through the valley as he flew overhead scorching the land below. Everyone ran for cover, Lord Zylo managed to get to Anri and whisk her to safety. There was no way to bypass them without casualties. Fang's towering flames dealt a deadly blow. The leg of one of the sentinels collapsed to the side, causing the giant to fall.

Fang landed on the top of the temple, with another roar, the sentinels retreated to temple and cemented themselves in their post. Fang landed nearby watching as the others approached the colossal doors. Dust shot out of the cracks, revealing a dark corridor. Its ancient stone walls cloaked in impenetrable darkness, until Lady Phoebe set ablaze the unlit torches. The flames were dim as they were swallowed by the temple's cavernous interior. Fragments of faded murals were etched into the walls. Scratches and dried blood sparked the imagination the deeper they ventured down the corridor. They came to a stop. The chamber in front of them spontaneously lit up. Its walls were covered in murals untouched by time's withering hand. The prince gently glided his fingers along the paintings. He was overcome with sadness.

The images depicted a mass genocide. Beings with almost translucent skin that glowed with a soft, inner light, giving them an otherworldly appearance. Their eyes, a kaleidoscope of colors. Much like the angels of Earth and LunaSol, their wings were magnificent. Shimmering with iridescent feathers they soared through the sky to safety. Hyperion butchered them. One of the images depicted him absorbing their light into his hands. The vengeful ruler of the heavens built his power off stolen life and energy. Once they were done observing the paintings another door opened, allowing them into another corridor. They descended further down and were stopped by another door with a mural.

It depicted the death of Orator at Hyperion's hands. The images told the story of how the Flame of Aterma was born. Three fires fused into one. Hyperion's, Orator's, and the alien race. Lady Phoebe approached the prince as he was deep in thought. She caressed his arm and could feel his tension and frustration. The images were disturbing and revolting. They had to press on. He placed his hand on the door, and it was extremely hot. His

427

hand was burned, and his blood marked the door. The intensely hot door opened for them.

Inside the room stood a terrifying beast; massive in size and towering an impressive ten feet. A masterpiece of divine craftsmanship. Standing upright with a muscular build and imposing stature of a human, but the ferocious majesty of a lion. Its head crowned with a thick red mane flowing like a royal mantle, framing his face. To their surprise, even with the intense heat of the room, the beast was imprisoned in a thick glacier of ice. The walls of his prison depicted a world lost to memory. Angelic writing, words the prince could read. Images of each of Chaos' descendants butchered in the name of personal gain. From Chaos the prince tracked back to an image that caused him to freeze in place. The Star of the Oricale. Under the image the words '*All Mother.*' He stared at it for ages until Anri tapped him on his shoulder.

She pointed to the far back of the room. A statue of Hyperion in his youth. The prince approached it. The sounds of gears caught his attention. It was a trap. He turned to warn the others, but it was too late. The door was sealed shut and the temperature increased. Zaos walked toward the statue of the god, the epicenter of the heat. It was home to angelic magic. Zaos and Anri could feel the unstableness of it. With Anri's assistance they used their magic to try and quench the heat. Anri placed her hand on the statue and whispered, "***Zamrznuti,***" sending a chill throughout the room. Water poured out of her pores and engulfed the statue in a glacier.

The magic of the statue reacted negatively to the ice and made it grow insanely in size. The sheet of ice now covered half of the room. They all ran for the stairs as it continued to grow. The bizarre ice engulfed much of the room. The creature's face was now covered. Anri and Zaos tried to reverse its effects and enraged the ice even more. The flat ice rose into spikes and jagged edges. Each attempt they made to stop the ice only made it get worse.

Everyone was worried, except the prince. His eyes were locked onto the blazing eyes piercing through the ice. He screamed and pointed at the figure in fear. Anri's mistake resulted in awakening another guardian. The ice shattered as the beast began to move. His body was now visible. His muscular physique was covered in red fur. The only thing he wore was a kilt. As it opened its mouth, flames erupted toward them. Lady Phoebe wrapped them in a telekinetic blanket to protect them against the flames. The creature was stronger than her and his flames more devastating. Lady Phoebe tried to hold on for as long as she could. Her mind was erupting into chaos. She could not sustain the barrier any longer. Lady Phoebe was disappointed; her abilities were obsolete compared to her opponent. The magnitude of its strength even surpassed her own. Anri and Zaos stepped in to reinforce the barrier. The flames were relentless; the creature sought to incinerate them.

The Eclipse Amulet tugged at the prince's neck. It flickered as if speaking. The prince called to Lady Pheobe to let him out. The barrier opened and the flames entered, as the flames broke through the prince drew on the power of the amulet. It quelled the creature's flames. Staring at the amulet caused the beast to bend the knee. He was done fighting. The massive lion-like creature balled up his fist and pounded on his chest. His name was Tamerimiri; a Leoion that was placed within the temple as a baby and trained by the angels. Leoions were created by the god Helios. They were used as slaves to build their kingdoms and then as soldiers in their wars against one another.

The prince informed Tamerimiri of Chantico's plot to get the flame. The prince tried to reason with him and explained the uncharted island was forced to reveal itself during an earthquake created by the goddess. Tamerimiri's rage exploded. He agreed to allow the prince and the others to enter the chamber of the flame. His motives were not pure. Zaos could see it in his eyes. Prince Alexander paid no attention to the smile that crossed his face. He followed the leoion toward Hyperion's statue. There was a hidden lever that he pressed, and the statue spiraled upward into a cavity that opened. Once the statue was locked in place the center of the room slowly opened. The hole continued to open and barely left any floor for them to stand on. Lord Zylo peered over the edge and could see the lake of lava that awaited them if they fell over. Tamerimiri pointed to a staircase that was a great distance down. He scaled the wall with his claw and landed on the steps.

Lord Zylo grabbed ahold of Zaos' waist and did the same. Lady Phoebe levitated down, while Prince Alexander and Anri mounted Shoxz and were the last ones down. The staircase led them thousands of feet into the depths of the planet. At the bottom was a door carved from the bedrock. At its center was an image embedded in the prince's mind; a flame with two swords – the very image on Soldiel's ring. Prince Alexander rubbed the carving with tear-filled eyes.

"You know this symbol?" questioned Tamerimiri.

"My father, well the man who raised me, Soldiel. It was on his ring."

"Awe, the leader of the Solaris Angels. Protector of the Flame of Aterma."

Tamerimiri placed his hand on the door and the carving lit up with flames. Gears turned and the door opened, inviting them in. Another flight of stairs descended deeper. They found themselves five thousand feet below the surface of LunaSol. At the end of the stairs stood an archway that gave life to a golden plated room. As they piled into the room, they soon realized it was a trap. At the center of the room stood three corpses. Three angelic warriors hardened in lava.

"You sought to betray us. Answer me!"

Tamerimiri sobbed and laughed at the same time. He could not answer. Another voice did.

"He brought you to your death. The Dominion Angels laid in waiting, ready to slaughter anyone who walked through those doors."

Their eyes were drawn to the statue she stood before. It was an elephante, this one was twice the size of the one on Venus Tower. The goddess, Chantico, stood before them in her natural state. Naked, her breasts exposed. The picturesque goddess wore unique armor around her neck with hieroglyphics painted onto it. It covered her shoulders and pointed out like spikes. Four chains connected the armor to her white satin skirt. The skirt had another piece of armor around her pelvis. The goddess flaunted her body with no regret. Each of her nails was four inches long. Anri and Zaos were on edge. Her powers were extraordinary and otherworldly. She toyed with the lava in her hand creating a ball. She smiled at the gawking prince.

"How would you have me judge this insect? These angels would have surely been swift and merciless. Would you have me do the same?"

A part of him wanted the goddess to kill the traitor. He contemplated it. He knew Chantico found pleasure in killing and he could not agree to it. His decision was made for him when Tamerimiri sprinted toward the goddess instead of the prince. He grabbed her head and pinned her to the wall. The goddess did not resist or struggle. Her body rested in his hand like a doll. He soon realized she was more than she appeared.

430

Chantico waved her hands, and the three angels dissolved. The lava could not burn through the floor. It was enchanted and glowed as Chantico manipulated it. She hardened the lava and imprisoned the Leoion. With each move he made the prison caused more damage to his body. The goddess laughed at his insolence.

"Tell me where the Flame of Aterma is?

Prince Alexander yelled for her to stop her assault on the poor creature, but she brushed him off. She would not stop until she got answers. Zaos and Anri could not use their magic. The goddess had the upper hand. She lost her patience and ripped the cage apart. Summoning all the lava back into her hand, she turned it into a spear. Tamerimiri's fighting spirit was still intact. He grabbed a hold of his swords and raced toward her. In his foolishness it cost him his arm. She used the spear to wedge herself between his arms and the tip of the spear ripped his arm straight from his body. It landed across the room. He collapsed on the floor in agony. Blood gushed onto the golden tiles revealing more angelic runes. His blood stopped in the center of the room. The pool of blood bubbled and intrigued her. She found a need for him, more importantly his blood. Her spear transformed into a scythe, and she ended his life. His head rolled into the bubbling blood and dissolved into it.

The room resonated with echoes of a booming sound. The puddle of blood animated itself and turned into a chalice. The top of the chalice had an opening for a key. Chantico approached the chalice and rubbed the keyhole. She looked up at the prince and laughed.

"The glory of the flame is mine."

The prince tried once more to plead with the goddess, "Stop this madness. It is too dangerous."

Chantico bellowed out to the prince to silence himself. She did not want to be disturbed. With the angelic runes affecting their magic, the prince could not allow Lord Zylo to get close to her. She was too powerful and would end up harming him. Chantico promised she would not kill them if they stayed out of her way while she transitioned.

"I will end my uncle's reign."

Her words only tormented them. She was the first daughter of Chronos, the brother of Hyperion. The tormented goddess walked away from the chalice, toward the scorched marks of the angels. Each of them held an item. Their holy relics were unscathed by her powers. To the touch they burned her flesh. As a goddess the runes had no effect on her, she was able to use magic freely. Manipulating them to her will, caused them to emit cerulean colored sparks that electrified her. She whimpered in pain. She extended her hand toward the other two items. The ring and the sword levitated toward her as well. The sparks intensified and burned at her flesh. The items reacted to one another. The cerulean sparks ignited and burst with even more energy, throwing the goddess against the elephante statue. The ring lowered itself onto the handle of the key as the key fused with the handle of the sword. The sword changed shape once the items came together. The steel tip of the sword was now key shaped. Lady Phoebe and Anri raced for the key, but Chantico raised a wall of lava around the chalice.

"I told you not to interfere. Now, you will feel the full extent of my power."

The goddess grabbed the sword and placed it into the keyhole. The chamber rumbled and the chalice sank into the ground. The opening grew with a diameter of one hundred feet. From the humongous opening came a circular plate held up by three elephante statues. The room stood in silence as the trunk of the oversized elephante touched the plate and flames erupted from it. The legendary Flame of Aterma was finally released. The hypnotic white fire towered into the sky. Its power terrified all those that gazed upon it. The cries of countless souls resonated from the flame. The prince dropped to his knees as blood trickled from the sides of his eyes.

"Take away the pain!"

The prince was the only one affected. Lady Phoebe and Anri could not help him. Zaos and Lord Zylo watched as Chantico drew closer to the flame. Her mission was placed on pause when the enormous statue came to life. Once the golden casing was destroyed, its red colored skin was revealed. It kicked the goddess into the air and the impact cracked the ceiling. The beast was an actual match for the goddess. It roared at the prince to leave the chamber before the voices tore away at his mind. The vindictive goddess flung her arm at the entrance and sealed it with lava. She rose to her feet and requested their surrender. The goddess was bleeding from gashes on her body. The Elephante did a number on her. Prince Alexander noticed a crest hanging around the beast's neck. It contained the name, Zaqiel. Her tusks were long and spiraled down to the floor. She rushed to the goddess and penetrated her stomach.

"I will never surrender to a pagan idol. I only answer to the rightful God."

"Your god is long dead."

Zaqiel released the goddess and stumbled backwards. The creature was unaware of the events that transpired in her latent state. The goddess was done for; she lost too much blood already. Chantico transformed herself into lava and attacked the beast, burning through her eyes. This allowed the wounded goddess to jump into the flame before anyone could stop her. Blind and unaware of her surroundings, she caused havoc. The flame reacted immensely. It roared out of control and sparks escaped the plate decimating the floor. Prince Alexander and the others scattered to avoid the impact. The flame returned to its normal state and expelled the goddess back into the chamber in her human form.

She quivered as she rose to her feet. She warned the prince of the impending doom. "He is alive!"

As the last word escaped her lips her face slowly turned to ash until her entire body faded. It was drawn into the flame. With the warning burning in their head, they raced to Zaqiel's aid. Only she could return the flame into its prison. In trying to do so, she angered Orator. His laugh could be heard from within the flame. With Chantico's powers he was able to manifest himself a new body.

During a visit to see his uncle, the other gods saw Orator as a threat. Hyperion, jealous of his abilities, fought to take them. Because of Orator's explosion, Hyperion's face was scarred. The flame was brought to LunaSol for the purpose of absorbing the life force of all living creatures as they passed into the afterlife. As he spoke, Nacilias' voice came through. He was mimicking him, which caused the prince to become enraged. Orator laughed at the prince's rage. His voice returned to normal as he explained that in Tartarus there was a door that allowed passage into the afterlife. It connected to the flame and fueled it with souls. The gate was destroyed and now the souls of the dead have no place to go and roam freely in Goul.

Locking eyes on Lady Phoebe, he drew closer to her. Flicking her hair back he gazed at her birthmark tantalizingly.

"I am amongst kin."

"If we are kin, then let me help you."

"Help me? I want to destroy all of you."

No one could fathom Hyperion's dark and demented hunger for power, but Orator was on another level. He truly had no regard for life. His body burst into flames and soared into the air, paralyzing them with dread.

"No one shall ever use me again!"

Orator blasted Zaqiel and dragged her soul into the flame. Magic was nullified and their exit was sealed. The room quivered at the flame's undeniable destruction. Orator's laughter echoed throughout the chamber. The gold-plated floors cracked and dropped into the abyss below. A massive lake of lava was hidden beneath them. The statues that held the flame up dropped into the lake and took the Flame of Aterma with it. The lake of fire shot up and destroyed the floor even more. They all raced for the only section of the room that remained intact.

The platform slowly tipped downward. Lady Phoebe held onto a loose tile as Prince Alexander extended his arm to her. Her heart was filled with dread; they were all going to die. His foolish decision to bring an Alulim with him to help only made matters worse. Now, he was serving her up on a silver platter. Lady Phoebe was losing her grip on the tile. The prince could see her aura pulsating with colors. He could not lose another friend. He was able to grab her arm and pull her up halfway before the floor caved even more. The prince could not react quickly enough. Her arm was ripped away from him as she fell into the Flame of Aterma. Screams and tears spewed and resonated in the chamber. The flame claimed her soul. With her soul added into the mix the flame raged erratically.

The lake bubbled as it crept its way up. It finally exploded into the sky and consumed what was left of the room. Each of the tiles finally gave way and everyone dropped into the pit below. The prince stopped breathing; all he could focus on was their descent into the cavern. The heat was too extreme, and it would not allow Shoxz to flap her wings. The closer they got to the flame the prince's amulet began to gain its power back.

The amulet surrounded them in a cocoon of energy. It protected them as they slammed into the Flame of Aterma. The flame reacted violently and grew more aggressive. The voices of Orator, Chantico, and Lady Phoebe could be heard around them. The rivaling energies caused an enormous amount of friction, which caused the flame to explode exponentially. It was unstable and destroyed the entire island sending them soaring into the sky. The impact knocked all of them out of the protective shield as it shattered. They were launched into the Sea of Hope at full speed.

Their lifeless bodies drifting above the waves. Fang's roars were a distant memory as he tried to collect the prince but could not as the waves tossed and turned. Zaos was the only one who woke up, noticed his sinking body, and held him up.

The prince coughed up water and slowly came to. They were washed ashore onto a nearby island. They could still see the aftermath from the island. Prince Alexander was cautious as the flame suddenly spiraled back downward and imploded, sending a massive wave of mist into every direction. Zaos grabbed the prince by his arm and ran for cover. All that was left was a huge cavern. The water circled downward and covered the opening. Zaos held the distraught prince in her arms as he wept for their departed friend. News would soon reach the shores of Weguard that the island was destroyed. They had to get ahold of the princess, otherwise she would believe them dead.

CHAPTER
35

PERSE

The prince called out to Fang, but his roars were no more. He cried out assuming the massive beast plummeted into the sea after the explosion. Zaos held up the crying prince, they could not stay on the beach. They were sitting ducks. The others were missing, and they had to search for their companions. Nestled in the secluded valley, shielded by an invisible veil lay a massive city in ruin. A jewel of time. Its stone walls were covered in burn residue and human ash. The Ruin City - Perse was a marvel of ancient architecture and culture. The capital kingdom of Lord Grevis was uninhabited.

A place where its cobblestone streets winded through a labyrinth of buildings adorned with intricate carvings and frescoes. Towering over the buildings were majestic temples and the grand palace, its spires piercing the sky, casting their shadow over the once bustling marketplace below. They cautiously continued to venture deeper into the city toward what remained of the palace. The prince absorbed his surroundings, examining the devastation. It reminded him of Weg. The energy in Perse was so strong when Zaos placed her hand on one of the statues, she was taken to the day the kingdom fell. Lord Grevis was already dead, and now vultures came for the plucking.

Atop the massive stairway leading into the palace, stood the progenitor speaking, "A reckoning is upon us. Every Ilihi shall be cleansed from this world."

Zaos glided to the edge of the assembly, her keen eyes and ears taking in every detail. The air was thick with tension, a palpable mix of fear and fervor emanating from the crowd, who hung on to his every word. His voice, deep and resonant, carried across the crowd like rolling thunder. He spoke of glory and conquest, painting a vivid picture of freedom that awaited them after his conquest. He declared the royals' enemies of humanity. His rhetoric was fiery, designed to ignite a passion within everyone, promising them eternal honor. His words inspired bloodlust, their hands gripping their weapons as they chanted.

"All hail, Alealam!"

Yet, amidst his rousing speech, and the rising cries for war, Zaos felt a chill run down her spine. Behind his spellbinding lips of oppression and salvation from the Ilihi, his dark ambitions manifested. Vocal legends of his existence were one thing, but witnessing him in the flesh defied comprehension, and language. The air was charged with an indescribable energy, a palpable force that both invigorated and terrified, saturating every atom within.

Zaos was ripped away from the scene and returned to her body. Prince Alexander stood over her as she collapsed in his arms. On repetition, the words, 'All hail, Alealam' were whispered. Her arm twitched first, catching the attention of the prince, then her eyes, until she finally was able to come to. As she tried to clear her thoughts of the vision, she sat in front of the prince and stared into his eyes. There was a sparkle unlike anything she had had since.

"Zaos, we have to move and find the others."

Nodding her head, she allowed him to help her stand and move further into the city. The aroma of earthy and woody tones immediately filled their senses. The closer they got they could hear the flames crackling and dancing. The smoky scent of burning wood filled the air. Anri, Shoxz, and Lord Zylo were huddled around the campfire trying to stay warm. Prince Alexander was ecstatic, they survived. Now that the cavalry was there, they were able to sit down in peace and replenish their strength. Anri filled the prince in on the aftermath of the explosion and where they ended up. The night sky was a canvas of wonder, for the first time the prince was able to see the cosmos so clearly. It was breathtaking. The moon hung overhead, a luminous orb casting a gentle, silvery glow over the landscape. Adding to the nocturnal spectacle, shooting stars streaking across the sky in a dazzling display of cosmic fireworks. As they burn brightly and then vanish, they leave behind a sense of awe and a reminder of the universe's endless wonders.

Each of them rotated guard duty to allow the others to rest. Day finally came, and they were ready to head back to the Palace of Perse. The golden statues that once lined the grand staircase lined the floor in debris. Five spectacular entrances remained. Faded carvings of Lord Grevis and his disciples were depicted on the entrances. The palace was built of concrete and stone. The symbols of the four winds were etched under their respective disciples. Lord Zylo ascended the broken stairs and Zaos wedged herself between him and the last step. There was unnatural magic at work. A trap.

She picked up a loose stone from the floor and tossed it toward the entrance. The stone rebounded and was launched across the city. Zaos' eyes turned completely black as she charged her hands with dark energy. She attacked the barrier and overpowered it. A rift opened, allowing them to enter the circular palace. Hidden behind the magical veil stood an enormous, vaulted ceiling that stretched skyward. It was held aloft by towering columns, each carved with delicate patterns depicting old legends. Candlelit, crystal chandeliers hung around the room casting a kaleidoscope of colors. Seated in the center of the room was a young, fair skinned man. His golden helmet commanded their attention. It resembled the head of a ram with its horns curled and extended backwards. A metallic staff with blue sapphires lining the rod was placed in front of him. His flowing green cathedral style cape covered the floor as he rose to his feet.

"There is nothing for you here, but death."

Insulted by his assertiveness, Zaos argued with the mysterious man and advanced toward him. Her confidence was struck when he tapped his staff on the floor and caused her to convulse with excruciating pain. Not even with her advanced powers could she withstand his magic. Prince Alexander tried to reason with the fellow, but he slammed the bottom of the staff into the ground bringing the prince to his knees. His magic was incomparable to anyone who practiced the Arcane Principles. The others dared not try to attack him, while he was controlling the prince's body. The prince knew what would grab his attention.

As the man approached the paralyzed prince, he noticed something tucked into his shirt. Standing in front of him, he raised the prince's head with the tip of his staff. Using the staff he lifted the chain revealing the amulet.

"By the great mother...It can't be!"

He called for the prince's amulet and examined it. The room was in an uproar. How could this man come to take possession of the amulet? The amulet could not be wielded by anyone outside of the Royal Family. He smiled at the prince and bowed.

"The fabled prince has returned."

"Who are you?" questioned the prince.

The guardian of the palace introduced himself as Sway, an Alulim who served as Lord Grevis' counsel. His arrival on LunaSol was unexpected. In his youth, he became a Warden for the Oricale and fought against those who tried to imprison her. When the planet was taken over, he fled and found refuge with an ancient breed of dragons, Sparked-Winged Magio. Already having mastered time manipulation, he learned magic from them and learned to create time rifts to travel the multiverse. During one of his trainings, he got lost in another universe. The Nebula in that reality was good. His story sparked a memory. Wade mentioned being in that universe as well before coming to LunaSol. It was known as Aura, but each of them knew the other existed. Their goal was to consume each other and become deities outside of time and space.

Zaos was very vigilant of Sway. Could he be trusted? She watched him as he interacted with the prince. Prince Alexander confessed his mistake of using an Alulim to help him battle against another, and he lost her in the process. Upon hearing their names, Sway tilted his head.

"Child, you truly believe Lady Phoebe is dead?"

"We saw her get consumed by the Flame of Aterma. We saw the explosion."

"You have no idea the raw power inside Lady Phoebe; you think some flame would harm her. If the flame was truly a bomb, we would all be dead."

Sway knew much about Lady Phoebe's origin. She was power manifested. Lord Zylo and Zaos looked at each other perplexed. In all their panic, they were blind. Hyperion used the Flame of Aterma to destroy the multiverse and create his own universe, so the explosion should have taken them all out, but it didn't. Sway laughed at how their smalls brains worked. He ordered them to follow him, he wanted to show them into Lord Grevis' throne room.

Anri and Zaos spoke amongst themselves. They worried about his motives. The prince followed him blindly up the spiral staircase that was to the left of them. Old oil paintings were hung on the walls as they ascended toward the throne room. There were only four openings in the walls facing each of the four winds. Lord Grevis' throne was a masterpiece. It was a stone settee lined with satins and silks. The prince was staring out of the window surveying the city when his name was muttered from the shadows. A mammoth of a man appeared from the darkness and made his way toward the prince. A crescent moon was etched onto the center of his chest plate. His face puzzled the prince; his features resembled Anri.

A breeze pushed past the prince as Anri raced for his arms. He was standing in front of Master Quatoz - Anri's twin brother. Since her astonishing revolutions during her altercations in the Pharaoh's court and again with the council members of the Palace of Otrant, it was exciting for them to see her happy. Anri believed her entire family was slaughtered during the civil war between the sister queens. Holding onto her brother's face she sobbed with relief.

"I am here."

Sway sat on the throne, while the others sat on satin pillows that lined the floor. Master Quatoz and Anri sat on the same pillow as they caught up. He was so happy to see his sister, but at the same time he was disappointed in himself. During the coup d'état, he arrived at his mother's throne room too late. Everyone was slaughtered and her body was never found. They presumed her dead. He was relieved to learn that Master Mukomo saved her and took her into hiding. Neither had the answers still as to why Queen Elizabeth betrayed her sister.

"There are players pulling the strings from the shadow," interjected Sway.

"What do you know about their family?" questioned Zaos.

"Only whispers, but two names continue to come up, Asphera and Eris."

The pain in the prince's arm returned. It was as if he was pierced all over again. What could his sisters have wanted with Anri and her family? Sway shifted gears. He had something to show the prince, a relic he brought through the spatial rift. He removed a dragon carved hourglass from his robes and brought it to the center of the room. He placed it on a ritual pillar. It was given to him by the last Arcane Dragon before its disappearance. Milk colored stones lined the hourglass. It reacted with the prince's amulet. Master Quatoz's gaze caught Sway's eyes. Something was not right. The emerald glow of the amulet encased the room, astral particles took form, revealing a meeting between three of the Divine Lords. An unsettling wonder crossed Sway's mind. What magic was at work here? Everyone observed the scene playout right before their eyes. Lord Grevis addressed the Divine Lords of his plan to build a tunnel from Jupiter Tower to Perseus. The town was located on the outskirts of Thunder Forest and would make it easier to travel to and from the tower unnoticed.

The three Divine Lords agreed that the tunnel would cut substantial time from having to deal with the residents of the forest. The prince noticed Lord Marlusha never made an appearance. Lord Grevis did not want word escaping to Lord Marlusha that they were going to build the tunnel. The three Divine Lords worried about their brother.

The sand in the hourglass was nearly settled at the bottom. The images of the Divine Lords began to fade, and they were returned to their present time. This information would give them an advantage. A tunnel beneath Perseus would allow them to infiltrate the tower before Lord Marlusha's army. The prince was anxious to leave, but Sway had other plans. He wanted to study the amulet and why the Aura stones on the hourglass were affected by it. He requested a week.

"We do not have a week," roared Zaos.

"Time is mine to control," smirked Sway.

Prince Alexander was intrigued to see what he could find out about the amulet. He agreed. Master Quatoz wanted to pick up his training. While they trained, Sway spent days analyzing the amulet. Flinging it into the air and stopping time around it, the amulet would react. Primordial arcane magic radiated from it. Arcane Dragons died off millions of years before the formation of Earth. How could its energy be this potent around a relic?

"Fascinating."

"What have you found," interrupted Zaos.

"How familiar are you with the Elder Dragons?"

The puzzled squint in her eyes said it all. Sway revealed that dragons have existed for billions of years. The Elder Dragons were composed of Arcane Dragons, Solaris Dragons, and Sparked-Winged Magio Dragons. They died off before the birth of Earth. Placing the amulet back on the pillar. He tried to peer inside of it. The stone held energy connected to Fang, but also the Trinity Angel. There was a hidden spark deeper in the stone. Sway grabbed ahold of the amulet, and it burned his skin causing him to drop it.

"What happened?" questioned Zaos.

"Get me the prince...NOW!"

Zaos raced out of the room to get the prince. He was in the courtyard training. Master Quatoz was in the middle of generating tentacles of water to attack the prince. The prince's body was encased in water that took the shape of a bear. Anri watched from the sidelines. She saw the look of despair in Zaos' eyes and followed them as they returned to Sway.

"My prince, I am sorry to call you with such haste, but I need to test a theory."

With a nod of his head, Sway handed the prince his amulet. With a wave of his hand, he levitated the prince into the air. He ordered everyone not to move. He instructed the prince to use the amulet against him. With his command he launched a beam of emerald light at him. The Aura Stones reacted.

"You are who I should be studying, not the amulet."

Zaos and Anri were confused, they surrounded the prince as they flooded Sway with questions. Sway would not answer them, but he did answer the prince.

"Do you know want I am?"

"An enigma, you are so much more than just one thing. You are the road map."

He ordered Prince Alexander to place the amulet on the pillar. He wrapped it in a time bubble before attacking the prince. Zaos and Anri tried to stop him, but it was all part of his plan. The amulet sparked with energy after each hit. Hit after hit, the prince tried to block him, but his magic was too strong. It got to the point that the prince drew his sword to cut through Sway.

"That right there."

Sway's words caused the prince to stop. "What?"

"Look at the handle of the sword, its radiating with arcane magic. It's in you. You have been touched by an Arcane Dragon?"

Binding him in magic he slowly approached the prince. He tapped his forehead and caused his eyes to blacken.

"Sway, stop, you will activate his angelic state. It's too dangerous," pleaded Anri.

"Angelic State? He is the Ja'eanko."

"What is that?"

"In our old tongue it means Child of the Cosmos. In this altered state he doesn't just have access to angelic powers. He also has access to every being the light of the cosmos touches."

"Prince Adam was wrong then," muttered Zaos.

Prince Alexandr's aura exploded with colors, and he was covered in a blanket of energy. It was unlike anything they had felt before. Sway moved his hands through the colorful energy that surrounded the prince. In doing so the hourglass activated and the sand began to swirl. Time in the room shifted and they were visiting the past again; the day Sway was introduced to Servilia.

"I am an Alulim, son of Callisto, grandson of Jean-Paul Brightheart."

"Why have you sought me out?"

"Alexander!"

Hearing his name caused Servilia to hold her stomach. For years she thought about him. What did this foreigner know about the baby?

"What business is he of yours?"

Sway held out an Aura Stone. As she stared into it, she could see his face. The prince, young and merry. The image changed and Drail and Hans appeared.

"He is thriving. He has family."

Servilia gasped and held her heart. He was safe and thriving. After all these years. Hearing it was still unsettling, if it landed in the wrong hands, it could be dangerous and unsafe for him. Sway's gaze never left hers. His intent was to bring the prince home. In an uproar, Servilia screamed and threw things. She would not compromise his safety until they could neutralize Lord Nebula.

"Lord Nebula is not yours to deal with. Prince Alexander is the light; we need to extinguish the darkness."

"He is a child."

"Servilia, that is why I have come to you. There is greater plan in motion."

Sway had traveled to at least three hundred universes. All of which had a different version of the Nebula in its various stages. Corrupt and dark, it consumed each universe until there was no one left to challenge it. Sway's activities drew its attention to the multiverse. After returning to his home world of Trion, he trained his body to jump further and further. He would be gone for years only to return and find out he was gone for hours at a time. Returning from one of his jumps he found himself in the middle of a civil war that broke out between the Alulim on this planet. The Wardens of Oricale were defeated, and she was imprisoned. Sway wounded, jumped through time and got stuck in the only universe where the Nebula was not evil. It called itself Aura. Singularly it knew more than any of the Nebula's. The Sentients never created the Titans, so Alealam was never born, and neither were Oricale nor her descendants. Other races evolved and lived in harmony under the ' *White Star.*'

The White Star taught him about Hyperion's betrayal and a splinter universe held apart from the others. Having foresight, she saw the child that could rival primordial deities. Wade was her first acolyte, but he failed to report back to her. Sway was allowed to jump through space and time once more to this splinter reality to help guide the child. If Lord Nebula was able to consume the child, he would have access to every reality. Servilia had to bring him home. It was her lips that whispered the prince's location to Eris.

The sands began to dwindle down and the vision disappeared.

"Miraculous. That spark, you are..."

"Sway, stop. We have company."

Staring out from the windows, they should see an army approaching the city. Cort was leading them.

"They have come for the boy!"

The Ruin City, Perse, was under attack. Hordes of creatures and Dark Servants could be seen from the palace steps. Sway would hold them off for as long as he could, so the prince could be led to safety. The prince ran for cover. Hundreds of ogres, trolls, and black orcs rummaged through the city for his scent. They moved with terrifying coordination, as if driven by a single, sinister will. The initial assault was swift and brutal. They blocked many of the exits with debris from the surrounding buildings. Fire raged on the outskirts of the city and made its way inward. They were surrounded on all fronts.

Master Quatoz mistakenly led the prince into an ambush. Four black orcs stood before them, reeking of putrid flesh and decay. The creatures were destructively huge, their skin was black and scaly. Once they set their sights on the prince, they collided with one another to pummel him. Master Quatoz saw a nearby well and could feel the water reserves beneath it. He raised the water from the well and decapitated the oversized creatures. Master Quatoz made a run for the well and leaped into it blindly. Anri and the others did the same and were led to an underground system of tunnels. They ran for miles undetected, until Master Quatoz was shot with an arrow. He stopped running and another arrow pierced his leg. Lord Zylo and Zaos jumped in front of the prince as Anri stood behind him.

Cort appeared from the dark abyss with a deadly smile. Prince Alexander was in his grasp. The traitor's son stared at the prince and took aim. Unlike his father, he was not protected by armor. An armored belt held his red silk tunic and pants together. His hair was pushed back into a ponytail. Cort brought with him two archers and four Bicornics. Zaos warned the prince of their toxic horns. The incredibly large rhinoceros-men stood a whopping six feet. Genetically enhanced creatures with steel weapons and armored plating. Their shimmering white horn added three more feet to them.

Cort ordered them to kill the prince's protectors and to save him for last. They rushed from his side and bolted toward the young boy. Zaos waived her hand at the ceiling and collapsed it on them. They picked up their wounded comrade and continued. Zaos laid him down after they reached a safe distance and tried to pull the arrow out. The arrowhead was drenched in tai-yne venom. The venom was dangerous and unique. It was resistant to magic and healing. The venom was already starting to discolor his arm; soon it would reach his heart.

Prince Alexander was surprised to see Anri crying. She was not one to show emotion. The death of her brother was certain. Lord Zylo did not want her to see it. Anri stood right beside him and caressed his face giving him kisses on his cheek and forehead. Her emotions were incredibly

446

dangerous in her current state. She was causing all of them to sweat profusely and drew it to her. Zaos intervened. It was too late for him. Retribution would come when they finally put an end to Lord Marlusha's plan. Master Quatoz whispered to his enraged sister of the location of the tunnel that would help them get to Jupiter Tower. Master Quatoz knew the risk of helping the prince and was ready to pay for it. He made peace with his maker as his veins darkened.

Anri screamed a hollow scream that made the hairs on their body rise. The sorrow in her voice crushed their spirits. Lord Zylo held her in his arms as she became overwhelmed with grief. There was an opening at the end of the tunnel, and he walked her toward it to remove her from the scene. They were led to an uncompromised section of the city. They raced for the outskirts and into the valley. Prince Alexander and Anri mounted Shoxz, as Lord Zylo raced into the open valley. Zaos exploded into dust and was blown through the air.

Cort and his army were a thing of the past, or so they thought. The prince broke through the boulders and made his way toward the open valley. He stared as they flew toward Perseus. He returned to the tunnel and lowered himself to Master Quatoz's ear.

"I have big plans for you!"

The last remaining Bicornic flung the dead body over his shoulder and back into the darkness. Cort returned to the valley and watched as they faded into the light of the sky. Prince Alexander was lucky he was not the target of the poisoned arrows. Why would they attack Master Quatoz and not him? Anri debated that question in her head as they flew closer to Perseus. Anri kept her composure and tried not to grieve the loss of her brother, but the prince could see the hurt in her eyes as he held her close. They shared similar pains. Lost never came easy, no matter how much you buried your emotions. It would eat away at your soul until nothing was left. Prince Alexander held her hand until they finally landed.

CHAPTER
36

WIND STONE

The town was infested with Dark Servants. The secret entrance was surely compromised. Without the tunnel, they would have to go through Thunder Forest to reach Jupiter Tower. Zaos enchanted new clothes for them to move amongst the townsfolk without causing mayhem. The town was filled with pastry makers. The sweet smell of cakes and breads lingered in the air. Their clothes were covered in flour. Anri and Zaos had netting to cover their hair. They were able to slip by and make it to the end of town where the forest began.

Thunder Forest, a realm untouched by time and modernity, captivated the imaginations of the townsfolk. No one dared to enter. The towering jacaranda trees, their gnarled trunks bearing the weight of centuries, form a dense canopy. The air is thick with the earthy aroma of moss and fallen leaves, the symphony of rustling foliage and birds singing create an atmosphere of serene enchantment. Amidst this expanse, a rare and extraordinary phenomenon occurs, cryanzanite unlike any found elsewhere in the world, grows directly out of the trees.

Cryanzanite, also referred to as thunder glass, a sight to behold. They gleam with an ethereal light emitting hues of amethyst. The gems sprout from the bark, their formations intricate and varied, resembling jaded shards and even some flowers. Legend has it that the stones were used in ceremonial rituals to harness the energy from the elements. Zaos walked the prince toward it and explained that it could only be created by a Thunderbird. They live amongst the stones and energize themselves. Zaos examined the stone. The forest was alien to them all. Those who venture into the forest never left a record of their findings.

Zaos could feel the energy pulsating from the trees. It was eerie and consumed her with paranoia. It was as if the trees had a heartbeat. She led them into the depths of the forest. Everyone stood close to one another. The pathway was very narrow, and they felt like they were being watched. Prince Alexander tripped on one of the stones setting off a cataclysm. The stone quickly grew and knocked into the surrounding stones causing them to grow as well. They raced through the forest, staying clear of the untouched stones. Nothing could stop the stones from growing and followed them until they crossed a nearby stream.

Standing in front of them was a man completely covered in crytanzanite. Zaos examined the body and requested Anri's assistance. She was in no shape to help. Her mind was twirling over the death of her brother. Zaos continued to examine the statue and could feel a soul within it. When she used magic on it her ears were filled with a high pitch sound. She left the statue alone and the noise subsided. The creatures that once inhabited the forest were also crystalized. Their souls were prisoners of the forest until the power source could be found.

Behind the statue was a stone pathway that led deeper into the unnerving forest. The center of the forest was home to sixty-foot trees. The sunlight faded to darkness and the stones were the only source of light. Their orchid glow mystified the forest. Prince Alexander and the others could not continue forward. The path finally ended, and they were brought to a high concentration of crytanzanite. Their beauty captivating. The lights cascaded through the air, reflecting a stunning show overhead. The prince's presence caused the stones to react. A voice broke free and paralyzed them with fear. Lord Grevis' voice echoed from the stones. Each word he spoke electrified them with light.

"*Those who seek passage into the sky, must deem themselves as light as air.*"

Anri interpreted the message the same way they did with the pillar previously. She stepped forward and used her magic to mimic the air. The

450

lavish lights were darted all over the forest and surrounded them in their glow. The stones liquefied and triggered the floor to react. It swallowed the liquid whole and sunk into the ground. Everyone screamed in horror. The orchid liquid took shape once more and penetrated through the trees and into the sky. It slowly took form and became Jupiter Tower.

Jupiter Tower was a stunning marvel with its orchid-colored glow. The enchanting structure defied the natural laws, springing to life as if it were an organic extension of the earth itself. Its base, a swirling mass of lilac and lavender, appeared to be rooted in soil. The walls of the tower shimmer with an otherworldly iridescence, creating a mesmerizing play of colors. Overhead, the clouds erupted with chaos and fury. The front of the tower was considerably different than the others. The others had staircases that ascended about three feet from the ground, but this one stood about eight feet above ground level. Zaos stared at the double-arched staircases that led to the high balcony.

The railing on the balcony was the only thing not comprised of crytanzanite. Staring down at them was an emblem molded from the iron. It formed a circle of feathers. The emblems of the royal families of LunaSol were all accounted for, except this one. As she examined it, it dawned on her. She saw it before in the library in Perse. While the prince was training, she was reading Lord Grevis' books. The sigil belonged to Uranus, the father of Hyperion. The Divine Lord took notice of the symbol when he started having dreams about it. At that point he did not know what to make of it. Once he learned the truth about Hyperion he went digging. Embracing his visions, he learned that he was created from Uranus' Horn, a relic he used to tame the winds. It imbued him with some of his memories and abilities.

Glass shattered sending shards falling over them. A feathered face peered above the symbol and screeched. A white feathered Massio Eagle leaped down into the field, its massive wings clipping everyone as it took the prince hostage. Flapping its wings, causing everyone to stumble, it soared into the sky with the prince in its claws. Anri enchanted her staff into a spear and launched it at the beast. It plummeted to the ground. Zaos raced to help him, but she was thrown back by an electrified whip. Dozens of them appeared from the center of the gate, lashing out at anything close by.

One of the whips entangled the prince's leg and dragged him toward the gate. While Zaos tried to save the prince, the others were sitting ducks. A flock of griffins swooped down from the sky engaging the others. Calling on her staff, Anri erected a barrier to protect them. Prince Alexander tried with all his might to hold onto a floor panel, but his fingers began to bleed. Zaos managed to dislodge the other whips, but the one holding the prince was draining him of energy and fueling the doorway. She wondered if the entrance was enchanted like Venus Tower, to accept a human offering. She picked the prince up and flung him toward the door. The electrified whip retreated inward and ignited his aura.

With one final burst of energy the door opened. Anri and the others killed as many griffins as they could before noticing the valley was decaying. The flowers withered and the grass died leaving a dark residue. Zaos turned to the valley and saw a Dark Rider in the distance. The plague reached the steps of the tower and slowly chipped away at the crytanzanite. The stone was durable and took longer to deteriorate. Anri lifted the prince's weak body onto Shoxz and entered the gigantic tower. Lord Zylo followed behind them as Zaos closed the door, never taking her eyes off the Dark Rider.

Inside the tower, the same orchid color resonated. It was dim casting shadows to dance and trick the eyes. From the corner of her eye, she noticed someone watching her. She turned slightly and realized it was a statue. It was made of ivory and gold. On the middle of her helmet was the likeness of a Sphinx. She wore a floor-length dress. Her breastplate bore the face of man blowing wind from his mouth. She was holding a bird in one hand and a shield in the other. The shield also had a depiction that startled Zaos to her core. She got closer to the shield and what she saw stunted her. It was the birth of Prince Alexander and etched into the bottom were the words, *Curse upon the Gods.* Zaos turned and yelled for Anri to come quickly. They all ran to her side and observed each inch of the statue. Lord Zylo was able to find the woman's name etched into the back corner.

"Ninlil - Lady of the Wind."

She was one of many statues. While they were preoccupied, prince Alexander regained consciousness. He watched as they searched through the statues. Zaos made sure the prince did not look at Ninlil's shield. The prince began examining them as well. They reminded him of the Valley of Possibilities.

The spectacular statues each depicted a history lost to them. One statue in particular caught Anri's eye. It was at the far back of the room. It was guarding a gigantic painting. Its beauty mesmerized her. The painting was a multitude of images comprised into one story. At the very top was an alluring female angel with her hands folded outward, holding a star pendant. Reminiscent of Queen Nimah. To her left side stood the image Gaea and to her right was another unknown woman. Behind the three of them was Hyperion.

Beneath each woman there were depictions of their children with their names written underneath them. Under the first unnamed woman was Lilith and Jesus. Under Queen Nimah was Celine, Zemata, and Osrian. Under Gaea was Anagar and Saturos. Further down there were two children cast to the side with their names scratched out. Tracing her fingers on the marking she spelt out the name in her head. Her hand trembled. It was true.

Zaos called on Anri. Unlike the previous towers, this one did not have a staircase leading into the rooms above. Each level was exposed to the other by a hole in the ceiling. In the center of the room was a spiral horn. Lord Zylo blew into it. A spring noise echoed throughout the room and the floor around the horn slowly descended. Flat metal sheets with holes replaced them and released a steady stream of wind. Lord Zylo stepped onto the platform and the wind glided him into the next room. They all piled onto the airlifts and were all elevated above.

The next floor was something out of a dream. The entire room was spelled to represent the universe. Lord Grevis was known to be fascinated with space. Zaos gawked at the moving planets and noticed the paintings did not represent their universe, but the previous one. Prince Alexander noticed a planet that stood out the most - Earth.

"What is this place?" he questioned.

The painting shook violently and retreated to the back of the room and reconstructed itself into a face. They noticed right away it was the face of Lord Grevis.

"No need to alarm yourselves. I will not harm you! This room has been enchanted with fragments of my essence. I can smell divinity. Where is the little prince?"

Prince Alexander stepped forward.

"It is a blessing to see you in one piece, but it saddens me to have to do this."

Lord Grevis' voice seemed to carry echoes of eons, telling stories of the cosmos and all the celestial beings that came before humanity. The

Divine Lord surprised the prince with his revelation. Prince Alexander was no mere Ilihi, but rather the son of Hyperion and Lady Eileen. Hyperion bedded the queen multiple times throughout her lifetime. Once she was aware of his sins, she came to the Divine Lords to rebel against God. They agreed at first until Lord Celeio learned about their sexual encounters. It is what started the divide between him and the queen which grew and allowed Asphera to gain him as an ally. When Lady Eileen found out she was with child she grew scared. She could not fathom he wanted an heir to bleed dry and gain more power.

No one truly knew if Lady Eileen caused the rebellion because of a lover's spat or out of anger for Hyperion's atrocities. In the end all of them were bonded with a common purpose. The prince's heart pounded with a mixture of shock and revulsion. Each thought echoed in his mind like a thunderclap. The room seemed to close in on him with the weight of this newfound knowledge. His father - *a god?* How could his mother bed him? What was she thinking? His stomach churned, a visceral reaction to the deception that had been his reality for so long. Did Drail know? Did Hans? What else was a lie?

Every memory of his childhood seemed tainted, as if dipped in a dark, oily film that settled over the joyful moments of his childhood. He was more repulsed with his mother over anyone. She was the vision of purity in every story, but she was anything but. How could his mother be so...imperfect? Clenching his hands into a fist, his nails dug into his palms as he grappled with the sense of betrayal. It wasn't just the lie itself that he was Sir Erin's son that disgusted him, but the implication that his entire life was a carefully constructed illusion.

Consumed in thought, his mind raced with questions, each one more unsettling than the last. Why was he a curse? Was he just a pawn on the board? Was his mother's love even real? A cold whisper in his ear paralyzed him.

"I can explain..." His mother's voice crept into his mind.

He looked over at Anri, disgust filled his eyes and twisted his features. She could see the pain in his face. Nothing would ever be the same again; his own father wanted him dead, a simple but fragile truth.

An explosion at the top of the tower interrupted Lord Grevis. It caused the painting to implode, revealing a hidden staircase behind him. The loud screeches over the tower shattered many of the relics. Leading

454

them into the stairway, Zaos followed it up toward the shrine. The platform beneath the altar was scorched in ash. Lord Zylo rubbed the ash in between his fingers and noticed fragments of bone. He showed the others and proceeded further up toward the shrine with caution. The stone beneath their feet sparkled as lightning erupted overhead.

To their surprise the stone was untouched and unguarded. A face was carved into each of the four columns, representing the four winds. At the top of the shrine were the remnants of a shattered egg. Running his hand over the marble stone, the prince noticed angelic runes. They lit up upon touch and silenced the screeching overhead. The guardian of the shrine was nowhere in sight. Zaos touched the floor and whispered the words, '*Zeig mir, was heir passiert ist*.' A shockwave hurled her to the edge of the platform. The shrine was enchanted to resist magic. The shrine was exposed to the elements. No railings around the outer rim to keep anything from falling over, Zaos' body clung to the side as the wind tried to claim her. Shoxz extended her wing to pull her in.

Anri approached the altar and noticed the stone was comprised of seraphinite and carved into a feather. As she touched it a ball of fire landed inches away from her and morphed into Cort. He punched the High Chancellor in the face before she could react. Lord Zylo rushed to Anri's side but was thrown back by a gust of wind. The dense and billowing sea of white and gray began to part as if responding to an unseen command. From the center, the clouds divided, the rhythmic beating of massive wings raged overhead. A celestial being of purple and yellow feathers, reverberating with power that shook the very atmosphere.

With each powerful stroke, its wings pushed aside the clouds, revealing patches of azure sky bathed in lightning. The edges of the clouds shimmered with a luminous brilliance. Each flap nearly flung them from the rooftop. Mounted on the creature was a hooded figure. Slender with a woman's frame. Anri noticed her nails were long, but one of them had gems designed on them. Her attention was drawn to Cort as he picked her up from the ground.

"Make any sudden movements and Artariz will fry you."

They were staring into the eyes of another Titan. Artariz was a Thunderbird, a six-winged beast, said to bring destruction in its path. Responsible for winds, floods, droughts, and fires caused by the lightning radiating from its body. Anri lowered herself to her knees in defeat. She would never survive an onslaught this close. Cort grabbed the stone out of ignorance, forgetting his father's teachings. Every stone was protected by a god.

His hand contorted and turned black as if the life in it decayed. The stone fell to the floor and cracked. Like the Fire Stone, a liquid oozed out of it and took shape into an old, blind, man. Cloaked in gray robes, he bore a striking resemblance to Lord Grevis. His hair was gray and wavy and extended to his pelvis. The spirit of the stone was Enlil.

The battle commenced between three formidable adversaries. Cort summoned whips of fire and lashed at the god. Enlil retaliated by summoning a hurricane, whipping winds around the tower causing everyone to seek shelter. Cort converted to launching fire balls. Pulling on Artariz' reigns, the beast, undeterred, sliced through the air like a bolt of lightning. Enlil redirected each fire balls toward the Thunderbird. The collision created an explosion of steam and sparks, lighting up the sky with a dazzling display. The tower trembled as the elements clashed. The prince struggled to maintain his flames as they were pulled away by heavy winds.

The hooded woman was not able to maintain her anonymity. A huge gust of wind pushed her hood back revealing her flowing blue hair and marble mask. Around her neck was a Nebula Stone. Prince Alexander looked up long enough to hear its familiar whispers calling to him. Enlil looked down at him, seeing the discoloration happening in his eyes. The air around them all thickened as the god sucked the life out of them. Ally became the enemy. Cort managed to muster one final attack. Breathing in deeply he exhaled a forceful jet of fire that caused the god to stumble and the hurricane to reduce its force.

Artariz swooped down from the sky with its electric aura at unparalleled speed and clawed at the unsuspecting god, ripping away at his concentrated astral form. As the clash reached its zenith, the tower trembled. With Enlil's demise, the hurricane intensified. Lightning painted the clouds as hail rained down like boulders. Artariz's wing was clipped, and her rider nearly thrown to her death. The woman leaped from the massive beast as Cort caught her. The Thunderbird destroyed the altar on impact.

Cort's companion was dazzling with her porcelain skin and blue lips. Her seafoam green eyes sparkled with every blink. She was fixated on the prince. Turning her arm into an icy scythe, she lunged at the prince and nearly pierced his chest if Shoxz didn't get in the way. Within the ice she was gripping a Nebula Stone. Its dark energy poisoned the Unicorn.

Prince Alexander held onto her crying and screaming. Cort grabbed the woman by her arm.

"What are you doing?"

"What you brought me here to do. I want them all dead!"

Her voice triggered Anri. Her words, the way she spoke. It was familiar. Knots tangled her stomach, like she was haunted by a faint memory. While in thought, the masked woman engaged Anri to break her spirit. The voice played over and over in her head. It brought her back to the day she was taken from her mother. The voice that tormented her dreams was from her very own cousin - Aquata. She led the charge against her mother. She slaughtered her family.

Cort tried to get close enough to ease Artariz from its slumber, but Lord Zylo and Zaos held him at bay. Lord Zylo managed to get close enough to Cort to rip out his throat, but Aquata was battling on two fronts. Her whip of water wrapped around Lord Zylo's neck and flung him into the air. Zaos cut through the whip with her daggers but was not able to stop Aquata. She launched a spear of ice that pierced her shoulder. Prince Alexander watched the light fade from Shoxz's eyes. He was all out of tears. He wanted blood. Cort was finally able to get close enough to the stone, but Prince Alexander kicked it out of the way and attacked him with his sword. Lord Zylo picked himself up from the floor and attacked too.

The epic showdown between Anri and Aquata was a spectacle of awe and wonder. Using the rain around her, Anri created tentacles of water to distract her opponent. Aquata was a blunt instrument of destruction. Concealing her hands in ice, she turned them into hammers and crashed through Anri's defenses. Waving her hands around she deflected her moves, but as powerful as Anri was, she could not inflict any damage on the traitor. Aquata was inches from piercing her eye with an ice dagger, but Anri managed to get her hand close enough to her stomach and launched her back toward Cort with a spell.

Lord Zylo and Prince Alexander circled them, but Aquata used the rain to create a barrier around them. Anri in all her glory was wounded. She stared at her cousin, who had the biggest smile on her face. She could not bring herself to look down. Her chest tightened. Zaos had healed her wound and noticed that the High Chancellor was in a daze. Blood seeped from the side of Anri's mouth. Further down she noticed an icicle dug inches from her heart.

Zaos rushed to her side and held her up. The icicle was infected with residue from the Nebula Stone. It was attaching to her skin. Zaos screamed for the others. Lord Zylo and the prince rushed to her side, leaving the stone unattended. Aquata grabbed the stone and mounted the Thunderbird with Cort. Placing the Nebula Stone on its forehead the crippled creature popped its wing back into place before taking off into the sky. Zaos tried to heal the gash next to Anri's heart. The wounds were deep and infected and could not be healed by magic. Lord Zylo and Zaos helped Anri to her feet. She would die if her wounds were not tended to.

Prince Alexander held the amulet in his hand. Still bewildered by its power, he chose to invoke its power.

"Fang. I need you."

The amulet clawed through the sky and decimated the storm overhead. Its emerald glow beamed like the day the prince first arrived on LunaSol. Over hundreds of miles the beacon could be seen. The immense pressure caused the platform to crumble. Lord Zylo tossed Anri over his shoulder and they made their way back down into the tower to seek aid. Another stone had fallen into the enemy's hands. Hope was just a faded memory. Lord Marlusha was one step closer to ending them all.

CHAPTER
37

HEART OF DARKNESS

After a bitter defeat, they hid in Thunder Forest for a week with no food or supplies. The poison consumed more of Anri's body. Her arm was nearly necrotized. Prince Alexander held onto his amulet praying for Fang to return to him. He had not mastered his telepathic control over his dragon. He did not want to. Fang was not a pet to control, but at this moment he wished he had more control over him. A spark of light flickered in the gem, then came a bellowing roar.

Breaking through the dense trees, Fang clawed his way through and landed inside the forest. Running to his companion, they rubbed their foreheads against each other. As the prince rubbed his hand against the dragon's chin he noticed healed wounds. Fang was attacked while they were separated. Rubbing the side of his face, he could see the dragon's mind. After the explosion he tried to grab the prince from the ocean, but could not get close enough without falling in. Fang returned to Seraqus seeking aid but was restrained by Princess Ionica's guards. They kept him locked up and abused him, trying to subdue him to her side. Fang burned or ate most of his tormentors. When he felt the beacon, he managed to break free and came looking for the prince.

Fueled with rage, Prince Alexander and the others mounted Fang and set their sights for the Empire of Seraqus. Leaving Valor Island, they had to pass over the chasm of the sunken island. Even with the time that had passed, the water was still back-filling. Smoke simmered from the depths and scaled the top leaving an eerie fog. The prince pulled on Fang's reigns and soared higher into the air. Eclipsing the sun's rays with each flap, he made it to Weguard. Encampments were stationed around the meadow. Princess Ionica's army readied for war.

As Fang neared the empire, shouting could be heard from the floor, "Dragon!!!!" This time they were met with resistance. The Royal Guard were equipped with electrified rods. Fang roared when he saw them. Weapons once used on him while in captivity by the princess. Princess Ionica was furious with her younger brother for leaving without her permission. Once dismounted, Anri was rushed to get medical attention. Fang was left in the courtyard, but once the prince and the others were inside, they were taken prisoner and brought before her highness.

"What is the meaning of this sister?"

"You have betrayed your station?"

Prince Alexander tugged at his restraints, but the guards held him in place.

"Since your arrival at court, you have been a thorn in my side. You have weakened our empire and only empowered the enemy. I have summoned the Royal Houses on a petition to remove you as prince. You have become a liability."

"Oh, please, you have been plotting this since the day you found out I was not an Ilihi. You want the throne; you can have it. We have bigger problems than that."

The room was in awe. The prince was abdicating the throne to his sister. They could not believe their ears. Prince Adam stood up.

"Sister, let the boy speak."

Prince Alexander's shackles were removed. His wrists were bruised. He rubbed them as he spoke.

"There are enemies left, right, and center. Lord Nebula is not our only concern."

Princess Ionica wrestled with his statement, "Who else is a concern?"

"Asphera lurks in the shadows. Saturos pledged allegiance to Gaea. Nathaniel Darkbloom has a hidden agenda, and that's just scratching the surface. High Magnus Kishib is a traitor amongst the Pharaoh's faction."

"We must rally together," replied Prince Adam.

"There is more. I can see it in your eyes," interjected the princess.
"Our mother was a liar."

Princess Ionica banged her hand on her throne. "You petulant child. How dare you speak of her that way? Our mother died because of you."

"So, you knew she had an affair with Hyperion?"

The room gasped with the news. Princess Ionica ordered all the guards out of her throne room. Caught in her own thoughts, she sat down allowing the prince to continue. He explained what happened at Jupiter Tower and the small hints throughout his time in LunaSol. The princess did not believe it until Lord Zylo advised that Anri could corroborate their story. The High Chancellor was in no shape to speak. She was still mourning the loss of her brother and the fact that she did not want to face the princess after eavesdropping on her scandalous secret.

"Is that all?" questioned Prince Adam.

"No, there is more."

Prince Adam and Princess Ionica were at a loss for words as they listened to their brother. He pulled out a scroll he received from a Frayjain when he arrived in LunaSol. He pulled on the golden string and the parchment was about two feet long. It contained schematics of how the four stones and four diamonds were created to contain the plague, but the final image depicted how they can be used as a weapon. Lady Eileen orchestrated it all. Her visions, her paranoia, her heartbreak. It was all her. She gave Lord Marlusha and Lord Nebula the tools they needed to take over, but why? It was the question on everyone's minds. Why would their mother want to kill Hyperion, but still end up leaving him a way to kill her son?

Her journal about him left many stones unturned but did leave some information behind. There were eight children anchored to him. Each secret revealed about their mother made his stomach turn sour. How could she tether his power to eight unsuspecting kids. Prince Adam asked if he knew who they were. Of course, he knew one of them, but he would not reveal that to them. He shook his head no. Finding the others were important, they could unlock his suppressed abilities.

As they continued to speak, a knock on the door caught their attention. Palar and Amaris had returned with news. Their spies revealed that Cort had returned to his palace and given his father the final stone. The Universal Splicer could not be used until the winter equinox. Lord

461

Marlusha needed a monumental solar event to harness energy from. To their benefit, the equinox was still a month away.

"Let us call a truce. I will stay my hand at this petition until we have put an end to this weapon."

"A truce. We should not even be at this point."

"Brother," called Prince Adam.

"Stop calling me brother. I don't even know you!"

Prince Alexander shouted at them both for being so blinded by power that they forgot how to be human. He used Anri's situation as an example and revealed her secret. Sister versus sister. A cousin slaughtering her family. Her brother dying before her eyes. Enough was enough. He already had two sisters that wanted him dead, he did not need a third. Hearing about Anri's past caused the princess to pause. Her own ward, her High Chancellor. How could she have lied to her for years? She could not let her brother see her anger. It would deter him from playing in to her hand.

Princess Ionica looked into his tearful eyes. Rather than focusing on supporting him and being a family, she was self-absorbed with power. Her heart could not forgive him, but for all appearances, she played the forgiving sister. Having always wanted her brother back, she made it nearly impossible for him to trust and love her. They were not raised together; how could she have asked for blind support and allegiance?

"Let us put this nastiness behind us. We are blood. We are family," roared the princess.

Prince Alexander was hesitant to take her at her word. He still felt some dark agenda within her, but for the moment he needed her. Princess Ionica could no longer remain behind her fortified walls and watch from the comfort of her throne. War was upon them. The prince and his comrades were exasperated. The princess ordered the return of her guards to escort them to their chambers and maidens were sent to draw baths and prepare their rooms.

The young prince turned to see his sister and brother escape to her room together. The guards rushed him, so he could not observe their actions. His bedroom was isolated from the others. It was at the far end of the hall. The bed was cemented into the ground and built from blue granite. It stood in the center of the room. White sheer fabrics cloaked the pillars of the bed. A small desk stood on one side of the room and a gigantic wardrobe stood on the opposite side. His room had a luxurious balcony overlooking the east side of the palace.

His bones ached, his vision was blurry, and his fingers twitched. The prince closed his eyes as he entered the bathroom. He took a beat before getting into the tub. Defeat after defeat required a long refocus of energy. When he was done, he gazed out into the open water as the sun cast its final light on the world before the moon took her place in the sky. The tranquil water below splashed against the palace tower with its sweet melody. The soothing sounds of the water enticed the prince even more and his eyes began to close. He tossed off his clothes and collapsed over the bed, sleeping the night away. It was ages since the prince felt such a relaxing sleep and since he was no longer astral projecting himself into the mind of others, he could finally enjoy it.

Night was about to become his enemy. The peace he enjoyed disappeared when Nathaniel Darkbloom dream-walked into his mind. It has been a while since their last encounter. Dark Servants lingered at every corner of his laboratory, but once they left his side, he was finally able to connect with the prince. With his red crystal in hand, their channel was open. He whispered the prince's name.

His eyes shot open. Lifting his head up, Nathaniel stood at the edge of his bed.

"Get out. Get out now!"

"I needed to see you."

"Stay away from me. You are a liar and a manipulator."

"I am all those things, but we have the same end goal for now. Lord Nebula is getting rather testy. While you have been distracted chasing your tails, Eris has the final star-piece to release Lord Nebula from his prison."

The prince's teeth shuttered at Nathaniel's warning. After the prince's stone was taken, only two remained and now they had them all. Lowering his head in shame, he was consumed in thought. Nathaniel was pressed for time. He could not waste a second more.

"Upon Lord Nebula's return, he will be weak during his transition. You will have a small window to take him out."

"You have already given him the power that he needs!"

"You are mistaken. The power of the Alulim and Potuliari that has been collected is fuel for the Universal Splicer. Lord Nebula will never lay hands on that kind of power."

A sigh of relief escaped the prince, before Nathaniel could utter another word, the connection was cut. Opening his eyes he stared at the ceiling. It's glacial reflection looking back at him. He turned over and rubbed his hand on the sheets envisioning Nacilias and Shoxz. He yearned to have them at his side, leaving Shoxz' body on Jupiter Tower was a regrettable mistake. Neither one had a proper burial. Not even Hans. He played over every death as he tried to sleep. His mind stumbled over the thought that everything they tried to prevent so far was for nothing. Prince Alexander kept tossing and turning, until his mind faded into nothingness, and he was at ease.

The prince drenched his pillow in drool as he slept. Excessive knocking on the door interrupted his phenomenal sleep. He was barely in any clothes as he held a blanket over his naked body and answered the door. A servant held clothes for the prince in her hands and pushed open the door.

"Those rags have served their purpose. I bring you fresh clothing and two armbands that your brother ordered for you. You will find shoes in the wardrobe."

The cotton was so soft in the prince's hands. She exited the room to allow him time to get dressed. He flung the sheet onto the bed and put the royal blue tunic over his head. The neckline started around his neck and as it got to the front dropped halfway down his chest. The sleeves were short and pointed. His pants were also blue and free flowing. The crotch was lower and allowed for agility rather than constriction. He was impressed with the outfit and took a liking to it. He opened the wardrobe and found a pair of black, high-top shoes waiting for him. With his outfit complete, he placed the strap of the sword around his body and entered the hallway to meet the others. The Royal Guard escorted them into the throne room where Princess Ionica and Prince Adam were already waiting.

The two flirted with one another, so they didn't see the others entering. Princess Ionica fed her brother a grape, as he lay sideways on her throne. Zaos cleared her throat to catch their attention before anything else transpired. Prince Adam quickly jumped off her throne, allowing her to take her seat and speak with them.

"Sorry for the fooleries. It has been so long."

Lord Zylo and Zaos turned to one another puzzled. The comment was very unnerving for them to hear. Rumors of their predilections were spoken of in the highest courts, but to see it up close was another thing entirely. They knew better than to mention anything in front of the unsuspecting prince. He was not familiar with the ancient customs of this world and the flares of passion between the sexes.

The princess rang her bell, and the throne room doors opened again as her servants brought in the High Chancellor. Anri was seated in a wooden wheelchair. Her arm was bound. The remnants of poison were still showing in the veins of her neck.

"The Magnus' are up to speed. What is our next move?"

"You have no moves. You are ordered to your quarters for recover," demanded the princess.

"Princess...but...why?"

"There is nothing for you to say."

Anri looked over at Prince Alexander. They both sensed she was being benched. The princess lost trust in her. She did not want to exacerbate the situation in front of an audience. The princess ordered the guards to sequester the High Chancellor until further notice. Princess Ionica revealed that overnight she sent word to the houses of Seraqus that she commanded to send their armies to march on Martilo. They would not sit back and wait for war to come to them. The garrison would meet at the Black Gates. Since they were uncharmed, an army could be led into the Valley of Shadows and surround the Black Kingdom.

A sudden hush fell upon those gathered in the room as an unexpected presence made itself known. The air grew colder, and the lights dimmed. From the corner of the room, shadows coalesced, swirled, and expanded like ink in water. From the swirling shadows, a figure began to emerge. Eris, tall and slender, her form draped in a cloak that seemed woven from the very fabric of night. Her eyes glowed purple with an eerie, phosphorescent light piercing through the darkness with an unsettling intensity. As she stepped forward, she glided through the air with grace.

Eris' voice, when she spoke, was a soft, haunting whisper that seemed to echo from every corner of the hall. "Forgive the intrusion," she began, her tone both commanding and enigmatic. "I come to you with a matter of urgency." The royals were wary and could not deny the gravity of her presence. As she took her place in the center of the room, the light bent around her and shifted in the presence of her darkness.

"What news do you have?" questioned Prince Alexander.

"Enough! I will not have it." Princess Ionica summoned shards of ice and launched them at her sister. In response, Eris summoned the shadows around her, creating tendrils of darkness that absorbed each of her attacks. The shadows twisted and turned, morphing into grotesque, nightmarish shapes that lunged at the others. The clash between the two sisters was not just a spectacle of raw power, but also a dance of elements. She brought the princess to her knees.

"Are you finished yet? Or should I kill you where you stand?" One of Eris' shadow monsters had the princess on the floor with its foot on her head. Prince Adam was chained by the neck while the others were restrained as well.

"Do not do this sister." The child prince roared out to his older sister. Prince Alexander knew Eris was ruthless, but he still pleaded with whatever humanity she had left. Looking back into his eyes, she nodded and allowed the princess to stand up.

"How cute. Reunited at last," Eris blurted out.

Zaos urged the prince to kill her. He ignored the comment and approached Eris.

"Sister, Speak and leave," demanded Prince Alexander.

"I have come here to warn you not to interfere in Lord Marlusha's plan," replied Eris.

"Why?"

"Mother's plan."

Hearing Eris say it out loud made the prince's stomach turn. She knew about her mother's plan all this time. How? The prince balled up his fist.

"You knew."

"I know more than you. Just like I know if you interfere and stop the machine from ripping open the void; you will ensure Lord Nebula's victory."

"We cannot allow him to unleash the plague," argued Princess Ionica.

"It will happen."

Prince Alexander and Princess Ionica stared into each other's eyes. What did she mean? Princess Ionica grew tired of her riddles. Before she could launch another attack, Eris was absorbed back into the shadows. The room was in an uproar. Eris knew more than them. The royals debated on

466

options and how to go about stopping Lord Marlusha's plan. The decision was not so cut-and-dry. Prince Adam and Princess Ionica agreed on a course of action, but Prince Alexander did not.

"To war!" both declared.

As they prepared their troops, Eris returned to Lord Marlusha's side. He stood atop the Black Kingdom. She watched as he approached the center shrine. It was already home to a Nebula Stone. He noticed her watching and called her to his side. She glided to him and gently rubbed his arm. She took the handsome devil from behind and kissed the side of his face. "They are coming for you!"

"I welcome it, but you should be more careful child. His eyes are upon us. He will seek vengeance for your betrayal."

"My betrayal? Do not forget, I know about your oath."

Lord Marlusha's eyebrows raised. How could she know the truth? She wasn't conceived when the oath was made. His blood ran cold. He continued to face forward staring at the altars as they radiated with luminescent colors.

"Leave me at once."

Eris cackled as she faded into the shadows. The Divine Lord descended back into the Black Kingdom. Cort and Aquata awaited their commands.

"It is time we ended this. Bring me the heart of this so-called Herald of LunaSol."

Cort bowed to his father and kissed his hand, "I shall not fail you."

Cort and Aquata left the throne room to gather his father's army. Massive trolls, black orcs, and all manners of foul creatures gathered outside the Black Kingdom ready to serve. Dark Servants and Magnus' gathered and prepared for war. Eris watched from the many mirrors in Tartarus, gliding her nail across the surface of the glass.

Returning to the looking glass that peered into the Empire of Seraqus, she watched Princess Ionica and Prince Adam devise a plan to betray their brother again. She could feel the distain resonating from their hearts. She would not stand for it. She smashed the mirror and descended into the darkness of Tartarus.

Prince Adam stood behind the princess and rubbed her shoulders. Nibbling on her ear, he slowly made his way down to her neck. Closing her eyes and letting out a soft moan, she embraced her urges. He moved his hands down to her waist and turned her around to face him. A look of panic crossed her mind. Could she do it again? Could she forgive him for abandoning her and finding another? The more she looked into his eyes the more she fell into lust. His hands, moving across her body, only made her want more. Hesitation was out the window. She fed into her cardinal desires. Sloppy with her affair she forgot to excuse her guards. Their passion flared and gave rise to an endless night of love.

With the winter equinox approaching Alexander took this time to train. Fighting through her wounds, Anri trained him. Zaos also took the time to experiment with her new abilities and partnered with Lord Zylo. Princess Ionica and Prince Adam secluded themselves the entire time.

When combat training was not in session the prince was trained in dragon riding. His new sleeker saddle was a gift crafted by the best blacksmith in Seraqus. The prince was having a hard time connecting to Fang. His siblings spoke the draconic tongue and commanded their beasts, but the prince tried to rely on his telepathic connection, but it caused more harm than good. Fang was rather agile and evasive. While on the offensive, the prince hesitated to strike allies, even if it was a simulation battle. Dragon fire was deadly.

For a month there was serenity across Weguard. The waiting was horrendous for the young prince. The day came when the royals left the empire with their army to meet with the generals – Lord Silverskull, Pharaoh Atemu-Nacus, and Lowe. Hearing about the invasion from her servants, Amaris decided to join the war council. The generals gathered tens of thousands of warriors, Ilihi, and Magnus' to aid them in battle.

Prince Alexander stood on the sidelines as each of them reported their strategies to take the Black Kingdom. Turning his attention to the floor, he could feel the ground trembling. The sound of a thousand hooves erupted over the horizon. The royals turned their eyes toward the hill overlooking the valley. As the golden sun began its descent, casting long shadows across the emerald hills, the air grew still. And then, from the crest of the highest high, there emerged the colossal lion, Narnarie. His mane shimmered like molten gold in the twilight. With a mighty roar, Narnarie summoned forth his legion of Fae creatures. The centaurs came first, their powerful hooves thundering against the ground. Half-human, half-horse, they galloped gracefully, their bows slung across their backs, ready to defend the realm.

Next, a swarm of fairies fluttered into view, their delicate wings glistening like stained glass in the fading sunlight. They danced through the air, leaving trails of sparkling dust that shimmered like rainbows. After them came the hippogriffs, a hybrid creature, embodying the features of both a horse and a griffin. The gnomes followed, small yet sturdy, their eyes twinkling with mischief and wisdom. They carried with them hooked hammers and dart guns. A group of dragoons, fierce and noble, marched in disciplined ranks, their armor gleaming. Following behind them were the dryads, dancing and twirling. From the rivers, nymphs ascended, their hair flowing like water. They moved with the grace of the currents. Finally, the Aiars, the massive tree humanoids, joined the assembly.

The soldiers got into position for battle, but Prince Alexander pushed his way through. Narnarie and Omega survived and brought the prince an army.

"I command you to lower your weapons."

"Brother, what is this?" questioned the princess.

"My army!"

Holding her composure, she ordered the others to stand down. Her hand trembled. The creatures of this world served no one. They abandoned humanity after the Holy War. Those that remained loyal to the crown, did so out of fear they would be imprisoned or killed. These creatures came to the prince's aid willingly.

The prince turned to Narnarie. "My prince, we await your command."

The prince, Zaos, and Lord Zylo attended to the new arrivals and set up an area for them.

The stars glistened over the valley like a blanket. The autumn leaves swung in the night breeze. Everyone prepared themselves for war. The peaceful sounds of the night were a thing of the past. Prince Alexander was once again alone in his tent. His brother and sister were nowhere to be found. The moment they were reunited they became inseparable. He was cast aside. He opened the green silk flap of his tent and stared out into the darkness. The sounds of sleeping men and the sounds of men in heat pulsated through the valley. Men had taken women into their beds and even other men. The young prince never felt the pleasure of another person. He was still pure and innocent. He returned to his bed and tuned out the world as he drifted off to sleep.

The following morning, the mighty sun rose. Princess Ionica was in her tent and Prince Adam was nearly naked beside her getting dressed. A servant of Lord Silverskull informed them that the generals awaited them. After getting dressed the princess addressed their armies.

"The day of reckoning is here. Lord Marlusha seeks to revive the tyrannical Lord Nebula and end the reign of man. We cannot allow him to persevere."

Her charming brother, Adam, followed her. "Lord Marlusha's army is our adversary today. They think they can strike fear in our hearts. Let us show them on this day, we are warriors united, and no one will stand in our way."

The cheers roared through the valley. It was Prince Alexander's turn to speak. The child could not gather the words to inspire thousands of people. He thought himself unworthy to address them. He stared at their faces staring back at him. What could be their final moments together startled his core. The world deserved peace and it deserved hope. The days of darkness and tyrannical rulers were over. The prince knew it was imperative that Lord Marlusha's bloodline be eradicated. Prince Alexander gathered his strength to speak and surprised his family.

"Today is not about defending me, or my family. Today is about defending all our freedoms. Lord Nebula will enslave this world and even go so far as to rid it of our kind. I speak to you, not as your prince, but as a fellow survivor. Darkness shall not consume us today. Fight hard and protect one another!"

Thunderous applause echoed amongst the warriors. The prince's words captivated them. Narnarie roared, signaling the other creatures to respond with their own calls and cries, creating a symphony of bravery and resolve. The sounds of drums erupted a great distance away. The bellowing horns spiraled into the air. The Black Gate opened, and the evil held behind its walls poured out like ooze. The air was thick with the scent of pine and seared earth, mingling with the faint aroma of death from beyond the wall.

They stood on the precipice of destiny, gazing into the heart of the storm that threatened to engulf their cherished lands. Lord Silverskull held his long sword in the air and roared, "CHARGE!" The soldiers marched into battle on their horses as the creatures moved with an almost choreographed precision. Their movements fluid and synchronized, guided by an unspoken bond and a shared sense of duty. Dozens of wings flooded the air as hippogriffs ripped away at the tai'yne's flesh. The massive dead dragons inflicted their own damage with their venomous bite. Orcs feasted on gnome blood. Centaurs trampled over goblins. The battle lasted for days as they broke through Lord Marlusha's defenses. The royals were dragged into the fighting as a fireball struck Prince Adam in the chest, knocking him back. Cort dropped from the sky like a fiery angel and took out the Royal Guard protecting them.

In one hand he held a fiery sword formed of tungsten and a shield forged of chromium. Dragonite runes were etched into his obsidian and crimson colored armor. His eyes were barely visible through his phoenix engraved helmet. He toyed with them and managed to keep Princess Ionica and Prince Adam on their toes. The princess could feel her energy depleting and left herself wide open for an attack. Aquata appeared from the moist ground and attacked the princess. She turned her hands into scythes and managed to break through the center of the princess' armor. Aquata deeply wounded her and grabbed her by the hair and dug her face into the ground.

Prince Adam was trying to fend off six minotaurs at once when he noticed his sister on the ground. Blinded by rage and love, he engulfed his hands in flames and tore through the minotaur's. The leader of the pact caught the brunt of it. His face was caved in, and heart ripped out. Turning to his sister, he saw Prince Alexander trying to hold his own against Cort, but he too found himself on the floor. The royals refused to use their dragons, because it would have been a bloodbath. Dragon fire knew no ally. Prince Alexander was crawling backwards as Aquata and Cort stood over him. Finding themselves in a cataclysmic confrontation, Prince Adam supercharged his sword to incinerate anything in its path. He drove it into the ground, summoning a pillar of flames that shot skyward, splitting the heavens. Aquata responded by draining the ground around her of its water, leaving it barren and dry and turning it into a spear. She launched it with so much force it ripped through the pillar and with a clench of her hand it crystallized and pierced the prince's ribs.

Cort turned away from Prince Alexander, allowing him to get to his feet and build distance between them. Staring at the battlefield, he saw countless bodies fall from both sides. It was a bloodbath. The Royal Dragons were kept from the fight until they made it deep into Martilo.

Before he could call on Fang, he noticed Zaos and Lord Zylo came to his aid. Zaos materialized from the dirt and managed to stab Aquata in the knees. Her knees buckled and she collapsed forward. This time the Elf of the Twilight was ready for her. She overpowered Aquata and spelled her into her human form. Aquata could no longer use her tricks to escape into water. Prince Alexander approached his brother who was bleeding from his mouth trying to gasp for air. Zaos tended to his wounds as Lord Zylo and Prince Alexander challenged Cort and Aquata. The battle was a mesmerizing dance of skill and strategy. Alexander, agile and swift, used this combat knowledge luring Cort into overextending his strikes. Cort, powerful and relentless, sought to overpower Alexander with sheer brute force. The air crackled with energy as they clashed against one another. Despite the intensity, both warriors remained focused.

At one point Cort got the upper hand. He head-butted the prince and impaired his vision. The prince dropped his sword, and Cort took advantage of the situation. He twisted and kicked the prince on the side of his face. Fire erupted in his palm and ascended his arm as he stood over the prince's body. Filled with joy, he failed to pay attention to his surroundings. Narnarie leaped on him and mauled at his flesh until he ripped off his arm. Screaming through the pain, Cort pushed his fiery hand through the lion's skull. Narnarie, though mighty, was not invincible. His blood poured all over Cort's face, forcing him to remove his helmet. As he lay on the floor trying not to cry, he pushed the lion's body off him.

In his pain he managed to get to his knees and cauterize the wound. The young prince screamed out as tears flooded his eyes. His hallow roar rippled through the valley like a boomerang. The skies darkened and wept with the prince. The humans continued fighting, but the creatures of LunaSol screamed and cried in his honor. They could feel his extreme pain running through the prince.

Prince Alexander ran to his side. As he knelt beside Narnarie's lifeless form, tears streamed down this face, mingling with the blood on the battlefield. He laid a gentle hand on the lion's mane, feeling the warmth that still lingered there. Blood dripped from his nose as the screams of the dead clouded his mind. He could not stand by and allow such an evil to exist in his new world. The light of his amulet intensified with each breath he took. His elemental powers were no match for the devilish fiend. Cort rose to the occasion and attacked while they were distracted. He summoned a serpent of fire that devoured Princess Ionica's servants leaving a trail of ash in its wake. The serpent turned to Prince Adam and opened its mouth.

The princess dug deep and focused on her anger. Her aura radiated blue as she absorbed the concentration of water in the air and ran for her brother. She held the serpent's mouth open and ripped it apart. Prince Alexander slowly rose from the floor as he watched his sister buckle and drop to her knees as blood poured out of her mouth. His heart and body were heavy and in utter pain. His anger once again got the best of him. Rather than forcing himself into his angelic state, he held his composure. Something odd was happening to him. He could hear everyone's heartbeat pulsating in his mind. His amulet glowed with fury.

His mother's voice once again pleading to him. "Do not do this. You will kill them all."

He rejected her and focused on the pulses. The aura surrounding each person and creature illuminated within his eyes. Cort attacked the princess again, launching spiraling fireballs. With a fluid motion, Ionica raised her hands, summoning a towering wave that rose to meet the flames, extinguishing them in a sizzling steam. The ground beneath them shimmered as Cort unleashed a series of fire whips, crackling with intensity. Ionica undeterred, twisted her hands gracefully, forming a protective barrier of swirling water that absorbed the fiery onslaught. It was a dance of fire and water. Cort would not let up, he conjured a ring of fire that encircled Ionica, attempting to trap her within its blazing confines. But Ionica was not easily ensnared. She leaped over it and transformed the ring into a fountain of steam, dissipating the flames into nothingness. Her counterattack was swift, as she summoned icy chards that glistened like the stars, sending them cascading toward Cort.

Cort grew tired of their elemental harmony of opposites. He summoned a fiery wall and transformed it into a blazing dragon. Prince Alexander watched and forced on Cort. A red orange aura flickered around him. The harder he focused on his adversary the more visible his aura became. He used his hands to bring his enemy to his knees. The image of Lord Nebula appeared in his head. He recalled the damage he inflicted on General Soldiel with the same technique. He tortured Cort, shattering his bones and subduing him. Aquata could not help her lover. She panicked and fled the scene.

473

Watching him in agony, he approached Cort and stood over his body.

"Please stop this. I surrender."

Lowering his face to his ear, he whispered, "I will not accept your surrender."

Prince Alexander's heart blackened with each bone he broke.

Aquata approached with the cavalry. A Bicornic charged at Prince Alexander and redirected his attention, causing the prince to lose his connection and release Cort. Cort surrounded himself in flames and was able to make a quick escape and add distance between himself and the prince. His attempt was futile, and he was caught off guard by Eris. She appeared from the chaos like a ghost and jolted her hand forward into his chest and ripped out his heart, before fading into the shadows again. No one noticed her, except Prince Alexander. She smiled at him and vanished as the battle continued.

His body collapsed on the floor causing his army to scatter. Aquata screamed out in sorrow. The love of her life was taken from her. Lord Marlusha would not be pleased. Without Cort to lead them, the battle was already won. Aquata called for a retreat to the Black Kingdom. Lord Zylo assisted the princess to her feet as she stumbled from the strain on her body. Another gruesome battle was over and ended in many casualties. It disheartened Prince Alexander to see the blood-stained battlefield. He wanted to go back to his simple life with Drail and a normal childhood. A loud bang sent a shockwave across the land and flung everyone back. They stared over the horizon, through the open gates as the Black Kingdom electrified the sky.

CHAPTER
38

RISE

The equinox was not for another three days. Could Eris have deceived them? The atmosphere trembled as the beam of light sliced through it, creating a spectacle of raw, unbridled power. Its intense, concentrated light was marked by a dazzling, almost blinding brilliance. The air around the beam shimmered and warped, distorting the view as if reality itself was bending. A high-pitched, otherworldly hum filled the air, growing louder as the beam's light intensified, extending further into space. As the laser continues its relentless bombardment, the atmosphere reacts violently. The vapor trails of the shredded clouds swirled into chaotic patterns causing lightning storms. The very particles of the air seemed to ignite and scatter, casting an ethereal glow over the fiery lands.

A malodor escaped the Black Gates and polluted the surrounding area. Shadow was cast onto the soldiers as they approached the enormous mountains that separated Seraqus from Martilo. The floor was covered in black clay and ash. The sky was covered in a thick layer of smog from the thousands of geysers that released toxic gases into the atmosphere. They covered their faces to avoid inhaling the venomous toxin. Stumbling over themselves, Lord Marlusha's armies continued to fight as they retreated to the Black Kingdom. The royals used their amulets to call upon the royal dragons. Their roars echoed over the horizon as their dazzling scales glistened against the contrast of the sky. Fire rained from the sky burning the opposition.

Not even the storm clouds could be seen through the smog. The dragons had to retreat as their visibility was impaired. Perched on the mountains, they roared and watched from a distance. The battle continued leagues in front of them. The Valley of Shadows was a wasteland. The ground was exposed to bedrock and made it harder to travel. Black acid jolted out of the geysers and coated the floor. The lightning storm overhead made it even worse. Each bolt that rained down from the sky decimated the ground and created new geysers. The closer they approached the Black Kingdom, the more they noticed it was an ambush. Lord Marlusha kept his most dangerous servants to protect his fortress.

Princess Ionica and Prince Adam seem unaffected by the deaths of so many. Watching as blood spilled to protect them, Prince Alexander grew squeamish. Being close to the humming sound of the beam of light made it harder for them to focus. Looking down at the floor, the young prince noticed his vision was blurry. He nearly fell off his horse. Words whispered in his ear. It was Nathaniel's voice again. Nathaniel would lead the prince into the palace undetected.

He dismounted Shoxz and turned to his brother and sister, "I must leave you here."

Princess Ionica dismounted, "What is going on?"

"Sister, just trust me."

"Be safe, little brother."

Prince Adam gripped the reigns of his horse, "We must stick together."

"Zaos and Lord Zylo will accompany me. We can handle whatever comes our way. I need you to promise me, if anything happens, that you rule with compassion, not fear."

Princess Ionica stared into her brother's eyes. In the back of her mind, she was excited. If he was out of the picture, she would be the herald the world flocked to.

"Go put an end to this," demanded Princess Ionica.

Zaos cloaked them with an invisibility charm. As they approached the Black Kingdom, the path was treacherous, jagged peaks stood guard over the ancient palace. Its towering spires and ornate stonework exuded an air of both majesty and mystery, whispering tales of centuries past. Winding through the narrow passages and over precarious ledges led them over lakes of lava. Each of their steps measured and deliberate. Any false movement could alert the lycanthropes that stood as sentries. The palace's formidable walls were constructed from weathered obsidian, sunstone, and iron. Before them stood a black-iron gate. Zaos tapped the gate and was thrown back. It was imbued with dark energy. The Eclipse Amulet lit up as the prince approached the gate. He placed his hands on the door, and it was like poison. His veins blackened and his fingertips turned purple. The light of the amulet blasted the door and repealed its magic.

Once inside the palace grounds, the atmosphere shifted. The halls were eerie and humid. Cauldrons and torches provided some light, but they had to be cautious, anything could be hidden in the shadows. Thousands of tapestries and curtains filled the labyrinthine halls. The flickers from the flame danced as they progressed slowly further. Silence was paramount, even the faintest misstep could reverberate through the grand corridors, betraying their presence. The prince could no longer hear Nathaniel's voice leading the way. Without him, they had to navigate the opulent maze. The Black Kingdom was known to house hundreds of Lord Marlusha's deadliest servants, but it seemed everyone vanished without a trace.

Besting the maze, they finally reached the throne room. The ceilings were hundreds of feet high and covered in red and black drapes that touched the surface of the floor. Portraits of his children hung from the walls. The cauldrons that lit their way dwindled as they entered another room. Prince Alexander could hear the earsplitting destruction above. He took his last steps and reemerged into the hub of that destruction, witnessing the devastating weapon.

The world trembled as the shrines atop the Black Kingdom made an impact with the tear in the universe. The sky was on fire. Space dust rained down around them like ash. As it hit the obsidian tiles it sparked like electricity. At the center of the four shrines each of the stones glowed. One blue, the other green, another red and one gray. The weapon was a force to be reckoned with. Lord Marlusha was standing in the epicenter. The shrine in the center was still not activated. He placed his hands on the black stone and fueled its power. His veins bulged and turned dark. Prince Alexander could feel the stone's energy. He was driven by an inexplicable urge; he approached the shrine cautiously.

As he stood near Lord Marlusha in a trance-like state, a strange energy began to pulse from its core, whispering to the edges of his consciousness. He could feel the tendrils of its power reaching out, slowly entwining with his thoughts and emotions. It was as though the stone had a voice of its own, calling to him with promises of boundless power and knowledge. As the energy continued to seep into his mind, his thoughts grew heavy and dark. His memories of his childhood were the first to be overshadowed by an ominous presence. Joyful events with Drail were distorted into painful fears. The stone seemed to amplify his deepest insecurities, clouding his judgment, and warping his perception of reality. He found himself questioning the loyalty of his closest allies, doubting the love of his family, and seeing betrayal and malice where there was none.

This time the stone was stronger. It had a volatile hold over his mind, covering it in a pervasive darkness that threatened to consume his very soul. The prince struggled to resist its malevolent influence, its grip on his mind tightened with each passing moment. Zaos and Lord Zylo slowly approached him and noticed he was talking to himself. The closer they got to it; they too began to feel its effects. It was relentless, feeding off their vulnerabilities. The battle within their mind was a perilous one, as the stone's energy sought to plunge them into depravity and madness. Lord Zylo grabbed onto the prince, but millions of voices scrambled his mind causing him to collapse.

Just as he hit the floor, Zaos heard footsteps. She turned and noticed Princess Ionica and Prince Adam. The princess grabbed an icicle dagger that hung from her staff and flung it at Lord Marlusha. It managed to slice the side of his face. The cut crystalized and slowly decayed his skin. Prince Adam encased his sword in flames and tried to sever Lord Marlusha's connection to the stone. The energy radiating from them shattered the sword inches from his forearms. The Divine Lord turned his head toward Adam and smiled, causing him to be flung across the rooftop. He shattered one of the pillars from a nearby shrine. Prince Adam barely had a pulse. The stone created a barrier as it fed on Lord Marlusha. It was preparing to activate.

With the barrier up, the stone's effect on Zaos and Lord Zylo diminished, but not Alexander. Zaos tried to break the enchantment by singing to him. As she sang, the stone reacted once more, but this time the humming noise turned to nails on glass. Before the stone could drain him of his life it released him, he was consumed by flames and descended into the floor.

Fang's roar ignited the amulet around the prince's neck causing him to slowly disconnect from the stone. Zaos grabbed Alexander and they all retreated into the palace.

"Are you okay?" she asked.

"I heard his voice," Alexander replied.

"Who?"

"Lord Nebula. He spoke to me."

The prince did not speak another word. He proceeded to walk down the steps again in a trance-like state and led them into a room where Lord Marlusha's body was clinging to life in front of a gold-plated, crystal-lined mirror. Zaos noticed it was not reflecting images from the room, but rather a shadowy corridor with eerie purple lights. It was a gateway. He tried to retreat through it, but it rejected him.

Princess Ionica demanded that he turn around. Running his decaying hand over the mirror changed its reflection. "Child, this place will be your tomb."

Princess Ionica slammed her staff into the ground and strands of water jolted from its core and wrapped around the Divine Lord, bringing him to his knees. She commanded Lord Zylo to get her guards at the bottom of the steps. He did as commanded.

Lord Marlusha laughed as he coughed up blood. "The stone is nearly energized."

Banging his hand against the mirror once more ignited his trap. The crystals around the rim shattered and leaked out a purple mist. The mist swirled and twisted, enshrouding the space in a thick fog. At first, it seemed harmless, but soon it became evident that this was no ordinary mist. The room, once a mundane space, began to morph. The transformation was subtle at first. The shadows grew darker and more defined, gradually taking the shape of a prison. The scent of flames that once filled the room was now tainted with the metallic tang of confinement. Rattling chains drew their attention to the center of this newly formed prison. Bound by glowing, spectral chains stood a humongous angelic woman. Her once radiant aura was dimmed, subdued by the oppressive atmosphere. Her face was pale like milk and her eyes blue like sapphires. Beneath her was a platform engraved with runes.

"Behold our great - *Queen Nimah*."

Prince Alexander demanded her release. Princess Ionica cursed and screamed as she watched Zaos approach the Divine Lord and helped him get up from the floor. The royals grabbed ahold of each other's wrist to stay close to one another. The elf was not herself. Her eyes were glazed over.

"What have you done to her?" questioned Prince Adam.

"She is the key to everything," responded Lord Marlusha.

Returning to the mirror, he banged on it again, causing the image to return to the dark corridor. Cutting into his palm he rubbed his blood over the glass, causing the portal to open. The royals took a step back as Lord Dark Lucus appeared before them; with his entrance, Lord Zylo and the princess' guards appeared from the hallway. Zaos snapped her fingers and ripped the guard's skin from their bones. Lord Zylo lunged at Lord Dark Lucas, but he dug his long sword into the lycanthrope's stomach and broke through the ground to keep him from getting free.

Lord Dark Lucus grabbed Zaos by the neck and placed her in front of Queen Nimah's prison. Only with her blood could the Nebula Stone run its course. It needed an offering, a being of light and darkness. Drawing his dragon-tailed blade, Lord Marlusha pierced the elf causing the mammoth of a woman to scream out in pain. The darkness that bound the Queen of Angels descended onto the platform and entangled Zaos. Her blood gushed over the floor, revealing spelled carvings that ignited the pendant around the angel's neck. Queen Nimah screamed out. Her voice shattered the walls.

"He shall rise!" laughed Lord Dark Lucus.

Lord Zylo struggled with the sword lodged in his stomach. Fading in between life and death as he was bleeding out profusely. Lord Dark Lucus was too preoccupied to notice Lord Zylo freeing himself. The great lycanthrope used the last of his energy to jump onto Lord Marlusha and push his claws through his skull before collapsing to the floor. Before the royals could intervene, Lord Dark Lucus waved his hand, and his shade appeared and bound them in darkness. It burned at their flesh as they tried to wiggle free. Zaos' blood faded into the runes and the floor descended, revealing another platform. It was a machine filled with dark liquid. The liquid ascended through the platform and into the angel. Once the machine was empty the floor returned to its normal state.

The souls collected by Nathaniel Darkbloom served their purpose and fueled the great angel. Now, it was time to use the full force of the stone. Lord Dark Lucus returned to the shrine. They were sitting ducks. Prince Alexander's face was flushed. Fueled by guilt, darkness consumed him, and anger took over. As his mind raced, a familiar voice called to him.

"Do not lose hope! I can put an end to all of this."

The very ghost that haunted his nightmares stood before him. The source of his paralysis pleaded with him. Queen Nimah could not be trusted. She had her own agenda. Prince Alexander refused her offer. The three royals held onto one another and drew on the energy of their amulets. Their auras radiated and broke through the darkness. The enormous angel stomped her feet as she screamed and cursed. Prince Alexander and his siblings raced to the shrine to see Lord Dark Lucus offering up Lord Marlusha's body.

With the final offering, his body turned to ash. The stone levitated above the shrine and encased it in darkness before extending to the other four. The energy beam was no longer and all that remained was a massive hole in the sky. Rings of clouds as far as the eye could see.

"Stop this madness, it's all a lie." roared the prince.

Lord Dark Lucus turned around, "Foolish boy."

"So, you know about the pact?"

Lord Dark Lucus raised his brow, "What pact?"

"This machine will not power Lord Nebula. It is meant to open the void and unleash those trapped behind it. Nathaniel fooled you all."

Lord Dark Lucus struggled with the truth, but he could sense the prince wasn't lying. He roared out as he grabbed his sword and shattered the stone. In doing so, a shock wave decimated everything in its path. Everyone was tossed back. A devastating light pierced the sky and forced open the tear. Queen Nimah's agony could be heard for miles. Prince Alexander took caution as he approached the shrine. The air around it was thick with toxic gases. His lungs nearly suffocated him.

The young prince moved deeper and deeper into the darkness until he reached the crumbling steps of the shrine. His amulet ignited even brighter, and his aura appeared like armor. As his light was eaten up by the darkness. Prince Adam and Princess Ionica feared the worst.

Grabbing his sister by her arms Prince Adam uttered, "We cannot let him die!"

Giving him a kiss on the lips, she agreed. They went back on their word and agreed to free Queen Nimah. Returning to the room below, it was filled with the echoes of sheer agony. The machine beneath her was once again filled with dark liquid. This time it was not black, but purple. Closing his arm, he shrouded his arm and his blade with flames. He lifted his blade but could not bring himself to destroy the machine. Princess Ionica saw the tears in his eyes, she glided behind him and held him by his waist, and she kissed the side of his neck reassuring him that he was not alone in this decision. He dug his sword into the machine causing it to malfunction and set one of her wings free.

Roars erupted from behind them as Dark Servants flooded the room and blindsided them. Their army had lost the advantage. Lord Marlusha's army had reclaimed the palace and were fighting to hold it. Princess Ionica was hit on the back of her head and the sapphire light in her amulet dwindled. Prince Adam was furious and managed to hold them back until he broke another wing free before a Dark Servant pinned him to the wall using magic. He watched as they forced his sister to her knees. Cursing and struggling to get free, he watched, as they punched her repeatedly in the face and kicked her and repositioned her again. The magic that imprisoned him kept his fire suppressed.

One of the cloaked figures grabbed the princess by her hair and pulled her head back. A knife was placed to her throat but before blood could be drawn, a dagger was launched into the head of a nearby Dark Servant. Pulling back his cloak, he had six more daggers that he used and disembodied the others. Adam was released from the wall and ran to his sister. Pulling back his hood, he revealed himself as Nathaniel Darkbloom.

"You would betray your brother and release her?"

Prince Adam was tending to his sister as he held her in his arms. He understood the consequences. He would strike whatever deal she wanted if it saved his sister. Nathaniel's devilish smile confused the prince. The royals stood back as the crystals on Nathaniel's forehead and hands sparked with passion. The markings on his arms radiated the same reddish glow as the crystals. He grabbed the chains and burned through each of them causing the angel to convulse. A white light escaped her pendant and in seconds Queen Nimah was gone.

"Be prepared to pay the cost when she comes knocking."

His stern warning festered in their minds as he made his escape from the palace. Prince Adam helped his sister to her feet. They climbed the stairs to the rooftop. It was completely covered in a cloud of darkness. A flickering green light could be seen at its center. The closer they got, the more they noticed the stones were drawing on his power to remain active. Consumed by worry the royals ignited their amulets and were prepared to sever the bound with their dragons to save their brother. In doing so, the dragons would die. Princess Ionica's amulet glowed a majestic blue, while Prince Adam's raged red. The beam of light cleared a path from them to see Lord Dark Lucus holding onto the prince's aura. Prince Alexander was in a trance and his veins were black.

Princess Ionica launched daggers of ice at Lord Dark Lucus. Each shattering upon contact. The demonic angel laughed. Using the shadows around him his agility was unmatched. He beat away at her and left her a bloody mess. Prince Adam fared better than his sister and managed only broken ribs. Holding onto his side as he coughed up blood, he looked into his sister's tear-filled eyes. A smile escaped her lips. Lord Dark Lucas picked her up by her hair, feet dangling and scrapping the floor like a doll.

"Say hello to your mother for me."

Before he could snap her neck, she dug a dagger into his eye. Screaming out in pain he flung her body to the edge of the platform. Prince Adam dragged himself over to his sister, leaving a trail of blood. Lord Dark Lucus approached but was blindsided by Pharaoh Atemu-Nacus and Lord Silverskull. As the three clashed, the tower trembled. Each blow sending shockwaves through the floor. Each swing of Lord Silverskull's sword brought the force of mountains crashing down, aiming to bury Lord Dark Lucus under the weight of the world itself. But he was a master of evasion, slipping through shadows and countering with strikes that seem to come from every direction. Pharaoh Atemu-Nacus ripped the floor apart and used it as shields to block the attacks. Having relied on his Magnus' for so long, he was excited to fight for himself for once.

While the battle raged on, Alexander's aura shattered. His entire body was covered in black veins. He could not stop its power. One final beam jolted through him and opened the beam even more. Clouds swirled around the beam and thundered and darkened. Tornados, hurricanes, and water sprouts formed across the world. The royal dragons perched on the mountains flapped their wings and soared toward the palace. Fang roared as the energy from the beam recoiled back to the tower causing it to crack. The impact even reached the battle below, tossing countless warriors around and damaging the foundation of the tower.

The pharaoh stumbled, which allowed Lord Dark Lucus to slice him across his chest. It burned through the armor and drew blood. Lord Silverskull got to him before the dark angel could plunge his sword into his chest. Rushing from the side with his shield, he pushed the angel over and rolled over his back, ready to fight. Dragon fire rained down from the sky as Narsacil and Maxsimo broke through the clouds. Princess Ionica and Prince Adam rushed to their dragons and mounted them. Lord Dark Lucus summoned dark energy into his hands to attack the unsuspecting dragons, but he did not account for Fang. His massive jaws broke through the clouds and ripped at his flesh. Not being able to cling to the tower, the emerald dragon had to release him and regain his stability as the wind pushed him around. His blood soaked the floor. His body was badly damaged. The once powerful angel whimpered for Eris. Without her he would surely meet his fate. Her magnetizing purple eyes glowed in the distance. With a flick of her finger, shadows consumed their bodies, and they vanished.

Narsacil burned the Water and Earth stones and Maxsimo burned the Fire and Wind stones. With their destruction the beam of energy withered away. Fang roared above the other dragons as he tried to get to the prince, but they would not make space for him. They did not want him to save Prince Alexander. Maxsimo wrapped his tail around the palace and tightened his grip causing the palace to break apart. Fang shot down and forced the two dragons to dislodge themselves. Princess Ionica and Prince Adam could not be seen from the floor fighting against the emerald dragon. They took their leave, leaving their brother to die alone.

The Black Kingdom's towering spires, now dislodged into pieces. The once-imposing walls, built from dark, glistening obsidian crumbled with the weight from above. As the wind howled, it carried the dust and scent of decay throughout the burning valley below. The prince stood on the floating platform, covered in his emerald aura as the ceiling below collapsed in a shower of dust and rubble, sending plumes of dark clouds spiraling into the air. Stone by stone, the walls crumbled, their structural integrity failing under the relentless pressure. As the palace disintegrated, it left behind a haunting silhouette against the sky, a poignant reminder of its former splendor and an example of what would come to those who challenged the royals.

When the dust settled, countless people from both sides were dead. Narsacil and Maxsimo landed near the entrance to Martilo, where their troops regrouped. Pharaoh Atemu-Nacus and Lord Silverskull accompanied them. They could not believe the prince and princess would leave their brother behind. It was not the time to speak about it. Could this really be the end? Did Lord Nebula truly win? These questions weighed on them. Adam ordered troops to search the site for any survivors. After hours of digging, they clawed through the debris and finally came to a small entry that glistened with light. Prince Alexander and Lord Zylo were found together. The soldiers grabbed them and brought them to safety. The destruction should have killed them, but fate was in their favor. They were still breathing rather faintly. The wound on the lycanthrope's chest was nearly closed. Seeing it floored the princess. How was he stitched up when they left him for dead.

Eris lurked in the shadows and watched as they gathered them from the debris. Her intervention with Lord Dark Lucus was not all she did before she escaped. She healed Lord Zylo before placing a protective barrier around the two of them. Her eyes darted to Ionica and Adam. They would pay for this. She made sure Alexander and Lord Zylo would live to see another day. In that moment she thought about her mother. She missed her. She wished she was still here.

"Mother, I hope you know what you are doing."

There was nothing left for her here. Light contorted around her, and she faded into the shadows. She returned to Lord Dark Lucus' side as he was being treated by a Magnus. The Uvali entered the cavern to witness the glorious return of Lord Nebula. Each of the colossal beasts bent a knee before the terrifying Nebula Gate. One of his Dark Servants approached the door and placed the final star-fragment into its slot. The stars glowed and released a purple liquid that connected them, creating the Nebula Star. Eris placed Cort's heart into the hands of the stone angel. The heart glimmered with life and powered the door.

The door slowly opened and the purple mist that was confined inside the gate oozed out and covered the floor. Eris touched the barrier holding the abyss back. It rippled with her touch and the eyes of the angelic statue above turned red and the abyss within the prison was discharged around them. Eris and Lord Dark Lucus took a step back as they saw a skeletal form exit. Much was covered in thick mist. The gargoyles that thrived in the darkness above fell from the walls as the dark mist collected their souls. It consumed the flesh from their bodies and slowly covered Lord Nebula bones. The room reeked of death. The eyes of the angel statue were now glowing purple.

Eris and the Uvali were spared from the darkness. Lord Dark Lucus fell prey to it as it ate away at him. The mist fed on his flesh. His armor burned away, and his bones dissolved into the cloud of darkness. Eris cried out immensely and tried to escape, but she was frozen in distress. The purple mist retreated to the nearly decaying man that stood before them. The Nebula Gate closed its doors, and the star-fragments were no longer glowing. Skeletal wings broke free from the darkness and fragments of skin grew onto it. It twisted and turned revealing the half-dead angelic warrior that once was Lord Nebula.

Lord Nebula's transformation was finally complete, and Eris was scared to look at him. He was nothing like she imagined. That prison stripped him to his core. His insides were exposed to the world. The angel had patches of white hair on his head. His nails were long and curled. When he looked at Eris, he had only one red eye to gaze upon her with. Lord Nebula was barely holding himself together. One of the Uvali lifted themselves from the floor and ripped apart Lord Dark Lucus' cape and used it to cover Lord Nebula.

Death and destruction in its true form was finally free to reign terror. He held his hand out to Eris to escort his feeble body out of the cavern. It was time for him to reclaim his throne. There was no time to waste. Darkness was coming for the land of the living. Lord Nebula was escorted to the throne room of Tartarus. Paintings of Lord Habagin and his family still hung on the walls even though they were slashed apart. She placed his feeble body on the throne.

"We have much to discuss."

Lord Nebula smiled at his subjects and gazed into the shadows. As the royals celebrated their victory, the Black Kingdom sunk deeper into the ground. Like a root taking life, the debris infected the earth and the plague sprung to life. It seeped into the soil, the water and branched out. With its release, Lord Nebula drew on its corruptive power. Princess Ionica and Prince Adam led those that survived out of Martilo into Seraqus and set up camp to rest. Prince Alexander and Lord Zylo were kept isolated. Pharaoh Atemu-Nacus and Lord Silverskull, both agreed it would be best if they disappeared. They did not know what his brother and sister were capable of doing. In the dead of night, they met with a group of elves and advised them of their plan to have the prince taken to safety for healing. The elves agreed and had the Aiars collect them with their roots and absorb them into the ground to keep the princess from seeing them leave. The ground opened a great distance from the camp and Forgon was waiting for them with Queen Asparaes.

"We cannot tell you what is going on, but the prince is still in danger. Hide him," demanded Lord Silverskull.

Both agreed to protect them and take them as far as they could. The Aiars gathered and took possession of the prince. Queen Asparaes used the pixies to charm them and hide their movements. Prince Alexander and Lord Zylo were placed in cocoon-like balls made of tree branches. The leaves within them stuck to their bodies and healed their wounds. Still in a coma like state, the prince's mind floated in the astral plane. Feeding on the plague gave him enough strength to feel his energy. He shuttered as Lord Nebula's voice penetrated his mind.

"I found you - son!"